FALL OF THE LAST DRAGON RIDER

FALL OF THE LAST DRAGON RIDER

Shawn Wilson

Podium

Cover design by Jack Nguyen

ISBN: 978-1-0394-5961-8

Published in 2024 by Podium Publishing
www.podiumentertainment.com

Podium

FALL OF THE LAST DRAGON RIDER

Prologue

"Prepare for next week. I expect to return quickly, but I do not want any issues. Is that understood?"

Both men nodded and bowed their heads low before sliding backward, keeping their faces from looking up.

"Now go."

Each turned, eyes still aimed at their feet, and scurried out of the room, ignoring the gaze they felt from both dragons.

Stioks turned his gaze toward his new dragon. Taerar was only a few months old, yet he was growing quickly.

You should have let me eat one of them. I am hungry.

"You are always hungry but fear not. You can go and find yourself some food in a few minutes. I must ensure you both understand what will happen next week."

Rising from his throne, Stioks moved to where Taerar and Juthom lay on the stone floor of the throne room next to each other.

He couldn't help but smile as he saw how quickly his dragon was putting on size. Even Juthom was surprised at how fast it was happening. Compared to the massive black dragon, Taerar was tiny, barely anything to be concerned with, but if his growth continued at the pace so far, it would only be a few years before his dragon would be worthy of carrying him. For now, he was too precious and had to be protected.

I don't want to go on this trip. It is too far, and I don't like flying for no reason.

A thrum came from Juthom, who knew what was about to take place.

Stioks moved until he was next to Taerar and leaned over, rubbing the brown dragon's scales and listening to him trill for a moment.

Then he squealed as Stioks poured magic into his touch, and a hissing sound came from where he had placed his hand.

"Taerar, never forget that you and I are bound, and you must obey me. If you do not, you will die at the hands of those who hate us. A Dragon Rider has sworn to wipe out the life you enjoy, and the small amount of pain you experienced once again is only a taste of what the two of them can do."

Pointing at Juthom, Stioks never took his eyes off his dragon, which had taken a step back, lowering its head.

"Look at your sire and see what they did to him in a sneak attack. Those scales that have never re-formed correctly testify to their devious side. That is why you must get stronger. You need to trust me, or you will never become the king you are meant to be."

The small brown dragon turned its head and gazed once more at the area Stioks had pointed out countless times. Taerar's mind struggled to believe that such a cruel person could be out there, trying to end his life and others. Yet the damage his sire had suffered stood as a testament to that fact. Dragon Rider Kaen and his terrible dragon Pammon wanted him and everyone else in this kingdom dead.

I will grow strong. I will not whine again.

Smiling, Stioks ignored the sound his skin made as it cracked and blood seeped from the wounds on his face. He stepped forward and held out his hand, waiting for Taerar to approach and lower his snout toward him.

"Good, I never want to hurt you, but I need you to understand pain. One day, we will save the land of those two and the others who follow them. Then you can rest every night without fear."

Trills came from Taerar as Stioks scratched the scales along his snout.

The cold wind had lost its touch, and Stioks smiled as he glanced backward, seeing Taerar tearing into a pair of cows and devouring them.

One day, that lie may be your undoing. If he finds out—

Who is going to tell him? You and I both know you won't, and unless we decide to have ale and bread while lounging together with that bastard and his dragon, I do not expect Taerar ever to learn the truth until it doesn't matter.

Juthom said nothing, flying higher into the night sky as they left his child below.

Are you sure this plan of yours is the right path? It may be too soon. There is still a lot of time to keep him hidden.

Anger flared within Stioks at the questioning of his plan, and he fought not to unleash it upon Juthom. Lately, the dragon had been testing him more. Since the day he bound with Taerar, it had been as if something was different, and it bothered him.

Those elves must be punished; I can no longer allow it to go unanswered. Grakgor Stormfist has told me how badly his orcs and goblins have suffered. He wants to blame me, yet it is still his undoing. I told him to wait, and I needed to cause a distraction to help remove the suffering his kind is under. A time is coming when I will need him and his troops again. That means I cannot wait any longer.

Juthom snorted, keeping his head down as he did. Only once had he accidentally gotten something on Stioks, and it had almost caused a divide between them that would have ended in at least one of them dying.

You know I am bound to you and will not go against you. My only concern is that when the time comes, we are genuinely prepared for the fight that is going to take place.

The wind swept away the rare sound of Stioks's laughter as his face bled.

Those two have no idea how much stronger we are now. When that next time comes, I plan on ending them both once and for good.

Looking at the cup in his hand, Kaen couldn't remember having crushed it.

"It's ok, it's not your—"

"It is!" exclaimed Kaen, cutting off Ava, who was trying to console him. He stood up and wheeled around, seeing her lean back at his sudden movement.

"Those people died because of me. They died because of my decisions! My inability to act and belief that perhaps we could live in peace!"

Tossing the broken cup across their room, he ignored the sound it made as the metal bounced off the stone walls and fell to the floor.

"How many have died because I believed Stioks felt he was beaten?"

Frowning, Ava shook her head at his question. "Thousands have died from the orc invasions these last few years, and you want to blame the man who gave us time to hold them off?!" Her voice got louder as she moved to stand in his face. "You have been working night and day for the last three years, fighting a battle that we wondered if it would ever stop! It has . . . for the first time in years, we have gone almost a month without a battle at those walls, and now we had one small moment of rest, yet you cannot help but still blame yourself!"

Kaen opened his mouth, preparing to reply, but Ava shook her head and held her hand up.

"You will wait till I am done." Her voice was deep, and Kaen could see the fire in her eyes. He loved that passion about her but knew that the words she was about to speak would not be easy to hear.

"Aldric, Hess, and Herb all agreed with your decision three years ago. For once, we were able to focus on living. The people of Ebonmount could live without fear of a dragon swooping down in the middle of the night and burning them alive.

"Yes, that was short-lived, as the orcs came months later, but even then, as the days and weeks passed and Stioks never came to help the horde that rushed against our defenses, people saw hope—a chance to win and live again.

"Even with our food problems, King Bosgreth is assisting us by teaching us how to grow food inside the cave with light orbs. Our people will eat while the orcs and goblins have to eat their own dead. Over a hundred thousand of their kind have died by our hands or by starvation."

Ava poked her finger against his chest. "You, Pammon, Amaranth, and Glynnis drove back the horde. Every mile cost them countless more lives. The forests and fields are littered with their corpses. They are now pushed back to the caves, and everyone expects you to do what you must. Even if more must die, everyone who has signed up for this next task believes their life is worth the cost. So do not dishonor those who have already died and those who still might."

Closing his eyes, Kaen slowly bobbed his head and took a deep breath, feeling her finger pressed against him. As he let it out and opened his eyelids, Ava stood there, her anger gone and smiling gently.

"I'm sorry, my love, I was just—"

"Being an eggling. I know. Hess and Sulenda both warned me you had moments like this."

Laughing, he reached out and put his hand on top of hers.

She rolled her eyes and sighed.

"Now, go outside and deal with your dragon. He is in a fit, and I cannot handle listening to both of you constantly complain to me."

Snorting, Kaen leaned over and kissed her on the head before turning toward the exit.

A cough came after a few steps, and he glanced back, looking to see what was wrong.

"You're forgetting something," she said as she pointed at the cup he had destroyed.

"Forgive me, my love," he replied, holding back the grin he almost let slip. Then he darted over, picking up the scrap of metal he had just created.

1

Plans and Students

Kaen read the reports Herb had given him as he waited in the centuries-old stone courtyard of the guild hall. The stones didn't show age, having been crafted during a time with magic long since forgotten.

Grumbling, he scanned the lines, seeing the information and data that worried him.

"Is that number really possible?"

Herb nodded slowly, pointing at a map on the small table. "If you follow this line and based on the data Tioanoe sent, I am afraid it is true. Her people are being driven back, and no end is in sight. Unless you and Pammon, or Amaranth and Glynnis help, I do not see how they can win."

You seem to forget every day is a battle. There will always be a problem that arises, and as the commander, you must make a decision.

Turning, Kaen stared into his dragon's golden eyes and nodded.

What do you recommend we do? You know what our plan is for tomorrow. Can we really spare Glynnis?

The real question is, can we afford not to let her help Tioanoe's people? If they fall and that army continues to grow, then we will find another enemy coming at us. Can we defend from three or four sides at once?

Scratching his trimmed beard, Kaen grunted in agreement. Pammon was right; he had been a different dragon since they returned from their trip three years ago.

Tell me, who should go with her? I would prefer not to send Phillip or Frederick since both are essential parts of this next assault.

I would send one of Herb's people with her. Three would actually be best. Have Herb send two mages and a ranger. Those three can create a lot of havoc and damage from the sky while limiting their risk.

Glancing at the map again, Kaen nodded, knowing Pammon was right.

"Pammon says you need to have two mages and one ranger go with Glynnis and help them. He will talk with her, but I expect she will gladly assist as always when Pammon asks."

Pulling out a notebook, Herb nodded as he wrote down a few things. "I know the ones I recommend. Let me see where they are and summon them. Would tomorrow work for leaving?"

Nodding, Kaen glanced at the preparations for tomorrow. "There is no time to waste. Every day is a chance for someone to catch wind of this plan and prevent its success."

Herb grunted and studied Kaen for a second. "You're carrying too much of this weight. The spies we uncovered are not all of them, and the chaos they caused the last few years has been hard on all of us. Don't shoulder this burden alone."

Kaen snorted and shook his head slowly as he scanned the documents one last time.

"You and Hess talk too much . . . both of you say the same thing. Still I can't help but feel I should have realized some of those reports were off. We didn't have time or the luxury to make mistakes like that."

"Yet who knew we would find so many mines with those damn glowing walls?" Herb asked. "Stioks mined the metal we were searching for from under our noses."

Bobbing his head, Kaen looked at the door. "We'll worry about that later. Thank you for all your help."

Herb remained silent as the last Dragon Rider in the land left. Everyone knew the burden he carried seemed impossible for one so young.

You know I do not like being a pack mule. What about my egg?

Pammon snorted and shook his head at Glynnis, curled around a silver egg.

Fifty yards away, Amaranth was doing the same thing with a bronze egg, watching them.

Kaen has people here who will guard the eggs and—

A small roar cut him off as Glynnis raised her head and shook it.

They cannot protect it for that long! Do you—

Pammon growled. Rarely had he growled like this, but in these moments, it was the only way to remind either of them who he was.

Lowering her snout some, Glynnis stopped talking and waited for what she knew would come next.

Instead, Pammon took a deep breath, moved toward her, and put his snout against her neck. She trilled from his gentle touch and gently returned the gesture.

Ava will personally be here while we are gone. Do not doubt that she will make sure no one bothers what is precious to me.

Amaranth snorted and shifted as she watched the two of them in their embrace.

Will you treat me the same as you have her? Last time, I was not given that kindness when I spoke out like that.

Pammon thrummed, moved to where Amaranth waited, and gave her the same gentle touch.

Glynnis's silver eyes glared at her competition for Pammon's attention.

His massive frame and size dwarfed the green dragon, even though she had grown quite a bit in the last few years.

When do we leave? Glynnis asked, smiling as Pammon moved back and turned to face her.

Tomorrow.

Moving back toward the cave entrance that Aldric had had his workers create for the two of them and their eggs, Pammon snorted before he leaped into the air off the cliff.

Promise me that neither of you will fight about this. Each of you knows that I feel for both of you. Do not drag me into these games you both play. There is no time for that right now.

Turning his neck so he could look at both of them at once, he gave a toothy grin.

And we all know those eggs are at least a month or two away from hatching.

Both females flinched at his words, and neither spoke as they looked at each other, wondering if one of them had told him that information.

Rest and eat. Tomorrow will be the start of a long ordeal for all of us.

Kaen could feel Pammon's frustration oozing off him long before he saw him coming to the courtyard where he was training students.

"You two ready?" he asked, watching Phillip and Frederick prepare to attack him.

They nodded and said nothing, moving to surround him from both sides, shields and weapons ready.

The two boys before him looked nothing like a sixteen-year-old should. Each was chiseled muscle from years spent doing nothing but preparing for battle. The time on the walls had transformed them from boys who learned about combat to young men who didn't flinch when it came. Each already carried a bronze token around his neck.

A year ago, they had taken the test during a lull, their accomplishments on the wall breaking a tradition and rule that had held fast for as long as most could remember.

As they came at him, neither saying a word, attacking in unison, Kaen couldn't help but smile.

Students and teachers stood by, watching the exchange of swords amongst the three of them. The pace was fast, as both boys didn't just use their weapons; instead, everything about them was a weapon. They used their shields, tossed out kicks and charges, and even threw dirt from the ground when they got up from being knocked down.

Their speed was exceptional, and their fighting skills were even more so. Both had over a twenty in their sword and shield skills. Each was dangerous in his own way, but combined, the two had taken down many of their teachers.

Oohs and ahhs, along with cheers and shouts, rang out almost as frequently as the sound of wood on wood did.

Kaen was always moving, always dodging and parrying blows and sending out the occasional attack to watch them respond accordingly. He was well beyond their level, and his speed allowed him to see everything coming, but it was no fun if they had no chance.

"Remember to take it easy on them," Hess, his dad, and their trainer had told him before this started.

Kaen could see Hess smiling at this exchange from the corner of his eye.

He gave the boys an opening, leaving himself vulnerable for just a second, and they closed in like hounds on a rabbit. Frederick came in high, requiring Kaen to focus on the sword making a straight line for his head, while Phillip came in low, his sword angling for Kaen's leg that he had left unprotected.

The crowd cheered when Phillip's sword barely touched Kaen's thigh before he pulled it to safety.

Neither boy smiled. Only a tiny turn of their lips displayed any emotion at all.

Both knew he had given them a chance, and they wouldn't squander it.

Their attacks came even faster now, and as they got close, Kaen saw when they unleashed their abilities.

Phillip's shield bashed against him, the force of it requiring Kaen to use his shield or suffer a broken weapon. As Kaen maneuvered to block the attack, Frederick activated his flurry skill, and his sword became a blur, five thrusts coming in rapid succession.

The actual strikes would be impossible to see for everyone but Kaen and a few rare people. His sword moved with his exceptional speed, deflecting each strike except the last.

As Frederick drove in, the final strike from his skill coming, Kaen dropped his own sword, grabbing for the boy's hand to take his sword from him.

From the corner of his eye, Kaen saw Phillip's flurry skill activate, attacking his hip and leg.

Grinning, Kaen stopped Frederick's attack, blocked two of Phillip's three strikes, and let the other three hit.

"Winner!"

The crowd of students and others cheered loudly as both boys immediately jumped back, away from their mentor. Each smiled at the knowledge that they had managed a rare feat.

"Well done, boys!" Headmaster Finn proclaimed as he moved toward the three of them, clapping his hands. "Well done indeed!"

Giving a slight bow toward both boys, Kaen winked, and each one dropped his sword and shield and gave him a salute before coming to shake his hand.

"Nice work, you two! Awe-inspiring use of the skills."

"You let us win," Frederick said. "We both know you could have stopped that."

Laughing, Kaen motioned to the crowd, which was still clapping, and their headmaster, who was almost upon them.

"That might be true," Kaen replied, bringing both boys under an arm, "but I'm not most people. Your combination would work against most people, so take pride in that."

They nodded and grinned.

When Finn got close, he shook both boys' hands and couldn't stop smiling at them.

"You two have grown so much! I cannot believe the men you two are becoming!"

Looking at Kaen, he gave a slight bow. "Thank you again for allowing me to participate in this!"

Clasping the man on the shoulder, Kaen squeezed him and shook his head. "You are due the honor of all this. It has been your gentle hand each day keeping these students on the path."

The older man's cheeks turned red from Kaen's praise.

"Well, ignoring all this, we must let these two celebrate with their fellow students before you whisk them off tonight."

"Promise me they will return," Finn whispered as he and Kaen stood side by side, watching the cluster of others congratulate the pair.

Not dropping the smile he wore, Kaen grunted. "That is a promise I can never make, and you know it. How many did we lose on the walls?"

Finn sighed. "Too many . . . will this end it?"

Kaen was unsure how to answer, as he felt Pammon's eyes upon him.

"No . . . it is one of many steps required to accomplish that task. For now it may give us a reprieve. Everyone needs a break."

Lying in bed, Kaen stroked his wife's cheek as she rested her head against him.

"When I'm old and fat, are you still going to love me?" she asked, gently running her nails across his skin.

"Maybe . . . I mean, you're already—Ow!"

He winced slightly as she pinched his nipple between her fingernails and lifted her head to look at him.

"Kaen Marshell, I would be cautious with the next words that come out of your mouth, or I might be the first to cut something off you."

He coughed, and the grip she had only hurt more as he nodded.

"As I was going to say," Kaen replied, clearing his throat before continuing, "I will always love you, and you will never be old or fat."

Ava rolled her eyes and grunted, letting go of the piece of flesh she was holding on to, and laid her head back on him. "At least you still have a little bit of sense left in you. Remember to use that in the coming days."

Nodding, Kaen pulled her closer.

The next few days were going to be no fun at all.

2

Secret Plans

Everyone was assembled in the courtyard of the guild hall before the sun was up.

Kaen glanced at the group of six and felt himself struggling to say something that would inspire them, knowing what they were about to attempt.

"I won't make a speech. You're here because I trust you with my life. We have a dangerous job that requires us to seal a cave down south. If successful we will repeat the process on all the caves. You six know what we are about to do. Do you have any questions?"

Each of them shook their head, no expression showing on any of their faces, as the light orbs cast shadows behind them.

"Good. Let's finish getting loaded and get out of here before dawn."

It had taken them only twenty minutes to load all the explosive casks onto both dragons' backs. Without Glynnis coming, Pammon had a few extra barrels on him, but the weight was not an issue with his size now.

These three are nervous.

Nodding, Kaen helped the last one get strapped in, took his seat behind Pammon, and hooked himself in.

That is why they are with me. Frederick and Phillip are experienced riders, and someone has promised me not to complain about three people riding on her this entire trip.

Hearing Kaen talking about her, Amaranth turned and looked at him.

I made that promise to Pammon, not to you.

And yet, would you prefer me to have him ask you or have me tell you to do this?

Frederick and Phillip didn't react when the green dragon shook her head and pulled it up quickly. Both were clipped in and the mage, Audrey, was cinched between them.

I will take that as a no.

Pammon thrummed slightly yet said nothing, knowing the threat of what Kaen was implying.

"Everyone ready?"

Phillip held up his thumb, and Kaen felt a double tap on his shoulder from behind Gilmun.

"I still can't believe I'm on a damn dragon. Holy ogre balls . . . Elnidith failed to describe how high up I am."

Kaen couldn't help but chuckle as he patted Pammon's neck. "She did tell me you had earned this, so enjoy."

Gilmun grunted, and he wasn't sure if that was a good thing or a bad thing.

As the sun rose above the mountains, they were as high up as possible in the sky, making their way toward the caves inside the mountain to the south.

You realize that once you go inside, I cannot help.

We have gone over this dozens of times. You need to be outside with the casks until it is time to bring them in. If something happens, you need to wait. I have a team I can trust, just like I trust you.

The bond didn't hide the frustration coming from Pammon, but he didn't bother to complain again.

Glancing down at the land beneath them, Kaen felt sad. In many places, the woods were burned to ash. Entire forests were gone, having been stripped clean or burned by the fires of the orcs, goblins, or Pammon when they came out to attack.

One day soon, you can help rebuild it.

Kaen nodded, seeing the burnt area surrounding Minoosh off to the east.

Every town on this side of the bowl was gone. Sections of the wall were constantly being rebuilt, and with this small break between the attacks, Kaen could see only a few small parties of orcs on the land beneath them.

Over there is a group we will need to remember. I count at least a hundred.

Using Pammon's vision, Kaen saw the group of orcs and goblins to the east, moving along a burnt section of trees, staying close to the edge as they traveled.

Where are they headed?

I cannot tell, and it has been a week since I have been out here. They might be building in the caves along the east and west, but the last time we scouted the outside walls of the mountains, no new openings were found.

That lake does provide a barrier.

And orcs never take a bath.

Chuckling as Pammon made a joke, he focused on the line of mountains they were flying toward.

Tell me I'm not being an eggling.

Pammon remained silent, and Kaen could feel the thoughts running through his friend.

We cannot keep fighting on every side. The rumor of Stioks attacking the wood elves a few weeks ago requires us to act. A year ago we helped hold back the orcs that attacked there. How much of the forest and how many elves died because we were too slow to respond? The spies that the king and Herb use are taking a week or more for new intel. Stioks is able to make moves and we are late in responding. We must act now, using that same delay in news and updates for Stioks to hear about it, succeeding while we can.

Scratching the scale on his friend's neck, Kaen nodded.

He felt Gilmun shifting behind him as the dwarf leaned his head against Kaen's back.

Looking over his shoulder, he saw the three riders with him, each leaning forward and hiding underneath the flying cloaks they had developed.

At least they aren't freezing too much.

We shall see when we land just how frozen they are.

The sun was on the far side of the mountains, less than two hours before it would disappear behind their massive stone wall.

"We need to move!" Kaen ordered as the seven of them ran toward the cave where the goblins and orcs that had been guarding the entrance lay dead.

Stay up high. Let me know if any large packs come toward us.

Pammon said nothing in reply, but Kaen could tell he was still frustrated at being unable to help with this next part.

The truth was that Pammon had grown so large that it required some adjustments to the new house they had built and to the cave entrance for both of the female dragons.

He was certain that his dragon had grown larger than Tharnok, but it was hard to say without seeing them side by side.

Not wanting to risk upsetting his friend again, Kaen ignored his desire to know how exactly strong Pammon had become. The few times he had asked last year for an update, even when explaining the reason why, Pammon would state being nothing more than numbers and not what he accomplished.

Simple Status Check with Skills
Kaen Marshell - Adult
Age - 23
HP - 2765/2765 (28%)
MP - 589/589 (28%)
STR - 49 (28%)
CON - 54 (28%)

DEX - 52 (28%)
INT - 46 (28%)
WIS - 40 (28%)
Skills:
Archery - 39
Brawling - 32
Daggers - 31
1H Sword - 31
1H Mace - 30
1H Axe - 30
1H Shield - 32
Spear - 30
2H Sword - 28
2H Polearm - 24
Staff - 22
Magic - 27
Mining - 21
Charm Resist - 30
Story Telling - 45
Haggle - 26
Dancing - 29
Dragon Riding - 28
Sneak - 21
Tracking - 22
Cooking - 27
Poison Resist - 19

As they ran toward the cave entrance, Kaen kept his bow out, an arrow ready in case they spotted another enemy.

"Stay low!" Kaen called out as the others moved to catch up with him.

Herb had complained about him bringing Phillip and Frederick along, but Kaen trusted them with his life. Over the last few years, they had spent a lot of time training and working together. Their commitment to him and their chosen path had actually made them more famous than he was in some ways.

So many parents had stopped telling their children they could be like Kaen the Dragon Rider but instead told them they could be like these two boys. Children and adults came up to them everywhere they went to shake their hands.

A memory of a horrible fight on the walls flashed through his mind.

Both boys had held back a break in an area Elnidith was trying to fill with anything she could as the orc horde pressed against it.

Phillip and Frederick had brought their roaming band of students to set up a half circle and led the defense that held back the horde. For over two hours, they stopped over two thousand orcs, bodies piling up so high that the orcs had to drag the corpses of their allies away to try to press their attack.

Finally, Glynnis came to dispatch the group outside the wall, giving them a chance to run carts with stone into the middle of the opening.

From that moment, both boys had earned a greater reputation than anyone else. That moment had pressured the adventurers' guild to allow them to test early.

"Clear!"

Kaen nodded and activated his night vision, seeing farther into the cave than the others could.

"You six, follow after a minute. I'll go ahead, and remember . . ." Kaen glanced back at the four under Phillip's command. "Stay quiet. Noise is our weakest link here."

Everyone nodded, and Kaen took off down the cave, hugging the wall and watching where he stepped.

His ability to see had improved over the last few years as he spent more time practicing the spell. Unlike the previous time he had ventured into a cave and risked not being able to see more than twenty yards, seeing down all but the longest sections of the cave tunnels was easy.

A few goblins had been hidden in cracks along the walls, and his arrows found each one in the eye.

He grumbled to himself as he continued in silence; he was still stuck at a thirty-nine. It hadn't mattered what he had done. Nothing seemed to raise it.

Hess's admission that it took almost a lifetime of practice and training to get above a forty had barely eased the pain of what he felt.

Focus. I can feel your mind wandering.

You're right. Just wondering why I can—

I know, but stop that. It doesn't matter. What matters is being safe so that we can get home to our mates.

It took a lot of effort not to laugh, but every time Pammon called Ava his mate, something inside him was tickled by it.

I'll make sure to mention that to my mate the next time I see her.

Pammon's laughter felt better than he could remember as it came through their bond. The last few years had been hard on him as well.

Coming around a bend, Kaen saw the area he was expecting. There was a massive black liquid wall shimmering in the cave's darkness. This time, instead of a few goblins being the protectors, two tier-two ogres stood a few yards from the entrance, looking bored and half asleep.

Moving behind the bend, he drew a second arrow and prepared for his attack.

[Twinshot Activated]

Kaen felt his lifestone burning as his energy flowed into the tips of his arrows. When they were glowing red, he moved from around the corner, unleashing both shots, which sank into each of their eye sockets. An explosion took place, and both of their heads were gone in a moment.

He had moved toward the beasts the second he let go of the arrows and drawn two more.

Two shrieks sounded out as the ogres fell, and Kaen saw movement on the sides. Goblins began to move toward the portal, and his first arrow dropped the one on the right.

Just a yard before the last goblin reached the black surface, the second one impaled the last goblin in the throat. It stumbled forward, hands clutching at the arrow, and moved through the black shimmering surface.

Dwarf balls . . . this is going to suck.

Kaen put the bow over his shoulder and drew his sword, his shield already on his left arm, as he ran to the portal.

Coming through it, he found the goblin dead on the ground, and no other goblins or orcs nearby.

Picking up the corpse, he stepped back through the shimmering side and looked out over the open area where the sounds of an army echoed off the stone walls. The glow of the fires created an eerie glow inside the massive cavern.

What?

Nothing. I was worried for a moment, but everything is fine. Prepare to land. I'll send the others back to you quickly so we can start bringing the casks.

A grumble came through their bond, yet he could feel Pammon starting to descend.

The light of their lightstones had told Kaen when they were near, and he waited by the wall just in case something came through.

"Everything went as planned?"

Kaen motioned at the four corpses he had stacked up on one side. "They decided to use bigger guards, but the smaller one still almost got away."

Both boys grinned for a moment and nodded. They were often underestimated for their size and age, but each knew that was a mistake.

"You just got here. We need to finish our plan. Return to the entrance. Drop the light orbs you have at intervals. Get those casks here as quickly as you can."

Kaen held his hand up to stop everyone.

"Audrey, Gretel, and Rorick, you are with me."

Gilmun cursed under his breath and took off after the two boys, who started jogging back toward the entrance.

After they were out of sight, Kaen turned and looked at the three with him.

"You have the hardest part coming up. Once they return with all the casks, we need to get them inside and detonate them. Everything will fall upon you to keep us alive until that happens."

No one flinched, but he could see their reactions. It was enough pressure to stand beside someone in a fight and know you were responsible for that person's life. Being told you were responsible for the only Dragon Rider alive was well beyond that.

3

Handle with Care

A smile lit up Kaen's face as he saw Phillip and Frederick carrying twelve casks on a specially made litter while Gilmun had three, two on his back and one in his arms.

"It's not fair," the dwarf said between breaths. "I got short arms and legs, plus I'm older . . . these two . . . they run me ragged."

Both boys grinned slightly before grabbing their litter and jogging back into the cave.

"It's ok, I feel your pain. Just know, only one trip left."

The dwarf snorted and took off after the two boys.

"He runs funny," Audrey said after the dwarf was out of earshot. "Like there is a stick or something up his arse."

"Maybe a short stick," Kaen replied, ignoring the laughter of the other two before returning to watch the moving black wall of liquid.

How are things outside?

Amaranth is keeping watch, but so far she has seen nothing. I'm assuming they made it to you already.

Yup. They are headed back to you. Soon this part will be over, and we can return home to our mates.

A groan came through their bond, and Kaen allowed himself to smile.

He was going to tell Ava what Pammon called her for certain.

"Now listen, we are going inside. Once there, we need to get these stacked along the wall so that it brings down a massive section of rock."

Kaen pointed at a few different spots on the small drawing he had made on a piece of paper.

"These points will need five casks each. There will be four over here. The remaining spots need three each. Do you have any questions?"

Gilmun raised his hand.

"If a fight breaks out?"

"If it happens, I will do what I can to defend while Audrey, Gretel, and Rorick provide support. You, Phillip, and Frederick need to get those casks in place. Start with the entrance first. We will go outward afterward. I would prefer to at least close the portal as we run for our lives."

The dwarf grunted and nodded.

"Anyone else?"

With no more questions, Kaen pointed at the portal. "I'll go through first. Count to ten, then someone comes after. Once we are all through, we will start having you retrieve the casks."

Each of the six had stumbled after their first time through. A few whispers and muttered words came from their lips as they stared across the open cavern and the massive amount of tents, stone buildings, and movement of bodies in the area.

The smell hit them as they realized the air was dank and filled with smoke and death.

"Hurry!"

Moving to the side where a small rock partially blocked the right side from view, Kaen motioned for the three support people to accompany him. "Stay here. This is your safest spot. Herb has told you what to do. You know the plan. Protect first. Kill second."

Minutes passed as the first set of barrels were placed. The second set was more challenging, which required them to move thirty yards in each direction. Kaen would keep an eye out, scanning across the multitude of creatures, nodding when he deemed it safe for the group of three to move, always holding an arrow ready to fire.

With the second set in place, Kaen motioned to the side he was on. "You three each grab a barrel. We will go the farthest out and then the next. Got it?"

They nodded, running back into the portal.

As they moved around the wall of the massive cavern, they waited and paused, watching as Kaen motioned for them to move forward and when to stop.

Sweat dripped down the three cask carriers as they approached the final ten yards where they needed to deposit the casks.

"Stop!" Kaen hissed, lowering himself and watching as the three froze and hid along the ground as low as possible.

A group of ten orcs was moving closer to them than the usual packs, carrying a massive stone on their shoulders. None looked at them, but Kaen knew it might get the attention of one of the orcs if they moved.

The minute stretched until the group passed them and Kaen felt safe enough to move.

When they were five yards from their final spot, the cavern erupted with noise. The sound of a bell ringing out and a green spell going toward the ceiling told Kaen what he feared.

Turning his head back toward the other group, which was almost one hundred yards away, Kaen saw a pack of at least thirty orcs and goblins rushing their group by the entrance.

One look told him everything he needed to know.

"We're screwed, give me the cask."

Gilmun hadn't moved even though he was the closest to Kaen, so Kaen went to him, grabbing the wooden barrel filled with explosives from his hands.

"Run and don't look back!" Kaen shouted. The dwarf stood there confused for a moment, so Kaen gave him a gentle shove to get him moving.

Taking three steps, Kaen threw the cask as far as he could across the cavern, not waiting to see it as he moved to where Phillip and Frederick were, both holding theirs out for him.

"Holy elf tits," Gilmun cursed as the cask flew over a hundred yards into the cavern.

"I said run!"

Halfway into Kaen's second throw, an explosion rocked the cavern.

The force of it knocked the other three to the ground while Kaen stumbled a step and finished his toss, not getting near the distance he wanted on it.

Kaen helped Gilmun and Phillip, lifting them both to their feet.

Their ears rang from the sound as another explosion echoed a second later, knocking the two off their feet again. Kaen winced in pain as his ears rang, a result of the force of the impact from the casks going off. Rocks fell and stones crashed down around them.

Kaen was the only one still on his feet as dirt and dust filled the air. Grabbing the dwarf and Phillip again, he pulled them to their feet. He looked where Frederick lay and froze for half a second. Blood ran down the boy's temple where a rock had struck him, and his eyes were rolled back into his head. On the ground, a stone the size of Hess's fist lay near the incapacitated young man, blood on one side of it.

Yanking a potion from his pouch, Kaen ripped out the stopper and poured it down Frederick's throat. The boy's eyes rolled back forward, and his mouth hung open as the sound of a bone popping back into place came from the side of his head. Four seconds later, Frederick held his hand against his head and let out a groan.

"Move!" Kaen repeated, motioning away from the entrance. Shoving Frederick ahead, he grabbed the last barrel and ran behind them.

Plan D!

Confusion came from Pammon as his friend tried to understand what Kaen had just said.

Plan D? We don't have a plan D!

I know! My other two plans are off the table! Give me a minute and I'll update as I can figure something out.

His night vision guided him along the wall, and he got Frederick up next to Phillip, who was trying not to cough from the dust.

"Keep hold of each other. Watch your feet!"

Gilmun stopped and waited until the three of them caught up, and after Phillip grabbed his shoulder, Kaen motioned for them to keep moving.

"We need to reach the other side!"

Kaen took the last cask and tossed it toward the middle of the cavern.

As it exploded, Kaen ran ahead with his bow out, letting Gilmun hold on to the back of his shirt for dear life.

Plan D is we make it out the other side of the mountain.

Pammon was roaring outside, and Kaen could feel his dragon's frustration like a raging torrent of water in a river.

Seeing a pack of goblins notice them, Kaen put his bow away.

We've been through worse. Trust me, we'll make it through this.

The orc pack wasn't prepared for what happened. Even as a group of twenty, Kaen had entered their midst and struck each of them down before they could cry out enough to draw attention to their plight. Heads were sliced off, and a puddle of red blood stained the rock they stood on.

Racing back to where his crew waited, Kaen motioned for them to keep going.

"I only have seventeen arrows left! We need to fight close if it comes to that. You three keep moving along the wall. I will defend you!"

Gilmun almost said something until Phillip pushed him from behind, keeping up the pace as Kaen watched where they ran. A cloud of dust was rising, and breathing was getting more difficult. The red and orange light from the flames turned the whole cavern into a soft, glowing light.

Another magical bolt flew into the air, exploding into a green glow that covered the cavern.

Figures became visible in the dust, and a few roars near them told Kaen they had been spotted.

"Shields and weapons ready!"

Everyone loaded their weapons and followed Kaen as they raced around the cavern wall.

Meanwhile, an army of figures ran toward them through the cloud of dust.

Kaen lost count as he cut down the creatures that continued to assault them. He was a figure of death, everything the legends had mentioned about being a Dragon Rider. The only problem was trying to protect his crew from the same horde that outnumbered them on every side but one.

Spells rained down on them from casters hiding behind the mountain of muscles. To get to them, Kaen had to leave the three he needed to protect. Not leaving them meant they were attacked by fireballs and more.

Phillip and Frederick were holding their own, neither flinching at the sight that would cause many battle-hardened men to buckle within seconds. Their time on the wall had made them numb to the shouting of the horde.

Each creature cackled as it anticipated feasting upon the flesh of those who had invaded their lair.

"Shield wall!"

Gilmun held up his shield as the boys stood on either side of him, using the stone behind them for protection as thirty orcs and goblins rushed at them. Swords, axes, and clubs rained down, but the three held fast, absorbing the attacks and using their swords to inflict damage. The number of enemies made it harder for the orcs and goblins to move quickly or defend as they pressed against each other, each one trying to be the one to land a killing strike.

Kaen didn't risk looking back; he was focused on the two Magus who had pushed a pack of over three hundred minions toward them. They were tossing spells at him, but his shield deflected each one, the flames that washed over it barely causing him any pain. Every swing of Kaen's sword cut down a path of goblins and orcs like wheat stalks against a thresher's blade. When his shield wasn't blocking a spell coming at him, it pulverized every creature he ran through, leaving a trail of carnage. Cries and groans came from the dying as he ran at his targets.

"Get the human!" one of the Magus cried out as a fireball came from its hand, aimed not at Kaen but at a group of orcs near him.

A pack of four orcs was almost upon him when Kaen realized what kind they were. The harnesses on their chests left no doubt what would happen as the fireball raced toward the screaming creatures.

Changing directions, he ran backward, holding his shield out before him, and a second later, the blast that erupted from the four orcs who had gladly given their life turned into a massive explosion, creating a thirty-yard-wide section of space without a single living thing.

Except for Kaen, who had knelt behind his shield.

Smoke and some flames licked at the exposed parts of his legs and feet, but Kaen smiled as he stood up, seeing the look on both Magus's ugly faces. The dragon armor he wore protected him against most of the effects of the magic.

Like an arrow, he sprinted at them, covering the now clear space, and was upon them in seconds.

They tried to shield themselves, casting barriers and other spells, hoping to buy time to find a way to stop the man who had withstood everything they had thrown at him. But he shattered their spells and unleashed attacks with his sword, dropping them to the ground, each of them now missing an entire leg.

As they toppled over, he moved quickly between the two, taking their heads off and sprinting back toward the buildup of creatures surrounding his friends.

4

What Lives in a Cavern

The piles of bodies the three had created aided their defenses but had trapped them against the stone, unable to move or strike out themselves. Frederick was in the middle, struggling to stand as a trio of orcs with spears overwhelmed his open side and landed strikes against his right leg. The three of them kept fighting, knocking weapons away and focusing on standing their ground while they waited for Kaen.

The crashing sounds and cries that grew louder than the shouts of excitement told them he was close. Bodies flew into the air. Parts of bodies joined that flight as Kaen ran through the cluster of monsters, smashing into and through them without hesitation.

The armor he wore was the newest gift he had received from King Bosgreth. The king had proclaimed that no finer suit had been made in centuries when he presented the chest piece and leggings made from the scales taken from Tharnok. For almost two years, the master craftsman in his hall had worked on the two pieces, forging special pieces of metal to bind the scales together and prevent them from coming loose.

Kaen longed for a helmet, boots, and gloves, but they did the job he needed right now. Every blow that hit him failed to penetrate, bouncing off or shattering the weapon. His own strength and stamina absorbed every blow without a problem.

The last ten feet between him and his men were the hardest, as he cut through the tightly packed orcs and goblins and shoved aside the corpses that already had piled up. Screams came with each swing, and soon he had created a path to the trio stuck in here with him.

When he saw Frederick's leg bleeding and how he was leaning against the stone wall more than standing on his own, a difficult choice arose. He had only two more healing potions remaining, and if he used one now, things like this would happen again, and someone would die.

As Kaen spun like a top, his shield and sword cleared a spot for him to maneuver; the creatures backed away with no leader to drive them toward him. Their hesitation shifted the battle, and a few minutes later, no creature remained near them, as the ones who could get away had run off, seeking help.

"How bad?" Kaen asked, seeing Gilmun binding his student's leg.

"I can't put weight on it. They cut the muscle and the tendon with their attack."

Phillip moved away, keeping watch as Kaen tried to read Gilmun's face.

"Thoughts?"

The dwarf grunted and motioned to the pile of bodies around them. "We're your limiting factor. Without us, you can easily escape or slaughter every one of these things. Protecting us may get all four of us killed."

Frederick nodded, motioning to his leg as Gilmun moved to help support him. "If you need to leave me, I'll fight as long as possible."

Kaen shook his head. This boy of sixteen years was as hard as steel, and his face showed no hope that Kaen would ignore the statement he had just made. He was ready to die if it meant the three of them might escape.

How hard did I push these boys?

"We'll go as a group. I'm not leaving you or anyone else behind."

Turning around, Kaen saw what Phillip was looking at.

"They're coming again," Phillip stated. "At least twice as many."

"Pick up Frederick and run. You can make two miles before you need a break, right?"

Phillip grinned as he turned, putting his sword into his scabbard and motioning for Frederick to do the same. "I can probably make it three. It's been a while since we raced."

Bobbing his head, Kaen resisted the urge to smile. "Gilmun, keep up, defend their back. I'll keep the patch clear as long as I can before returning to you three. If it gets bad, put him down and defend yourselves. I'll find you."

Without waiting for them to respond, Kaen was gone, running faster than any animal the boys and dwarf had ever seen.

Frederick winced as Phillip grabbed him, throwing him over his right shoulder while keeping his shield in his left hand.

"This is going to suck for you," Phillip declared as he started to run, squeezing his friend as tight as he could, hoping to keep the bouncing to a minimum.

"Goblin shite," Gilmun shouted as he raced after the boy. "I've got short legs, remember that!"

Where are you? I can sense you, but you are still deep within the mountain. It is like you are shifting directions, sometimes coming toward the other side and other times running through the middle of it.

Kaen ignored the question. His sword was pointed at a pair of cave trolls that blocked his path. A flame surrounded his sword as it carved the flesh from their skin. The smell was horrible, but the noise they made as he carved them into pieces that didn't regenerate was far worse.

Once both of them were dead, heads split in two and hearts pierced, he raced toward the pack of hobgoblins that were running toward his three friends.

Arrows plinked off his armor, and Kaen ignored the creatures who couldn't understand why nothing they tried seemed to take him down like it should.

They had moved slowly along the cavern wall for over an hour, only now realizing how expansive it was. They had already traveled twelve miles through the cavern as it snaked inside the mountain. Some areas were a mile wide, and others as much as three.

Phillip was doing his best carrying his friend, who gradually got weaker with each passing moment.

Catching up to the hobgoblins from behind, Kaen slaughtered them, watching as the ones farther ahead heard the sounds of their dying brethren and turned, finding the same fate coming for them.

I have no idea . . . it's been over an hour, and we still see more caverns ahead. It does twist and turn.

You need to be careful.

Chuckling, Kaen ignored Pammon for a moment. A few more orcs were getting close to his men.

Each time they stopped and rested for a few minutes, Kaen considered using a potion, but the fear of not knowing how much farther they had until they reached the exit kept him from doing so.

"I'm fine," Frederick said with a grunt. "My offer still stands if you—"

"I don't, and stop asking," Kaen replied, cutting the boy off. "We will make it. All of us. Now drink and eat while you can. We have less than a minute."

Phillip was covered in sweat and gore. The fatigue of carrying his friend was starting to show. Gilmun looked even rougher, but the dwarf wasn't about to complain when two boys, over a third younger than he was, continued to keep a positive attitude.

As they started running again, Kaen heard a roar from the direction they were heading.

"What in a goblin's teat was that?" Gilmun asked, tossing his empty waterskin to the ground.

Shaking his head, Kaen shrugged. "Something tells me we are about to find out."

* * *

Two miles later, a towering monstrosity that had to be an orc came into view. Kaen realized it had to be close to twenty feet tall. It carried two massive hammers, each over half its body's size, chains attached to their shafts, and a belt around its waist.

"Impossible," Gilmun gasped, almost tripping as he ran.

"What is it?"

"A siege ogre . . . but those things haven't been seen since the old stories."

Kaen's mind searched to remember anything he could about one of these, but he had never heard of them before. Gilmun's statement of how long it had been since one had been seen made him concerned about what other things might stand in their way.

"You three keep on the path you are on. I'll move off to face it."

"Sure that's a good idea?" Gilmun asked. "Not that I doubt you, but those were rumored to be able to crush dwarven walls with a few strikes."

Glancing back at the dwarf, who was gasping for air, Kaen gave him a wink before drifting to the left. "Would you rather I let it come over here and you two fight?"

A coughing fit came over Gilmun, and Kaen heard Frederick give a small laugh.

Not waiting for a reply, Kaen took off ahead, clearing out the creatures between his men and the ogre.

I wish you were here. This is about to get interesting.

A hint of concern and worry came through their bond, not blocked by the amount of stone between them.

What are you going to do?!

Smiling, Kaen sliced the head off an orc while smashing through another one.

Fighting a new ogre. He is about half as tall as you are.

I swear if you—

Yes, mother, I know. Don't die . . .

Pammon grumbled as Kaen moved toward the monstrosity thundering toward him.

For a brief moment, he understood how Hess must have felt those five years ago when death was so close.

Don't say it . . . I can feel that thought!

A hammer whistled over his head, and the other one followed behind it, slamming into the rock and shattering it. Pieces flew through the air, shrapnel from the power of the blow against the mountain floor, and cracks ran at least ten yards in each direction from the point of impact.

Coming out of a roll, Kaen raced toward the ogre, who moved far faster than he had expected for something so large.

The only hit he had landed so far had cut just a few inches.

This thing's skin is tougher than anything I have fought so far.

Another hammer strike came at him as the ogre used its momentum again to spin, the weight of the hammer making it act like a top.

Each head of the hammer was solid metal, almost as tall as Kaen, and wider as well.

Occasionally, a foolish orc tried to rush in and help, but it was turned to paste by its own ally, who didn't care that it killed one of its own.

Standing his ground, Kaen held up his shield, preparing for the first attempt at blocking the hammer swinging low along the ground.

A cracking sound rang across the cavern, echoing for miles, but the immediate impact and sound left Kaen struggling to stand for a moment. The effect of the shield and its steadfast ability held true.

Someday I hope to see what that armor in the vault offers.

The ogre also appeared stunned, the sound of the impact disorienting it. It pulled on the hammer that had collided with Kaen's shield and noticed that a massive three-foot section was missing, split from the main part, and lying on the ground.

As he glanced at his feet, Kaen realized he had slid along the rock about ten feet from the strike, judging by the trail of scratches. He raced to the ogre's arm and sliced at the wrist holding the broken weapon. He then ignited his sword with his magic and cut deeper with the magical assistance.

The ogre shouted in pain as its wrist was sliced and a tendon got cut. Not waiting for it to recover, Kaen drove his sword into its leg, slightly above the ankle, and leaned into it, running the blade around its entire leg and severing most of the muscle and all of the tendons. The creature howled in pain as its leg gave way, and the massive ogre crashed to the ground, sending a cloud of dust into the air.

Running from under the ogre as it fell forward, Kaen glanced toward his men and saw a pack of four tier-two ogres racing at them.

"Hairy dwarf balls," he muttered as he ran, leaving the massive ogre alive but injured.

5

Underground Troubles

Kaen watched the ogres chase after his men, running backward and trying to keep as much distance as possible.

The only good news was that most of the orcs and goblins had not followed them. The large clumps of their dead allies convinced them not to chase unless a stronger ogre made them.

Sheathing his sword and swapping it for his bow, Kaen sighed.

Eight arrows . . .

There was no other option, and he knew it. The distance he needed to cover before the ogres ran them down was too great.

Kaen drew two arrows and sent his mana into them, charging them so they crackled with electricity. He ran, holding the shot ready and dodging the few creatures that stayed in his path.

As the creatures came into range, he paused, slowing down just enough to feel comfortable with the distance the shot needed.

[Twinshot Activated]

Both arrows flew across the cave, lightning arcing once or twice between the arrowheads as they traveled toward their targets.

The two ogres in the front of the pack took the arrows in their sides, jerking for a moment as the power of the lightning coursed through them, causing them to stumble and roll. Both ogres behind them slowed down and glanced toward Kaen, who had put his bow away and was running full speed again with his sword drawn. The one in front pointed at Kaen as it continued the chase after Phillip and the others.

A chain ogre with two massive axes came running toward him, planning on slowing down or maybe even injuring the man that had just crippled their siege ogre.

No time could be wasted, so Kaen kept running, even as the ogre prepared to swing at him with both axes.

The moment Kaen leaped at the ogre's head with his shield out, it realized that at no point had this human planned to dodge or block its attack. As the axes swung toward Kaen, the shield crashed into and through the ogre's face, leaving a trail of blood, bones, and brains as Kaen flew over its shoulders. The massive corpse thudded and rolled along the ground, with no head to be found.

Landing and rolling to his feet, Kaen took off toward the last ogre about to reach his friends.

Phillip stopped, ignoring his aching muscles and lack of air, and dropped Frederick on the ground.

"Stay!" he shouted, pointing at the man trying to rise and pull his weapon. "Gilmun, with me!"

The dwarf nodded, ignoring the spit and snot in his red beard as he drew his weapon and tried to get a few more breaths of air into his lungs.

"Plan?" he gasped as they stood side by side, taking a few steps toward the charging ogre.

"Stay alive. Kaen is coming. We just need a few seconds."

Gilmun nodded, watching the ogre that was racing toward them. "Tier two?"

"Think so . . . has armor, though . . . not sure . . ." Phillip replied, taking deep breaths as the last bit of distance separating them from the rushing ogre disappeared.

It roared, swinging the colossal sword it had in a wide arc.

Phillip read the movement and judging by how fast it had charged, he knew it would be at an angle he could most likely deflect.

As he raised his shield, using both hands for support, the blow bounced off his shield slightly, sending the boy to the ground in a roll.

Gilmun didn't wait, rushing forward and slashing at the ogre's leg with his sword.

As its sword swung and the momentum carried it around, the ogre lifted up its right leg to kick the dwarf charging it.

Knowing he had just put himself in harm's way, Gilmun lowered himself, sticking his sword along the edge of his shield and preparing for the incoming blow.

The ogre's shin caught Gilmun as he had gotten close enough to minimize some of its momentum, but it still drove its leg into the sword, crashing into the shield and sending the dwarf flying through the air.

A thud and a groan came as Gilmun slammed into the wall, sliding down its rough exterior and landing on his face.

Howling, the ogre turned, glaring at the dwarf and the piece of metal lodged in its leg from Gilmun's sword, which had snapped during impact.

It hobbled over toward the dwarf, lying face first on the ground, and roared, lifting its sword as it prepared to stab downward.

Phillip approached its injured leg, not shouting like so many might. He had learned that if an enemy doesn't know you are there, let it find out the hard way.

He activated his flurry skill, and five thrusts landed in rapid succession on the ogre's leg, severing its Achilles tendon.

The leg buckled, and the ogre fell forward, its sword clattering along the ground as it went down.

Not wasting a moment, Phillip unleashed multiple strikes and attacks at its side. As its armor lifted, the exposed skin was quickly covered in deep gashes.

A hand came back as the ogre tried to swipe, and Phillip saw it coming and stepped away, slicing with his sword and cutting off four fingers from the hand that had tried to strike him.

Off balance and out of position, the young man moved forward, years of fighting experience flowing through him as he moved. His sword came up and through, catching the ogre in the throat.

Dancing away, the creature fell face first as it tried to grab the wound that was gushing blood and cracked its own face into the stone floor.

Breathing heavily, Phillip lunged forward once more and drove the sword down into the base of the ogre's neck, severing its spinal cord.

"Good work."

Phillip spun, seeing Kaen standing there with a slight smile.

"Just doing what you taught me," replied Phillip as he cleaned off his sword and went to check on Gilmun, who was groaning as he stood up.

"How bad are you?" Kaen inquired as he checked on the dwarf.

"A few broken ribs," he said, and then coughed, wincing, as blood oozed from his mouth. "Maybe a punctured lung."

Kaen reached into his pouch and pulled out a healing potion. "You and Frederick will both get half. I only have one left."

The dwarf nodded and took the potion, drinking half and reacting as everyone did when they were healed.

Kaen moved to Frederick, who was turning white as the blood loss began to impact him.

I'm an eggling for waiting this long . . .

"Drink this," Kaen ordered as he helped the boy swallow the liquid.

After they had recovered slightly, Kaen turned and saw Phillip gazing at the cavern around them.

"They haven't pressed the attack . . . Why not?"

"I'm not sure," Kaen replied, wondering the same thing. "We have killed a lot, and I just took down what I can only guess was not one they had intended to send to fight . . . still . . ."

Phillip turned to his mentor and laughed. "I think you mean *you* have killed a lot. At least a thousand or two?"

Rolling his eyes, Kaen gave the boy a gentle punch to the shoulder and grunted.

"We need to get going. I don't want to waste this break."

Phillip turned and moved to where Frederick was standing.

"You ok?"

Frederick nodded and gently tapped his leg.

"Bleeding has stopped, but I'm still light-headed. I think I lost more blood than I realized."

"How are your ribs?" Kaen asked Gilmun.

The dwarf twisted a few different ways and took a few deep breaths. "Healed, tender but not broken."

Glancing at Phillip, Kaen grinned. "Who do you want to carry?"

"You take Gilmun. We both know he's heavier than he looks."

The dwarf scoffed and snorted, unsure if that was an insult.

Without hesitation, Kaen moved to the dwarf and scooped him up like a parent might a child.

"Hey!" exclaimed Gilmun, who had no time to react as Kaen put him over his shoulder. "I'm a grown dwarf!"

Kaen laughed and turned to see Phillip taking a moment to get Frederick.

"On second thought," Kaen said as he swooped over and grabbed Frederick, who was caught off guard by his action. "I'll carry them both. Let's go!"

Not hesitating, he turned and took off, listening to both men complain as he carried them while he ran.

You are getting closer. I can feel you.

Since they had started running, they only had to stop and fight three times. Phillip could keep the pace Kaen set a lot longer without having to carry his lifelong friend.

Gilmun and Frederick had forgiven Kaen for putting them down, realizing the amount of ground they were covering and the speed at which they moved.

I have noticed the same thing. Are you outside the cave?

Yes, I am above it, though. When you finally get here, you might find an angry dragon waiting for you.

Chuckling to himself, Kaen kept running, knowing that soon enough they might hopefully see his dragon.

Twenty minutes later, Kaen slowed and set the two men down.

"That isn't good," he said, pointing at a massive pile of dead orc and goblin bodies that were covered by rocks and stone. "They blew up their own exit."

"Never easy, is it?" Gilmun complained as he glanced behind them. "What now?"

"Clear a path and then our way out. Make sure no enemies are around that can attack us."

The dwarf started to grumble until he saw both boys moving to follow Kaen.

"Elf tits, you three are impossible!"

Kaen and Phillip worked on the rocks while the other two kept guard.

Only a few orcs and goblins had been dumb enough to come close to them. A single ogre had moved near them, causing everyone to get their weapons and prepare to fight, but the group with it backed away, moving out of sight.

"I'm not a fan of how this feels," Gilmun said as he continued to watch. "What happened here? These bodies aren't new."

Kaen threw boulders like they were pebbles, no longer getting shocked looks from the dwarf, who had never seen the man's true strength. "You're right. They sealed themselves in, not leaving a way to escape. Obviously, something happened within the ranks that caused enough of them to try to desert or go elsewhere."

Phillip smashed some rocks with a war hammer he had found near the bodies and continued to grind away at the pile. "This is going to take time, isn't it?"

Kaen nodded. "I've worked enough rock to know this won't be cleared today. Gilmun, go ahead and rest if you can. We'll need to take turns keeping watch."

The dwarf grunted and then sighed, "Fine, but don't blame me if something sneaks up on us while I rest."

Everyone laughed; a small break in the mood that had been heavy since the plan went sideways was just what they needed.

While the three of them slept, Kaen continued to grab boulders and chuck them across the cavern. The sound of them hitting rock and rolling away was a steady rhythm as he kept up the pace he knew wouldn't overexert him.

His hands felt different as he removed his gloves to do the work. It had been ages since he had such a task, and for this brief moment, buried under a mountain and doing something so mundane, Kaen was at peace.

You feel different.

That is because I forgot how much I enjoyed the quarry, even when all I could think about was getting away from it. The work was honest and made me better because I did it.

Does that mean you and I are retiring from this work to open up a quarry?

Kaen chuckled and felt Pammon join him in the moment.

I'm an idiot, aren't I?

Pammon didn't reply, and Kaen continued to toss rocks, choosing carefully to avoid a rockslide.

No . . . you are not an idiot. The plan was dangerous, and there were many ways it could fail. I know the loss of the others hurts, but you may have discovered something even greater by doing this.

Are the orcs and goblins blocking their own troops in?

Pammon's agreement with that statement trickled through their bond.

What could cause them to treat their own like that? How bad must things be for them to turn on each other?

Kaen picked up another boulder and threw it, hearing it smash into the ground. Moving away, he watched as several rocks shifted for a moment and then stopped.

Let me get back to work. I see the spot I need to clear. After that, perhaps I can find us an opening.

Be careful. I have your side covered out here.

Smiling, Kaen grabbed the war hammer that Phillip had found and set to work on a few stones he knew would be the key to the next part.

6

Tight Moments

After crushing rocks for an hour, Kaen felt everything was in place.

The others were awake, amazed at how Kaen had never slowed down. Each strike of his hammer was deliberate and precise, rocks cracking and shattering under the force. Yet none of the strikes broke more rocks than Kaen wanted to break.

"We need to back up. This might cause a rockslide."

Seventy yards away, Kaen pulled out his bow and infused the nocked arrow with magic. It grew bright, maintaining a red glow.

He loosed the arrow and it struck the point that he had aimed for, exploding and sending rocks in every direction. The massive blast echoed through the cavern, bringing a reaction of noises behind them.

"It sounds like the orcs and goblins are preparing to return!" shouted Gilmun as dust drifted from the massive rockslide.

"Let's go, and watch your step!" Kaen shouted, putting up his bow and pulling out his sword.

The dwarf coughed a few times as the dust bothered his still-healing lungs, but Kaen led them along, past rocks that shifted as they climbed over them.

"Up there!" Phillip called out as he pointed to the top of the pile.

Kaen also saw it; they had found an opening at the top of the mountain of rocks.

A massive collective roar came from behind them.

"Those things waited for us to clear a path!" Kaen shouted, pointing at the opening. You three go! I'll hold them off!"

None of them argued as they clambered over the rocks, making their way up and into the opening, which was only about four feet wide. Kaen watched as a horde of orcs and goblins gathered at the base of the rocks, looking up at the four of them as Kaen backed away slowly after his men.

Down below, the number of creatures continued to swell, well over a thousand and more coming by the second.

Pammon, we are about to be coming, and things will be nasty!

He could feel his friend moving and thought there was movement near the mountain's exit.

I'm here. Just make it to me.

Every creature seemed poised to begin climbing up the rocks after him and the others, yet they waited. Not looking a gift horse in the mouth, Kaen dashed up the pile of boulders and rocks and caught up with the other three, all on their hands and knees, climbing through the gap.

Phillip had a light orb out and was leading the other two; some areas were getting tighter, so that there were only a few feet of room instead of the initial four.

"Holy elf tits," Gilmun called out from behind Phillip. "It's like being in a mine!"

"There is an opening, but it's going to be tight. Like real tight!"

Already struggling with the lack of space around him, Kaen put his sword away and affixed his shield on his back. Between it and his bow, they were already catching on rocks that jutted each way.

Using his night vision, he could see just how tight things would get.

The other three had the advantage over him. He was thicker than any of them and saw the trouble the tight space was causing.

"You ok, Frederick?"

A grunt came from the boy, but he was obviously struggling to keep moving forward.

"I can't breathe, it's . . . it's hard to focus."

"Focus on my back!" shouted Gilmun. "It happens in places like this. Ignore the rocks. Keep yer eyes on my back and nowhere else."

"It's just so tight . . . like it's crushing me!"

The panic in Frederick's tone was easy to hear, and Kaen squirmed behind him. "You have to go forward. There are over a thousand orcs and goblins behind us. I'm right here. Phillip is in front. Pretend this is just another training exercise, and focus like Gilmun said."

The shouts of creatures coming up the rocks they had just climbed added to the moment, and the young boy shook from fear.

"Breathe, slowly, in and out. It will be hard at first, I know, but breathe."

Gilmun's voice was low and slow. Even over the thundering cries behind them, the dwarf backed up slowly so he was within reach of Frederick.

"Follow me. Focus on me, and we can get out of here."

Wedged in the tunnel, Kaen knew time was running out. Soon the creatures would come climbing into the hole, and he would be limited in his ability to fight back.

"Frederick, remember that promise you made all those years ago on the street? You told me you would give everything to be like me. Today is the final test. Show me all these years were worth it."

A second passed, and Kaen saw the young boy change. His breathing returned to normal, and the tremors that had begun to consume him stopped.

Frederick began to move slowly, picking up speed as the dwarf before him moved ahead.

No one said anything, ignoring the sound of goblins entering the opening about twenty yards behind them.

Phillip was grunting, and Kaen couldn't see what was happening, but he had an idea why.

"Moving . . . a few . . . rocks . . ." Phillip shouted. "Wedged good. It's tight up here, Kaen."

Already the path was closing in on him and his weapons were catching on everything.

The same fear that Frederick had a moment ago tried to overwhelm him. He couldn't turn around, and backing up wasn't going to be an option much longer. Barely able to look behind him, he saw the creatures and their yellow glowing eyes staring at him, some being forced ahead by whatever monster was pushing them ahead.

Rocks were being dragged away from the opening, widening it up.

"Keep at them. I need to take off my bow and shield."

As he slid back a few steps, the creatures' shrieking rose in the tunnel, and Kaen ignored them and the pit in his stomach.

Are you ok? Your heart is racing.

It's tight down here. Worse than you can—

Kaen cut off his words as he reached a spot and finally got his shield off his back. Laying it on the ground ahead, he fumbled for his bow, ignoring whatever had struck him from behind.

I'm working on getting out of here. Just know there are thousands behind me.

Pammon was concerned, but a thread of strength flowed through their bond.

Smiling, even in the darkness of the hole, Kaen felt his friend giving him support.

Thank you.

Always, now focus on what you need to do.

Putting his bow on his shield, Kaen slid them along the rocks, helping them over the spots that blocked the path.

"I'm out!" Phillip shouted, his words echoing through the tunnel.

Kaen could see the light ahead. A few dips and turns blocked his view of the path he knew had to be between him and the exit.

As he squirmed and wove through it, the rocks felt like a monster, wrapping its massive hand and fingers around him and squeezing. Breathing was challenging as he saw the opening ahead.

"Grab my shield," Kaen grunted, struggling to fill his lungs.

Gilmun squirmed into the opening ahead and grabbed the shield with his fingers, blocking out the light from Phillip's orb.

"Focus on this next spot," the dwarf warned. "It's tight; I can see it in your eyes. You can do this, just like your student did."

Wanting to laugh, Kaen just gave a slight nod. The dwarf was earning his reputation at this moment, helping them get through a spot they might have floundered at without his calm demeanor.

Seven feet from the opening, Kaen saw the other three looking at him, looks of concern and hope fighting for space on their faces.

A small area of rocks pinched in tighter.

"You able to widen this?" Kaen asked, his voice barely a whisper.

"Not quickly," Gilmun replied. "This next part will be hard for you. Do you trust me?"

Looking at the redheaded dwarf and seeing the truth that lay deep within his eyes, Kaen nodded.

"Good. Here's what we need to do." Gilmun turned to Phillip. "You need to climb in and be ready to grab his hands. Toss that orb in so it lands near that spot so you can both see. Frederick, you and I will have to pull them both. I know we're still hurting, but we must do our part."

Leaning back over the hole that led to where Kaen was waiting, Gilmun smiled. "It's time to pretend to be a dwarf, Dragon Rider Kaen. When Phillip is in place, I need you to wedge yourself. Get into that spot and keep your hands ahead of you. Use your toes to push. Then the hard part comes next. You will feel crushed, unable to breathe, but we both know it isn't true. Once Phillip has your hands, he will tell us, and I will give the call. Now watch."

Gilmun leaned over and put his hands against his chest.

Somehow, Gilmun expelled even more air, his hands not moving and inches appearing between them. For about twelve seconds, he held it like that before he started to shake. Another seven passed as he trembled, and the dwarf finally took a deep breath.

"You will have to do that. You will have to expel all the air from your lungs. It will burn, and your natural reaction will be to take a deep breath. Fight it. You cannot do that while in that spot. Use your feet and use those toes. Drive as we pull. Do you understand?"

Kaen nodded, calming himself and grateful for the thread of strength coming from Pammon.

"I'm ready."

Gilmun nodded and pointed toward the opening, where Phillip bent down and tossed the lightstone inside.

The bright light almost made things worse, as Kaen's shadows made the small path feel even tighter. Phillip climbed in, keeping a small smile as he inched forward.

It looked like the young man wanted to say something, but he didn't; instead, he kept his eyes focused on the man who had trained him. When Phillip was close he held his arms out, waiting for Kaen.

"I'm in position."

Gilmun grunted and pointed at Frederick, who moved to the other side of the opening and prepared to grab Phillip's ankle.

"Strong but gentle, don't jerk," Gilmun warned as they got into position.

"Ok, Kaen, move forward, and Phillip, tell me the second he has your hands."

Kaen used his feet, pressing against rocks that seemed to slip as he dug his toes in, his armored shoes feeling like weights that held him back.

The rocks caught against his dragon-armored chest and legs, but inch by inch, he got closer till his hands were clasped around Phillip's.

The world was so dark, even with the light of the orb, as the weight of a mountain pressed on every side of him.

"I got him!" Phillip shouted, his voice seeming loud in the chamber of rocks.

"Blow everything out!" shouted Gilmun. "Phillip, say when!"

Kaen's breaths were already short and quick. Barely any movement of his chest or lungs was possible. His whole body screamed, and his mind was raging against him.

Closing his eyes, he focused as Hess had taught him so long ago—on the target before him and letting everything else fade away. His lifestone burned gently, reminding him of the strength inside.

Forcing every bit of air from his lungs, Kaen felt a little space starting to form around him, the smallest amount of room finally there.

"Now!"

Seconds stretched on as Kaen felt his body pulled, his arms lengthening his body and those massive shoulders and traps being wedged against his head. He tried to not crush Phillip's hands and wrists as he held on, feeling his body get stuck in the tight embrace of stone.

"Pull!" grunted Gilmun as Kaen fought the urge to take a breath. His mind was swimming from needing to breathe, and his lungs felt like they would obey its desires.

His toes dug and pressed, and he was unable to use his legs like he wanted. Only the tiny movements of his ankles and calves seemed to work.

The sound of rocks scraping across his armor filled his ears as Phillip tugged and twisted his arms, trying to shimmy his mentor through the gap.

Kaen's eyes watered; he wasn't sure if he could hold on much longer without taking a breath. Even if he had wanted to, he knew nothing would come, which would send him into a state of panic as the rocks hugged his chest.

Finally, his body surged forward a few feet, wrenched free from the mountain that wanted to hold him forever. He gasped for air, feeling the constraints against his torso gone.

Stale, dirty, old air filled his lungs, yet every bit of it felt better than he could remember air having ever been.

"There we go," the dwarf grunted as they continued to pull him and Phillip into the opening on the other side of the fallen stone.

Lying on his stomach, Kaen forced himself to roll over, his lungs filling up as much as possible half a dozen times before he forced himself to get up.

"Remind me I never want to be a dwarf in a mine," Kaen joked as he saw the other three smiling at him.

"I hear that," Frederick replied.

Kaen stared back into the hole behind him and the movement he saw inside.

Slowly, he gathered his bow and arrows.

7

How One Should Act

Kaen infused his arrow with power and sent it flying down into the tunnel.

The explosion shook the rocks he was standing on and he hopped down as quickly as possible.

"You three ready?" Kaen asked as he looked at them, each wondering what had taken him so long.

They nodded, and Frederick moved to the front, holding up the one lightstone they had left.

We are on our way.

It's about time. Amaranth has been pestering me this whole time. Apparently, I have been acting like a mother hen, she says, with how I have been worrying about you. She said it is fine if I act like that with our children but not you.

Chuckling, Kaen followed behind as the four of them jogged through the cave.

Pammon was outside when they reached the exit, the sun's light spilling through the massive entrance. Running forward, Kaen hugged his dragon, who trilled slightly for a moment before stopping when he saw Amaranth staring at him. High above them was the sun, already past the midday point.

"That long?" Frederick asked out loud, shielding his eyes from the brightness.

Any movement along the swamp?

None. I sent Amaranth out to scout a little, and she saw nothing but the occasional animal. She wasn't happy when I made her return without hunting. I tried to warn her about the birds, but . . .

Kaen nodded, scratching his friend's neck for a moment longer before facing the others.

"I know it's been a long time. If you need to relieve yourselves, do it now. I want to fly all the way back to Ebonmount before we land."

The men nodded, each seeking a place for a little moment of privacy.

Amaranth, we will need to use Flight Burst to reach the capital quickly. Is that going to be a problem?

The green dragon huffed, expelling a massive breath out her nose as she glared at Kaen.

Why would it be a problem? I haven't been the one waddling around all night, anxious at your return.

Kaen thumped Pammon's neck as his dragon groaned.

I will remind you of those words in the coming weeks when you complain that I do not show you as much favor as Glynnis.

The green dragon moved closer to Pammon, who turned and matched her gaze as she puffed out her chest.

Kaen moved back, taking in the difference between them as Pammon had now reached a state where he was almost twice her size.

Would you hold that over me?

Pammon leaned down and put his snout close to hers.

He breathed on her and slowly touched the tip of his nose against her.

Whatever was conveyed between them was no longer something Kaen was given access to.

Based on Amaranth's reaction and how she and Pammon intertwined their necks a moment later, things appeared well between them.

How bad was it?

Flying over the destroyed forest, Pammon had waited at least a while before asking the question Kaen knew was on his mind.

Things went bad. We were fortunate to survive the initial blast that sealed the side we came in. There were still thousands of orcs and goblins in there. The attacks have stopped, so something must be happening on their side, but it looks like they have trapped one of their most potent ogres in the cave.

Listening and thinking, Pammon continued to speed across the sky, occasionally checking on Amaranth, who was still behind them.

They had dug out of those caves multiple times when we destroyed some of them two years ago. Why stop? Why bury their own?

Kaen didn't have an answer, and knowing that Pammon was just as confused bothered him more.

What would it take for a kingdom to do that to its own people? If Aldric decided he needed to cut off everyone outside by bringing down the wall in the pass . . .

Something horrible is coming?

Kaen nodded, the dread both he and Pammon shared flowing between them.

Do you finally believe me that the time for us to go on the offensive is now?

Knowing how often Pammon had told him this truth, and he had ignored it, Kaen gave up his notion that victory could be obtained some other way than by taking out Stioks.

Yes. We need to see Aldric.

"I don't think I ever remember being so tired," Aldric declared as he stifled a yawn. "Parenthood isn't easy. I had heard it was difficult, but experiencing it now . . . it is harder than I imagined."

Chuckling, Kaen sipped the diluted warm wine the king's men brought for them.

"I still can't believe you finally remarried and had a child."

Aldric gave a slight grin and shrugged. "I blame you. This whole 'living' and enjoying those moments of peace is what brought this on."

Setting his cup down, Kaen remembered the wedding and how it had brought joy to the kingdom during its first year of fighting the orcs. News of the king's new wife being pregnant rallied the people during those hard times, and now a prince gave hope for another king like the one they had known.

"We need to talk about what I found and how bad things will be. Herb should be here soon, but I must talk to you about something else."

Aldric set his cup down on the table and leaned against it. The eight-foot-long table was in the room they had used to track troop movements for the last few years. Every wall was covered in maps copied from ones Kaen had made.

Wall sections under repair, those defended and one with straw men on them to help look like real guards, decorated the room.

"I cannot sit back and wait any longer. I had hoped that with the news of dragon eggs and then us getting more riders, we could easily win the battle when it was time to face Stioks, but waiting is no longer an option. I must go and face him."

The king's face usually never flinched no matter what news he was told, but his left eye twitched a few times. "You're serious about this. I can see it in your eyes."

Nodding slowly, Kaen stood up and moved to a map that showed the mountains with all the caves.

"This cave is sealed on both sides. We sealed the inside portion, but someone sealed the other side. I haven't checked, but it would appear that this explains why the number of orcs attacking has decreased over the last few months. There is no reason why the orc king would just abandon this fight after so long."

Aldric tapped his finger against the table. "You think they are regrouping . . . since Stioks has attacked the elves, you believe things may start again."

Kaen knew his eyes answered that statement as Aldric read him. Moving to a map on the wall, he pointed at a section far to the southeast. "Somewhere out here is the orc king. I need to find him and destroy the threat before it regroups. It will be easier than attacking Stioks first. If I can take out this threat, it will make what comes after easier."

The sound of Aldric's chair scraping against the stone floor seemed louder than usual as the man got up to study the map. "It seems like a gamble. We have no idea how far away that place could be, and there is no telling what might be out there numberwise. Would you risk being gone that long and flying out there alone?"

"Do you have a better idea?" Kaen asked.

Shaking his head, the older man frowned, scratching a chin with the slightest amount of stubble. Kaen realized that Aldric looked thinner than he had a few weeks ago.

"You've lost weight."

Aldric's eyebrows rose slightly. "People are hungry in the kingdom. I cannot continue to hide inside my walls and eat while they don't. We have already cut rations inside the castle. The food plots we are trying to grow inside the mountain are taking longer than we had hoped. Even with the envoy King Bosgreth sent to assist, we are months away from having enough food for everyone." Pointing at the map of the kingdom's defenses, Aldric sighed. "I'm just grateful the dragons have been willing to eat the orcs and goblins, as we both know there are not enough animals to continue feeding them as one might desire. Soon we will run out of food if something doesn't change."

"The war of attrition," Kaen muttered, remembering what Elnidith had warned him of over six months ago. "We are starving, and they know it."

Returning to his chair, Aldric plopped down, picked up his cup, and took a slow drink. "War is ugly, and this one has gone on longer than we had hoped. If the elves and dwarves hadn't helped, we would have been done half a year ago.

"My advisors have done everything they can to help. You know how I felt when I learned about two people who were working for our enemy."

Kaen nodded as Aldric scowled. The older man took a deep breath and let it out slowly, working through the anger and frustration of finding spies within his own walls. Not wanting to rehash the past, Kaen moved on with their discussion.

"Which is why I need to attack the orcs and their army. If I can end their ability to keep up this assault, we can start getting back on our feet."

"And Ava? Have you told her about this plan yet?" Aldric asked.

Frowning, Kaen returned to his seat. "She wouldn't like it, but I know she will see the wisdom in it."

Unable to hold back, Aldric started to laugh, his voice echoing off the walls as he showed a rare moment of joy. "Kaen," he said after wiping a tear away, "I hope for your sake things happen as you dream they might. I am afraid whatever foolish notion you have will be worse than you can believe. Not telling your wife of your plans leaves you open to other problems."

Are you sure he is awake?

Why would you ask me that question? You know I can tell. He is inside the main room.

I know it just feels weird knowing you can tell that about Hess. When we get close, let him know I'm coming.

I'm grateful you finally acted as you should have a while ago. It is time to stop beating yourself up for the mistakes of the past and move forward. No one can force me to do anything if I have learned anything over these last few years.

Smiling, Kaen glanced down at the sleeping town. The moon was out, and light orbs glowed dimly in the streets as people rested.

For years, sleep had been a rare commodity. The horde attacked at all hours of the night. Their vision allowed them better success at night, and it meant everyone was up, ready to defend.

Children grew up without parents, which burned his heart more than Kaen wanted to admit. So many lives had been lost. So many families had been broken.

Let it go. You have saved more than most could have imagined. Together, we have done all that we could.

Kaen nodded, blinking back the tears that he felt forming.

So many new children had joined his academy because they had no family to return to. All those years of planning had provided a home for children growing up as he had—with no parents.

In the rare moments when he got to visit, their statements of being just like him tore his heart to pieces.

He was done pouting and defending.

Tomorrow he would be the one to bring the fight to his enemies.

Hess says he is ready for you. He also said to make sure you do not wake up Callie or Sulenda, which will make you suffer.

Patting Pammon's neck, Kaen grinned, the anger he had a moment ago gone.

That girl is just like both her parents.

Yes . . . yes, she is, and that is a scary thing.

8

Fatherly Advice

Waving away Hess's attempt to pour him a cup of watered-down wine, Kaen sat in a chair, glancing around the rare empty room of the Dragon Rider's Inn.

"Why are you out here?" Kaen asked, noticing how age had finally caught up with his dad.

"The office is stuffy, and when I sit out here and close my eyes, I can remember the good times we've had here. I remember the day we arrived in town and sat in that booth," Hess said, pointing at the one booth that had never changed in the entire remodel of the inn. "I remember how you wowed the people with your story and stood on the bar like a fool."

Letting out a chuckle, Hess took a small sip of his drink before setting it down on the table.

"So, what stupid thing do you have planned? Pammon won't tell me what it is, but I can feel something, and the way you're sitting tells me you won't be here long."

Snickering, Kaen grinned slightly and leaned against the table. "Let me tell you what has happened in the last few days, and then I'll tell you my plans. After that, you can tell me if I'm right or wrong in my decision."

Refilling his drink, Hess shifted in his chair to get comfortable. "Will my opinion change what you are going to do?"

Kaen shook his head.

"Well, then, Dragon Rider Kaen, tell this old man a story worthy of being told in this inn."

Hess picked at his teeth with his tongue. The wrinkles on his face had started appearing a few years ago, and his age was evident after the injury to his arm.

Folds of skin made mountains as he frowned, not happy with the results of the cave collapse or the plan to seek out the orc king's domain.

He scratched his head for a moment, considering the plan and options before them.

"Do you really think you can find it?"

Shrugging, Kaen pointed at the map he had placed on the table a few minutes ago. "This is the only section we haven't explored, and I'm not sure where else it could be. None of the reports from our spies in Luthaelia mention an actual kingdom of orcs there. They have told us about groups seen taking people away, but always to the south. That points to this area."

Hess nodded, studying the map and never losing the partial scowl he now wore.

"And Ava?"

Chuckling, Kaen shook his head as he crossed his arms, leaning back in his chair. "Aldric asked me the same thing. Why does everyone seem to think this will be an issue?"

"Because she is your wife. I know you seem to think she understands you must do certain things because of who you are, but that doesn't mean she will be excited or content to let you do this."

"So you don't agree with this plan, then, because of her?"

Hess groaned and stood up, shaking his head, stretching as he rose. "No, your plan is one of our few options. You and Aldric are right. If this doesn't end soon, disease and starvation will become our biggest problems." Hess pointed at Kaen and gave a weak smile. "Just remember to ask her about this instead of telling her. It will go better."

"If only I had gotten that armor from King Bosgreth sooner. Think of the difference it would have made against the initial rush of enemies."

Hess shook his head. "Let it go, son. They torched a massive section of the forest, removing the ability to use it against them. Their siege weapons were a threat to you and the other dragons. Focus on what you can do now, not the mistakes and choices we didn't make."

Standing up, Kaen nodded, moved to where Hess was, and embraced him. Even though Hess was still taller, Kaen again realized how much time and all this work had taken a toll on his mentor and dad. His massive body had shrunk enough that, for the first time in a long time, Kaen realized the truth of something he had missed while lost in his concern for his past mistakes.

Hess is getting old . . .

A chuckle came through their bond, and Kaen smiled as they broke the embrace and gave Hess a gentle tap on his shoulder.

"Love you, Dad. Thanks for the advice, as always."

Cocking his head to the side slightly, Hess studied Kaen's expression and slowly began to nod as he smiled. "I doubt you'll listen, but I'm glad I could offer some. Love you too, Kaen. Be safe."

Rolling up the map, Kaen started toward the door. He then winked, and when Hess saw it, Hess groaned.

"Don't you dare let him do that!" Hess shouted as quietly as possible.

Through their connections with Pammon, a thrum began to grow, and even with the noise-dampening runes, the cup on the table vibrated.

"Holy dwarf balls, Kaen, Sulenda is going to kill you!"

At the door to the inn, Kaen laughed, then ran to where Pammon was waiting outside.

You better get out of here.

Or what? Sulenda won't hurt me. Only you and Hess have to fear her.

Pammon leaped into the air and the few people who had stopped and watched from a distance waved at the two of them, giving a slight cheer.

Take me home. I need to talk to Ava.

Pammon groaned, and Kaen could feel his dread at that statement.

You're not afraid of Ava, are you?

Only one person besides you can hurt me; that is her, and you know it. Please don't make me suffer because you are an eggling. Hess was right. Ask, do not tell.

"Why are you asking me? Usually you don't."

Kneeling next to her as she sat in a soft chair, Kaen wore the same smile he'd had since he walked in the door. "I didn't want to tell you what I was thinking of doing. I wanted to know your thoughts and whether you agreed with this decision."

Tapping her finger against her lips, Ava studied Kaen for a moment before turning and looking at Pammon, who was sitting inside the huge room. "Hess . . . you talked to Hess first, and he told you to ask, didn't he?"

Pammon thrummed, and Kaen saw Ava smile as he lost his. "Perhaps my dad gave me some marriage advice."

Snorting, Ava shook her head but never stopped smiling. "At least you listened. I guess I shouldn't be too upset about that. I'd make you promise not to get injured, but we both know how well that last promise held up. Are you sure you're not rushing into this after losing the others in the cave?"

Wincing from the reminder, Kaen shook his head, seeing Ava realize that her comment had hit a nerve.

"No, but we all know what happens if another six months or more of fighting occurs. Food is our greatest threat now, if we cannot stop the flood of orcs for good," Kaen replied. "Children like Callie and the others need a place they can grow without fear."

Groaning, Ava took a deep breath before letting it out. She turned toward Pammon and rolled her eyes. "Some dragons spoil that child; why shouldn't you make this about her, then?"

Why do I always get blamed for spoiling that redheaded child?

Both Kaen and Ava laughed as Pammon grumbled.

"Fine, Pammon and I will go get ready. I'll return soon, my love."

Years of combat had provided Kaen with one of the greatest tools in life. The harness system he had for Pammon was constantly evolving as his dragon grew and the needs of combat shifted. It took less than ten minutes to put on the straps, saddle, and four baskets filled with arrows.

I need to thank Hess and Herb for really streamlining this process.

As Herb said, necessity is the mother of invention. Now, then, how quickly do you want to get there?

It's been a few long days, and I'm actually planning on sleeping a few hours, if you don't mind. Are you good on food?

Yes . . . My displeasure of nothing but orcs and goblins has well surpassed its limits.

Then just fly toward the spot we talked about. You pick the path. I'm going to rest.

Are you asking me or telling me?

Groaning as Pammon regained altitude, Kaen patted his friend's neck before leaning back in his saddle and lying flat along his ridge.

Do you mind if I sleep for a little bit?

Oh, I don't mind. I just wanted to make sure that I got the same treatment as Ava.

Sometimes, I think you get the better treatment. Besides, Amaranth and Glynnis always listen to you.

Pammon began to thrum, shaking violently as he flew.

I'm sorry. Are we talking about the same two female dragons? They don't ever listen to me. Every discussion turns into a battle of wills, and I never win, even when I get my way.

But it always looked like—

Trust me, I never win. I often envy how you and Ava discuss things, and you always come out ahead.

It was Kaen's turn to laugh as he lay against Pammon's back, shaking his head.

I guess we both don't get our way . . . Does Hess . . .

At the same time, both started to laugh, Pammon thrumming louder and Kaen starting to tear up slightly.

It is a good thing we can escape for a few days.

You did see how Amaranth acted when I left. Needless to say, had Glynnis been there, I'm not sure she wouldn't have come with us.

But someone needed to guard the eggs since we weren't sure how long we would be gone.

Exactly!

Both of them said nothing for a moment as Pammon reached the altitude he would fly at. Beneath them, the world came alive as the sun appeared in the east.

We should appreciate the fact that we are suffering together. Not that I would have it any other way.

I can't imagine having two babies soon . . . the thought of two egglings . . .

Pammon's spine lurched momentarily as a shudder traveled through him.

I'll do my best to spoil them like you will someday spoil mine.

We are in trouble, aren't we?

Yes, Pammon. . . . Yes, we are.

9

Seeking What's Hidden

Thank you for letting me sleep. I can't believe I slept that long.

Pammon said nothing, but Kaen could feel the affirmation of his comment through their bond.

How long will it be till we reach the border of the area we know?

We will arrive a few hours before the sun rises tomorrow. How far do you want to explore?

We have to search until we find it. Otherwise, we are wasting time and leaving our people defenseless against what might keep coming. Surely we can find some trail leading deeper into that section.

We thought that two years ago and found nothing. It may be different since it appears that they are no longer invading.

Kaen considered the truth of that. If the orcs and goblins had been in the cave for as long as it appeared, the question now was where they had gone before the way in was sealed off.

I guess I should have listened when someone said we should have checked a few months ago to see more troop movements.

Yes, but someone was acting butthurt all the time and not listening to his wife or his dragon.

The amount of sarcasm that came through their bond as Pammon spoke was impossible to miss.

I can only apologize so many times . . .

That doesn't mean I don't take the opportunity to remind you so we don't fall into the pattern of bad choices again. Now, let's focus on what we need to do: eat and rest. Now that you are awake, I am going to use my skill to cut down on some of our travel time.

[Flight Burst Activated]

The surge of power that flowed through Pammon and the speed they now experienced was far beyond what it had been three years ago. The size and strength of his dragon still amazed Kaen every day. Growth had slowed the last year as food became scarcer and the dragons were forced to eat the orc army more and more. Occasionally they could eat a higher-tier ogre, and there was a noticeable difference in growth in the females. Still, Kaen started to wonder if Pammon was reaching a limit to how large he could become at his age.

I'm only six years old, and your thoughts run everywhere. We both know I am the size Tharnok was. And don't ask.

I wasn't. I'm just thinking of things we need to figure out. Are you still ok with Phillip and Frederick being the first to attempt to be there when the eggs hatch?

There are no other options. We both know that no one else has shown the conviction they have. Based on what you told me about what happened inside the cave, there should be no doubts. Even Frederick's fears were not enough to prevent him from taking this chance. You were almost frozen as he was.

Kaen gently patted the scales on Pammon's neck as he leaned against it, feeling the wind rush over him. Beneath him, the world sped by at an alarming rate.

Only twenty-seven candidates are still alive after all those fighting to take the test next month. None of them are over sixteen . . . Then there are still over one hundred fifty students with lifestones who will be ready in another year. Did I do right by this?

Frustration flowed from Pammon.

There was no other choice. We have talked about this multiple times. Without the "Dragon Children" as your people call them, the wall would have never withstood the assaults. The guards were overwhelmed and the constant barrage of attacks that lasted for over a month wore everyone out.

People forget that even you and I need rest. When we were gone for a few hours to sleep, it wasn't easy on Glynnis or Amaranth. Each of them was pregnant also and that required them to rest.

So do not feel like the kingdom can only succeed with you. The truth is they are all exhausted. We suffered from spells that made people weak and sick. The initial attack killed hundreds of guards we had not expected to lose, all to a spell no one knew was coming.

When wives, children, and your students defended, the walls held. Sometimes we must be willing to understand that everyone must fight. I remember a young boy who was not as prepared as these children are going into a cave against goblins.

Smiling, Kaen remembered that moment and the lessons learned the hard way.

And you are sure Amaranth and Glynnis are ok with those two choices?

Pammon stayed quiet for a moment. Minutes passed, and Kaen could feel him struggling to answer that question.

Amaranth is fine with the decision, while Glynnis has a problem with it. One was used by the council and saw firsthand how their actions and words contradicted the truth. So her fear of other Dragon Riders is not there because she has seen how you act. Even when you make foolish mistakes, she knows you are fighting in the interest of others. Plus, she has sworn herself to you.

Glynnis still hesitates, as the idea of her child being bound to a person still feels like a form of slavery, like the people we encountered on the island. She won't fight against it, but I think it has to do with the candidates you have chosen.

If more eggs come and the decision arises again, they will be more hesitant if the boys do not work out.

Kaen thought about the conversations he had had with both dragons, telling them his desire and wishes about Phillip and Frederick. There had been a moment when he felt Glynnis would never give in, but he also remembered when Amaranth stepped in and defended him.

Do they really fear my ability to command them?

Would you fear a person who can make you do anything with just a single command?

Pammon's question left no doubt on how the two felt.

So do they fear me or—

It is both. You have earned their respect, but I can always feel the fear that hides beneath their scales. You know, for a few weeks, I struggled with those feelings after you commanded me to fly away. My very will was crushed like a deer between my teeth. I had no chance. It was as if everything I was disappeared at that moment. There is a part of me that struggles to know what I would do if you used that power again. When you tossed away that jewelry, it proved to me you were worthy of that power you hold.

If you used it to enslave the will of my kind . . . I am not sure I could ever forgive that, no matter the reasoning. Some might ask, "Aren't the results worth the price?" Aldric asked you once and had you not stood up to him, I would have. Would you trade all the lives of your family and friends if it meant stopping this war?

You know I wouldn't . . .

Then do not dwell on that idea again. Know that I am forever grateful we didn't fly to the island of my kind and enslave them. Be better than the one we are fighting, who we both know would not hesitate to use that power. I know why you did it, and I agree with the decision, but that power is still like Stioks.

How can you compare the two of us?!

How many people in the kingdoms he rules over wish they could resist his command? Yet they have no power to do so. Saying no results in their death—or worse, the death of those they love.

Considering those words, Kaen remained silent, letting the wind wash over him.

It's never easy.

Thrumming, Pammon gently shook his head as he sped through the sky.

We were not chosen to have an easy life. There was one brief moment where I considered selling my own soul and telling you to do what I knew was wrong. Thankfully you are a man worthy of me. Now rest, stop worrying about what might happen, and focus on what is before us.

Two days of traveling with limited sleep left Kaen and Pammon in a sour mood. The forests and the swamps they searched through had provided constant problems.

Mosquitoes plagued them every second they were on the ground, and even under Pammon's wing, they found their way to every inch of Kaen's exposed skin.

Food was difficult even for Pammon to locate, and the few animals he found almost never felt worth the time or energy to fly down and eat them.

Halfway through the second day of searching, a path appeared deep inside the swamps, and as the sun began to set, small fires showed in the distance.

You see those?

Activating his lifestone, Kaen closed his eyes and looked through Pammon's eyes, seeing the dots of fires spread across the land to the southeast.

How many fires are there?

Thousands . . . I think we have found what we are looking for.

As they flew closer, a castle came into view. Even in the darkness, combined with the moon and the lights within the castle, Pammon easily saw what was before them.

There are a lot of weapons on those walls that appear designed to take down a dragon.

Based on the number of defenses, they have no love for Juthom and Stioks. What do you want to do?

Flying high in the night sky, they looked at the army below them. Spread out for miles all around were campfires and tents, with goblins, orcs, and ogres everywhere.

Fires flickered as what must be an orc blacksmith banged on weapons and armor, preparing the army for battle.

There must be over a hundred and fifty thousand, maybe two hundred and fifty thousand. We have barely killed one quarter of their forces.

I'll ask again because the real question is now: What do you want to do? Can you really fight against that?

The frustration of knowing there was a chance of another three years or more of siege so close to Ebonmount had Kaen's lifestone starting to burn. If he was right, Stioks planned on working with them, and both forces would attack together. The odds of their kingdom falling were too high.

Together, we can easily take out enough of them to let them know we are done waiting.

Thrumming, Pammon nodded.

How do you want to do this?

They spent an hour studying the army beneath them, and Kaen and Pammon knew the castle would be hard to break. At some point, they would obviously draw the attention of those inside, and neither had any idea what might actually come from within the walls.

If the siege ogre was any indication of things to come, there were probably horrors that would make it seem like a minor threat.

We will hit from the south. I'll start by sending arrows into the camp, causing confusion and killing as many as possible. I have almost four hundred arrows.

Kaen sighed, knowing that he had only six arrows designed to fight dragons. No one had found any more of the metal required for them, and the constant fighting had prevented them from searching for more. Aldric had given the little bit he had in storage to help his cause.

Just tell me when you want to engage. I will do my part. You do yours.

Smiling, Kaen nodded and drew his bow back.

Perhaps I can finally hit forty . . .

The chaos that erupted beneath them as Kaen sent arrows charged with lightning into the camp, mixed in with ones that exploded, seemed to pale compared to the fighting along the walls in Ebonmount.

Every shot killed groups of ogres, orcs, and goblins as they began fighting amongst themselves, trying to find out where the attacks came from.

When a higher-tier orc or ogre showed up, Kaen took them out with a single explosive shot, preventing leadership from controlling the troops they were responsible for.

By the time he was almost out of arrows, Kaen had killed over three thousand troops.

It's much easier when one doesn't have to worry about destroying a wall or injuring their own troops.

Are you sure you are ready for this?

It's time for us to bring the fight to them. You lay a path of fire to the side and draw their attention. I'll do the rest.

Swooping down, Pammon used his breath to ignite a path of fire over fifty yards long before swooping back up into the sky.

No one had noticed Kaen as he hopped off Pammon's back when the dragon paused momentarily at the end of his trail.

Kaen took off with the sword and shield in hand, charging to the west at the first orc he saw.

By the time the shout had been raised in the camp, Kaen was cutting a path through the army on the west side of the flames Pammon had created, a row of bodies littering the ground behind him.

Do not celebrate just yet. They are coming to you like flies on stink.

Let them. Tonight we will strike them down.

From above Kaen, in the darkness of night, Pammon roared, and as Kaen's sword took off two heads from goblins who had looked up, Kaen let himself smile.

There was killing to do, and he would be the instrument of death.

10

Always Listen to Your Dragon

Popping a cork off a potion, Kaen drank it, letting the injuries that were overwhelming him go away in the silent yell that always came.

We should consider that we have done enough and go.

Kaen glanced at the field. The sun was up, and countless corpses lay in piles surrounding him. The creatures he had just killed were nothing he had ever heard of before, and as he drew closer to the castle, two more stood near the gate, chained and appearing ready to come at him.

What are these things? They disappear from my sight and then appear so close . . . if it weren't for your vision, I would have no idea where they were.

They are nothing we have ever seen, and the fact that one almost tore your arm off should make you cautious to continue to press this attack. We have dealt a major blow, and we need to go.

Am I being an eggling if I say I want to stay and fight and push to the king of the orcs?

He sliced down two more ogres that rushed at him, both tier-two but no match for his power and speed.

I mean, I did hit forty with my sword in that fight. Should I try my bow against them?

We need to go. We may be at our limits. If Stioks hasn't pushed against these . . . LOOK OUT!

Pammon's cry rattled his head, but Kaen saw the massive cloud of green gas coming at him. Turning, he run as fast as he could away from the cloud that rolled across the ground and high above it.

I'm not sure I can outrun this . . .

Panic flooded their connection as Pammon swooped down to where Kaen was.

Reverberating through his mind was the memory of a spell resembling the one Stioks had cast the day they first fought.

I'm coming. Keep running!

Pammon swooped down, corkscrewing as he tried to get to Kaen as quickly as possible.

Glancing over his shoulder as he ran, Kaen saw the cloud sweeping over the orcs and goblins, watching them drop and choke, none standing back up after falling down.

Pammon was too far away, and Kaen knew it. He had been foolish, allowing his anger to cloud his thinking, and now he was about to possibly be killed because of it.

I'm almost there!

Speeding past the horde that ran away with him, having seen death approaching, Kaen realized there was a kind of magic he didn't know about.

Pammon was so close, but the cloud was almost upon him, stretching across the ground.

Hold your breath and run!

Filling his lungs once more, Kaen felt the cloud wash over him, and his skin immediately began to itch and burn. His eyes watered, and everything inside him wanted him to scream in pain, sending out the breath that he held so dearly in his lungs.

Jump!

Knowing what Pammon wanted, Kaen leaped into the air, driving with all his power as he felt the talons gently grasp him before they swept him into the air.

Trails of the magic cloud swirled around him as Pammon flew higher, his wings sending away the green gas that seemed to kill so many without concern for who it was.

Almost out of it! Hold it!

Only now did Kaen realize how high the cloud had risen—it was well over a quarter mile high.

His chest heaved as his body wanted him to retch. He wanted to scratch at his face. Mucus dripped from his nose and eyes.

It was hard to see as his vision went white.

Breathe!

His lungs rattled and shook as he pushed out the air inside him and quickly gulped down more. Each breath burned. Even though they were out of the cloud, it was as if somehow the magic had penetrated him.

[Disease Resistance Skill Acquired]
[Disease Resistance Skill Increased x10]

The pain and feeling subsided for a moment, but it was still there, crawling along his skin.

Talk to me! Kaen!

Blinking back the tears and mucus, Kaen wiped his eyes.

It took a few times, blinking and trying to look around, for Kaen to realize what was wrong.

I can't see . . .

Pammon roared, his voice thundering across the land as he flew to the west.

At all?!

Concern and worry hit Kaen harder than any weapon ever had. He felt the fear inside Pammon.

I cannot see from my eyes. I can see from yours, though. I . . . I'm sorry, Pammon . . . I didn't—

No! Do not give up. Be ready. Use my eyes. I'm going to send you up into the air, and you will get on your saddle. We will fly home. Someone there can help you.

Had Kaen not been able to feel the doubt in Pammon's voice, he might have believed this was possible.

Stop blaming yourself, that gas attack couldn't be something you planned for!

Pammon ignored Kaen's plea, pushing himself to his limit and keeping his Flight Burst skill activated for as long as possible.

Had he seen the speed at which the cloud passed beneath them, Kaen would have understood what concern and worry can allow one to do.

Pammon's fear dripped off him every second they were flying. No matter how much he tried to convince Kaen that everything would be ok, underneath it all was the lingering doubt.

Over this time, Kaen gained seven more points of disease resistance.

In less than a full day, Pammon reached the Ebonmount border and aimed for the cave with Amaranth.

I need you!

What is wrong?

Kaen is injured, and I need you to try to heal him. It may be like what Elies had.

When Pammon spoke those words as he flew toward the cave entrance, Amaranth was up, moving from both eggs and darting toward the open space.

Hurry. Every second counts!

* * *

Kaen groaned as he lay on the ground. He had gotten off Pammon, who immediately left, flying to find Ava.

You are a fool. I know Pammon is worried, but I am not sure I can heal this.

Kaen lay still, feeling the magical power of Amaranth flowing through him.

What is different? Is it too late?

There is dark magic in this. I have only seen magic like this once, but it was not this evil. It has a taint to it.

Had Kaen been able to see, he would have noticed Amaranth's look of concern, her eyelids almost closed as she concentrated on trying to heal the rider of the dragon she cared for.

How many of their own did they kill with this?

If I had to guess between them and my actions, at least a quarter of their army is now gone. Once the cloud came over me, I couldn't see how much farther it spread. All I know is that they considered me worth that cost.

Of course they did, scoffed Amaranth. ***You are worth more than their entire army. If you died, Pammon would have raged, and Glynnis and I would have left with our eggs, leaving you and the others to deal with everything that came after.***

You would abandon the kingdom?

A grumble came from Amaranth, and Kaen could sense the frustration from her.

What do I have here without Pammon? He is my mate. You are his rider. Together, you both give Glynnis and me a reason to stay. Without you two, no reason exists for us here. Staying would only put our eggs at risk, and we all know that giving them to Stioks is not a wise decision.

Kaen started to move when he felt a talon push against his chest.

Lie still and stop talking. It is hard enough to see if I can do anything without the distractions of conversing, and it is harder when you move.

Kaen lay still, sighing, doing his best to hope for something he realized might never happen.

"Kaen!"

Ava's voice carried across the stone walls and floors as he heard Pammon's talons slide across the floor.

The sound of footsteps approaching him told Kaen there was more than just Ava there.

I brought Ava and her father. I need to rest, but I won't leave. Is there any change?

No . . . Amaranth isn't—

Do not worry. No matter what happens, I will be here.

"What did you do?" Ava asked, her hand touching his side as she knelt beside him.

Letting his lifestone burn, Kaen looked through Pammon's eyes and saw Ava leaning over him, tears falling from her face. Next to her was her father, carrying a bag over his shoulder and getting ready to kneel next to him.

"I tried to end the fight . . . I . . ."

Swallowing the lump in his throat, Kaen felt the weight of what his choice had caused. A blind Dragon Rider. A kingdom that needed him, and now, once word got out, they would be even more vulnerable.

"Tell me what it was," Lord Hurem said as he began to open his bag. "Ava told me Pammon said it was a cloud of green. What other effects did you have?"

Watching himself from Pammon's perspective felt weird. He saw his father-in-law pulling out a book and laying it on the floor beside him. Kaen could hear everything, but to see it like this, he felt overwhelmed by it all.

"My skin itched like I wanted to scrape it off me. My eyes burned, and mucus ran from them and my nose. Everything felt on fire, I guess. The orcs and goblins who breathed it didn't make it more than a few steps before they fell to the ground."

The older man nodded, flipping through the book after he handed Ava a small notepad and pen. She took it, and Kaen saw her writing on it.

"Do you feel the effects of it still?"

Shaking his head, Kaen reached up and tapped his chest. "I gained Disease Resistance. I'm currently at a level seventeen."

A smile broke through his concern as Lord Hurem and Ava looked at each other in shock.

"A seventeen . . . well, that explains why it no longer seems to be bothering you, but still . . ." The older man trailed off as he flipped through a few more pages. He reached into his bag and pulled out a jar of something yellow.

"This might sting, but are you ok with me trying something?"

Holding back a snappy reply, Kaen nodded. He felt the man opening up his eyelids, watching it through Pammon's eyes.

This is very weird . . . seeing what you see and feeling it.

Be quiet and focus. I'm tired and would close my eyes if you weren't using them.

Surprised by the short, snappy reply, Kaen felt Pammon's exhaustion. He had pushed himself to make sure they got to Ebonmount safely.

Lord Hurem filled a dropper with some of the yellow liquid from the jar, held it over Kaen's open eye, and administered a few drops. Kaen tried to not react as pain erupted, burning all the way to the center of his head.

"Holy mother of goblin humpin'! That shite burns!"

"It's good that it does," replied his father-in-law as he put the remaining liquid back in the jar and closed it. "If it didn't, we would be in trouble."

"Does that mean—"

Her father cut Ava off as he held up his hand and gave a sharp shake of his head. "For now, I will put a poultice on his eyes and wrap them up. We need to get with the adventurers' guild and see what they might have to help with this. For now, Kaen, you need to rest. Judging from how Pammon jerked while flying, you can stay here."

I'm going to close my eyes. I need to sleep.

Not waiting for a reply, Kaen felt the world go black.

Fear gripped him at that moment when he realized that he was blind without Pammon.

A hand squeezed his shoulder, and Kaen felt a pair of lips against his forehead.

"It's ok, my love. I'm here. Rest."

11

Consequences

The sleep that came was not restful, as Kaen repeatedly relived his mistake. Most of the time, he died. Sometimes Pammon died because of his choice.

When he woke up, covered in sweat, he immediately touched his face and felt a bandage over his eyes.

"Leave it alone," Ava's voice rang out. "Father says it will help. For now, just trust the poultice and rest."

You are safe. We are all here.

Pammon's voice and the hand on Kaen's shoulder calmed the fear rising inside him.

Use my eyes if you want. I can feel what you are feeling.

Letting his lifestone smolder, Kaen sighed as the black void of his vision was replaced with what Pammon saw. He was still lying on the stone floor, a small piece of cloth under his head and a thin blanket over his legs and torso.

Thank you. More than you might realize for this.

That is what I am here for. To continuously support you.

"I'm going to stand up," Kaen announced, putting his hand on Ava's. "I can see through Pammon's eyes, and I need to see if I can figure out how to walk and move like this."

"Are you sure?" Ava asked as she glanced at Pammon, who nodded.

"Yes, and you should know you look even more beautiful when seen through the eyes of a dragon. Every strand of hair that is out of place shows up—"

A fist punched him in the arm, and Kaen laughed, seeing it coming and letting it hit.

"Gah, you're such an arse. See if I help when Pammon isn't around."

Grabbing the blanket, Kaen set it to the side and rolled over to his hands and knees.

His body felt weird as he tried to move based on what he saw through Pammon. It took a moment, but after a minute, he was able to stand and not keep rocking as he felt off balance from the view.

"You look like a toddler who has just learned to stand," teased Ava.

Amaranth and Pammon thrummed, finding Ava's comment funnier than Kaen's.

He ignored them and turned to face Pammon. Seeing himself and how he looked almost made him shudder. His face had a few boils, and his beard was splotchy and missing some patches.

Touching his face slowly, Kaen saw Ava wince as he did.

"I had hoped you might not realize—"

"How awful I look?"

She nodded, moving a step closer to him. "It's all over. I lifted your armor slightly but didn't try to remove it. Father said he was surprised at how well your body defended against the spell. We both believe it has to do with Pammon and your connection as well as your lifestone giving you resistance to it so quickly."

"Help me take it off?"

She helped him as Kaen struggled to undo the pieces. Standing still was hard enough, so he let Ava do most of the work.

Eventually, everything but his underwear was off.

His entire body was covered in boils and splotches. None of it hurt, yet the view of it made his stomach almost roll. Even though he was a mountain of muscle that reminded him of Hess years ago, Kaen felt like he looked like a monster.

You are fine. She does not care how you look. She is just grateful that you are alive, as am I.

But—

No buts. Rejoice in the fact that you are alive and that it appears you will recover. Lord Hurem said that you will regain your eyesight at some point. He is certain. For now, you need to rest.

Ava moved up next to him, and Kaen saw her as she reached out to touch his arm.

Flinching, he moved, his directions backward, his arm slamming into her and sending her into the table before she fell to the ground.

As she landed on the stone floor with a thump and a cry, Kaen's legs weakened and he fell to the ground near her.

"I'm sorry! I didn't mean to!"

Ava nodded and brushed herself off, wincing.

"It's ok. I am fine," she said.

Realizing that he had just risked injuring her, Kaen backed away and began to sob. He let his lifestone stop burning and found comfort in the darkness.

You need to stop this!

A hand touched his shoulder, and it took everything he had not to pull away.

"This is my fault! All this happened because I didn't listen to Pammon and leave when I should have. I look like this because of—"

"Please stop, my love." Ava's voice was breaking, and he felt something wet against his skin. "I cannot bear to see you in this pain. I don't care how you look. I care that you are alive. Does Sulenda care that Hess doesn't have an arm?"

"But I have to defend against—"

"You are not alone. This isn't just your fight." Ava's voice had changed to the firm tone she used. "Stop thinking you must do this alone. Stop believing that every time someone dies, it is your fault. Everyone in this kingdom is willing to lay down their life if it means others can live. You have done all you can, and it is time to stop believing otherwise.

"For three years we have fought shoulder to shoulder on the walls. We defended against the never-ending onslaught of creatures that attacked. How many nights have we spent fighting on the back of the dragons? Remember, I'm here with you the entire way."

Her hand squeezed his shoulder, and he felt her moving around him. Even without his sight, he could sense her coming to kneel before him, a hand on each of his shoulders.

"We swore to love each other no matter what and to defend the other. Let me help defend you from yourself and the belief you seem to have that only you can win this battle."

"But . . . Stioks is a—"

"A man . . . just like you. A man who allowed himself to be foolish and overconfident and look at where it got you. He will make a mistake. He will get cocky, and when he does, we will make him pay. Together."

It was true. Stioks and Juthom had made a mistake once, and they were almost able to end this war then. Surely the man would make another. When he did, it would be the moment to act.

You are lucky I let you marry her. She is far wiser than you are.

Kaen began to laugh.

"Pammon reminded me why he let you marry me. He said it was because you are much smarter than I am."

"Of course I am," replied Ava, her tone matter-of-fact. "All women are smarter than men."

Amaranth thrummed, and Kaen could hear Pammon groan.

"Now, if you don't mind, let me help you to a chair so you can sit while I get you some food."

Sitting there, letting Ava feed him some porridge, was more challenging than he imagined.

After about five bites, he tried doing it on his own, feeling the bowl against his lips and scooping it into his mouth with a spoon. Occasionally, Kaen felt some food fall against his chest or lap, but he didn't care, ignoring how he must look.

"You know I don't mind helping," Ava said as she took the empty bowl from him.

"I know. It's just . . . not knowing how long this may last, I need to try to do some things for myself."

He couldn't see Ava nod but felt Pammon agreeing with that statement.

"Fine, then I'll leave some clothes here and come back later. I must return to our place and get a few things together. Pammon can take me."

Wanting to say something, Kaen bit his lip. The tone of her voice told him she wasn't pleased with how he was handling this.

You look like an eggling trying to move after hatching . . . you are flopping—

"Please stop," groaned Kaen as he lay on the floor, pulling up his pants. "I know it doesn't look pretty, but I'm doing my best."

I'm not making fun of you. I'm simply stating how you appear. I already offered to help guide you, but you made it clear how you feel about help.

Ignoring Amaranth's statement, Kaen tied his drawstring with minimal issues, after a lifetime of doing so, not requiring him to see it.

Reaching slowly along the floor, Kaen felt around for the shirt he had misplaced while trying to put his pants on.

A slight thrum came from the green dragon across the room.

After a few moments of no success, Kaen sighed. "Am I anywhere near it?"

No . . . go to your right, about four feet . . . more . . . more . . . now a little to the right . . . there.

Kaen felt the cloth shirt brush his outstretched fingers and grasped it quickly. He pulled it to himself and started to put it on, realizing it was on backward when the shirt was tight against his throat.

It is funny to believe you are the famous Dragon Rider who commanded the council to stand down, unable to—

Amaranth stopped talking when Kaen turned to face her.

He knew where she was, able to feel her presence somehow, and he glared.

"Do I need to command you to be quiet?" he asked, his voice expressing displeasure at how she was talking to him.

I shall refrain from further teasing. Forgive me. I thought since you and Pammon did it, we would be ok with a little fun.

Grunting, Kaen forced himself to take a deep breath and let it out slowly.

"I'm sorry . . . I am on edge, and you do not deserve to be talked to like that. Forgive me."

He heard her talons coming across the floor toward him, and a moment later he felt her breath against him before her snout barely touched his forehead.

Forgive me. I should have been kinder to the one who freed me. Now sit still and let me see if I can assist with your injury.

The warm touch of her healing spread over him, running through his body.

She focused it on his head, and it was like a gentle summer breeze blowing through his hair and over his face. It calmed him, taking away some of his worry and angst as the magic flowed through him.

Time seemed to stretch on as he sat there, enjoying the peace that came from whatever Amaranth was doing.

When it stopped, he felt a slight gust of air from her nostrils.

Whatever that poultice is seems to be working. I can sense it doing something, but you still have at least a week before you may recover any sight at all. Your skin is also healing itself. In a few days, I expect those boils to be gone.

"Doesn't your magic heal them?"

No . . . those are different in some way. Elies had something like that, but it was a darker magic. A common thread exists between them, but both are resistant to healing. It is like . . . flying into a powerful storm. It is possible, but the time it takes to fight the wind may not be worth the effort. It would be best to wait it out and save your strength. You are stronger than Elies was. Your lifestone is different.

Kaen nodded, knowing the truth of what she said.

Turning, he looked toward the entrance to the cave where they sat with both eggs.

"Pammon is returning."

Yes, I can sense him too.

"He likes you."

Kaen's statement caught Amaranth off guard, and she choked for a second before regaining her composure.

What has he said? What do you mean?!

Grinning, Kaen shook his head. "Just know he cares about you both. Even though he isn't sure how to show that or tell you, be gentle with him. For so long, it was just him and me. He didn't have another dragon to relate to. When Tharnok came along, it wasn't a close relationship. Every day, he was trained to be a fighter. Now . . . now he is learning to love."

The slightest trill came from Amaranth for a second before it went silent.

Only the sound of wind and her breathing could be heard for a minute.

Thank you. You surprise me every day. Somehow you have given me hope even when I know you are missing yours.

Holding his hand out, Kaen waited. Amaranth moved forward, putting her snout against his hand.

Scratching it gently, Kaen nodded. "Family does that."

12

When Life Hits Hard

The absence of vision made knowing what time it was difficult. Not needing as much sleep amplified Kaen's frustration as he listened to Pammon.

You need to come with me. Sitting here will do you no good.

"But if people see me, it will—"

It will be impossible. I will not fly near the city. For now, we need to get you out of here. In a few hours, we can go pick up Ava. She said she wanted to pack a few things and rest.

Frustrated, Kaen sighed. "Fine, we can fly for a bit, but I don't want to be seen by anyone. If word gets out—"

It will not come from me, Pammon interrupted, moving closer to Kaen. **Stop complaining because I won't let you chase a chicken and get on my back.**

A chuckle escaped Kaen's lips, and he groaned.

What is this about a chicken? Could he not catch one?

Amaranth's question sent Kaen and Pammon into a fit of laughter as Kaen followed Pammon's neck until he found the groove he knew to grab onto. Years of practice allowed him to do this in his sleep, and now, with no way to see, Kaen found himself sitting exactly where he belonged.

I'm still confused about this chicken. Is it a real chicken?

It was a chicken. Back when Pammon was young. He wanted to eat it, but I never let him.

So this is one of those jokes you two share . . .

Pammon thrummed, vibrating beneath Kaen's legs.

It is. Do not worry. One day, we will joke about things that make you upset.

That doesn't seem very wise.

Family often doesn't seem to care as long as the others think it is funny.

Amaranth snorted.

Go fly. I will guard both eggs until Glynnis returns. When she does, I will need some time to be free.

Hearing the click of Kaen's harness, Pammon turned and moved to the edge of the cave entrance.

When she gets back, we can fly together.

A trill came from inside the cave as Pammon leaped into the air.

She will hold you to that, teased Kaen, feeling the familiar scales on Pammon's neck as the wind rushed against him.

Kaen felt awful after Ava made him drop her off at their old place to collect items. She told him to listen to Pammon, as he was acting like an eggling.

You are being stubborn. Stop holding back and use my eyes. Why ignore what we have and limit yourself?

Tired of Pammon's pestering for the last hour or so, Kaen gave in, letting his lifestone burn so that he could see the world through his friend's golden eyes.

A calm flooded Kaen's mind as the world below him came alive. The world moved beneath them in the light of the evening sun. Carts flowed in the streets, and people walked along the sidewalks.

Everywhere Pammon's eyes moved, Kaen saw life and felt connected to it all.

It appears that I was right, as usual. Next time, you should just obey my advice the first time I offer it.

Ignoring Pammon's words, Kaen lost himself in the moment. All the panic and fear disappeared as he saw the world beneath him. Life went on, and he knew that in time, things would also return to normal for him. He had things to accomplish.

That is it. Let go of the frustration you feel. Let me do what I can. It has been a long time since you just enjoyed our time in the sky. The kingdoms has been dependent upon us since Elies and Tharnok passed. Without them there to protect from Stioks we became the wall that holds back the waves of oppression.

How did the two of them ever manage to stay so strong for so long?

Pammon's mind wandered as they flew.

I don't know. We have chased enough false reports, and the knowledge that the spies have been working within our kingdom cost us greatly those first few years. When Herb's people found the caves with the same portals as the ones to the south, and all the mines empty, we knew just how far ahead of us Stioks has been. We've gone in circles sometimes. Even though the attack on the orc king didn't go as we planned, we have learned more than we want to admit. Now we know why so many continued to crash against our walls.

Pammon, I caused this . . . my actions at the orc castle and today when I pushed—

It was an accident. Ava will not blame you. I need you, and she needs you to be the man she fell in love with. Bold, brave, and committed to protecting others.

Do not beat yourself up about this. The kingdom needs the Dragon Rider who fought back the horde, not the one who cries on my back right now.

What do you mean?! How can you say that right now?!

Because I am your dragon and your friend. Because we are bound. You and I know you have acted like a whipped dog, moving with your tail between your legs this last year. Every day has been a battle of your spirit due to regret.

Ava and I won't be able to deal with you if you sink deeper into regret. Stioks won't have to worry about defeating you because that will happen on your own.

You don't understand! How many have died—

How many have lived because of the sacrifices you have made? What would happen if you had attacked, and we died? How many more would have perished? This isn't a game we can play of what if. Deal with the task at hand.

Your wife needs you right now. She needs her husband to be present and strong. When the time comes, and you can change gears, that time isn't now.

Kaen sat there feeling like Pammon had slapped him across the face.

His heart hurt in so many ways, yet the truth of what Pammon had just said fought against every emotion that wanted to keep Kaen encaged. His soul was defeated, and Kaen realized that he was tired.

I will try . . . I cannot promise to always be strong, but I will do what I must for Ava and you.

13

Commitment

Pammon flew to an area along the mountain and when he spotted a cliff large enough for him to land, he set down on it, his massive wings flapping and fighting against the wind that wanted to push him off.

Why are we stopping here?

I want to do something, and we are going to make a pact. Glynnis had mentioned to me that dragons once created something to mark special places and moments long ago. Together you and I can do that. We can choose from this day forward to be different. To no longer live in the past and to focus completely on the future. No matter what life throws at us.

Sitting on his dragon's neck, Kaen felt confused but watched through Pammon's eyes as his dragon moved to a massive rock pressed against the mountain.

What are you fighting for?

No more families hurt . . . no more families broken . . . to keep them together . . .

Kaen's lifestone began to burn.

Remember how you felt when you thought Hess was going to die. Remember that moment. Let those feelings overtake you.

Goose bumps appeared all over Kaen's body as he remembered that day. The moment Pammon had told him Hess was about to die and that he was going to have a daughter. In that moment, Kaen relived all that pain and hurt, and those fears and a clear thread of why it had mattered so much swept over Kaen.

His lifestone surged, power flowing through him and making his body pulse with energy.

Yes! Give it to me! Let me have all of that!

Kaen grunted and put both hands on Pammon's scales. He could no longer reach around his dragon's neck, which had become so broad as he had grown. Sliding his hands along his friend's scales, Kaen embraced Pammon as much as he could, letting each scale he felt along his skin act as a conduit for what he was about to do.

Face pressed against a scale, Kaen gave it all to his dragon. He felt the power leaving him, pouring through that connection.

Heat began to rise inside Pammon, hotter than any other time Kaen had felt before. The very scales he was embracing felt like the heat of a forge.

Inside Pammon was a torrent of emotions and strength. Kaen could feel Pammon's sadness and hurt, along with a commitment to the goal they had agreed on years ago.

And then the power came out of Pammon and through his mouth.

Seeing through his dragon's eyes, Kaen watched as a flame so hot it was only blue a few yards passed the tip of Pammon's snout before it turned white and then almost vanished. It was still there, but Kaen could only see it because of how Pammon's eyes saw everything.

Like an almost invisible stream of fire, it poured out and began to heat the rock Pammon had focused it on.

Together, they watched the stone change color, turning a bright red, and then it started melting. What seemed like forever was only a few moments, but everything changed as the rock became a hot pile of some weird material. Once it reached an almost white stage, Pammon cut off his flame and quickly moved forward, pushing his talons against the rock, pressing down on it with all the force he could muster.

Pain surged through his dragon's talons, and Kaen was about to cry out, but he heard Pammon say no, not through words but through their connection.

A hissing sound rose, and a few heartbeats later, Pammon pulled back his talons and looked at the stone, which was turning clear.

What is that?!

Dragon crystal. It is only capable of being made by a dragon with a rider. No other dragon can gather the power I just had without one like you pouring your strength into me.

Kaen watched through Pammon's eyes, trying to ignore the pain he felt coming from Pammon as he poured his own life into his friend. The rock suddenly became absolutely clear.

How . . . why . . .

Words failed Kaen as he understood what his friend had done. Joy flooded him, and he squeezed his friend's neck.

Thank you.

Pammon snorted, and Kaen realized his dragon was crying.

Today we will no longer cry because you are blind. Instead we will rejoice because you are something new. Stronger because of the pain. I will do anything for you.

And I you.

Pammon turned his neck, focusing his wet, golden eyes on his rider, who sat on his body.

Then promise me to stop this path you have been on lately. Let go of the pain and hurt from the weight you force yourself to carry. Today, be free. Be the boy who called out to me when I was a hatchling, and the man to whom I swore my life. You are a king. Act like one.

Unconsciously, Kaen sat up and grabbed his chest with his hand. It throbbed with pain and hurt as he realized just how bad he must have been for Pammon to speak to him like this. He chose this moment, knowing he could be open to hearing the truth.

You have my word. I will do everything I can to be the man worthy of calling you friend and Dragon Rider. Forgive me for being an eggling.

Pammon thrummed and moved his head forward, putting his nose into Kaen's chest and then pulling back when he realized how hot it still was as he heard the searing of flesh.

Sorry, I did—

Kaen grabbed Pammon's jaw and held him in place, letting the pain of his friend's mouth stay there just a moment longer.

We both needed to feel this.

When Kaen let go, Pammon grinned, seeing how Kaen's jaw had changed in just a moment. It was firm and set, committed to a path both knew they needed to take.

Let us return to our mates.

Amaranth had been upset and healed both of them but said nothing else once Pammon had told her what he had done. She looked at him differently as he curled up around her, encircling her entire body with his massive one.

You are different . . . what changed up there?

Kaen has remembered what is required. He will no longer be the coward and fool he has been playing at for the last while. As of today, he will be the man this kingdom and land needs.

Pammon gently wrapped his neck around hers, listening to her trill as his scales slid across her own.

Tomorrow we must leave, and you need to take care of Ava. He will tell her what must be done. He must go if he is to act upon the promise he made. You will need to be the wise one I know you are and guide her during these times. I am grateful that you and Glynnis both gave her a tooth.

Still trilling, Amaranth closed her eyes and let out a soft groan.

You are wiser than I give you credit for. Doing this with me, touching me like this, and then telling me you must go, all while also giving me a task that we both know only I can accomplish . . . Tell me where you are going to go.

We need to try to find Glynnis. It has been a while, and I had expected her to return. Now is not the time to be weak, which means we must either help her or ensure she is on her way back. While I am gone, I entrust you with what I hold most dear.

Amaranth shuffled slightly, her trilling stopping as she rotated her head to see Pammon's golden eyes looking at her.

Some might be upset to hear that a human female is more important than anything else.

Pammon thrummed and squeezed his neck around hers a little tighter.

I did not say you were not important . . . you simply like to hear me say that you are.

Amaranth began to thrum slightly as her head moved up and down.

And yet you still have not said those words . . .

Snorting, Pammon growled slightly before releasing a blast of air from his nose.

If I didn't know any better, Ava has been causing you to act more like a human. However . . .

Unraveling his neck from Amaranth's, Pammon moved till his snout was just a few inches from hers.

Amaranth, you are important to me, and I am grateful every day that we were able to rescue you all those years ago. I look forward to hundreds of years spent with you by my side.

Pammon watched as her eyes changed color. They had begun to change since she got pregnant. Neither she nor Glynnis knew how or why, as dragons told very few stories about one's eyes ever-changing.

The copper color they were becoming sparkled as she touched the tip of her snout to his.

And I look forward to many more flights with you across the sky. Now embrace me again and sleep. I can feel the exhaustion seeping through your bones.

Pammon winked as he encircled her neck again with his, and they laid their heads down next to each other on the stone floor.

Across the room, Kaen smiled as he held Ava. He could feel what Pammon felt at that moment.

Tomorrow would be a new day.

Ava had not been excited at the news of their departure, but she accepted it.

Kaen was different and she could sense it.

Even though he was blind, he walked like a man whose eyes were locked on a specific purpose. Best of all, Kaen acted like he had actual hope.

So when she kissed him goodbye, the pain she felt of seeing him blind hurt less. Knowing her husband was acting like the man she had fallen in love with made all her pain less painful.

We need to go and see your mother. She told me to fetch her today. Amaranth informed Ava.

"I can stay here until you get back," Ava replied, wiping a few wet spots from her cheeks.

I will not leave you alone. You are family and I will not abandon family.

Turning to look at the green dragon wrapped around the two eggs, Ava saw those massive eyes, green at the moment, staring at her.

"When did we become family?" Ava asked, a slight laughter escaping her lips.

Pammon reminded me of that, and I have been remiss to acknowledge it. You have shared your home and everything else with me. I have never been treated so nicely by most of my kind, yet you did not attempt to make me feel like anything less than you. I thought . . .

Amaranth paused a moment, unwrapping herself from the eggs, and began moving toward Ava.

I thought that perhaps you might use Kaen to make me obey. To force me to do things I might not want to do. You never have. Today, you reminded me of the woman that you are. I might have bonded with you if I had known you as a hatchling. I sense a kindred spirit in you. That is why I will make you a promise.

Amaranth was now only a few yards from Ava. She lowered herself to the ground and slid her head along it until her snout was just a foot from Ava's.

If you promise me to help both of our mates to act as the kings they are and love us as they should, I will treat you as if you were my rider. If I hear it, I will always answer your call and defend you and yours as if they were my own egg. Do we have a deal?

Ava stood there, not realizing for a moment that her mouth was open as Amaranth approached her and she heard the words echo in her mind.

Reaching out with her hand, Ava tried to hold it still as it trembled. Tears rolled down her cheeks as she put her hand against those green scales.

"I would be honored to consider you family and even more honored to call you a friend."

Ava took her other hand and pulled out a necklace with two dragon teeth attached. Smiling, she took her hand off Amaranth's snout, moved her hand to the tooth she knew was from the green dragon, and pressed hard with it into her palm. It began to bleed, and Ava then put the hand back on Amaranth's scales.

"I promise to protect you just like I would Kaen or Pammon. I also promise to protect your eggs and those who hatch from them."

Amaranth trilled, a green glow surrounding her as she poured power into her snout. Ava's hand on her snout glowed, as did the tooth on her necklace.

Wait . . . I am almost . . .

The glow got brighter around Ava's hands and she stood there in shock. Then the tooth she held dissolved, vanishing into nothing, and Ava felt a presence growing in her mind.

We are bonded as much as we can be. Pammon told me of this and you are worthy of what it costs.

You can hear me as Pammon does?

I can feel you when we are this close. Now, wipe those tears and let us go see your mother.

Laughing and wiping her nose, Ava nodded. She then suddenly threw both arms around Amaranth's snout.

Thank you . . . Thank you more than I can say with words.

Your heart says them for you. Now . . . let us go do what females must do. Be strong and make sure those males do not screw up the world.

Ava burst into laughter and nodded. She wiped a few more wet spots from her cheeks as she moved to where the saddles were kept.

Kaen and Pammon had returned to Kaen's home and picked up some equipment to replace what he had lost. His dragon-scale chest piece and leggings were fine, but the rest of his clothes had fallen apart from the spell that had touched him.

Outfitted for battle, Kaen set off, eyes still wrapped like a blind man but without feeling defeated. He knew that Pammon was right. It was time for him to be the person he had been chosen by the world to be.

Two days had passed with hard flying, and Kaen could see how bad the land below them had become. The southwest part of the desert and the rotted wood area had spread farther north, the infection of the land seemingly shifting more and more every day.

It has gotten worse than the last time we were out here.

With Amaranth and Glynnis pregnant, their ability to fly here when reports came in wasn't an option. We were already struggling to keep the orc army at bay. Aldric's and Herb's scouts didn't report back this kind of rot the last time they came out here. Evil plans must be in motion and speeding things up.

Kaen rubbed the scales he had touched thousands of times and said nothing. There was nothing to say, and he was here, doing what they both knew must be done.

An hour later, Pammon felt someone reaching out to his mind.

Glynnis is ahead! They are fighting!

[Flight Burst Activated]

Kaen leaned forward, hugging his dragon's neck as Pammon took off without warning. The moment Pammon spoke, Kaen knew what he was going to do.

What did she say? I cannot feel her or reach her.

Since she arrived, there have been nonstop battles. She says she has seen over twenty thousand kobolds.

That number seemed impossible, but Kaen knew it had to be true. All the fighting they had done against the orcs and goblins had taught everyone how to count armies quickly.

I'm assuming there is more? I can feel it inside you.

There are very few towns left out here. The report from Tioanoe is that there may be less than five thousand total people alive now. The fighting and the lack of food have gotten to them as well. Most children and older adults have fled toward the sea, hoping to find somewhere in that kingdom that might take them. Or at least a place to rest.

That report burned inside Kaen. He knew he was to blame for things getting this bad, and he blocked out the emotions that tried to bury him under an avalanche of guilt. There was no place for those feelings. He was here, and now they would do what they could to help fight and save Tioanoe and her people.

Fly fast . . . we will bring death to those kobolds.

[Flight Burst Expired]

Kaen felt like he was watching a massive group of ants as he looked down at the kobold army to the west.

I think there may be more than twenty thousand . . . Glynnis, how are you holding up?

If you two had not come today, I would have had to abandon these people. There is little left I can give. Sleeping has been almost impossible unless I fly away, and when I do the kobolds attack, killing everyone I leave behind. The people Herb gave me are out of arrows and exhausted. Getting mana or sleep for them appears to be just as impossible.

Where is Tioanoe?

Pammon's eyes shifted. The place he was looking at was so far away that even his vision couldn't see it all.

She is there. I can tell where Glynnis is.

Let me see the armies again. I want to consider something.

Pammon's vision swept back to the tiny dots that moved slowly but steadily over the barren land. A long line stretched from east to west as they pushed up and to the west, driving out anyone and anything they came across.

How long can you breathe fire if you leave nothing left with your widest fan?

Pammon thrummed, well aware of what Kaen was considering.

I can hold on for about a minute, a little longer if you share your power with me. That would let me send out a stream about twenty yards wide.

And they are walking in a row, that is what? One hundred yards or so wide?

About that . . . it is miles long, and it will probably work.

I cannot help, Glynnis chimed in. ***I have already exhausted the little I had today. Every day, I have pushed myself till there was nothing left. I even have a few holes in my wings and am hoping Amaranth can help heal them.***

Stay close to Tioanoe and the others. We are going to be there soon, but first, Pammon is going to teach these kobolds a lesson about his strength.

Pammon laughed, thrumming as he prepared to dive toward the ground.

Be ready to give me your power when I say so. Part of me has missed fighting like this.

Kaen chuckled at that statement. It brought back memories of when Pammon and the other dragons had to stop their breath attacks on the orc army because they had brought in massive weapons designed to bring down Pammon and the others. The first few days had been painful and glorious. In the initial attack from the woods, a spell that came from some wand killed most of the guards on the wall, yet Pammon had easily taken out ten thousand troops with his breath attack. The orcs had pulled back and regrouped.

When they saw the siege weapons coming out of the forest, both knew that fighting would be different.

No siege weapons in their army?

There are no trees for them to use, and the land would have worn them out. My greatest weakness is that they have casters who have a weakening attack. It feels like you are swimming through water. Each time it was cast, the air above them looked like a cloud of smoke, and flying into it earned me the scars I have. Now I have to be careful where I attack, and they keep their casters with the strongest forces.

Kaen considered that knowledge, and it bothered him to hear that.

An attack designed to stop dragons? Why would a kobold army have such a thing?

It is because Stioks must have a hand in helping them. He doesn't fear them because he uses spells like the ones we saw that day we fought. If I had to guess, the attack the orcs used from their castle would most likely not affect him . . . He is—

Teaching them how to stop us . . .

For all these years, Stioks has invested in this moment. Today, we shall show them how ill-prepared they are for us.

Kaen grinned, rubbing his friend's neck as they dove toward the ground.

Today, you shall show the world once again just who you are, my friend.

Pammon thrummed as he dove from the sky.

14

Old Friends

The sensation Kaen felt as he experienced destruction through Pammon's eyes almost overwhelmed him. His lifestone burned, and that power was shared, causing the fire that came from inside his friend to burn hotter and last longer.

Pammon came from the east, just enough off the ground and at a speed that his fire would fall under him as he breathed, covering a solid twenty-yard-wide section.

The screams and shouts were lost behind them as Pammon flew.

For almost a third of a mile, a blanket of fire cut off the south side of the army from the tiny section on the north side, unable to cross the fire that would take minutes before it might burn out.

Give me more . . . I have a little left, but I need more . . .

Kaen focused, feeling how tired Pammon was, watching a patch of two hundred yards be safe from the destruction Pammon was bringing.

Recalling his purpose, Kaen took a deep breath and let his power flow through the bond.

Pammon took a massive breath, and then another long stream of fire, this time a shade darker than before, came out of his snout. It burned to a crisp the kobolds he engulfed with it, and another thirty seconds or so of fire was spent, covering at least another four hundred yards of death.

Hold on . . . I am out of flames, but I am not done yet.

Kaen gripped the strap that lay on his legs with one hand.

Do you want me to shoot a bow? I can—

For now, let me do this. The time may come when you need to use the limited arrows we have—there are more than we prepared for. Let me use my size and strength.

Kaen realized what Pammon was about to do, held back from warning him about how dangerous this was, and stopped. He had done enough foolish things, and Pammon had been right each time. If Pammon felt this was his time to shine, so be it.

Gripping the strap with both hands, Kaen watched as Pammon lowered himself and picked up more speed. His dragon angled himself slightly, his massive back claws and feet acting like a plow in soil, tearing up the army under him.

Half a mile passed with almost no drop in his dragon's speed, and then Kaen noticed Pammon's eyes shifting more to the west.

Up there! Do you see that group?

Kaen did because Pammon saw it. A massive army of kobolds had come together and were attacking a walled-off town. Above it, Glynnis was doing her best to keep the kobolds from surrounding it, but a gray mist hung above the main army attacking the south wall.

You aren't showing off to impress me, are you?

Pammon ignored Glynnis's comment as they angled toward the troops. His eyes searched until they found what Pammon had been looking for.

There are the casters, two different groups. Look at those kobolds next to them. They are a lot taller and covered in armor.

Remember the archers stationed before them as they advance. Between those two groups, I need help getting close with that spell active. And the arrows they use are not like most of the normal ones.

When Glynnis said those words, Kaen's brain started to become active.

Pammon, can you—

I'm on it.

As if he were using the telescope that King Aldric owned and had shown Kaen one night, Pammon's vision zoomed in on the archers in front and looked at the arrows on the back of the pack before the casters and larger kobolds.

Holy dwarf balls . . . those are like the arrows Hess was making me.

Those are just the tips, though, not the entire arrow.

Still! That means we found out where some of the ore that has gone missing has appeared. Stioks has gifted them the very weapons we created for him.

Forget that for now. We will be fine. Now is your turn. Take your bow and your arrows. I will get you into position and be your eyes.

Angling up, Pammon moved higher up into the sky, letting the army he had been destroying from behind get a small reprieve. When he reached about three hundred yards above the casters they needed to attack, Pammon began to hover.

Tell me what I need to do.

Kaen unhooked his bow from the clip next to him, pulled it up to his chest, and smiled. He didn't need Pammon to show him what he was doing.

Just keep your eyes on our targets. I'll do the rest.

A wave of satisfaction came through their bond, and Kaen pulled an arrow from the quiver tied near him.

He let his power flow into the tip and sent a shot toward the ground.

The white-tipped arrow arched, flying through the air before landing about thirty yards from his target. The kobold it impaled exploded, and a blast radiated out from it, taking out more creatures in a ten-yard radius.

A little off. You were—

I got this. Let me do it.

Kaen took another arrow and let it go, watching it fall and, this time, get closer. It hit within fifteen yards and sent another circle of death to those near the one he hit.

Turn slightly to the south and move back for a little.

Taking a deep breath, Kaen watched the chaos ensuing down below. He could see the casters and others looking up at him, but nothing they had would reach Pammon. Their attacks were worthless.

Glynnis, do you realize you could have dropped rocks or trees upon them from up here?

No reply came for a moment, and Kaen wondered if she hadn't considered that.

There aren't many trees or large rocks around here, and I'm not as large as Pammon. Flying around here with them would have been difficult for me.

True. Just wondering.

Pammon thrummed slightly and stopped when Kaen loaded two arrows.

What? Why did you do that?

Kaen grinned, ignoring Pammon's question.

Let me shoot and be quiet.

There, in the blackness of no vision, Kaen breathed in slowly and then exhaled. He had cut his ability to see through Pammon's eyes. He knew where his targets were and exactly how he needed to shoot. The time for him to do this on his own was now.

Both arrows began to spark, lightning infusing them as Kaen poured his magic and power into them. After ten seconds, he let the arrows go.

[Twinshot Activated]

Only then did Kaen allow himself to see through Pammon's eyes.

His friend was tracking the two arrows as they fell to the earth. The casters and warriors had begun to spread out some, moving in different directions, but it didn't matter. Kaen had seen them and how they were responding to the threat above.

Both arrows struck simultaneously, each hitting a different kobold, and the lightning and explosion they produced did precisely what he had planned for.

He didn't need to hit a specific creature. All he needed to do was hit a particular area and let those black-tipped arrows with their mana-infused spell inside them do the rest.

They landed sixty yards apart, each creating an area of destruction over forty yards in radius.

The ground exploded as the power he had infused went out in a circle, sending bolts of lightning that arched from each kobold to the next. When it struck the taller kobolds in their metal armor, they acted like an amplifier, arching even more and catching other kobolds.

[Archery Skill Increased]

That was glorious . . . did you just gain a point in archery?

Kaen felt the weight of so much training, practice, battles, and more vanish from him as he saw that notification.

[Archery Skill Waiting To Be Chosen]

Kaen?

Yeah . . . sorry, I just . . . I finally hit level forty in my archery skill, and now I can finally choose an ability.

How about you worry about that later and focus on what we are dealing with now?

Kaen snorted and started to draw arrows rapidly, each time pouring power into them momentarily before sending them down below.

The cloud is starting to disperse! I can come help!

Wait just a little longer. There are still a few archers, and I want to make sure that it is safe.

Five minutes later, the army beneath them was running away in fear. They fled once both dragons swooped in and began tearing them to pieces. Without the casters and the archers to protect them from Glynnis, it became a scene of destruction that lasted several hours as both Pammon and Glynnis ate their fill of the bodies of the creatures beneath them.

"By the spirits, what happened to you?"

Kaen smiled and shrugged as Tioanoe ran toward him as best she could. All over, she had bandages and cuts. Behind her were a few dozen other warriors who had come to see the dragon and rider that had saved their lives.

"I'd say you look awful, but you might not believe I can see all the bandages you wear," joked Kaen as he bowed slightly. "Sorry for the delay in coming . . ."

Tianoe snorted and shook her head as she gazed up at Pammon. "You have grown as well . . . perhaps we shall let the two of you pass through our land without payment."

A thrum came from Pammon while Kaen groaned slightly, remembering the first time he had entered their land.

"Forgive me for how long it took to help, though . . . the reports I had didn't tell me it was this bad."

She nodded slowly, and Kaen saw her spin a small colored bracelet on her arm. Pammon's eyes let him see it clearly beneath her fingers, and he felt a twinge in his gut.

"Krudae . . ."

The color on Tioanoe's face changed a little as she realized what she had done. "Yes . . . she has departed this world and now sits with our ancestors. She had much honor for the numbers she had sent before her."

Kaen moved forward, able to walk much better after practicing, stood before her, and extended his hand.

As they clasped forearms, Kaen smiled and gave a slight bow. "I will pray that your ancestors know how great she was. She almost took down a Dragon Rider."

A coughing fit, followed by some sniffing, plagued Tioanoe for a few seconds. "Dragon Rider Kaen, you honor us greatly." Turning, she motioned to Glynnis, who had collapsed near Pammon and appeared asleep as his dragon moved beside her. "The dragon you sent along with the others has been a great ally in our battles. I know they are tired, and the things your dragon friend has done will be sung for many lives to come. Now tell me, how are things in your kingdom?"

Frowning, Kaen scratched his neck and then tsked his tongue against his teeth.

"Let me grab some food to share with you and your people. Then we can talk about what is happening here and at my home."

She gave a bow and then turned, whistling, her fingers moving momentarily. A dozen of the female warriors behind her took off, running into the town, each smiling even though they were covered in wounds and blood.

"You never fail to share what you have. I am grateful as always. Please, if you will join us in our last city, hard choices must be made."

Kaen nodded and turned to look at Pammon.

I'll do my best to not stumble and fall.

I have no doubt you will do fine. Tell her I will always remember Krudae. She was a fierce warrior for one so small.

Kaen jogged to catch up with Tioanoe and put his hand on her shoulder. "Just so you know, I am blind. Right now, I can only see because Pammon is here. Once we go inside your walls, I cannot see."

She looked back at Pammon, who nodded slightly before resting his head near Glynnis.

Glancing out over the battlefield, she noticed that the warriors appeared to be making sure all the kobolds were dead. She tugged her ear for a moment.

"Then we will eat out here. They will understand when I tell them you must remain to protect your dragons."

Laughing, Kaen gave her shoulder a squeeze and bowed. "Thank you for that."

"No, Dragon Rider," Tioanoe replied, her voice strong and steady. "We thank you for honoring your promise. Today, we are prepared to die and hope our children and older ones might live. Now we believe we can see them soon. That gift is far greater than you will ever know."

Smiling, Kaen held back the pain he felt at how he understood more than she realized.

15

Leadership Choices

Experience had made Kaen pack an entire basket of food. He knew it was the one thing people didn't have in times of war, and even though it was most of what he had stored for his trips, he shared it willingly, seeing the eyes of those who got a small piece of meat and some hard bread.

Each one bowed and thanked him for his kindness before moving off to enjoy it while they waited for a pot of broth that was being cooked to satisfy their hungry stomachs.

"So you believe this is the work of the other Dragon Rider? Do you believe there will be a break from our battle?"

Kaen slowly let out the breath he had been holding as he studied Tioanoe's face in the light of the fire. Pammon was kind enough to keep one eye open so that he could react to everyone who had offered him thanks.

"My honest answer is not for long. Today, they suffered greatly, but they will regroup, and their tactics will change. I cannot keep Glynnis out here forever, as she needs to return soon . . ." He paused and leaned close, motioning her to join him. "She has an egg and has to protect it and be near it."

Kaen smiled as Tioanoe's mouth fell open, and she leaned her head to get a better look at the yellow dragon that had defended them this past week.

"Will she allow someone to bond with it?" she whispered.

Kaen nodded. "I have two young men who are ready. Over the last five years, both have proven themselves to be someone I could trust with that power and responsibility. Sadly, it will be a month or two before the eggs hatch, and even then, it will be many months before either of them can ride their dragon."

She nodded and tapped her chin a few times while staring into the evening sky. “Imagine riders again, protecting the land . . . it seems like a dream we will not want to wake up from.”

“There is still much I must do . . . we all must do. Stioks is active, and I have no doubt, after seeing what I saw here and holding those arrows in my hands, that he played a role in your downfall.”

The woman spat on the ground, grimacing at that news again. “What did we ever do to that man? He has never come to our lands, and we would have allowed him free travel!”

Sighing, Kaen shook his head. “Stioks doesn’t care about that . . . in fact, I think he only cares for himself and some dream or vision he has in his head—a place where everyone obeys him absolutely.”

“So what do you think we should do?”

Her question frustrated Kaen, as neither of the two choices was good. Each would mean they would lose a part of who Tioanoe’s people were. Both could still result in their entire group being wiped out.

“The answer isn’t simple, and you already know what one of my choices would be if not both.”

She grimaced and turned her eyes to the burning fire between them.

“Go join our people who have fled north and try to find a place there . . .”

Kaen nodded. “Or . . .”

She sighed, picking up a small stick, breaking it a few times, and then throwing it into the fire. “Or move to Ebonmount and try to survive there.”

“Neither of which promises that your people will be who they are now. Both have problems and may change you and your people forever,” Kaen replied. The question is, what do they want? I know you are a proud and strong group. There are still plenty of woods to the north where game and opportunities lie. However, we also know that the king who owns them will one day come, demanding tribute or more.”

Neither spoke as she chewed on his words for a few minutes.

“Being a leader isn’t great, is it?” she asked, frowning.

Kaen chuckled and shook his head. “So many think being in charge is the greatest position one can have. A worthy leader loses sleep and more because they always care about those they lead. Life shifts from becoming about them to everyone else. They sacrifice everything to ensure that the people they are responsible for have what they need. And the choices they must make . . .”

Kaen smiled as she looked at him. Pammon was there, listening and watching.

“We have to learn not to regret it when our decisions don’t go as we had hoped. We cannot live in fear of not making another decision lest more people suffer. Sitting by, choosing not to choose, is far worse. Chaos breaks out, and people lose faith in their leaders. When that happens, everything falls apart on the inside."

"You sound like you are speaking from experience," Tioanoe said. "Is that what happened?"

Kaen nodded. "It took a great loss and some words from a stubborn old friend to help me realize it. Instead, I will do what I must because I don't want another to suffer like you."

She was staring at the fire again, nodding slowly.

Minutes passed as neither said a word, each considering the choices to be made.

Eventually, Tioanoe stood up and stretched. "I will decide in the morning when the sun rises." She went to a knee and touched her head to the ground. "Thank you, as always, for your friendship."

Kaen smiled and gave a slight nod. She moved off to join her people, who had moved back inside the last town they called home.

After she was gone, Kaen stood up and moved to where Pammon was waiting for him.

I am still determining which path she may choose.

Kaen smiled and scratched Pammon's snout.

I don't think she will choose either of those.

Do you think she will stay and fight?

Tapping his finger against one of Pammon's scales, Kaen realized he had tilted his head up toward the sky even though he couldn't see.

Scratching his beard, he shook his head.

No . . . she will choose a path she will come up with. I know she never wanted power, but she also knows the burden of it better than most. She will be a great leader if she can protect them long enough to survive.

Moving to a small space between Pammon and Glynnis, Kaen sat down and leaned back against the two of them.

Thank you again for being stubborn and wise.

Pammon thrummed once, stopping when he remembered how late it was and feeling Glynnis stir slightly.

Thank you for listening and doing what you must.

Kaen scratched a scale, took a deep breath, and scooted himself back until he was snug between the two dragons. Letting out the breath, he smiled.

Remind me that tomorrow when I tell you my next plans.

A groan came from Pammon as he snorted.

Go to sleep.

Grateful for the morning and the need to arise, Kaen found himself rested even after a few of the nightmares that often plagued him.

Tioanoe was waiting for him outside his camp with a fire going.

"Part of me wants to ask what it is like to see through your dragon's eyes. The other part of me really wants to ask how you go to the bathroom like that."

Kaen started to howl with laughter, and even Pammon thrummed, having heard her question.

"Both are different . . . I won't say I have ever hidden anything from Pammon before, but needing his assistance with the second question was beyond either of our imaginations."

She chuckled and nodded. "I have decided what we will do."

Kaen stood where he was, crossing his arms and waiting for her decision.

"We will go collect our older and younger people and then move to a place mentioned in stories long ago. A place that lies between both the elf kingdom and the kingdom of the waters. There, we will grow strong again and perhaps be able to come back here in a few generations and start over. We also may decide that is the next place for us: living in a space where neither kingdom holds much power and may ignore us, waiting for the other to deal with us."

"That is a wise plan," Kaen said, smiling at her. "I told Pammon last night you would choose your own path, and I am glad that you have. When will you leave?"

"The preparations have already begun. Everyone who can is collecting supplies that we will take with us. It will be a hard journey, but you are right. The enemy won't wait forever, and we need to be gone while we have your protection. They will wait a few days or maybe even a week to see if you are truly gone before attacking again."

"Then I will let you and your people do what you must. Pammon and Glynnis will eat a few more of the bodies before we go. I also have things I need to do before returning to Ebonmount."

Moving toward her, Kaen held out his hand once more and smiled as she took his forearm. Both of them pulled forward in a small embrace.

"Know that if you ever need my help, I will do what I can to answer the call," Kaen said as they moved apart.

"I, too, will do what I can to help if you need it. Until then, I will pray to our ancestors to watch over you and your dragon as you protect this land."

She bowed once and turned, never one for long goodbyes.

Kaen chuckled as he and Pammon watched her walk away.

She is in a much better mood today than last night.

It is because she has found her purpose and drive, like you. People are best when they have a goal they know is right and work toward it.

When did you become so wise? I still remember an eggling who wanted to eat a chicken because he thought it insulted him . . .

Pammon growled and closed his eyes, keeping them shut so that Kaen couldn't see where he was moving.

Walking toward where he knew Pammon was, Kaen realized he was centered even in the darkness. His mind allowed him to use his other senses to pick up where things were and what he had seen.

You are not going to make fun of me now, are—OUCH!

Pammon's eyes flew open as he yanked his head from where it had been resting on the ground. Kaen stood a few steps away, smiling and waving his hand in the air.

Dang, your scales hurt . . .

My scales! You slapped me!

Kaen started to laugh as he felt Pammon diving at him with his head.

He rolled to the side and was on his feet, prepared for the change in direction as Pammon approached him.

They collided, Kaen grabbing as much of Pammon's snout as he could. He was pushed back along the ground but did not give up his grip on his friend.

How are you doing that?! You're not using my eyes!

Pammon pulled back the other way, and Kaen let him get dragged again before letting go and rolling to his feet.

I'm not sure, but my lifestone is acting weird. It's like I can somehow sense what is going on around me . . .

I swear if you get a skill, I will make you walk home.

Laughing, Kaen walked straight to Pammon and stopped a foot away.

It only works with you right now. I just know where I am and what was around me . . .

Snorting, Pammon stood up and moved away from Kaen toward the kobold corpses.

Well, I'm going to get breakfast. We need to leave anyway. What is your plan, oh great Dragon Rider?

The sarcasm of Pammon's question oozed through their bond, but Kaen ignored it.

We need to check on the elves . . . something tells me the report that came in a few days ago may be even worse than here.

16

Difficult Revelations

So . . . you've been quiet. You're going to tell me what you're thinking about.

Kaen smiled. He knew what he wanted to do the moment they were in the air, and he had some time to finally check the choices for his new archery skill.

Archery Skill Choices
[Fan Shot]
[Homing Shot]

Looking at the two choices, Kaen considered the best option.

I'd like your opinion about a skill selection and which one you think I should take.

A hint of curiosity swept through their bond, and Kaen chuckled slightly as Pammon continued to fly into the sky.

I can choose Fan Shot, which Sedel used in that archery contest. It has many uses but also goes through arrows quickly. The other is Homing Shot, but if I remember correctly, its cooldown is brutal.

How bad are we talking?

Twenty-four hours. Fan Shot has a thirty-minute cooldown.

And does the homing shot do what it actually says?

From the two books that I read, it will track and follow its target, but it's not like I can aim for a specific part of the body. It simply strikes whatever it hits first.

So if someone knew that, they could use a shield or even a weapon to block it?

Exactly. So against a shielded warrior, it would be better to fire it off behind them and let it come around from behind. Otherwise, it would make a direct straight line for them and run into their shield.

Pammon was weighing the choices with a different mindset than Kaen was.

One considered it from a dragon's perspective, while the other considered it from an archer's point of view.

What would happen if one of those was fired at me and I took off in Flight Burst?

I have no idea. The book only stated the obvious information about it. It doesn't avoid walls, but it simply tracks the target. If you step to the side, it will turn around in an arc and come at you. If trees, a wall, a mountain, or anyone else gets in the way of it behind you, then it will be gone.

That sounds like a terrible skill to shoot from the air. It would crash into the ground.

Yet it sounds like a great skill to shoot from the ground into the air or in the air at something already in the air.

Pammon grumbled as Kaen continued to toss out possible scenarios on which skill might work best when.

I'm tired of trying to figure this out . . . do you have to pick now?

Nope. I just thought I would ask your opinion. I was going to wait to talk with Hess and maybe Herb, but I have no idea. We carry a lot of arrows, and that means Fa—

No more . . . please. My head hurts, and it's not even my skill.

Laughing, Kaen nodded and then let out a sigh.

I'll stop talking about it . . . it's just that I waited so long, and now that I finally have a forty in archery, I can—

Kaen froze, realizing again something else he had forgotten.

Sensing Kaen's elevated heart rate and how he was moving behind him, Pammon turned and saw Kaen unhooking his bow and holding it in his hands.

The locked part of your bow . . .

[Inspect Bow]
Bonded Bow of Archer - + 5 to Dex + 3 to Archery
Unlocked: Rune of Piercing - Arrow penetrates all armor and defense by 30% more.

Holy dwarf balls . . . the arrows provide a thirty percent bonus to penetrating all armor and defenses . . .

Pammon said nothing, continuing to stare at Kaen as they flew to the north.

That seems really powerful. Tell me I'm wrong.

You aren't wrong. Imagine what that would do to even you . . . Imagine if I had that when we fought Tharnok or Juthom . . .

This changes some things for sure. At least you had Tioanoe collect all

those arrow tips from the kobolds. Hopefully there is enough for a few more arrows.

Kaen nodded, holding the bow his father had made for him so many years ago. Pammon had turned his attention back toward the sky where he was rapidly climbing, and all Kaen could do was feel its power through his hands.

Thanks, Hoste . . . you always keep looking out for me.

The first day flying north toward the elven kingdom reminded Kaen of all the life that still existed. Everywhere, trees grew tall, and Pammon mentioned how many deer and boars he saw inside the forest. When they camped, it wasn't long before Pammon caught one for Kaen to cook once Pammon had eaten his fill. Skinning a deer and gutting it was not something he wanted to do while he couldn't see.

How much longer are you going to be blind?

Kaen sighed and looked toward Glynnis, who was reclining on the ground near Pammon.

I have no idea, but hopefully it will be no more than another week or two. I'm not supposed to take the bandages off, and in case something happens, I have two more in my supplies so that I can put them back on.

Glynnis snorted and shook her head.

Why do men always rush in and fight first, not paying attention to what might be around them? You could have picked up some rocks or trees and dropped them on the castle.

Pammon erupted in a thrum so loud that every bird within a hundred yards leaped from the trees and flew away.

After his dragon had settled down, Kaen chuckled a little bit.

You got me there. As you said, I didn't use my brain. I was angry and upset and thought I was invincible. Now look at me. One mistake cost me my vision.

Remind me again why we are going out here. I thought you said the elves were not under your protection after what they tried to do to you.

Pammon snorted, and Kaen shrugged.

That was their old king and his daughter. They have been dead for three years. I have been remiss in checking in on them as I should have. The elves helped as much as possible, sending supplies and food during our battle with the orcs. Sadly, their land still suffered the loss of their tree.

Kaen turned his attention to the fire and the food cooking on it. He had only cut off the tender strips of meat, so the food was cooking quickly, and he knew it would be ready in another minute. Pammon, as always, was more than happy to eat the rest of the deer.

I just wish I had known about their tree . . . who knew a single thing could provide that much power to a kingdom . . . now their land produces far less, and the elves seem to grow older faster.

Has it really been half a year since we have been there?

Seven months and a few weeks, but not that I kept count. Still, their elders have been kind and understand my reservations about coming that often. They still profusely apologize every time we come.

Bosgreth has been the greatest asset of all. We still need to visit him, and then, at some point, I need to stop in and check on the wood elves . . .

After the elves, you need to go home for a bit, though. Ava will need you, and you need to be with her. Do not forsake your obligation to her because of the duty you feel you owe.

Pulling one of the sticks off the spit he had built, Kaen nodded and took a bite of the meat, sucking in air as the hot meat burned his tongue slightly.

I'm a dragon that breathes fire, yet I don't try to swallow something I know will burn my mouth.

I've always wondered how that works.

Glynnis's head popped up, and a slight trill came from her.

I can tell you! It's the saliva! As a dragon begins to . . .

Kaen closed his eyes and relaxed against Pammon. He and Pammon had no idea that Glynnis would spend half an hour talking about how each dragon had different saliva that protected them based on the magic they used. She also knew about the glands in their mouths and along their throats. If they had to kill another dragon, Kaen was certain those glands would be useful in some way to the adventurers' guild or Lord Hurem.

With Pammon's eyes closed, he could only embrace the darkness of the world around him. He listened to the sound of the insects and the crackling of the logs becoming embers. He could smell the smoke and the clean air of the trees here. The land smelled different from the battlefield and town just a day ago.

Without his eyes, it was as if every one of his other senses was on overdrive. When he concentrated, he could hear and smell better. The meat had tasted amazing, and Kaen could taste the wood he had speared it with, the oils in it having escaped from the heat and coated the inside of his dinner. He had never noticed these small things, even though he had experienced most of them hundreds of times.

I'm not saying I want to be blind forever, but I wonder what I could learn if I tried while I was.

As he fell asleep, Kaen decided to visit Master Bren when he got back and see what the man might be able to teach him.

Something is wrong . . . can you smell that?

Kaen nodded. He had started to smell it almost the same time Pammon had.

There is smoke up ahead also. The clouds . . . a haze beneath them of whatever must be burning.

We had a fire once that did something like what this feels like . . . it was a massive lightning storm that ravaged one of the territories after a dry season. So much was destroyed.

Pammon, can we speed up but not use your Flight Burst?

He felt Pammon's wings begin to beat faster and watched as the green forest below them and up ahead suddenly stopped, a massive line in it that was burning and rotted.

Stioks . . .

The land's appearance at the edge of Pammon's vision reminded Kaen of the spell that had missed the two of them the one time they fought. Not only did the land look rotten and diseased, but it had also been burned.

This is recent, Kaen. Get your bow and be ready. Glynnis, stay near me and be sharp. Don't engage if we find the two unless I tell you. If so, harass and always dodge. Do you understand?

I do.

Kaen felt anger rising up in Pammon as they continued to fly toward where the capital of the elves should be.

If it looks this bad this far out . . .

Then no one will be left alive. You and I need to end this . . . we need to attack him.

Kaen felt the hatred in Pammon overtaking him and forcing him to desire the same thing as his dragon.

Wait . . . we need to wait.

Are you going to hide again?! Look at what he has done!

Kaen winced, almost as if Pammon had taken his tail and slapped him with it. The pain he felt from that comment flowed through their bond, and Pammon immediately knew what he had done.

I'm sorry . . . it's just . . . when I think about him and see what Stioks has done, I cannot help but become enraged. Every part of me wants to tear him apart, and now . . . many of these people welcomed us and fed us.

I know, and it's ok. You're right. I'm not going to hide anymore, but we need to find out what we can do here and then return home and plan from there. You and I know that right now is not the time for this fight. If I cannot see, I cannot fight back, which would put us in a dangerous position if Stioks found out.

Pammon didn't reply, but Kaen could feel his acknowledgment of the wisdom behind that statement.

Just promise me when the time comes, we end this. Once and for all.

I promise.

17

Changes

They scouted for half a day, flying high above the land at the edge of the clouds, knowing this was the safest spot to travel while looking for Stioks and Juthom.

Everyone and everything is dead . . . we haven't seen a single person alive . . .

The pain in Pammon's tone barely compared to the rage his friend felt at that truth. It was hard enough for Kaen to keep his own emotions in check. He was angry. Angry at himself and at what that man and his dragon had done.

We need to get home. If no one has reported the extent of this damage yet, we need to.

As they circled around, Kaen struggled to comprehend how he was going to fight someone so powerful that they could do this. The amount of magic Stioks must have boggled his mind. He had a few tricks with his bow, but when his tricks ran out, the fight in the skies was not in his or Pammon's favor.

Why would a man and a dragon do something like this? Isn't this a waste of so much land and food? How much more will he make look like this?

Kaen tried to consider what he might tell Glynnis. It had been hard to describe to them how bad Stioks had been. Neither one of them had really seen anything the man had done, and the orcs they fought were just creatures bent on destruction. No matter how hard a fight it had been, they weren't Stioks.

Both female dragons considered those words meaningless even when others told stories around them. They had lived in a land with dragons over five hundred years old. They had seen what power and destruction was truly like. Every dragon knew that death was a possibility if you tried to go outside your area and encroach upon another's land or food.

All those times I tried to tell you about this man and his dragon, and you thought it was nothing, this is only the start. I promise you that. He will do this to the entire land you have flown over if he is not put down.

Kaen felt Glynnis moving up next to them from the back position in their formation. Pammon turned his head and watched the yellow dragon as she pulled close and gazed at the two of them.

Forgive me. I did not realize just how demented he was. This makes what Tharnok did look like nothing, and now . . . now I will help you no matter what.

Pammon nodded and turned back to scan the ground and skies.

Do not take this wrong, but get back into position and keep a lookout, Glynnis. We must be cautious here. Kaen and I both know the power of a well-executed attack when one is distracted.

The yellow dragon said nothing, moved back into her part of the formation, and began keeping watch, as Pammon had asked.

Grateful for the rest and food since they had flown nonstop, they returned to Ebonmount. They had no desire to take any more risks, so they didn't stop for the night. If they were caught on the ground, it would mean death for at least one of them.

When the mountains came into view, all three sighed in relief, knowing that they would need to rethink how they traveled and stopped every time they left the bowl.

Do you think Juthom and Stioks worry about us like we do about them?

I'm not sure, but I doubt either of them are fools. I would expect they rarely stop, either. Juthom most likely feeds himself before they fly, and he wouldn't need to worry about food as much as we do.

Pammon was right. The war had less impact on Stioks's kingdom. Some had tried trading only to find out the hard way that that only brought death and worse. Their spies had told them that the people were oppressed and that those who were still alive worked in horrible conditions, but they had food. There were massive plots of food growing and being stored all over.

Kaen had read the reports multiple times about the two factions within Luthaelia: those whom some might call fanatics and followers of Stioks, and those who were unable to escape.

Let's visit Ava and Amaranth first. You both need to rest, and I need to see my mate. After that, we can seek out the others and discuss what needs to be done.

Kaen felt his heart skip a beat as he saw Ava standing beside Amaranth, waiting for them to land. As he climbed down from Pammon, she ran toward him, an actual smile on her face.

Something is different about her . . .

Yes . . . I sense it, too.

"You better stop talking about me and hurry up and get over here," Ava shouted as Kaen climbed down the last few scales before dropping to the ground.

He raced toward her as she approached him. Ava barreled into Kaen, throwing her arms around him and squeezing tight.

"I've missed you, my love," she whispered into his chest.

"I've missed you as well," Kaen replied, using a hand to lift her chin up and kiss her. "You seem in good spirits. Did your mother cause that?"

Ava groaned and shook her head before motioning to the other side of the cave.

Kaen only saw the head motion as Pammon was kind enough to keep an eye on Ava while he moved near Amaranth.

"Pammon, if you would . . ."

Kaen felt his dragon's gaze shift across the room. Over at a table, his mother-in-law was reading a book and ignoring the two of them.

"She seems happy," Kaen said, his voice low and slow.

"Stop that. Mother is fine and giving us a little privacy before she comes over. Now stop worrying about my mother and tell me what happened while you two were gone."

Rolling his neck and finally getting it to pop, Kaen grabbed her hand and began to walk toward Lady Hurem. "How about I tell both of you at once? That way, I don't have to worry about repeating myself."

Ava chuckled. "You have learned a lot in our years of marriage."

After kissing her on the forehead, Kaen walked toward the table with his wife on his arm, thankful to be home and have a moment to relax.

The two women sat stunned at the news of Roccnari, neither saying anything as Kaen described the horror of what they had found.

"Pammon was ready to go and seek out Stioks and Juthom, but thankfully, I convinced him that until I can see, now is not the time. I'm left with little choice, though. Sooner rather than later, we must take the fight to him."

Lady Hurem's expression never changed as she considered what Kaen told them. Ava was wrestling with controlling her temper and grief.

"I wish we would poison him or burn him down or something!" Ava shouted, slamming the small wooden table, causing all three of the cups on the table to knock over and spill. "I'm sorry," she gasped, her mood shifting again. "I'll go get a cloth."

Before Kaen could say anything, Ava was on her feet and moving to the other side of the cave where the cabinets and chests were filled with things.

* * *

"Part of me wishes I had taken her with me. Putting her at risk—"

Lady Hurem held up a hand and cut Kaen off. "You seem to forget that my daughter, your wife, is a very skilled mage. Why limit yourself when you travel? Nothing binds her here except your fear of her getting hurt."

Ava was almost back at the table when her mother smiled at the two of them.

"Kaen was telling me how tired he is. Would you two be ok if I get a ride back to my house and let you nap?"

Rarely did Kaen have to bite his lip to keep from smiling, but at this moment, he did, knowing full well that what she had just said was a lie, even if it was what he wanted.

"Oh, I can ask Amaranth to take your mother. She would be happy to do that for me."

Choking for a second, Kaen turned his head and listened for an answer. "I'm sorry. Did you say Amaranth would do that for you, and she would be happy about it?"

Ava chuckled and moved to where her husband was and slid her arms around him before kissing him on the neck. "There are a few things that happened while you were gone. I'll tell you later."

Amaranth moved toward the cave entrance as if he had asked her himself.

I shall take Lady Hurem back to her estate and will see if I can find something for myself and the other two to eat. Do you both require anything?

Kaen knew that if his eyes weren't bandaged they would be bulging at what Amaranth had just said.

I am fine, but thank you . . .

He heard Amaranth's huff, and then Kaen saw through Pammon's eyes as Ava and her mom walked over to where the green dragon was.

Closing his connection to all but Pammon, he felt his dragon reacting before he even asked a question.

It is not my place to say, but just know that your wife will have something to tell you.

Why can't you tell me? Why keep it a secret?

Something came through their bond, and Kaen couldn't understand the feeling. It was like remorse and frustration all mixed together.

Does your mate ever require you to not tell another person something because it is not your place to tell it?

You know she does . . .

And now you know why I cannot tell you any more.

Grunting, Kaen shook his head and walked over to the bed.

Sitting on the edge, he began removing his boots and sliding out of his dragon armor. As his arm came up, his improved sense of smell told him precisely what he didn't want to know.

"Dear spirits, I smell . . ." he muttered to himself.

He stood up, moved toward the cave wall, and began to walk with his hand on the edge of it.

Do you want my help?

No . . . I need to do this on my own.

If you were about to trip over something, should I say so?

His foot hovering in midair, Kaen cocked his head and then lowered it back down, slowly shuffling with both his feet. After walking about a yard and not hitting anything, he turned to where he knew Pammon was. A low thrum echoed through the cave, and Kaen lifted his hand, giving Pammon the middle finger.

Frustrated, he stormed along the wall until, about twelve steps in, his foot caught a few bags stacked along the back of the wall and he tripped, falling onto the cold hard floor.

I tried to warn you . . .

Coughing and trying to keep from laughing, Kaen rolled over to his knees and stood up.

You did . . . is there anything else in my way until I reach the water spigot?

No . . . you are fine now, but just stay along the wall. I don't want you tripping over my tail.

Ignoring his dragon, Kaen shuffled until he found the wall again and, after a bit, made it to the water. He heard Ava's soft footsteps coming, and he smiled.

"He said you weren't using his eyes," she complained.

"I'm not. I could hear you coming even if you tried to be sneaky."

"That's no fun . . . I wanted to scare you!"

"And watch me fall over again?"

She laughed and came up, wrapping her arms around his bare chest. As she pulled close, she let out an *ewwwww* before taking a step back. "You smell like the backside of a horse . . . would you like some help washing?"

"I would be honored if you helped me, my love."

Kaen climbed into the small tub as Ava turned on the water, finding the right temperature for him.

"I didn't know I'd have to take care of you so soon," Ava joked.

Kaen laughed, forgetting for a moment the conversation they had just minutes ago.

18

Being Behind in Preparation

Kaen could feel Aldric's and Herb's gazes even though Pammon was lounging on the floor of the cave behind both men.

Each had sat there mulling over the news of what had happened to the elves and tried to consider what it might mean for Ebonmount and others.

"This spell that he cast at you when you fought and missed . . . was it with a wand?" Aldric asked.

Shrugging, Kaen picked up his cup and sipped the watered-down wine. "I honestly don't know. Hess had mentioned it, and after hearing how many Fiola had used in the defense of her cave, I had wondered, but is it even possible for him to have that many? How long would one take?"

Herb grunted as Aldric looked at the short man beside him. A scowl was set on Herb's usually cheerful face, and he was rubbing his head again, more hair missing over the last few years from this habit he had acquired since becoming the head of the adventurers' hall.

"We have to remember that what we know about Stioks is limited, but he is the strongest mage in all the lands that I am aware of. Before he became who we all know him as now, his family was powerful and a long line of adventurers. Some said he was kin to the king. When the guild banished him officially because of some tests he had conducted on his own, there might have only been one close to his power, and now . . . Selmah is never going to be able to help beyond teaching."

Bending down, Herb grabbed his small backpack near him and dug out a piece of paper and a pen. He started sketching a few things as Aldric leaned over to watch.

"Now what I'm drawing is . . ." Herb's voice trailed off as he looked up at Kaen and realized his mistake. "Ahh . . . uh . . . can Pammon come look at what I'm doing so you can see? The visualization helps a lot."

Kaen chuckled and nodded, and a sigh came from across the cave as Pammon left his spot between Amaranth and Glynnis, moving to peer down at the paper Herb was drawing on.

"Sorry . . . I got excited and forgot," Herb said as he bent over the paper and made a few more marks. "Now look here. This wand is set on a pedestal like the one we have in the adventurers' guild with the crystal sphere. I've marked these four spots around it where mages would stand and pour magic into the item. With a wand, it's different than most other items, and I know Hess told you a little bit about the process, but the limiting part of a wand is here."

Herb put his finger next to a small diamond shape he had drawn inside what had to be a wand.

"The crystal that is used for the wand is critical. Only certain types work, and most are small because finding them and forging them takes time and money . . . when the wand is used up, the crystal shatters, turning the piece of wood or metal into scrap.

"I know the wand Fiola must have used, and when I say it was considered one of the priciest wands the elves had, know that it was. Its gem inside was larger and purer than most that have been found in the last several centuries. The spell that was used in it had been infused by a mage with power on par with what Stioks was most likely at within the last few years."

Moving his finger to the next set of drawings, Herb grunted and added a few arrows pointing from his four circles that represented the mages.

"Each of these mages has to maintain a steady stream of power infusing to the crystal at all times. If someone falters or stops, then that wand is finished. What usually happens is most wands are one-shot wonders. With four mages, you can comfortably keep this going for a while, each of them funneling power inside the gem indefinitely. You can rotate mages as long as there are always at least two, adding a steady stream of power."

Kaen was enthralled, considering what this might mean for what he could make or what he might face.

"Here's the problem, though . . ." Herb said with a sigh as he flipped the paper over and began drawing again.

Kaen watched through Pammon's eyes and felt the worry that came from his dragon when both of them realized what Herb was drawing.

Stioks is using a dragon to empower wands . . .

Aldric leaned forward, his face showing the concern he now had as he, too, knew what Herb was drawing.

As the man sat back and tapped the pen against the paper, he frowned even more before sighing. "I'm afraid Stioks must be using one or both of his dragons to help with this process. As you know"—Herb pointed at Pammon, who was looking down at them—"a dragon has an enormous supply of mana and power, well beyond what you and I do. They can infuse that wand at a greater rate, and with two dragons and every caster Stioks can summon, including himself . . ."

Herb's voice trailed off, and only the sound of the wind across the cave's opening could be heard.

"How strong could that make a wand?" Kaen asked. He licked his lips, concerned with the answer that he might have seen firsthand.

"I'm talking about things that haven't happened in a thousand years," replied Herb. "Dragons have been unwilling to do this, for lots of reasons. Imagine someone with an endless supply of dragons and a crystal of a decent size. The power that wand could have could . . ."

"Destroy a kingdom," Aldric said, finishing off where Herb had stopped. "It would appear we might need to start working on some of our own."

Herb shrugged. "We have a few in the vault. Each only has a single use and is nowhere near the power of what Stioks could possibly possess. To create anything like what he might have would require . . ." Herb's eyes drifted over to Pammon and the two female dragons who were feigning sleep.

I'm not sure how I feel about being used to make a weapon like that . . . if it gets into the wrong hands . . .

Kaen nodded, understanding Pammon's reservations about this task.

"I can't say they would be on board, and I'm sure you can imagine why, but how long would it take to make something as powerful as what I described if you had a dragon's help?"

Herb leaned over and began writing some numbers on the paper. He glanced up at Pammon and then turned toward Kaen.

"This is a personal question, but if I may, how much mana do you and Pammon both have?"

Kaen smirked, and a groan came from Pammon.

"Is this a bad request?" Herb asked, looking back and forth between Pammon and Kaen.

Shaking his head from side to side, Kaen blew a raspberry.

Are you ok if I look?

Fine . . . I will not share all of mine, but you may tell them I have over three thousand. Do not make this a habit again. We both know what that will lead to.

I haven't looked in years, and you know how hard it was for me not to look when I hit forty on archery the other day.

Yes, I know. Now, answer his question so we may understand his thoughts.

[Simple Status Check]
Kaen Marshell - Adult
Age - 23
HP - 2765/2765 (28%)
MP - 589/589 (28%)
STR - 51 (28%)
CON - 54 (28%)
DEX - 52 (28%)
INT - 46 (28%)
WIS - 40 (28%)

"Sorry," Kaen said after finally responding. "We don't share this, and I haven't looked in years for different reasons, but Pammon has over three thousand, and I am over five hundred."

Aldric's and Herb's eyes went wide, and each cleared his throat as they glanced at each other briefly.

"Th—three thousand?" Herb asked, his voice cracking.

"That is what he said."

"And you're above five hundred?"

Kaen chuckled, hearing the doubt in Herb's voice. "Yes. I mean, I'm almost six hundred bu—"

"Holy dwarf balls," Herb cursed, sputtering as he stared at Kaen. "I . . . I can't remember the last time I heard of someone being above five hundred and you say that so casually."

Motioning with his finger at Pammon, Kaen grinned. "Blame him. Most of that is from him."

Both men nodded slowly, and Herb, after closing his eyes and shaking his head for a few seconds, bent over and began writing numbers.

Kaen watched the formula the man was working on, and he could almost understand it. Although many things didn't make sense, he could see where Herb was going with it.

That number there is the required mana for each rank, isn't it?

Kaen smiled and nodded.

Yes, and the other one, I believe, is the potency, and I think there are charges in the column he is writing.

[1 Intelligence Gained]

What was that?

Kaen began to cough and covered his mouth as he did.

Both men looked at him, and Kaen waved away their concern for his sudden fit.

I . . . I just gained a point of intelligence . . .

Well, I expect you to not act like an eggling after knowing you have gotten smarter . . .

A thrum came from Pammon, and both men turned to glance at Pammon and then back at Kaen.

"What are we missing?" Aldric asked, a slight smirk on his face. "Obviously, it's something."

"I'm not sure you really want to know," Kaen declared. "If Hess were here, I'd gladly tell him, but you two might think I'm being a braggart."

He couldn't see how Aldric scrunched his eyebrows and stared at him. The king scratched the stubble on his chin and then leaned back in his chair.

"You gained a stat increase, didn't you?"

Kaen snorted and nodded. "I did . . . how did you figure it out?"

"I'd like to say I'm smart and understand what Herb is writing, but if you didn't and just figured it out . . . combined with what I know about you and Hess and the competition he joked about over the years between you two, it just makes sense."

Herb mumbled under his breath about damn Dragon Riders before continuing his work.

"I guess we won't make Herb use six hundred since that would mess up all of his work so far," joked Aldric as he put his hands behind his head and relaxed, waiting for Herb's final results.

"Maybe six months . . . a wand with one charge could be done in three, and two charges in six months . . . three charges would require a year."

Kaen glanced at the numbers that Herb had circled and the final column he put side by side.

"So based on that possibility and the fact that Stioks has been preparing for years . . ." Kaen said, trailing off as he did some math in his head.

"We're in a lot of trouble," Herb replied. "If he managed to get hold of three gems worthy of the spell you mentioned, he could have three wands with three charges each. That also means—"

"There could be even more that were produced before he killed my father," Kaen declared as he interrupted Herb. Scratching his beard, Kaen felt a weight pressing down on him but wouldn't give in. No matter the odds, they had to win. He had to win. "So what do you two want to do to help against this knowledge?"

Both men looked at Kaen and didn't answer, each trying not to wince at the memory of Hoste.

"What can we do?" Herb asked. "We are behind, and there is no way we could compete with that kind of power or speed unless all three of your dragons decided to help."

Pammon growled, and Herb winced slightly.

"I can ask, but it is a decision they must make on their own. As I've said before, I won't force them to do anything. This doesn't mean you can't start working on something else. There are mages here; even a wand or two might mean the difference when whatever we fight takes place. Someday, we all know that we must march on Luthaelia, and when we do, you will need whatever help you can get."

Aldric stood up suddenly, catching Herb off guard.

"He's right. I'll head home right now and get my royal court working on something. Expect an answer from me within a few days."

Kaen nodded and stood up, holding out his hand and giving a goodbye shake to Aldric.

Herb grabbed his paper and pen and stuffed them into his backpack. "I'll work up some ideas as well . . . perhaps in a few days, I might have an answer," he said, his voice not conveying the same sense of surety as Aldric's had.

"Good. Now Pammon and I will take you both back. I need to get a few things done as well."

19

Breaking Limits

Grateful for his strong constitution, Kaen ignored the bruises and red marks all over his body and continued to focus on the sound he heard coming toward him.

His sword barely blocked Phillip's attack, and a slight sound told him to take a step back.

The kick missed as it came low at his legs, a foot grinding into the dirt slightly, and Kaen lifted his shield, preparing for what he could hear coming at his head.

The attack changed as the sound vanished, and Kaen recalled what he had learned from the other attacks he had endured.

Trusting his instincts, Kaen spun to the left and whirled around, his sword following, and he heard Phillip's feet against the ground, trying to maneuver out of the attack Kaen was launching.

Kaen began to swing his sword in a pattern, listening for the slightest noise as Phillip backed up or shifted on his feet. He could feel it, sense it, and know just how far the boy was from him.

With his position firmly in his mind, Kaen's sword danced to a pattern of swings and thrusts. Each one came fast, slightly faster than Phillip, but the loss of vision made Kaen feel that the speed difference was ok.

The boy's shield blocked attack after attack, letting Kaen know precisely where his opponent was.

Seizing an opening he felt was there based on how the shield deflected his sword, Kaen dashed forward, his blade coming in for a thrust.

He could hear Phillip ahead and trusted the image in his mind. His sword came straight at the boy, striking like a viper.

No sound came from hitting Phillip's shield or a blow against the boy.

Suddenly, Kaen's sword was stuck, and he felt a blow to the top of his head.

"Dead!" Bren shouted.

Kaen sighed, and his sword came free.

He activated his lifestone and immediately saw through Pammon's eyes what had happened.

That boy is better than you ever were at that age, teased Pammon as he began to thrum. **He baited that so well. Even if your swords had been real, he would have lived while you died.**

Kaen groaned softly as he gave a slight bow to Phillip, who was smiling as he wiped some sweat from his eyes.

"Trapping my sword with your arm and side was a brilliant move. I'd like to say I never saw it coming, but . . ." Kaen trailed off, both of them laughing at his awful attempt at a joke.

"I still can't believe how well you fight even if you can't see," Phillip replied, watching Bren walk over toward them. "I was trying to be quiet, but you never lost my position."

Nodding, Kaen turned to see Bren coming at the two of them. He had aged a lot in the last few years. Bren had fought on the wall some, remembering why he had given up a life of adventuring and instead wanted to train people. The older man had opened up about the nightmares he was having again, seeing people die on the walls. A light had dimmed in his eyes, but the man seemed different today. Bren sounded different than he had in years.

"Phillip's right," Bren declared as he got closer. "Your footwork has improved, and I can see how you tracked him better. Against most people, I doubt they would have held you off as long or thought of trading the loss of an arm and their side to kill you."

Phillip nudged Kaen a little and chuckled. "I'd gladly give up an arm if it meant defeating you. I won't brag, but I managed to get a point in shield and swords from that."

Kaen snorted and grinned, knowing that the young man was vastly outpacing him in different ways. His lifestone wasn't special, just a standard one, yet the boy's commitment to the cause seemed to somehow push his ability to the limits. Even Hess had repeatedly commented that it was weird how fast Frederick and Phillip progressed.

"Tell me, Kaen, what did you do wrong?"

Kaen tried to consider what Bren was asking, knowing that the simple answer of being unable to see wouldn't be enough. He replayed what he had done in his mind, and after about twenty seconds into the fight, he groaned.

"I only ever attacked with my sword . . ."

"Exactly. Even though you have a shield and legs, you never used them for anything but defense. Phillip used all three, and you should have picked that up at some point and done the same." Bren stopped his commentary for a moment and moved to stand right in front of Kaen. "Stop using Pammon and get into the ready position."

Kaen turned his lifestone off and felt the darkness overtake him. Spreading his feet out, bending his knees slightly, and adjusting his hip, he felt comfortable even without being able to see.

"Raise your sword and shield."

He brought both up, holding them near each other. Turning his head just slightly, he inclined an ear toward where Bren was.

"I'm going to attack. I'm just going to use my hand. When I do, don't break it, but stop me. Are you ready?"

Kaen nodded, focusing every ounce of attention through his ears.

Thwack!

Pammon thrummed, and Kaen reacted, yanking his head back as a hand slapped his cheek.

"Try again."

Getting into position again, Kaen got ready, and a few seconds later, he felt the impact against his leg from Bren's foot.

"Again."

Groaning, Kaen felt overwhelmed. Over fifty times, he had been hit, and not once had he heard or sensed Bren's attack coming. It made no sound. There was no clue about where it would impact.

"Tell me what you are doing wrong."

"I have no idea," Kaen replied, not trying to hide his frustration in his tone. "I can't hear you or sense you at all. Every time, I just get hit."

"What are you trying to do? Just hear me?"

"Well, yeah, what else should I be trying to do?"

Bren started to chuckle, and Kaen felt his temper decrease slightly as Bren laughed for a moment. It had been so long since the man had laughed. Even though he was upset at his failures, Kaen needed to hear this man return to who he had been.

"How long have we trained together?" Bren asked, his hand suddenly on Kaen's shoulder.

"It's been over five years."

"In all the times we have trained, when have you not been trying to use your lifestone to cheat and get ahead? I can tell that even now, you aren't. Why are you limiting yourself?"

Kaen lowered his shield and sword, feeling like he was being chastised for not doing what he had gotten into trouble for always doing. "Wait, you want me to cheat like that?"

Bren started to laugh and then began to cough because he laughed so hard. "Kaen . . . you're blind. By the spirits, son, use your damn lifestone!"

He is right.

Did you think the same thing?

I could lie and say yes, but I actually did not. You wanted to do this your way. Bren is right . . . using your lifestone has always been your way.

Kaen took a deep breath and focused. He felt his lifestone burn with power and then took one more breath, making it burn even hotter.

Every one of his senses became sharper, and as Kaen settled back into position, he could feel the presence of Phillip and Bren around him: their scents, their breathing, and the slightest shifting of their bodies as they stood still. Kaen was almost certain he could hear their hearts beating inside their chests.

Slowly, a world around him began to appear. The ground beneath his feet was somehow there in a weird way. It stretched for about fifteen feet around him before fading into darkness. He could make out a slight shape of the other two, their bodies almost like tiny green lights forming a person. He couldn't see Phillip's weapon or shield, but he could see how he held his hands and arms.

Then he saw it. Bren's hand shot forward toward his left side, and Kaen raised his shield, blocking it with barely any strength.

For the slightest moment, Kaen thought he saw a smile appear on the outline of Bren's body.

Then a flurry of attacks came.

Bren moved with a speed that defied his age, a speed well beyond what Phillip was capable of and a skill honed over a lifetime of combat and training.

His hands and feet darted out in a variety of attacks, including leg sweeps, double arm punches, a flying kick, and more. Each time, Kaen easily blocked and moved slightly, avoiding the strikes and attacks.

Bren moved near Phillip, and Kaen saw the young man's arms move. The young man tossed his weapon and shield to Bren, and in a moment, Kaen knew what was coming.

The sound of wood on wood echoed across the courtyard as both men didn't hold back, Kaen no longer just defending himself but also attacking.

Kaen sent a leg sweep that Bren easily dodged. Bren then swung his sword at Kaen's outstretched leg, requiring him to yank it back quickly or allow it to be hit. Their shields collided as they both used them for leverage and position.

Unsure of how much time had passed, Kaen saw Bren's green outline change for the briefest moment. A bright light welled inside his chest and raced toward the arm holding the sword.

Kaen knew what had happened.

That bastard used a skill.

The sword became a streak of light aimed at him, but Kaen did not react to the wooden weapon. Instead, he danced with the body and knew how that arm worked. He could see each thrust and swipe aimed at him. His shield sounded like raindrops as the sword struck it over and over.

Another light blossomed inside Bren's shape and raced toward his legs and shield arm.

Kaen braced, knowing what was coming.

Bren slammed into him, and the shields bashed together. The cracking of wood filled his ears, and Kaen felt his shield falling apart.

Heavy breaths came from Bren, and Kaen saw his friend and teacher going for a combo he hadn't seen in years. It had surprised him and cost him a duel, but now Kaen recognized how the man shifted and prepared, seeing the power of Bren's lifestone sending out waves of light to each of his limbs.

The flurry that came felt slow this time. Even though Bren was attacking with a speed most would never hope to defeat, Kaen knew he would survive this onslaught. As the seconds ticked by and a string of kicks, punches, and sword thrusts came, Kaen dodged or parried each of them.

A final surge of light came and ended, and the moment it did, Kaen smiled.

He went on the offensive, his sword, broken shield, and legs coming at Bren just as fast as the trainer had attacked him.

Ten seconds later, he stood over his trainer, breathing hard as he held the sword to the man's chest.

"Dead!" Phillip called out.

[Magical Energy Detection Learned]
[Magical Energy Detection x20]
[Sphere of Detection Gained]
[World Sight Gained]

Kaen moved back, breathing rapidly as the area that he was able to detect grew by another ten feet.

There, on the edge of it, he saw Pammon's head. A dazzling display of magical energy and power that was almost overwhelming flooded his vision as he saw his dragon in a whole new way.

By the spirits, you are . . . powerful . . .

What did you just gain?! I could sense something surge inside you!

It's like I can see a limited range around me. I can sense life and energy. It's—

"Kaen, what in the spirits happened?"

Bren's question cut him off, and Kaen looked down at the man he still had pinned to the ground. Tossing the sword away, Kaen extended his hand and helped Bren up.

"I did what you said. I cheated, and now . . ." Kaen paused, turning his head slightly each way. "Now I can see you two even without Pammon."

"Holy dwarf balls," Bren muttered, chuckling as he dusted himself off. "Have I ever told you how much I hate how you do that?"

Kaen laughed and heard Phillip laughing as well.

"Yes . . . yes, you have."

20

Fatherly Advice

"I won't ask because I'm not sure I understand what you just said," Bren said as he tried to figure out what had just happened. "I expected you to do what you always do, but not like that . . . not like . . ."

"Able to see your abilities and block them?" Kaen answered. "That last ability you used . . . it's a level forty skill, right?"

Bren chuckled and nodded. "Blade Dance. Most won't ever get that option, but somehow I did. The fact that you blocked it and, not only that, anticipated every strike was what I couldn't believe. If you had your vision, I figured you could probably stop me now, but knowing you were blind and doing it . . ."

"That's the same one I took at level forty," Kaen replied, grinning from ear to ear.

Bren groaned, knowing that not only had Kaen found a new way to see, but he also had acquired a skill in half the time it had taken him.

Phillip came over, and Kaen realized he couldn't see expressions. He allowed his lifestone to reduce itself to a slight smolder and switched to Pammon's eyes.

There on his young trainee was a smile that reminded Kaen of the day he offered each of them a lifestone.

"What?" Kaen asked as he faced Phillip.

"Nothing," the boy replied. "I just can't figure out how you do what you do. Ever since that first day we met, the way you smelled, learning it was because you trained so hard. Frederick and I both believed we could be like you if we trained hard enough. No matter what . . ."

Phillip sighed and then chuckled as he looked at Pammon. "We both knew there was going to be a limit because you had a dragon, yet we never let that stop us. Even on the days everything hurt, we pushed each other . . . Had it not been the both of us, I'm certain we wouldn't have made it this far.

Then, when you made us that offer to give us a chance to bond with a dragon egg . . . it . . ."

Phillip began to sniff, and tears started to drop to the ground. He lifted his head, ignoring the streaks they caused on his dusty cheeks. "It told us we had finally accomplished what we had promised you. We had worked hard enough to prove how committed we were to this kingdom and everyone here. It's why we never doubted we would make it through that cave. Even when things were bleak and our dwarven friend shared his doubt, we both knew you would push through. Knew you would get us home."

Wiping one cheek, Phillip smiled. "Now here I stand, having dealt with the fear and frustration of knowing you are injured and yet seeing you push yourself to get better, allowing no excuse to hold you back. I'll admit I wasn't sure I could offer much, but knowing that you trusted me with the secret of your injury and felt I could . . . it means more than words can express. Now you have proved why we know someday this land will be free. I just watched you do the impossible. I'm not sure how, but it gives me hope that my dragon and I will be able to push through those moments when all hope seems gone and come through stronger on the other side, because I have watched you do it."

Kaen stood there silent, not sure if Phillip was finally done talking. When Kaen realized Phillip was, he smiled and reached out, grabbing the young man and giving him a hug. He felt Phillip sniff a few times as he hugged him back, more tears on the young man's cheeks clearly visible through Pammon's exceptional eyesight.

"I cannot be more proud of you and Frederick, and to hear you say those words . . . knowing how broken I was for a while. Thank you. I will continue to try to be worthy of emulating."

Kaen saw Bren moving toward them both, and the older man slapped each of them on the arm before grabbing it and squeezing.

"All this talk is going to make me cry, and I don't need to do that. Just know I'm proud of both of you. This kingdom would be long gone if it weren't for men like you."

Kaen sat on Pammon's back, feeling the wind against his face, not caring that his jaw was sore from smiling so much.

I have not felt that level of joy from you in a long time. Perhaps getting blinded was the greatest thing that could happen to you.

Kaen chuckled and gently rubbed his friend's neck.

It took me being blind to finally see how blessed I am.

Where to now?

Back home. I need to get a few more things to bring back to the cave. Ava seems content staying in there, and I have some items being brought by. We also need to have a chat with Hess later today. Can you retrieve him?

I guess I could torture myself with a visit. Would you like me to bring the other two?

Kaen couldn't help but smile at that thought. He knew how much Callie loved being around all three dragons. She had seen the eggs once and almost had to be dragged away.

That sounds like a plan. Tell Hess to bring some food and we will eat here. Maybe even a bedroll if they would like to spend the night.

A rumble came from Pammon, and Kaen started to laugh as he felt his dragon's feelings through their bond.

That is if you don't mind doing all that. I know you are not a pack mule.

I was about to say some unkind words, but since you asked nicely, I will refrain. There is no point in ruining the moment.

Kaen nodded. For the first moment in a long time, he felt like he was breaking free from the prison he had locked himself away in.

"Kaen!"

Grinning, Kaen stood off to the side where he had finished setting up a small privacy screen for the bed he had brought over on Pammon.

He had listened to Pammon tell him how Callie was talking and how excited she was about getting to see all three dragons and both eggs.

His little sister raced toward him, seemingly not concerned that his eyes were covered with a cloth, and jumped up, fully expecting him to catch her as always.

Scooping her up in midair, he laughed and hugged her before tickling her neck.

"What's wrong with your face?" she asked, her hand reaching out to touch his eye covering after she stopped giggling.

"Oh, I hurt my eyes, but I'll be fine in a week. This is just to help them heal."

He could see her looking at him and moving her head slowly from side to side as Pammon kept his eyes on the little girl the dragon loved more than he admitted.

"Hmm, it makes you look less ugly," she said, eliciting a round of laughter from all the dragons and adults present.

"I can't help it if our parents are ugly . . . at least you don't look ugly like they do," Kaen replied as he gave her a quick kiss on the cheek and then set her down on the ground.

He saw her biting her lips as she stared at the dragons and the two eggs.

"You want to go and see the eggs as well as Glynnis and Amaranth?"

She nodded, her head moving so fast a woodpecker would struggle to keep up.

"Go ahead, they said it is ok."

Squealing with glee, Callie took off running toward the egg Glynnis was curled around.

"You sure they don't mind?" Hess asked as he came forward and gave Kaen a hug.

"Pammon told them it would be ok, and so they don't mind. They understand you are family, and as such, neither one minds. Besides, that egg is harder than one might imagine. I don't see her doing anything to it."

Sulenda groaned as she moved over and hugged Kaen after embracing Ava. "You say that, but we will have to listen to her jabber about those eggs and her desire for one. 'Surely my brother Kaen will let me have a dragon . . .' She says things like that at least twice a day."

Kaen chuckled, letting Sulenda go from the massive squeeze she gave him. Unable to see her face, Kaen could tell she was probably not excited about how he looked.

"If I said I'm starving and we should eat first, would you three mind?"

"I'd rather eat now while it's warm. I won't tell you how excited Sulenda was to finally use the meat she had been saving."

Kaen smiled as he moved to the table and sat in his chair.

"Well then, if you don't mind, I need some advice, Dad."

Hess looked at Ava, who rolled her eyes but nodded while helping Sulenda with her pack. "You two boys have fun. We'll get dinner finished up."

The four of them sat watching Callie race around the room, climbing over Pammon and laughing when he scooped her up in his claws and set her down somewhere else.

"Hard to imagine this would be a sight that wouldn't surprise me," Hess said, picking at his teeth with a bone. "Who knew three dragons would be a common thing in Ebonmount?"

"I, for one, am glad she is here," Ava chimed in. "I have missed getting to see all of you, and hearing her laugh does me a lot of good."

"Did you two ever figure out what skill to pick?" Sulenda asked.

Hess glanced at Sulenda and shook his head. "It's not easy. Both have advantages, and each has a weakness. Kaen knows what he wants to pick, but he can't commit to it."

Sulenda and Ava looked at Kaen, who no longer used Pammon for vision but instead let his lifestone help him see the energy within their bodies.

"It's true. It took me all these years to finally hit level forty. Fifty could be decades away. The right setup with Fan Shot would allow me to send out so many arrows, each of which I think I could imbue with energy. If that happened, the potential for fighting is hard to compare. It works from all angles and has good uses when I'm on Pammon. That said, one of the problems is how it would actually work on Pammon, and it could only be used while facing behind him or in a diving attack. Otherwise, his head or wings would get in the way."

Sulenda snorted. "You have gotten a lot smarter since you barged into my office all those years ago."

Kaen squeezed Ava's hand gently as they rested them on the table together.

"I try . . . but still, Homing Shot could be a game-changer against Stioks or any other dragon in the right environment. Hess says it travels as fast as an arrow the entire time, and it would keep chasing that bastard until it hits something. Combined with the penetration rune on my bow and the ability to charge an arrow . . . I may only need one shot."

"Do you believe it would be that easy?" Sulenda asked, leaning against the table.

Kaen sighed. "Nothing is ever easy, but what matters now is I have heard from Hess and his thoughts. I'll make my decision soon enough. I want to practice with whatever I choose sooner rather than later. Let's not worry about that problem and enjoy our time together. Ava had me pick up some tiles if you are interested in a game."

Hess nodded, and Sulenda groaned. "As long as the two of you aren't on the same team, yes! Both of you cheat when you play!"

"I would never do that," protested Hess as he winked at her.

As Hess and Sulenda playfully squabbled, Kaen leaned over and kissed Ava on her cheek. "I love you and want you to know that."

She smiled and kissed him back, this time on his lips. "I love you too. Now, don't cheat unless it's with me," she whispered.

21

Special Connections

The night with Callie, Hess, and Sulenda had been a salve that both Kaen and Ava needed more than they realized. Seeing the little girl curled up between three dragons, a hand resting on one of the eggs as she slept, reminded them both how precious life was.

"Can I come again soon?" Callie asked as Hess clipped her in between Sulenda and him on Pammon.

"Anytime I am free, and if Mom and Dad say it's ok," Kaen replied. "Just make sure that you are doing your work and helping out around the inn. If those chores aren't done, you won't be able to come."

Kaen saw the grin on Callie's face and heard her already bugging Hess about when she might come spend the night again.

Grateful that Pammon was watching the three, Kaen saw Hess roll his eyes as he chuckled.

"Love you, son! You two take care and don't be afraid to stop in when you are able to make public appearances."

Kaen waved at them as Callie squealed with glee when Pammon walked toward the opening of the cave. Her screams of delight echoed after Pammon had leaped off the edge into the air.

"She is a handful," Ava muttered, squeezing Kaen as she snuggled closer to him. "Is that why Hess looks so old now?"

Giving her a kiss on the forehead, he sighed, feeling the world go dark as Pammon's eyesight no longer helped him where he was.

Kaen focused, finding the right amount power that his lifestone needed to be filled with power, and saw the world of energy flowing around him.

The stone floor was there, barely visible with a single line that somehow marked the part he stood on. It didn't matter if it was dirt, stone, or carved bricks. Each time, the landscape showed up with a view that had been impossible to describe to Ava.

Next to him, squeezing her tightly, he saw his wife, a body filled with more green lights than Phillip or Bren had. It left him with a few questions about what exactly he was seeing, but until he could surround himself with more people, the answer wouldn't come anytime soon.

"Now that they are gone, we could head back to bed for a few . . ." she said.

Kaen glanced down at Ava and even though he couldn't see her face, he saw the energy inside her moving slightly faster than before.

"I would enjoy that," he replied, lifting her chin and kissing her on the lips.

A thrum behind the two of them was soon joined by another, and Kaen heard the sound of claws on stone.

We shall go and find ourselves some food.

Amaranth's tone made him laugh, and he used his hip to gently bump Ava. "Did you ask her to leave?"

Ava snorted and began pulling him back to where they had set up their bed. "Sometimes a woman has to take charge."

Kaen gently stroked Ava's hair as she lay on his chest.

Her lips kissed his skin and Kaen groaned slightly, always ecstatic anytime she touched him. He had never known how amazing it could be when someone you loved reached out on their own accord and put their body against you.

Kaen's chest rose a few times as he held back a laugh.

"What?" Ava asked, running her fingernails up and down his stomach.

"I was just thinking how lucky I am to have you and what a fool I was before you."

She laughed, poking him gently in the side before returning to gently run her fingers over the contours of his exposed abs. "You are wise to realize how lucky you are . . . now what exactly was it that made you a fool?"

"You sure you want to know?"

"I'll trust your judgment to not say something you shouldn't," she replied, kissing him again on his chest.

Taking a deep breath, Kaen shifted a little on the bed and drew her closer. "Growing up with Hess I never really got to experience a physical connection with anyone. I fooled around with a few girls in the village, sneaking a few kisses, but no one every really connected with me. Also, Hess was not a great example at the time for how to relate to women.

"Looking back now, I can see how he missed Sulenda and was struggling raising me. That led to him showing me the wrong way to flirt with women. So when we moved to Ebonmount, I tried to emulate him. I had seen his bravado and his lack of fear with them. I saw how they responded to his larger-than-life actions."

Kaen sighed. "So I tried to flirt with every woman I could. Compared to Minoosh, this place was filled with women who seemed interested in me . . . even if it was for the wrong reasons. I even flirted with a woman old enough to be my mother, and I'm grateful she never allowed it to go anywhere."

He squeezed Ava, then leaned over so he could kiss her head. "All that changed when I met you. None of the other girls mattered. I only wanted to be with you. It drove me crazy not knowing who you were, and when I finally did, I was certain you would see me for the bumbling backwoods boy that I was.

"Yet here I am, with you and realizing how blessed I am. The only person I desire to touch me like you do is you. Just having you here in my arms, our skin touching each other, fills me with a happiness that is hard to describe."

Ava started to laugh. "Oh, I'm pretty sure your happiness was evident earlier."

Kaen snorted and pulled her up toward him, kissing her on the lips again. "Perhaps I can show you that once more."

Lifting her eyebrows, Ava smirked. "Perhaps you can."

Perhaps next time you could give me a warning when you are going to be doing that.

The tone in Pammon's voice and the angst he felt through their bond caused Kaen to start laughing harder than he had expected.

I had not planned it. It was Ava's idea. She even got Amaranth and Glynnis to leave.

I am well aware of that . . . they both tracked me down, knowing what would be taking place between you two.

I didn't sense any major problems on your end from that.

That is because I was nice and blocked what we did from you and Ava . . . unlike some who forgot what we agreed upon . . .

Kaen groaned, still snorting at the fact that he had forgotten to do that.

Sorry . . . it had been a while and I—

I understand. Just remember, when you fail to do that, I do not want to be responsible for scaring the populace like that again.

His mouth fell open and Kaen began to imagine where Pammon must have displayed their mating flights.

Do I want to know?

Oh, I am sure that you will hear about it eventually. I was caught off guard and the east side of the city got a view I doubt any of them expected to see.

I'm sure bards will sing of your exploits in taverns all across the city now.

Kaen was laughing and he could tell that Pammon did not find his joke nearly as funny as he did.

Are you doing better now? Amaranth has told me it was safe to return.

Sitting there at the table in the cave, Kaen tried to decide how to answer that question. Ava was across the room, washing a few things, and had told him to stay put since he would not be much help without his vision.

I am ready for what must come soon. The time is limited, and we both know that eventually I must act. I owe Amaranth something. I'm not sure what, but the bond she formed with Ava has changed her. Since then, I have felt a strength in Ava that's different than before.

Pammon was flying east of him, and Kaen could feel something coming through his bond. A concern he hadn't felt before.

Do we want to have this discussion while I am not near you?

Kaen tried to imagine what Pammon was talking about, but nothing came to mind that he felt needed to be discussed.

I'm lost. What is it we need to discuss?

A moment passed and Pammon said nothing.

Let me finish what I and the other two are doing, and then we will return and talk.

What are you doing right now? Eating?

A sense of humor flittered across their bond.

I will do that later. Right now I am providing the farmers with my magical crap.

Kaen started laughing, his voice carrying over the empty cavern.

Shite! I feel bad for them . . . the smell . . .

Yet every time I come, they bow and smile with looks that are worthy of my crap. We both know it is the only reason why food supplies have kept up for so long.

Kaen scratched his newly grown beard. Pammon was right. The amount of crap those three dragons produced had been a godsend. The farmers had taken it, excited to handle such a disgusting task, having been told how well it worked.

The first few fields they used it on had outproduced every other field and allowed for two crops instead of the usual one.

Every orchard and fruit tree in the kingdom received a steady supply.

Tell me they aren't still mixing it with water . . .

They are. That smells worse than I want to admit. The number of barrels they fill with that concoction would fill your house from floor to ceiling a few times over.

Groaning, Kaen recalled the one time he had been present when they demonstrated what the heads of the agricultural group had achieved. The stench had brought back nightmares of the one time Pammon had sharted inside his room in Roccnari. It had taken weeks for the smell to go away, and those poor elves had turned green. The only good thing was that it had kept Huethea from invading his personal space for a few weeks.

Kaen winced at the thought of that kingdom now. The destruction he had seen and the knowledge that any elf who had lived was hiding in the forests around their old homes or on the road toward Ebonmount left a bad taste in his mouth.

What are you thinking about?

I'm thinking that I need to heal quickly. Every day I can't see and am unable to do what I must is another day some innocent will be injured.

Kaen tapped his fingers on the table, knowing that he needed to get better.

The sound of Ava's steps echoed slightly as she came toward him and he activated his lifestone, seeing her enter the range of his new way of seeing the world after a few seconds.

He smiled and considered how amazing she looked composed of green magical lights that outlined all the curves of her body.

"Why are you smiling?"

Kaen chuckled. "I'm just thinking you look exceptionally amazing."

He heard her snort and moved his chair out slightly, tapping his leg for her to sit down.

After she plopped down on his lap and put her arms around him, Ava leaned forward and put her lips near his ear.

"I just thought of something while I was over there and . . . it seems foolish but it may actually be something only you can do."

Pulling her close, Kaen laughed. "Do I need to tell Pammon to stay out longer?"

She pushed against him, her head shaking. "No . . . but we will need him to take us somewhere."

Intrigued, Kaen felt Ava shifting slightly on him, excited about something.

22

Enduring Pain

"That seems like a foolish idea, but like you said, it might actually work."

"I know!" Ava exclaimed after Kaen heard her idea. "I mean, think about it. You have a poison-resist skill and a disease-resist skill now. Almost no one ever gets those because no one can endure those things and survive."

Kaen scratched the side of his cheek a few times, feeling his nails dig deeper than usual and trying to remember the last time he had trimmed them.

"So you want Pammon and Amaranth to take us to the adventurers' guild and let people use magic on me . . . all with the hope that I can gain a resist skill to those types . . . if I didn't know better, someone might think you were trying to finally kill me."

Ava pinched his side, ignoring the fact that Kaen barely reacted more than a slight shift at her touch.

"But it makes sense if you really think about it."

Kaen nodded, still not exactly sure how much he wanted to stand there while people used offensive spells on him. Ava was right that he might never know when a fire or lightning-resist ability might be useful. Especially if fighting dragons.

"I guess we will have to talk to Pammon and the others in a moment. They're almost here."

"I know," Ava declared. "You seem to forget that I can feel her when she is close enough."

Kaen nodded. It would take him some time to get used to that.

Have you done something to upset your mate? It seems like this idea should warn you to sleep with one eye open.

Pammon thrummed, not caring that Kaen wasn't laughing at his joke.

Seriously, though, it makes sense and you know it. Are you willing to take me there?

We have nothing else to do at the moment. Amaranth has told me she is already on board with this idea even if I was not. So whenever you are ready we can go.

"Looks like we are ready here," Kaen stated, shifting the backpack he already had on, knowing that Pammon would fly him regardless of the way he felt.

"I'm already ready!" Ava shouted, and Kaen swapped his vision to Pammon's eyes, seeing that Ava was already latched in on Amaranth.

Those two . . . what is it you wanted to talk to me about? Does it have to do with the two of them?

Slightly but no. Climb on and we will talk on the way.

At some point you need to let Ava be bound to a dragon. If we survive this and when more eggs come, you need to allow her to become a Dragon Rider.

I thought we had decided it wouldn't be good for her to do either of these two. Why now?

Because the longer you wait, the more she will question why you have not let it happen. Years will pass and she will age and since we do not know how many more eggs will be hatched here, you cannot risk not giving her the first chance at the next one. I can only imagine how you will feel as you watch her grow old . . . the pain you will experience when you have to bury her and have another century or more to live.

Tharnok shared with me how much it hurt Elies when a woman he had grown fond of died. After that he swore off those kinds of relationships.

The guild was quickly approaching, and Kaen knew he only had about another minute before they landed.

I do not have a problem with this. So what do I need to do?

Tell her. Let her know that when the next eggs come, the first shall be hers. Tell her why you want her to have it.

Did Amaranth tell you to say this?

Pammon snorted, shaking his head at Kaen's question.

She mentioned to me the need for you and Ava to be joined like this. She knew I would tell you what I have because Amaranth knows how much I care for both of you.

Sighing, Kaen tapped the scales on Pammon's neck as they prepared to land.

I know. Thank you for telling me this.

Pammon thrummed slightly as the ground raced toward them.

Just know, I am looking forward to seeing Ava's idea in action.

* * *

Kaen began to regret agreeing to the plan Ava had come up with.

His body was sore and the smell of burning flesh was worse, as his nose was now more acute when it came to scents.

Still, he was amazed at how right his wife had been.

Two healers were standing by and Amaranth was just a few yards away, occasionally healing him when he needed it.

Ava had not been excited that Herb required her to be the one to test this out. Her fire magic control was good and so she had sent small attacks with barely any power at him for a few minutes.

Eventually Kaen had told her to try harder, and the first fireball she sent left Kaen without any chest hair.

He saw the next fire spell enter his view of magic and wanted to dodge it, knowing that he could, but instead he stood there, taking another hit to his midsection.

[Fire Resistance +1]

"Eleven," Kaen stated, not allowing himself to groan or his voice to crack.

"It's coming faster!" Ava shouted in reply. "The stronger the attack, the faster your skill gains have been!"

You should see the look of excitement on her face. It is almost as if she is enjoying taking turns with the other two mages to burn you.

Which is why I'm not using your eyes to see that . . . I can't say this feels great, but the truth is most of these spells do less than a sixth or so of my life per attack. The others barely did anything.

Do not worry. Once you hit twenty, I will get involved.

Kaen groaned, nodding to Ava even though he couldn't see her, and he saw as the next spell came, striking his stomach.

You do look quite amazing in those shorts Herb found for you. I understand why you didn't want to wear your dragon armor.

Kaen grunted, motioning with his hand for another spell.

It's because . . . Pain came through the bond as a fireball from Ava struck him in the stomach again, sending flames over his body.

[Fire Resistance +1]

Sighing, Kaen held up his hand for them to stop and turned to Amaranth. "Can I get a heal, please?"

The green dragon moved forward with her snout; it began to fill with power and Kaen stood there in awe every time he saw it. The magic flowed from inside the dragon's chest, up her neck, and to the tip of her snout.

He saw it flow from her and into him the moment she put it against his chest, breathing better as the burns and sores disappeared.

Your natural healing is amazing to watch when combined with my spell. I do not remember any dragons recovering so naturally as you do. Ava was wise to pick a mate with a strong constitution like yourself.

Kaen began to cough and Pammon started to thrum.

"Thank you," he finally got out after catching his breath.

Your wife has ruined that poor dragon. The things she tells me now . . . I'm not certain which is worse, her or Glynnis.

Kaen motioned for another spell, tightening his core and waiting for it to come.

As I was saying, the fire resistance the greaves and chest piece give would most likely hinder the potential gains I have had so far.

Well, you do look foolish standing in those leather shorts and that bag over your head.

Kaen grumbled. He had only looked once at the spectacle that he was. Herb had found a pair of fireproof shorts used by some crafter that could withstand most fire spells. They fit him well. The bag over his head came from the same blacksmith, again resistant to fire. It smelled like coal and burnt metal and now the scent of burnt flesh.

The things we do to get stronger . . . Elies would be proud.

Kaen felt a sense of pride come through their bond.

You honor him even now by your willingness to endure anything.

Kaen let Ava lead him to their bed and when he felt it bump against his legs, he plopped down on it.

Amaranth was almost asleep as well, and Kaen had seen just how tired Ava and the green dragon both were.

The light that shimmered inside them and was trapped by their skin was almost gone. Each had used everything they had to help him in this endeavor.

Once he had hit level twenty and no more gains came, Pammon had taken over.

The pain still lingered in his mind as Amaranth healed while he put his hand into the small fire his friend had created on the ground.

His flesh had started to melt away, his muscles feeling like they wanted to vanish only for the healing that Amaranth had poured into him to regrow it as it vanished.

No pain in his life had compared to what he had felt in that moment.

Every ounce of willpower kept him from pulling his hand out.

Pammon had poured his own life force into Kaen, giving strength in that moment.

Kaen winced as he felt the pillow against his face, remembering what he heard Ava say once they were done.

"I've never heard a man scream as loud or as long as you did."

He couldn't recall screaming. His lifestone was burning with every ounce of power that he could hold on to through the pain that wanted him to black out.

The skill gains had flown by so fast at first.

Time had lost all meaning, but he saw when it said his Fire Resistance had evolved at thirty. It felt like it had happened quickly, but the world felt different in that moment.

The pain diminished slightly, his flesh not dissolving like a piece of paper thrown into a fire. It took longer for his skin to vanish, and instead it bubbled and warped in weird ways before being reshaped to how it was supposed to be around his arm and hand.

Everything had been a race against time. How much he could endure, how long Amaranth could heal him, the amount of life force Pammon could share.

Slowly the burning lessened and as he hit thirty-nine it began to almost feel cool against his skin. The fire burned but not like a flame.

It was more like a cold burning sensation. Metal so cold it would burn.

He asked Pammon to do it once more. Make fire that was slightly hotter.

Without protesting his dragon had done it. A stream of what Kaen could only imagine lava felt like emerged, drenching his arm from the elbow down.

He had shuddered, screaming once more, but then it came.

[Fire Resistance has evolved to Dragon Breath Immunity - Fire]

The pain stopped.

The burning stopped.

No longer did his flesh melt away.

No longer did Amaranth have to heal.

The flames did not bother him at all.

Pammon had been in shock just as much as he was. Neither was sure it was even possible.

Herb had called him insane. The truth was that Kaen knew he was.

Yet there were no other options.

This fight would require everything, and Kaen couldn't risk being weak.

Carefully he had wiped the dragon fire off his arm.

He could finally use Pammon's eyes again to make sure that no flames were left on him.

Once it was all gone his lifestone gave out.

Pammon had cut the strength he had shared.

It took Ava and Herb and some help from Amaranth to get him onto Pammon.

The flight over here felt like a dream.

Lying on the bed felt better than anything he could remember in so long.

Then sleep came.

And he relived the pain of the past moments.

23

Uncovering Things

The day after, they all did nothing. Still recovering from the previous day's events, Ava had repeatedly ensured that Kaen had no lasting problems with his left arm, which he had put inside Pammon's fire.

Amaranth and Glynnis spoke in a different tone when Kaen talked with them. When he asked how long they thought the eggs might take to hatch, they confirmed it would be a few weeks.

Soon, Phillip and Frederick would need to stay inside the cave and wait for the moment when the eggs hatched.

There would be no time to get them if things moved quickly.

Kaen remembered how quickly Pammon had hatched. One moment, he heard his friend's voice in his head. The next moment, the egg cracked, and a tiny copper dragon was before him.

"My parents are expecting us. If we don't go, we know how they will act the next time we see them."

Kaen groaned, stretching in bed as he lay beside Ava, enjoying her scent. He had never realized until the last few days just how she smelled. There had always been a scent, but now he could easily recognize it even when other scents were around.

"I know . . . do we have to get there early, or can we just show up right before dinner?"

Ava elbowed Kaen, earning a grunt from him. "I would like to spend a little time talking with my mother before we just sit down and eat. Some mothers and daughters are like that."

"Fine. I guess you should ask Amaranth if we can have her take us. Pammon has been struggling to avoid destroying every inch of your parents' courtyard when he takes us."

A moment passed, and Kaen knew what was happening.

"She said she would be happy to. Now sit up and let me help you get dressed. I need to make sure you are wearing something presentable."

Kaen tapped his eye covering. "Isn't this good enough?"

Groaning, Ava pounced on top of him. "No . . . you need more than just that. I don't want to share more of your body than I must."

Kaen laughed, pulling her down and kissing her.

It took a while before they were ready to get dressed and go.

Lord Hurem had been anxiously awaiting Kaen's arrival, evident from his sitting in the courtyard, reading a book, and facing the direction they always came from.

"It was nice of you to come a little early!" he exclaimed. "Your mother is waiting inside for you to help her with something, my precious daughter!"

Ava smiled and kissed her dad on the cheek before waving at Kaen and heading toward the door, which would take her inside.

"Let me assist you. We are just going over to the table."

"I can see a little. Just lead the way, and I will follow."

Lord Hurem cleared his throat as he stared at Kaen. His eyes narrowed as he took in his son-in-law, with bandages still over his eyes. "How can you see? Have you disobeyed my instructions, taken the bandages off, and tried looking?"

"It's a long story, but no . . . just something I've picked up in the last few days. I'll tell you more after we sit."

Kaen watched Lord Hurem scratch his chin for a moment before turning sideways and slowly approaching the table.

Unable to help it, Kaen laughed and moved quickly, reaching out, putting his hand on his father-in-law's shoulder, and pushing him. "Don't worry about me, and stop walking like that."

"Remarkable!" the man gasped.

Kaen didn't need eyes to see, knowing the man had a smile on his lips.

"Now, I don't believe you would lie to me, but you haven't tried opening your eyes yet, have you?"

Kaen shook his head slightly as he watched the green outline of Lord Hurem's fingers remove the pads that were over his eyes.

"I have not. Ava has changed the bandages and pads a few times, but only to put on more salve and clean bandages."

"And you can still tell me how many fingers—"

"Four."

Lord Hurem snorted, still checking every few minutes that Kaen could see. "What you are describing is impressive. I believe there must be books talking about it somewhere, lost for a thousand years or more. Though I guess, knowing who you are and what you always seem to achieve, this might be something new entirely."

The warm washcloth felt exceptionally wonderful as the man washed salve from his eyes. It was always pleasant when Ava had done this. The area around his eyes had become sensitive to touch after being protected by the pads and wrap.

"Now listen. Cover your eyes with both hands and slowly open your eyes. If it hurts or becomes too much, close your eyes and we will cover them for a few more days. Better to be safe than sorry."

Kaen nodded. His heart was pounding as he desperately wanted, no, needed to be able to see normally.

Slowly he put his hands over his eyes and took a few deep breaths. Calming himself, he opened his eyes slightly. It felt like he was pulling his eyelids apart. They were somewhat stuck together from the salve, and remained shut even after a good washing.

"Can I borrow that rag again?" Kaen asked, forcing himself to relax and close his eyes again.

After a few more wipes with the cloth and letting it sit for a minute, Kaen felt ready to try again. Once more, Kaen held his hands over his eyes and was able to pull apart his eyelids. The brightness of what he saw through the tiny cracks between his fingers was almost overwhelming.

"Relax . . . breathe," Lord Hurem said. "I can tell by how your face is scrunched up that it is a lot. Keep the amount of light to a minimum. I probably should have taken you somewhere darker. Would you like to move?"

Kaen shook his head slightly and continued to breathe. Closing his eyes for a moment, he cracked them again. The light felt so bright that it was almost as if he had a lightstone next to his eyes.

Something draped over his head, and the light immediately almost disappeared.

"I put my shirt over you. That should help some. Look down and try now."

Kaen opened his eyes more, needing a few seconds to open them completely. He had to blink multiple times as tears came out, lubricating everything.

He made a tiny crack between his hands; this time, the light he saw was less overwhelming. He exhaled the breath he had been holding and continued to open his fingers slowly.

It took minutes to adjust after each slight increase in space.

Unsure how long it had been, Kaen finally slid both hands from over his eyes. Occasionally he had to squint, but he could see his legs as he stared at them. The brown leather pants his wife had put him in had a few drops from the fallen tears.

He had never imagined how excited he might be to see a pair of pants, but it felt exhilarating. The fringe of the shirt was a dazzling bright light, a reminder that it was different under this shirt than when he took it off.

"Hold up and wait," Lord Hurem ordered. "Don't just rip that off. Tell me what you see. Is it clear or blurry? Do you see multiple images of everything?"

"I see two legs in a pair of brown leather pants."

A chuckle came, and Kaen saw a hand appear beneath the shirt. "How many fingers am I holding up?"

"Two."

"Just two, or do you see an afterimage, like another copy elsewhere?"

Kaen shook his head. "I only see the two you have held up. Both look clear, and I can tell you just got your nails trimmed."

Kaen heard his father-in-law sigh. "Alright. Close your eyes, lift your head, and when you're ready, let me know. I'll take the shirt away, and we will try this again."

After finally opening his eyes, it was hard to close them, but Kaen forced them shut. Sitting straight, he held up a thumb and felt the shirt come off his head.

"Now, slowly open your eyes . . . slowly!"

Kaen shut them quickly as the light had hit him worse than Pammon's head-butting. He knew that he had messed up, trying to open them completely.

"Sorry."

"Not as sorry as you will be if you get a massive headache. Trust me, son, I don't want you to suffer any longer than you must, but this isn't a race. Small steps."

Nodding, Kaen slowly cracked them open, repeating the process, and after what felt like forever, he could see his father-in-law and Ava standing before him.

"Well?"

"You look amazing," Kaen replied. "Better than I had remembered."

Ava and her father both snorted and shook their heads.

"Kaen, I'm glad you think I look amazing, but is everything still clear?"

Coughing, Kaen nodded. "Yes, sir. Thank you. It is still a bit bright, but I can see fine."

Lord Hurem nodded and stood up, collecting all the materials from the table.

"Good. I'll be back. You two can sit here and enjoy the garden while I retrieve my wife."

Kaen turned, more excited than he realized to be able to see his father-in-law depart.

A hand brushed his, and Kaen turned to see his wife smiling at him.

"You should see yourself," she said.

"Forgot how good I look?"

Ava snickered, making a face. "It's . . . you know I love you, right?"

"Why do I feel there is a *but* to this?"

She nodded, her smirk transforming into a full-blown smile. "Let's just say we need to get you a mirror . . . there is a two-inch strip of white that wraps around your face and—"

"Holy dwarf balls," Kaen cursed. Glancing around the courtyard, he found a silver tray on a small table with some glasses on it. Moving quickly, he took the glasses off the tray and held it up, looking at its polished surface.

Looking back at him was a man with a tan, weathered face, except for a solid two-inch white section.

He slowly put the tray down and looked at Ava, who was biting her lip. Her eyebrows were all the way to the top of her head. Kaen could tell it took every ounce of her self-control to not laugh.

"Will you still love me if I'm ugly or look like a raccoon?"

Unable to resist, Ava burst out in laughter, wiping a few tears as she nodded.

"Gods, yes . . . that is exactly what you reminded me of . . . a cute little raccoon."

"Have you ever actually dealt with a raccoon before?" Kaen asked. "Because let me tell you, those things are not cute. They are mean and vicious, and they will fight you."

Ava continued to laugh, and then Kaen saw her glance around him.

He turned to see Lord and Lady Hurem walking toward them after entering the courtyard through the main house door.

His mother-in-law missed a step when she saw Kaen; she grabbed her husband's hand to regain her balance. A well-hidden smile flashed briefly before being pushed down into her normal elegant look.

"Kaen, I am excited to hear that you are well!" she called out as they approached him. "Even if it looks like you are in need of a little sun."

Kaen shook his head, unable to resist smiling when he saw his mother-in-law grinning. He would gladly endure the looks and jokes because he knew it was now time to settle a few things.

24

What Does an Enemy Hold?

Lying in bed with Ava, Kaen couldn't help but smile as he stared at his wife's face.

"Go to sleep," she groaned. "I can feel your stare."

Snorting, Kaen kissed her on the head. "I'm sorry. It's been so long since I've seen you with my own eyes, and I just can't help it. Everything about you is beautiful."

"Turn that light off and let me sleep. You wore me out, and some of us aren't always a bundle of energy. Besides, you have a lot to do tomorrow."

Kaen sighed and leaned over, tapping the lightstone till it turned off.

"Fine, just remember you are the one who told me to go to bed."

Kissing her husband's chest, Ava nodded. "I did, and I'll try not to snore tonight as well."

Kaen smiled as he lay back on his pillow, eyes still open, even in the cave's darkness.

With his vision back, there were many things to plan and do, but the world felt like it was heading in the right direction once more.

Kaen had allowed Aldric and Herb a moment to tease him about how he looked before making them sit down so they could discuss some things.

"It's good to see you healthy again," Aldric declared as he pulled out a stack of papers and handed Kaen and Herb each a few pages. "I got my people who are skilled in the art of magical crafting to give me some information on what we have in our vaults and what we could potentially create in the coming months and years. Each page is broken down into possibilities as well as current items and supplies."

Kaen couldn't help but be impressed by the detail of Aldric's report and by how much the man had stashed away inside the palace vault.

"Are all these things listed available for use?" Herb asked.

Aldric frowned slightly, and the look he gave Herb spoke volumes. "Most of what we have that is crafted isn't that strong in power, as you can see. The few items that are would not be something we can just give out to anyone. They would be limited to men like yourself or Kaen. Their value is likewise . . ." Aldric stopped and stared at his copy, tapping his finger against the table several times. "I guess cost doesn't matter anymore. If we don't win this war, all the money in our kingdom won't be worth anything. Besides, we all know right now it's almost worthless already."

Herb nodded. "It's gotten bad. The elves who have shown up are destitute, needing a place to stay and work, and it is already difficult to support the population we have now. Their money has no value outside of the metal, and without Roccnari to trade with, I'm not sure how long it will take for coins to have a value again."

"Any news from Golden Edge?" Kaen asked.

Grimacing, Aldric shook his head. "The last two caravans have come back with less each time. Now, with the destruction of Roccnari, travel is going to be even worse. They have continued to gouge us, and the quality they have given is often lacking. I think that you have somehow upset their king."

Kaen rubbed his face. A yawn slipped out and Kaen felt embarrassed by it. He had stayed up way too late letting his mind wander.

"I think he is allied with King Vorlack across the sea. I'm not sure how we can fix our relationship with King Germain. Right now, if he isn't going to help us, we need to stop wasting time there. That's another problem for another day."

"Every day has enough problems," muttered Herb.

"You're right," Kaen replied. "Now, what about the guild? Do they have anything to offer or help with?"

Herb sighed and pulled out a piece of paper from his pack. "The bad news is that Roccnari was our main guild for producing magical items. The elves' natural affinity, combined with their high magical proficiency and long lives, led to them doing most of the work. I have hopes that some of the members are still alive in the guild hall there, but from what I have heard, it may not be possible to gain access or for them to leave for a while."

"Why is that?" Kaen asked.

"Whatever spell Stioks unleashed has left a trail of magic that causes an illness or disease. Anyone who stays inside that area for any length of time acquires it. It can then spread before that person dies. Some of the elves who arrived showed signs of illness and were quarantined. Most are dead, and some of the workers who helped with them are now getting sick."

"Is it spreading within the kingdom?" Aldric asked, his tone rising an octave.

"No. For now, it has not spread. It doesn't appear that people live long once they get it. Maybe seven days. I can only imagine that there are going to be many corpses along the road, and those will need someone to dispose of them."

What kind of man would create something so deadly and horrible . . . We need to stop him soon!

Pammon agreed, his affirmation of Kaen's statement coming through their bond.

We need to be cautious, though. We don't know a lot, and it is concerning to hear about this spell. It makes me wonder what was used on you and what the orcs have.

Do you still believe it was a wand or that they can cast this spell on their own?

I believe it must be a wand. What I saw, the way the spell grew and destroyed, makes me think it must be something Stioks gave. Both of them used theirs around the same time, which also makes me wonder if they have been working on creating them for many years or just recently. The only attack similar to this was the one they used the first day of their attack. If the orcs had that kind of weapon a year or two ago, I do not see how they would have held on to it. Do you?

Kaen found himself nodding. The line of thinking Pammon had done was correct. If he had access to that kind of weapon, it would be the first thing he might use.

How many do you think they might have left?

Kaen felt Pammon trying to decide on some things, and he began to chuckle as he felt the dragon's frustration at not being able to come up with an answer.

A cough brought his attention back to Herb, who was smiling at him, giving the same look he always had when Kaen and Pammon were talking.

"Sorry, but I think Pammon just figured something out. Give me one more minute?"

Both men nodded, able to see a glimmer of hope in Kaen's expression.

How many of those weapons would you give a group like the orcs? If they only used one but had two, three, or ten more, what would stop them from using them on Stioks's kingdom?

Imagine if they destroyed not only Ebonmount but Luthaelia as well. Sure, Stioks would be upset, but without people or workers, it would put him in a challenging position of power. So I believe they must have had one recently.

This means they might be seeking a replacement from Stioks. It also means he will most likely be informed soon of what I suffered.

Which means we might need to prepare for defenses.

Kaen groaned when he knew Pammon was right.

"Pammon believes, and I agree, that the orc kingdom most likely only recently acquired the wand they used against me. We both believe that Stioks is no fool and would not give them multiple uses of that spell lest they get brave and use it against him. That means most likely he has only recently acquired them or is now finishing off the process of building them."

"That would mean we aren't so far behind, then," Aldric said. "Which also means we shouldn't worry about him suddenly showing up and doing the same to us."

Herb replied, "Do you really want to risk that being true? Imagine if we are wrong, and that does happen. Even if he didn't get close to the capital and used it instead on a town or the farms, we would be devastated at the loss."

Kaen nodded. "We also need to prepare for Stioks to arrive. Pammon is right. By now, the orcs will have reported to him what they did and how they used that attack. He will believe the kingdom is weak if he believes I am weak. Combined, those two points make it likely the man will indeed come here."

Grabbing a pen, Aldric flipped over one of his papers and began scribbling quickly on it. He wrote for over a minute before looking up at both men watching him.

"Ignore me. If this is true, I need to write down some things we need to prepare. I must ensure that certain things are done within the kingdom to protect it and the people."

"Do what you must," Kaen said. "Pammon and I are going to check on a few more things today after this meeting, and tomorrow, I plan on heading toward Luthaelia. We need to show ourselves, and I am planning on taking Amaranth and Glynnis with us."

Kaen saw Herb's reaction and knew that the men didn't want to consider it. Without dragons to protect them, the kingdom was left in a very weak position, especially against a wand or some other spell with the kind of destruction Stioks obviously had. This was why Kaen and Pammon had stayed in the bowl for most of the last three years. Anytime they left, everyone knew a spy was probably on their way delivering that information to Stioks.

"How soon?" Aldric asked, not looking up from the writing he was doing.

"How soon what? Till I leave?"

"No," Aldric replied, shaking his head. How soon do you think Stioks might arrive?"

Tapping the table again, Kaen knew the truth of that question and what it most likely was. "Honestly, any day. That man has been a step ahead of us. He has been playing a game of strategy against the kingdom for years and been winning . . . Twice I have managed to get the upper hand. Once when I attacked him and again when I returned with Amaranth and Glynnis. Now . . . well, let's just say I'll be ready to meet him if word reaches me that Stioks is here."

Aldric grunted, turned toward a servant thirty yards away, and motioned for him.

The man ran to the king and gave a bow as he arrived.

"Go tell the mages to activate the wards."

The man bowed and sprinted away, which told Herb and Kaen how concerned their friend was.

"Are you going to risk those even while Kaen is here? Surely you know that they won't last more than three days."

Aldric turned and stared at Herb, seeing the concern and worry in the smaller man's eyes. "For three days, we can know if we are under attack within seconds of him crossing those mountains. That gives all of us here a chance to react. If Kaen leaves tomorrow, it will give me two days to form some kind of defense and hopefully be able to defend at least a portion of the people I am responsible for . . . a number that has decreased more from the start of the war and is now going up with the people seeking refuge."

Suddenly, Aldric frowned and groaned. "Forget that. I need to shut the pass. Only certain individuals will be allowed to enter it for a few days."

Herb started to protest, but Aldric shook his head and raised his hand. "You get to deal with adventurer things within the kingdom. I must deal with others. I know you won't like that, but for now, I must. Imagine if Stioks sent people in with a wand like that—someone crazy enough to use it and not concerned with preserving their own life."

He pointed at Kaen. "Someone already came here and spent a long time waiting to strike at him. They were willing to die for that chance to weaken us. Do you doubt I am wrong about how much worse things can get now?"

Herb's face changed about seven times in four seconds as the man struggled with what he felt and knew was the right decision for the people. "Fine. You do what you must. I will make sure our adventurers do what we can."

Aldric nodded and stood up. "I know there is more to discuss, but I have to act right now. There is no time to waste."

He turned to Kaen. "Be safe tomorrow. As always, I am grateful for the man you are and try to be."

After the king had gone, Herb stood up and collected his papers. "He's right, Kaen. Your father would be proud of you."

Kaen stood silently as the short guild master walked off toward a door, leaving Kaen and Pammon alone in the castle's courtyard.

Swallowing the lump in his throat, Kaen turned and saw Pammon watching him.

No turning back. It's time.

25

Testing New Things

"Ready?" Kaen shouted.

"No, but I don't have a choice!" Hess yelled back, still jogging away from him.

Kaen chuckled as he looked at the man he called Dad wearing full plate armor, holding a massive shield, and moving toward the four-foot-thick stone slab they had buried in the field's ground.

"You know he wouldn't bet on what is going to happen," Bren said as he stood a few feet from Kaen, watching the event about to take place.

"I know. He told me he was concerned about this test but wouldn't let anyone else do it. How long has it been since someone has seen this skill in use again?"

"Hundreds of years . . . maybe if you asked the wood elves, they might have someone who recorded it, but most . . . no . . . I can't recall the last time someone in the human race has had it in a thousand years."

I'll make a bet that he loses his other arm.

Kaen groaned as Pammon watched from his spot as well. Amaranth was down near where Hess would be, just in case something horrible happened and his dad needed healing.

Why would you say that?

The image of Hess trying to hug people with tiny arms just seems funny . . . he is still a large man . . . just imagine it.

Kaen closed his eyes, picturing what he believed Pammon was thinking about, and started to chuckle.

That is so wrong, but it is funny . . . I'll tell him what you said.

He will laugh as well. Now focus and be ready. He is almost to the spot.

Kaen looked across the massive field. Hess was getting close to the three-hundred-yard mark and was about to reach it. Near him was Phillip, holding a stick with a red flag on the end that was currently pointed toward the ground.

"Hopefully he is as fast as he thinks he is," mumbled Bren. "I haven't seen him run in a while."

"This was his idea. I had other men offer to be the test subjects, but he wanted to see it firsthand," replied Kaen as he pulled an arrow out of the quiver and slipped it into position.

"At least it's just a regular arrow."

Kaen nodded. He could see the broken ones that had impacted the stone from his earlier shots. A few chips and cracks from where they hit, but nothing had happened to the stone.

Phillip began to wave the red flag, and Kaen took a deep breath.

"They're ready. You tell me when, and I'll let them know."

Kaen drew back his bow and focused on Hess. It felt weird aiming an arrow at him. His dad was ready, legs slightly bent and apart, that massive shield before him.

"Count to three. I'll go on three."

Bren waved the flag once, reaching the left side as he said, "One!"

Kaen saw Hess move slightly, his eyes focused on the man he loved.

"Two!" Bren shouted as his flag hit the bottom of the swing to the right.

"Three!"

[Homing Shot Activated]

The arrow sped faster than Kaen expected. He had just acquired the skill this morning and wasn't sure how fast it would fly. It streaked toward Hess, not flying up and in an arch like he had imagined but in a straight line as if pulled by a rope right to the man he cared about.

"Holy dwarf ba—"

Bren never finished his curse as the stone brick erupted in a pile of dust and debris.

He is fine. Amaranth says it cracked the stone but didn't go through.

"He's ok," Kaen told Bren as he turned and motioned toward the stone. "I want to go see where it hit."

Both men started running toward the stone and saw Hess and Phillip standing off to the side, inspecting it.

"I can't believe how that flew," Bren declared as they ran to the others. "It doesn't fly like a normal arrow would over a long distance."

Kaen nodded, replaying everything that had happened when he activated the skill.

"Two feet . . . it penetrated two feet," Phillip informed them as they arrived. "The arrow isn't even broken."

Kaen looked at Hess, who had his plate helmet off now. "You ok?"

"I won't admit I had second thoughts when Bren signaled two, but son, that thing hit with some force, and the speed was incredible."

"I'm glad to see you aren't too slow in your old age," Kaen teased as he leaned in closer and studied the arrow he had fired.

The shaft wasn't splintered or cracked like the others. Even though it wasn't a special arrow, just the standard one Kaen shot for practice, it was somehow infused with a power that prevented it from getting damaged.

"Have you tried to pull it out?"

Hess shook his head. "I didn't touch it. I figured you'd want to see what it looked like yourself."

Kaen put one hand against the stone, grabbed the shaft as close as possible to where it was embedded, and tried to pull. The arrow didn't budge, and Kaen tried to gently twist it, yet it still held fast.

"It cracked the stone," Phillip pointed out, utterly aware that Kaen could see that. "It's not on the back side, but it traveled almost halfway through the stone. That's incredible!"

"And the hole is only as thick as the arrow," Hess added, pointing out the obvious. "I've only seen that happen when shooting hay targets."

Kaen's mind raced, considering what this skill might actually do.

"How many arrows now?"

Hess glanced at Kaen, seeing the expression on his face and knowing what he really wanted to know. "Two . . . only enough for two. That gives you how many now? Four?"

Kaen grunted in agreement. "I pray it will be enough."

The sound of fighting rang out over the grounds. Shouts and orders were barked as both sides clashed. Those in the front of both groups died the quickest, unable to stand against the swords, spears, and axes that broke the defenses they hoped would keep them alive.

What had started as such a frantic-paced battle ended in less than five minutes.

"Frederick is going to lose," Hess declared as he watched the two squads of students dwindle. "His team is outnumbered now."

"Maybe," Kaen replied, watching the battle continue. Each had started with fifty troops, and Phillip had employed a flawless wall technique that cost Frederick's team more losses at the start.

Knowing his team's limit, Frederick countered and sent a group of five that darted around the initial clash and cut down part of Phillip's men from the side, causing a break in the wall that allowed one area to surge ahead.

When Frederick's troops surged, they overreached, collapsing their defenses in the middle, and found themselves split. Phillip's troops now gladly used their number advantage to wedge deeper into their enemies.

Once marked with the red paint that came when a hit from the weapon struck someone's head or chest, the student fell down, pretending to be dead. If an arm was lost, they had ten seconds before tapping out.

Phillip still had eight troops pushing against Frederick's four, staying within the allowed space. Two men had a shield and a spear for Frederick, while the other two had an axe and shield.

"They've used the boundary well so far. While it might not seem realistic, natural defense provides an advantage, as you know," Kaen pointed out.

Hess nodded, rubbing his stump on his arm and recalling the circle of trees he used in a similar way.

Cheers and shouting were heard as the students watching called out for the team they wanted to win.

Frederick and Phillip stood a dozen yards away from their team, giving orders and encouragement.

"There," Kaen said as he pointed at a shift in Frederick's team.

Hess chuckled as he watched the four students remaining charge the two on the boundary to their left, overwhelming them and cutting them down before the other six could come to their aid. They shifted again, using the boundary as a barrier, and began to give up ground, moving toward the next corner along the line.

One of the axe users for Frederick's team stumbled, their shield and axe moving out of position, and two of the attackers for Phillip came at the man on the boundary line.

A tsk came from Kaen as he saw one of Phillip's troops take a spear to their side, falling over without delay. The other one found themself hooked by the axe and dragged over the boundary line with Frederick's person.

One of the watchers shouted, "Out!" and called both students gone for having stepped over the rope.

"Three to four . . . so fast," Hess said. "It's scary how they have learned and adapted."

Kaen elbowed his dad and shook his head. "You've been training them. What do you expect?"

"Kaen, those students are thirteen years old. They have better tactics and execution than most imagined possible. It's unbelievable. Even Aldric has done what he can to mimic the success of your school in his own troops." Hess paused as he spoke, watching the exchange of attacks slow down as the students realized that every mistake now mattered.

"They are like this because this is all they have known for five years," Kaen replied, wincing when another one of Phillip's soldiers got caught out of position and took a spear to their foot. "Ten seconds . . ."

The student and his allies knew they were about to be at a disadvantage, so the one who was going to be dead used that for the squad. They ran and slammed themself into the shield of the axe warrior holding the outside edge into the field, waving their sword at the spear holder next to him.

Phillip's other troops moved with them, one darting around their friend about to be dead and scoring a hit on the side of the axe wielder.

Both students fell to the ground, leaving three versus two.

"Wanna bet?" Kaen asked as he watched the remaining two shield users thrust their spears out, getting some room between themselves and the remaining three who backed up.

"The other two only have axes and a sword. I'm not sure they understand how to win."

Kaen smiled when the two with spears turned and ran toward the boundary.

The three realized what they were doing and took off after them, knowing it would be bad for them if they reached the corner of the ground.

"That one's a keeper," Kaen said, pointing at the axe user, who dropped her shield as she ran and tossed it at the retreating spear user. Neither looked back, instead trusting that the twenty-five yards they needed to cross would be doable with the element of surprise.

The axe flew true, striking one of the spear users in the lower back and sending them to the ground.

"Ouch," Hess hissed as only one person remained for Frederick's team. "Only good news is that's Abagail. She won't make it easy on those three."

Kaen snorted and nodded. Though she was only thirteen, her skill with a spear was exceptional, one of the reasons Frederick had chosen her. Now she stood a few feet from the rope lines and held her spear against her shield.

Kaen watched as she stayed low and ready as the three approached.

The one who threw their axe only had a shield, and per the rules of the game, they could not trade weapons or acquire a new one.

"This won't last a minute," Kaen said as he watched the three approach Abagail. "I'd wager a silver coin on her."

Hess shook his head. "I won't take that bet."

Kaen laughed, and both men started to move closer to the field, walking slowly as the roar of the students grew, everyone knowing the end was about to be over.

The three students on Phillip's team had her wedged back, setting themselves for the attack they were about to launch.

They came as one; the girl with no weapon charged Abagail, her shield held out before her, trying to bulldoze into her.

Abagail dropped low, angling her shield while driving her spear out to the attacker on the right.

The poor girl ended up getting flipped over Abagail as she thrust upward when their shields connected, sending the girl out of the area. The attacker on the right had to stop their charge, seeing a spear coming toward them.

Abagail knew what was coming from her left but had already committed to her plan.

She thrust herself toward the attacker on her left, their axe coming at her and catching her arm with the shield. Knowing it would catch, she yanked on the shield, wedging the blade so the student couldn't pull it back, and thrust her spear into their exposed side.

"Ten seconds," Hess said as the axe hit Abagail's side.

Kaen began counting off the time in his head.

The last student for Phillip began to back up, hearing the order from their leader.

Abagail let go of her shield and ran toward the other student, thrusting her spear quickly and precisely, even though she only used one hand.

"Five . . . four . . ."

Kaen ignored Hess, well aware of the time in his head.

Frederick's student was also aware of the time as the entire school chanted loudly. The chant echoed across the walls of the training grounds, and both students knew exactly how much time was left.

Abagail thrust her spear toward the lower leg of the last student she faced, and Kaen winced when they naturally moved their shield low to block it. Hess's tsk cut off his count as Abagail did what she was known for.

Her spear froze midstrike, and she adjusted her hips and arm, driving up and out, sending the wooden tip of the spear right into the clavicle of the boy who had made one costly mistake.

The tip connected as the students counted ONE, and when the judge whistled, the ground went silent, waiting for the verdict they all believed would come.

"WINNER! FREDERICK'S TEAM!"

An ear-deafening roar filled the school as Abagail held her spear high and smiled. Phillip's last warrior fell to the ground on his knees, tears beginning to form as he realized his mistake.

Kaen saw Frederick and Phillip smiling and nodding as they moved toward each other to shake hands.

"She learned that lesson from you," Kaen shouted over the celebration.

"Which one?" Hess shouted back.

"Commitment even unto death."

26

Alarms

Every student was excited to meet Kaen personally after the skirmish was over. Those from ages nine to sixteen were just as ecstatic when he took the time to shake each of their hands and encourage them.

Even though it took a while to get through all of them, Kaen knew the importance of that moment as he saw how the students reacted.

"I'm proud of you, son," Hess said as Kaen waved goodbye to the last group. "Seeing their faces light up proves that today was worth it."

Kaen nodded, his eyes darting over the grounds as the students approached their classrooms. "How many have we lost?"

Grunting, Hess moved up next to Kaen and frowned. "Too many. Over a hundred. The battles on the walls cost us more than we wanted, but without them . . ."

"And the number of kids with lifestones?"

"Sixty-three," Hess replied. "At one point, you know we were well over one hundred and fifty."

Some of the older students were sparring, their class focusing on things they had seen today. In the group of twenty were a mix of a few dwarves and two elves.

"How many dwarves are part of the school so far?" Kaen asked.

"Thirty-two or thirty-three. I'm not sure which one. There are also only twelve elves in the school. You, of course, know why."

Nodding, Kaen ignored that problem.

Stupid people and their old ways of thinking . . . there is no elven homeland right now. Everyone should be learning . . .

"That's fine. For now, keep me updated on the food situation. I'll see what I can do to help."

Kaen turned and gently punched Hess in the arm as he started to walk toward Pammon. "You're doing a great job here."

Hess scoffed and shook his head. "Organized chaos is what this is. Never in my life would I have imagined teaching an army of children how to fight."

"And yet you already have Callie here, learning how to. Sulenda already told me how she feels about that."

"It's the only way, and we both know it," Hess shot back, his face turning red. "No one can sit back and wait. Everyone mus—"

"I know," Kaen replied as he stopped walking. "Things are going to get worse before they get better. You taught me how hard it is to succeed. She'll come around. Do what you must to protect my sister, just as I will."

Sighing, Hess just nodded, not saying a word as Kaen walked away.

"Amaranth told me how the practice went today. Does its success make you feel better about choosing that skill?"

Kaen nodded and smiled at Ava as he held a piece of fruit a few inches from his mouth. "I'm glad it went the way it did. I need to remind you that I'm unsure how many days I'll be gone. Try not to fight with your parents or Sulenda while I'm away."

Ava leaned across the table where they were eating and tapped the table near Kaen. "Don't worry about the women in my life. Just worry about the one who will be here waiting for your return."

Chewing the bite of the apple he had bit off, Kaen offered the rest to Ava. She shook her head. "I'm ok. You're going to be the one without a nice cooked meal."

Kaen didn't hesitate, biting off a large piece, and smiled as he chewed.

Hurry!

Kaen cursed as he pulled on his leggings and cinched them around his waist. Ava had already grabbed his bow and arrows, holding them by Pammon, who was shifting anxiously from side to side.

The sound echoed loudly in their cave as the shrill of the runes sent their warning sounds across the entire bowl of Ebonmount.

I'm almost done! We still have to figure out where he is!

Pammon snorted and stared at the entrance to their home in the mountain. Through the bond, Kaen could feel rage, concern, and anxiousness, all fighting to be the strongest.

Stuffing his feet into his boots and stomping them against the ground, Kaen ran the last few steps toward Pammon, tightening the belt that held his sword around his waist.

Ava grimaced. The warning cries of the wards woke them up, and Kaen struggled for the briefest moment to determine whether it was a dream or actually happening.

We are ready to go. We'll be in formation as we get altitude. I suggest we stay close to the mountains at first.

Kaen grunted as he grabbed the bow and arrows from Ava's outstretched hand and kissed her quickly.

"I love you!" she shouted as Kaen climbed onto Pammon, and the dragon began to move toward the ledge, not concerned that his rider was yet to be strapped in.

Every second counts. Hold on!

Kaen used the strength of his legs to keep himself in place as Pammon leaped off the edge and began to beat his wings, taking them into the air and angling south to follow Glynnis's advice.

Glancing behind him, Kaen saw the yellow dragon coming out of the cave first, followed by Amaranth on her tail.

How long till we are high enough?

Too long. Clip in and hold on.

Kaen grunted and put his bow in his mouth, biting down as he grabbed the two clasps and the loop band and slipped them into place.

The moment he was secured, Kaen braced his core and felt Pammon activate his skill.

[Flight Burst Activated]

Glynnis had taught Pammon this technique, and he mastered it rather quickly, earning praise from the female dragon.

The mountain flew by them as they sped through the darkness.

Fighting the force pressing against him as Pammon flew upward, Kaen grabbed the bow with one hand, making sure the arrows didn't spill out of the quiver against his leg.

Almost there. Hold on a little longer!

The stars were bright in the night sky, as the moon was completely absent tonight and for a few more evenings to come.

This is a perfect time for those two to ambush . . . How are we going to find him?

Look where the lights in the sky disappear. You can see where one passes, and they vanish.

Amaranth's wisdom had been shared by Tharnok when they had trained. Kaen realized how much he still didn't understand about fighting a dragon.

Can you tell which side of the bowl they came from yet?

Once we are in position, I will see if Aldric has the direction marked.

Kaen glanced down at the land below him, the lights around the walls of the keep roaring brightly and more lights appearing around the town.

Every second mattered, and when Pammon finally grunted and their speed returned to normal, his dragon shifted in the air, flying flat and high above the world below them.

We are in the thinner air. Stioks can't stay up here like we can. Smart thinking.

Pammon felt insulted that Kaen hadn't realized this was his original intent, and that feeling oozed through their bond.

Look down below. Aldric has the signal set up.

Igniting his lifestone, Kaen changed his vision to Pammon's and saw the blue glow that pointed to the east.

You two form up on each side, spread out four hundred yards. You both need to fly low enough that you can spot the changes in the sky. I'll be the bait.

We will protect you.

Pammon snorted as they angled toward the eastern side of the bowl.

How far are they beneath us?

About a mile. They are lowering themselves now.

Is that too low? I mean—

Let us handle this side of things. They need to be low enough to try and spot Stioks, and we need to be high enough for him to see us. I will do what I can to try and see Juthom. You must do your part to be ready for when the attack comes.

Pulling a normal arrow out, Kaen didn't say a word. He could see the arrows and knew the four metal ones were closest to him in the divided quiver. Right now, he regretted having practiced with Hess today. There was no way to use the skill he had planned all their attacks around.

ON ME!

Glynnis's scream echoed through his mind, and Kaen saw a green bolt of some spell flying through the sky.

He's below me!

Pammon roared, diving down toward the ground where he knew Glynnis was.

I can see them! They are attacking from below and behind!

Kaen cursed to himself as he realized they had been beaten at their own game by Stioks.

They had spent the last hour scouting the area they knew he had come from, and now it appeared that Juthom must have been skimming the ground below, hiding in the darkness of the trees and waiting to attack.

There! I see them!

Kaen called upon his lifestone and let it burn, power roaring through him and into Pammon. He saw Glynnis flying with everything she had through his dragon's eyes as another green bolt of magic flew toward her.

Keep going! I will be there!

Pammon's concern overwhelmed Kaen, who felt something akin to when Ava had been hurt. That moment showed how much his dragon cared for Glynnis, as the barrier Pammon kept up most of the time was gone.

He's fast! I'm trying!

Kaen tried to guess the distance and speed they were diving at and did the math. There wouldn't be a better chance if Pammon could come from the right angle.

Can you come at him from behind? I'll have the be—

I will not leave her in danger. Take the shot or don't. I won't wait!

Pammon was headed for a midair collision, and Kaen only now realized it.

Keep going the way you are coming! Dodge what you must, but lead him in that direction!

Glynnis didn't reply, but as Kaen watched the shape coming toward their yellow dragon through Pammon's eyes, something felt off.

Wait . . . why is Juthom so slow and—

Pammon ignored Kaen's question, pulling his wings closer and diving for the collision he had prepared for.

Kaen stopped using Pammon's eyes and began to search around them and above.

They would slam into Juthom in twenty seconds, but Kaen felt an itch in his mind he couldn't scratch.

Then the stars behind them vanished for a moment.

Look out!

His cry was too late as a stream of green magic raced toward them.

Grateful for the shield he had equipped as they flew, Kaen held it up and braced for what he could only imagine was behind that bolt of magic that struck them.

Heat, power, decay, and pain washed over Kaen, and Pammon roared as the magic ignited his backside.

It smelled like rotting flesh, and Kaen could see his friend's scales bubbling, affected by whatever magic had struck them.

Pammon's wings faltered and Kaen reloaded his bow, the arrow he had held for so long falling into the night.

Kaen was angry and furious as he saw the black dragon coming for them, hot on their tail.

I have to land soon . . . something is sapping my strength.

Kaen ignored Pammon's plea and trusted the power inside him to help with what he was about to do.

The arrow glowed with power, red to white, changing to blue and eventually to black.

Dive. Amaranth, help Glynnis! It's a female dragon on her!

Sending the arrow flying as Pammon dropped toward the ground, Kaen watched it slam into some part of Juthom. A roar echoed above them, and for the briefest of moments, Kaen felt hope that things might shift in their favor.

A green bolt appeared and raced toward them.

Pammo—

Stioks and Juthom were too close, and whatever affected Pammon had limited his ability to dodge in time.

The bolt tore into Pammon's backside, a garbled roar coming from his dragon's mouth as they began to roll in the air.

I need . . . to land . . .

Kaen held another arrow, fighting the two different forces that pushed against him. The downward momentum and the spinning action as they rolled through the air made it almost impossible for him to pull back the arrow, but he did.

Every muscle in his lower body and core was tight. He took a deep breath and held it, focusing on the spot where he could just see Juthom's outline.

Infusing the tip with as much power as he could manage, his head swimming from the force, Kaen let it go, wishing he had been able to infuse more energy into it.

It shot toward Juthom, and when it exploded, Kaen saw the dragon's outline appear in its light.

There on the black dragon's backside was Stioks, covered head to toe in black armor that seemed almost to absorb light.

Kaen swore he could see a smile through the man's black helmet.

27

A Test of Strength

Pouring his strength into Pammon, Kaen gave all the life force and power he could.

Within a few seconds, his dragon began to control the roll they were in and smooth out their descent.

Flashes of lightning lit up the sky above them, and Kaen saw the shape of three dragons fighting in the air as roars echoed from above.

Thank you . . . I can stay in the air for a—

Left!

Pammon folded and adjusted his wings, not wasting a moment, and used his skill.

[Flight Burst Activated]

A hard bank turn sent them flying out of harm's way as another green bolt appeared and fired past them toward the ground below through the dark sky.

[Flight Burst Expired]

Ignoring his desire to smile, Kaen could clearly make out Stioks now. The battle in the sky above them provided light and a glow that radiated off Juthom's black scales. The dragon and his rider had overshot their position, and Pammon's sudden move had sent them flying farther away than both would have wanted.

Use your flight skills and maneuver around and behind them! They're turning, but we got a little bit of room.

Kaen could feel the weakness in his friend's body as every stroke of Pammon's wings seemed to provide less power than expected.

I am feeling better, but I'm unsure what spell he used. It doesn't do damage like I thought it would, yet somehow I feel weaker.

Kaen glanced at his quiver and cursed.

I only have four of the dragon arrows and a dozen more of the regular ones. I'm going to use one of the dragon ones and see if I can hit him.

There is a rider of some sort on this dragon up here. This dragon is a yellow female!

Kaen wanted to ask questions, but his position left him no time.

The arrow he held was meant for a dragon, and he was going to risk using it. Time wasn't on his side, and he knew it.

Drawing the arrow back, Kaen filled it with power, letting the entire arrow turn black as he scanned the sky, looking for Juthom.

His body roared with the power of his lifestone, and every ounce of rage inside threatened to overwhelm him.

This bastard attacked because he thought we were weak! We are going to kill him!

Through their connection, Pammon's rage mixed with his, and both were intent on this moment being the last time Stioks would draw breath.

Power vibrated through the arrow, and Kaen waited, allowing the fight in the sky above them to show where Juthom was.

Hold on!

Kaen's world spun as Pammon was attacked from underneath. Juthom slammed into them from below, using the same thing Kaen had hoped for on them.

Both dragons spun through the air as each clawed and snapped at the other.

The impact sent his bow and arrow flying from his hands, lost in the darkness of night.

Fire roared around both dragons as they tumbled through the sky, shredding scales and snapping jaws at each other's necks and the riders who sat on their backsides.

A gust of black flame roared over Pammon's body, and Kaen felt it burn, smelled the leather, and the rest of his harness melted away from beneath him.

"STOP!" Kaen shouted at Juthom.

The fire paused for a second and then immediately started again.

He resisted my command!

Grasping onto the two scales around him, Kaen held on tight, not wanting to fall from whatever height they were at as the dragons continued their assault on each other.

Pammon roared, his breath burning all over Juthom. Kaen felt a massive weight break free as he saw the dragon fall backward and head toward the ground.

End this!

Pammon responded with another roar, diving after the dragon as his flames burned along the black dragon's scales.

Juthom rolled over as he fell toward the ground, diving toward the land beneath them, trails of fire wisping behind.

Shoot him!

Pammon's request pained Kaen, who knew his bow was gone. All he had at the moment was his sword and shield.

It fell, and— Kaen glanced around and then groaned. *Everything is gone . . . the arrows and the rest. Only my shield and sword are on me now. His fire, it burned . . .*

Kaen let go of the scale on Pammon's neck and squeezed tighter with his legs, feeling his body with his free hand.

His hair seemed untouched, and even though he smelled smoke and burnt things, Kaen realized that his body was not injured.

I am absolutely fine. The fire did nothing to me . . .

Focus! They are beneath us, and I am going to do something stupid!

Kaen started to ask when he realized what it was and leaned forward, wrapping his arm around Pammon's neck and grasping between his hard scales with his fingers.

[Flight Burst Activated]

The moment Pammon felt Kaen's fingers in his scales, they shot forward, now on the offensive. The massive bronze dragon came down upon Juthom, his back claws raking across the dragon's body, narrowly missing Stioks, who sent a green bolt into Pammon's underside.

Both dragons roared, and Kaen felt the power sapping from Pammon again, his body weakening once more as a green mist covered them from underneath.

[Flight Burst Expired]

Black and bronze bodies tumbled and twisted, each trying to recover from what had just happened as their bodies collided.

Kaen could see gashes in Juthom's scales, blood flowing from them.

As they flew past, a glow began to cover Juthom, and Kaen felt a pit form in his stomach.

Brace yourself!

Kaen felt the impact as they slammed into the treetops, loud eruptions of limbs and trunks shattering from Pammon's weight and force.

Off to the side and behind them, Kaen heard more trees being destroyed as Juthom smashed into them.

Time seemed to last forever as Kaen felt his dragon being beaten by the trees as they fell deeper into the woods, thicker tree trunks now snapping off as they crashed down upon them.

It took less than twenty seconds for them to be on the ground. A long row of trees snapped off at different heights, pointing to where Pammon was breathing heavily.

Kaen slid down from his dragon's neck, surprised to find himself unhurt.

Are you ok? What is hurt?!

Pammon snorted and then coughed.

In the low light and that close to his dragon, Kaen could see cracked and missing scales, long furrows of claw marks, and a few tears along his dragon's wings. The acidic smell of blood filled the air.

I'll be fine . . . I just need a moment. They crashed, too, off to the south.

Kaen nodded, checking his shield, which was still attached to his forearm, then reached for his sword.

It was stuck, the thin layer of metal having melted the scabbard around the blade Elies had given him. Somehow, the belt had not burned when everything else had.

It was then that Kaen realized only his chest and leggings were still intact. His boots had burned off, and his bracers were gone.

Anger and pain filled him with the realization that a gift from his father had been burned away to oblivion.

I'll be back!

Kaen started running through the forest of trees, listening to the sounds coming from the south. He heard a noise that echoed through the trees.

It sounded like a dragon screaming in pain.

I'm coming! Wait!

Ignoring Pammon's call for him to stop, Kaen continued to run toward where he had heard the sound of a dragon's cry.

His lifestone raged inside him, and he ran with no fear of what had to be coming up soon. It had already been a mile, and he was running so fast that if it hadn't been for his night vision, keeping up with the constant maze of trees and rocks that littered his path would have been impossible.

Another scream came from his right, and Kaen shifted his direction again.

I'm close! Can you fly?!

His lungs didn't seem fatigued at all. He had covered a mile in only two minutes, and every bit of power flowed from his lifestone into his legs.

No. Surely, you can hear me coming.

Kaen slowed for just ten steps, turning his ear and listening to the forest behind him.

Now that he had stopped focusing on Stioks and Juthom, the sounds of trees shattering and the ground shaking reached his attention.

Do not hurt yourself!

I will not abandon you in this fight!

Kaen felt how far away Pammon was, and he could tell that the life force of his dragon was very low. His heart was torn, knowing he couldn't help Pammon and fight Stioks at the same time.

If I can defeat Stioks, this is all over. Trust me!

A massive flicker of light and a horrible scream and roar came from the heavens above.

Kaen took off running again in the direction he had been headed.

What was that?

Pride and joy gushed from their bond.

They have killed the female dragon. Glynnis and Amaranth are both hurt badly, according to Amaranth. They will land, heal, and try to join us.

Kaen smiled, feeling the battle shifting. Stioks was alone. Only one dragon stood between Kaen and Stioks, and he would end it tonight.

The scene before Kaen was not the one he expected.

Fires had been burning, and their light showed him exactly where to go. The forest was in flames, and Kaen ignored it as he ran through the fire, feeling the heat but remaining uninjured because of the skill he had suffered to earn.

As he burst into the small burning clearing, Kaen almost tripped.

There was Juthom, his body on the ground, chest heaving, and a green magical chain of some kind wrapped around his snout.

Next to him was a brown dragon, much smaller than the black one, which was taking massive bites from the black dragon's backside.

Its eyes turned and saw Kaen, an anger burning inside them.

Stioks turned, taking his eyes off Juthom and the dragon that was ripping massive mouthfuls of flesh off the dragon he had been riding.

"Dragon Rider Kaen . . . thank you for delivering yourself to me."

Stioks's smile sent a shudder as blood dripped from the bottom of the man's chin. He held a sword ready and a shield that looked to be made like his, only composed of a bundle of red dragon scales.

"What is . . ." Kaen's words froze in his mouth, but he already knew the answer before asking it.

"This is my dragon, Taerar. Taerar, say hello to the man who just ended your sire's life."

The brown dragon swallowed the massive bite in his mouth and then roared.

BURN!

It opened its mouth, and Kaen saw the fire forming inside its throat.

"STOP!" Kaen yelled, holding out his hand, forcing his will upon Taerar.

The brown dragon froze, choking on the fire it was trying to summon and unable to overcome what Kaen had commanded.

Stioks growled. "That is not possible . . . you cannot be!" The black-armored man turned and held up his hand as he looked at his dragon. "You are mine. He cannot control you. Be free!"

As if a stone wall that had been holding back a dam of water broke, the young dragon's throat worked again, and it roared, sending massive blasts of fire at Kaen.

Kaen smiled, standing there as he held up his shield before his face, allowing the fire to wash over him.

Ten seconds of fire poured out around him, and the ground and trees behind were hot and blazing. Ash even burned away from the power of the flames.

"How?! How?! It's not possible!" Stioks screamed, seeing Kaen as he stepped toward them through the fire.

The man held up his hands, and a huge green cloud began to form. Kaen knew what was coming. Time was short, and he had to act.

Willing himself, Kaen dashed toward Stioks, his sword, still locked in its scabbard, held out as he prepared for a fight that would determine who lived or died.

28

Difficult Choices

As the green spell left Stioks's hand and rolled toward him, Kaen leaped, every ounce of power filling his legs, jumping higher than he had ever managed before.

Thirty feet in the air, he flew over and past Stioks, coming down toward the ground close to the brown dragon, which was turning and roaring.

Stioks moved faster than Kaen had expected. His black sword came toward him as Kaen landed, spinning, and their swords collided.

Sparks flew, and a piece of Kaen's scabbard broke off, finally revealing the blade under it.

"I've seen a blade like this before," Stioks taunted as he unleashed a flurry of attacks with his sword. If I remember right, that man is dead, as you will soon be."

Ignoring Stioks's apparent attempts at distraction and trying to make him act reckless, Kaen calmed himself, forcing down the anger and hate that was fighting to control him, instead listening to all the instructions Hess and Bren had drilled into him.

Their blows rang out, metal upon metal, swords against shields, as the forest sounded like a blacksmith's forge, the peal of their strikes and parries echoing through the trees.

Kaen quickly realized that for the first time in his life, the man he was fighting was on a different level than anyone he had faced.

Gray hair stuck out of his black helmet around his face. Even though this man was older, his speed and strength spoke of why he was so feared.

Kaen countered every attack he threw, and both held back from using their skills as they studied each other's fighting styles.

When their swords collided, it only took half a dozen strikes before Kaen's scabbard broke off, revealing the sharp edge of his sword, now free from the shackles that had hidden it.

"You're good," Stioks taunted as he parried blow after blow with what seemed like ease. "Well trained in a variety of styles and techniques. Kudos to whoev—"

"Shut up!" Kaen shouted, driving forward and giving two feints before unleashing a combo attack with his sword and shield.

The smile never left Stioks's lips as he parried and blocked, shifting his feet slightly and countering with his own combo, five blows and a kick that came in rapid succession and took every ounce of concentration Kaen had to follow and block.

He's higher skilled than me . . . possibly by—

"Don't overthink it. It will cost you!" Stioks exclaimed. With a sudden shift in his attack, his sword moved much faster than Kaen had expected, drawing a slight cut along his bare right arm.

Kaen wanted to curse and shout back but knew it wasn't worth the distraction.

Stioks then struck with an attack that hurt far worse than any injury Kaen had sustained so far.

"Another Marshell that shall fall by my hand . . . I guess this is justice for what your father did to my friend's granddaughter."

Kaen stumbled, the words catching him off guard as his mind tried to absorb what Stioks had just said.

Stioks didn't waste a moment. His shield slammed into Kaen and sent him sprawling backward. The man's sword came at him with deadly accuracy, and another gash appeared on his sword arm, up near his shoulder.

"Oh, you didn't know?" Stioks's eyes sparkled in the light of the fires, a sneer upon his lips. "You look like her. Her grandmother was the spitting image of Madalyn . . . she was beautiful and proud. Stubborn, I hear as well."

Kaen's arm felt weak and slow as he tried to fight back, trying to clear his mind, yet inside him the words hammered against a wall of pain and hurt that Kaen had built a long time ago.

"What about her family?" Kaen shouted, lunging recklessly with his sword.

Ignore him! I'm coming!

Pammon's voice filled him, stilling his trembling spirit, and Kaen felt a strength coming between their bond.

Stioks sensed it and grunted, shaking his head as he stopped taunting Kaen. A green glow surrounded his sword, and Kaen leaped back, trying to give himself room against the attack he believed was coming.

Stioks's black sword came at him so fast that even with his speed, Kaen couldn't keep track of every strike.

Blood flowed down each leg where the blade had pierced the dragon scales against his thighs. A wound was flowing from his side. Three strikes had made it through his defenses, each of them shallow but doing their job of slowly sapping his strength.

"She died . . . had something I needed. Like so many who were nothing more than tools. It's a shame your entire family is dead."

Kaen screamed. His lifestone was hotter than ever before. The words tore at his being, and Kaen couldn't take the pain of them anymore.

[Flurry Activated]

He went on the offensive, his sword coming at Stioks with every ounce of power he had. Power flowed through it, lightning dancing off the blade, and Kaen saw a look of surprise as the man before him moved back, realizing the attack wouldn't be normal. Stioks's sword glowed and each slash and thrust was deflected. The man had used a skill to cut off his attack.

Each parry sent an arc of electricity through the man. Every time their blades connected, lightning flowed through the blade, and Kaen saw Stioks wince as the power he infused through the blade jolted his opponent.

Rage filled Stioks's eyes, and Kaen saw his sword hand begin to glow green.

"Two can play at that game," Stioks grunted, pushing through the pain coursing through his body.

A cloud of magic erupted around Stioks, and Kaen felt his body convulse and shudder.

[Diseased]

The notification startled Kaen as he stumbled, and Stioks's grin returned. Stioks pressed his advantage, sword and shield slamming and slicing at Kaen without wasting a moment.

[Shield Bash]

Kaen's attempt to knock Stioks back or off his feet failed when the black-armored man's shield flashed green, blocking the attack.

Loud crashes came from the woods, and as Kaen fell backward, Stioks stepped on Kaen's sword hand, pinning it to the ground. Kaen tried to roll, bringing his shield to slam into Stioks's legs, but the older man deflected it, jabbing his sword through Kaen's left shoulder and into the ground.

"You're weak, just like your father," Stioks snarled as he leaned over and glared at Kaen. "I killed him the same way, watching him squirm beneath my boot as I took my time. You will die the same way, a sad testament really to a man I had respect for."

Kaen screamed in agony and pain as the older man drove the sword deeper, burying it into the ground and slicing the muscles and ligaments that allowed movement of Kaen's shoulder.

[Crushing Kick]

Kaen's right foot impacted Stioks in the leg, causing the man to stagger back a few steps. It made Stioks's black glove let go of his sword, leaving him pinned to the ground.

Rushing forward, the older man put his right hand against Kaen's chest, pressing down on him. A green glow began to appear, and Kaen felt the magic starting to seep through the armor he wore. The scent of rotting flesh filled his nostrils, and the memory of how Elies had smelled struck him.

"Yes . . . this is the same spell . . . I can see that you recognize it."

Kaen's strength began to fail him as the spell ran through his body, and when the young Dragon Rider tried to use his weapon on Stioks, the older man knocked it aside with his shield.

Stioks laughed and slammed his shield down over and over on Kaen's unprotected arm, only stopping after he heard the sound of a bone breaking.

The right hand still glowed green, an eerie glow of magic running up the man's arm and to his chest.

"You're strong . . . far stronger than I would have thought, but you were a fool! Waiting gave me time . . . time to grow stronger and find my own dragon. Now he and I will cleanse this land from the curse you bring upon it. The world will prospe—"

A crashing of trees stopped the speech Stioks was giving as he drained the life from Kaen. Pammon fell from the top, landing next to the small brown dragon. In a moment, his massive mouth snapped forward, chomping down on the younger dragon's neck.

Panic surged from Taerar, and Stioks turned, seeing the sight before him. His body shook from fury and rage as Pammon growled, his teeth squeezing tighter. Those soft scales of youth began to crack, and blood appeared as Taerar thrashed in Pammon's jaws.

Be still, or I will end you!

Taerar froze, realizing there was no escape.

Stioks growled and held up his hand. "Release him!"

A thrum began to echo from the fire that burned all around them. Trees everywhere burned, and Pammon's golden eyes locked with Stioks's, and the two stared at each other.

You cannot control me. Save your power for the weak. Now release my rider, or your dragon will not draw another breath.

Stioks fumed as he stared at Pammon. His hand grew brighter, a green light fighting the orange flames for dominion in the darkness, and he held it inches from Kaen's face.

"I can just as easily end your rider's life," Stioks replied, a sneer appearing as he spoke.

You can, but we both know how this moment will go. Your story will end. Kaen will be hailed as a legend who gave his life to end yours. Your dragon dies the moment he dies, and you will die after.

"You will die as well!"

Pammon thrummed again. The young brown dragon was limp, doing its best to not move as the jaws around its throat held it firm.

I would gladly give my life for this moment. My rider had one goal, and it is stopping you. Now, release him.

Stioks's arm trembled as the spell's power in his hand flickered, waiting to be released.

"Why would I do that? Once I do, both my dragon and I will be dead."

Pammon's golden eyes narrowed, his lids closing slightly.

I will make a promise even though every part of me wants to end you right now. If you free my rider and go, I will not kill you at this moment. I will give you the same chance I am giving your dragon. Another day to plot and plan.

Time passed as the light of the fires illuminated them all. The bronze scales around Pammon's jaws showed the restraint Kaen's dragon fought against. He had a simple desire to snap the threat in half. Stioks could see the look of terror in the young brown dragon's eyes, trying to see what the man who was his rider would do.

Stioks's chest heaved as he glared at Pammon, knowing that if they fought, he would lose, especially after his dragon died. He was well aware of how that death would impact him even if he didn't value life as most riders did.

Kaen was sweating, fighting against crying out as part of him wanted Pammon to end Stioks, even if it meant death. His soul, however, cried out, wanting to live and see Ava again. Pinned to the ground like a babe, Kaen knew he wasn't nearly as strong as he had hoped. His heart was torn as knowing who Stioks claimed to be ravaged those memories long locked away. How could he come from a man so evil and be so different?

Stioks took a deep breath and let it out, never releasing the spell he held.

"How shall we do this? You will release my drago—"

No! We both know you are as trustworthy as a snake. You will remove your sword and walk to the other side of this clearing, and once Kaen is up and behind me, I will release your dragon.

"Why should I trust you?! How do I know that you will—"

Because you have no choice where you can even hope to get what you want. If you do not, forever, you will be the villain who died in a foolish

attempt. Run away and hope to get stronger. Know that we will be coming and prepare for that. When the time comes, we shall see whose dragon is stronger and whose rider is better.

Stioks glared, seeing Pammon's gaze, and rage overwhelmed him.

He screamed, roaring as his face cracked, blood running from the fissures that appeared. When his rage subsided and wisdom took over, Stioks gave a very brief nod.

"Swear that you will allow Taerar and me to live and flee. I will trust you if you swear on your rider's life."

Don't . . . don't do it.

Kaen's words pricked Pammon's pride and heart, but he ignored them. He knew Kaen wanted him to end Stioks, and he knew Kaen wasn't concerned with the consequences.

Focusing his connection only with Kaen, Pammon shifted his golden eyes to his friend. To his rider.

If you die, I may ravage this land far worse than he ever would. The risk then is too great. The people here might suffer in ways we never dreamed of. I cannot allow that to happen. What if I killed Ava in my rage?

Pammon felt Kaen's life fading and knew there was no more time to argue.

I, Pammon, swear on my life and my rider's life that if you release Kaen, allow him to join me, and no longer fight us at this moment, I will grant you and your dragon the freedom to escape.

Stioks frowned for a moment and then smiled. "Very well. I accept."

The magic in his hand disappeared, and he leaned over, grabbing his sword and pulling it free from Kaen. Kaen cried out as blood poured from the wound.

Pammon growled, his teeth sinking deeper into Taerar as the young dragon began to cry and twitch.

"Sorry, I needed my sword," Stioks said, sliding it into his sheath and walking toward the other end of the burning clearing as if out for a stroll.

Kaen fought to stand, feeling Pammon's strength fill him as he made it to his knees and got on his feet.

Moving to hide behind Pammon, Kaen watched as his dragon growled once.

Be smart, little one. Run to your rider and fly away. No matter what he says, do not turn back. If you do, I will end your life.

Opening his jaws, Pammon turned his head and freed Taerar's neck, blood oozing from all the broken scales.

Without hesitating, the brown dragon raced toward Stioks, who glared at him, his displeasure for how this all worked written across his face.

The man climbed up on Taerar's back and looked over his shoulder at Pammon and Kaen.

"Until we meet again. Just know next time I will not lose!"

Taerar struggled as he leaped into the air, the wound on his neck making it hard for him to fly in his usual manner.

Kaen struggled to stay standing, watching the man he despised more than anything fly away into the night sky.

"Are you sure that was worth it?" Kaen asked as he coughed.

Only time will tell. Hold still. This is going to hurt, and we need to go now!

29

Learning the Truth

Pammon flew through the air, holding Kaen in his front talons, doing everything he could to not crush him or injure him more.

I am almost to you! Be ready to heal him!

I wasn't strong enough . . .

We will deal with that problem later. For now, hold on. Glynnis and Amaranth are close. She will heal you.

Kaen fought to keep his lifestone burning. He felt weak, and the fire inside was struggling to burn. His loss had weakened his resolve, and now he felt like the mountain he believed he could climb was impossible to surmount. If Stioks toyed with him this easily, it was no wonder his dad had died at the hands of that monster.

He was so strong . . . so fast. How much stronger was Elies?

I can't answer that now! My strength was almost gone, and it took everything I had to appear that I could win in a fight against him. Had he waited me out, I would have had to sacrifice you.

Kaen felt the truth of what Pammon was saying. He had no strength left to give. He was almost out himself. Pammon was utterly weak as well.

Juthom is still alive.

Yes . . . for now, we will leave him where he lies. If he dies while we are gone, so be it. He will never fly again.

Kaen saw Glynnis and Amaranth in a field through Pammon's eyes. Both were covered in blood, scales missing, and wings partially torn. Pammon's left wing had a large gash in it, but hopefully, it would heal more in time.

Stay back. I'm not sure how well I will be able to land.

Amaranth touched her snout to Kaen, a green light illuminating the tip and where she touched his shoulder. The sound of flesh rejoining and bones and ligaments reattaching filled Kaen's ears as he fought back the pain. The screams he let out filled the night air.

The green dragon was panting, and Kaen knew she had to be at her limit. He had no idea how much energy she had spent. Both she and Glynnis were injured more than he had imagined.

You need me to heal you next. You are on vapors and can barely move.

Pammon grunted. He had one eye open, watching as Amaranth healed his rider.

Once his shoulder and arm are fixed, you can do what you wish to me. Pammon paused a moment, his nostrils twitching as he breathed. **How bad is the spell?**

Her eyes changed colors, turning gold and then green.

Later, I can work on it . . . he should recover . . . in time. For now, you both will need rest.

Pammon snorted and closed his eyes. "Rest . . . I have rested far too much. That is why tonight went the way it did. "

In his mind, Pammon was going over the battle they had just fought. He had practiced aerial combat with Tharnok and his two mates, but tonight was a lesson he hadn't been prepared for. Fights during the day were completely different from those at night. Flying higher left one vulnerable to an opponent beneath them. Their ability to strike first was critical, with no way to see who was below them.

Why were the yellow dragon scales black? Who was her rider?

Glynnis turned her attention from Kaen to Pammon, shaking her head a few times before responding.

It appears to be someone with a wand. They tried to use it when we got close, but I think it only had a few charges. Once Amaranth and I attacked, the rider died quickly. The scales were covered in some type of black liquid, which hid her true color. This was definitely well-planned.

Pammon knew that was true. The tactics employed were those of someone skilled in the art of fighting. If what he had learned from Kaen was true, Stioks had to be over seventy years old. The knowledge and power this man possessed felt off.

Kaen. He has a stone like yours.

Panting, Kaen nodded. His shoulder was sealed, and he could move it. His wrist was working as it was supposed to, as well. Rising to his feet, he felt slightly weak.

Slowly! Do not fall and hurt yourself again! I will not heal you if you do.

Kaen chuckled. He was waiting to walk as he felt weak, knowing it had to do with whatever spell Stioks had cast on him.

[Ailment Check]
Diseased - Life-draining magical rot infects your body, limiting natural recovery and healing. Left uncured, your body will decay.
Weakened - Thirty percent of strength, and speed is reduced.

Kaen stared at the notification and struggled to imagine how Elies survived so long with these effects.

Did Tharnok ever tell you how bad Elies's infection was?

Pammon raised his eyebrow slightly, watching as Kaen stumbled toward him. Amaranth was lying next to him, her head pressed against his neck, and a faint green glow was coming from her.

Yes . . . what he told me was not good. Do not worry. I am sure Amaranth can heal you once she recovers. You have her. Elies did not.

Kaen made it to where Pammon was and ran his hand across his friend's scales. He could see the gouges and tears along Pammon's flesh, realizing how bad dragon fights were when two large ones got within range of each other's talons.

Rest. I'm here.

Pammon breathed out slowly, and Kaen knew he was going to drift off in a moment. He looked at Glynnis, who was sitting off to the side, watching the three of them.

Glynnis. Are you ok?

I am . . . I just . . . today was something I had not personally experienced before. Female dragons rarely fight because we are deemed too valuable. I had seen a few males fight from a distance before, but actually having to do what I did tonight . . . it was more complicated than I expected at first.

Kaen watched as she moved closer to them and settled down next to Pammon.

The truth was that the female was soft. She flew poorly, and I could tell she did not fly often. She was a little older than me, and her size was a bit of a challenge, but once I took out her wings, the fight was over.

You two were amazing. Thank you again for what you did.

A slight trill came from Glynnis when Kaen praised her, but she stopped when Pammon shifted.

Rest. The morning will come soon enough.

Kaen groaned, stretching slightly as the sun's rays struck his face.

Pammon and the other three were still sleeping, exhausted from what they had done the night before.

I wonder how far Stioks was able to get before his dragon—

That thought made Kaen wince as the truth of it hurt. Stioks had a dragon because he had fallen into the man's trap. That was why Stioks had asked for a truce.

I should have seen that coming . . .

Standing up, Kaen felt weak still and wondered how long it might last.

Looking at himself, he realized he was a mess. He was covered in dirt and blood, with a slight stench of rotting flesh and body odor. With no shoes on, a pair of dragon pants, and a chest piece, his appearance was awful.

Fingering the holes in his armor, Kaen sighed. He had known they would be broken and damaged one day, but it came earlier than he had expected.

If only I could get that case in the vault to open . . .

Kaen muttered to himself. He had cut his hand, hoping that blood would activate it, but it didn't. No matter how hard he had hit it again, even with an empowered shot, the glass case withstood everything he had thrown at it.

You are not controlling your thoughts and ruining my sleep.

Kaen glanced at Pammon, who had both his eyes open.

"Sorry. It's time for us to go. The whole kingdom is going to be in a panic."

Pammon nodded and then grimaced. He turned his head and saw Amaranth's snout glowing much brighter as she touched his side.

Hold still. There are a few things I need to do before you start trying to fly around.

Grunting, Pammon held still.

I'm going to look for that female that we killed. I am hungry, and I know that will be worth finding and eating.

Kaen rubbed his tongue against his teeth and considered what Glynnis had just said.

That is a really good idea. Pammon and I can fly back to where Juthom fell. I need to retrieve my sword, at least. I'm not sure where my bow is or if it survived the fall.

Well, wait until I am finished. It will only take a few more minutes, and then we can go our separate ways. Will we meet back at the cave?

Yes. Pammon and I will need to talk with the king. As soon as you are done eating, you two can calm Ava's nerves.

Amaranth snorted.

You have no idea how hard that will be once I tell her what happened. And before you ask, I will not lie for you.

Pammon thrummed, and Kaen groaned. He was going to lose on all sides.

He is alive. Barely but still alive. Be careful when we land.

His body is broken. Look at that. A tree is stuck through his side from when he crashed.

Disgust came through their bond from Pammon.

Stioks discarded him as if he were trash. After all that dragon had done for him, the man allowed his new dragon to begin eating Juthom while he was still alive.

* * *

Come to gloat or finish me off?

Kaen heard Juthom's voice in his head as they landed behind him. A massive blaze had burned, and now the trees were gone in a large area around the fallen black dragon.

Pammon can end your suffering. I will not grant any other mercy besides that for all you have done.

A slight thrum came from Juthom before it was cut off, a wheezing sound escaping his nostrils as blood flowed from them.

I would do it all again. This is the life a dragon desires above all things. You will never understand that.

Kaen moved slowly around Juthom, now getting a full view of the size difference between Pammon and the older black dragon.

Yes . . . I can see it in your eyes. Your dragon is larger than me. Somehow, you two grew . . . A cough and blood from the dragon's snout stopped him for a moment. ***Stioks believed you two were weak . . . not worth the time . . . How little did he realize when you two attacked us outside Roccnari that day. If I could laugh, I would, but the pain is too great. Now . . . now you two are trapped. Neither of you knows what is coming, and I'm not sure you can match him.***

Pammon leaned over his head, casting a shadow over Juthom's snout. Gold eyes peered into the darkness of Juthom's eyes.

What is coming?

Why should I tell you? Would you threaten me with pain? Every day since I made a pact with that man, I have felt pain. Pain you cannot begin to imagine. There is a reason why his family does not accept him. He tortures them and others. No one is safe if he believes you have failed or slighted him.

Slowly, Juthom adjusted his head and looked at Kaen.

He wanted to break you. If he had his way, you would be in a cell in the castle they built for him. Every day, he would torture you until you died . . . like he did your father.

Kaen's heart skipped a few beats as he moved closer toward Juthom until a gaze from Pammon made him stop.

What about my father?! What did he do?

Juthom laughed, thrumming and ignoring the coughs that came and the blood that flowed.

I will tell you, but it will cost you. When I am done, you must promise to kill me quickly. End the pain that even now Stioks leaves me in.

30

Mercy Given

What pain? How are you in pain?

Blood flowed from Juthom's nostrils and out his mouth.

Make the promise, and I will answer those questions. I could last for days here until animals picked me apart, unable to stop them. Make that promise, and I will share with you all I know.

Kaen looked at Pammon, and he saw his dragon nod. Sitting on his haunches, Pammon stayed close to Juthom, always prepared to act in case the black dragon surprised them.

I swear I will end your life quickly if you tell me what you know.

Juthom closed his eyes and sighed.

Very well . . .

Your father was as unprepared for Stioks as you were. When he approached me decades ago, I had considered fighting him, yet something in my mind told me it would not be easy. His power and use of magic is beyond what most can believe.

While most use fire or lightning or even rare water magic, Stioks specializes in death magic. Everything he touches dies. Even people he loves.

Juthom winced, not because of the pain but because of the memories he had.

He made a pact with me. If I would lend him my strength and let him ride me, he would find me females. I would be allowed to roam as I wished and eat whatever animals I desired. He promised me gold and riches beyond my dreams, so I agreed.

Slowly lifting his left talon, Juthom pointed to a scale on his chest. A slight bit of magical power flowed through his talon, and Kaen saw a green shimmer appear over the scale.

He bound me and him together through a magic I cannot describe. The pain of it almost made me break it once it started, but from the moment he touched me, I knew I could never kill him. I could not touch him. To do so would end my own life.

Carefully laying his talon back on the ground, Juthom took a few short breaths.

We found females, fighting the last of the males in the area and proving my worth. They followed me gladly, seeing the power and purpose we had. Each was promised great opportunities if she produced an egg. One day, he got impatient and wanted more females, so my chance of siring an offspring would increase.

He ran into a silver dragon who proved harder to tame than he had expected.

Juthom opened his eyes and looked up at Pammon.

She was your mother. Proud, mighty, and magnificent. I could not convince her to join me willingly, so Stioks tried by force. She is the one who burned him into how he looks now. I was surprised he let her live, but he was so angry at his defeat and what she had done that the only punishment worthy of his rage was imprisoning her for as long as he did. He taunted her daily, showing her how close she had come but failed. All he did was keep the fire inside her stoked for the day she escaped.

A thrum escaped his body for a few seconds before the pain made him stop.

Your mother was a magnificent creature, and I can see the same regal side in you.

Pammon snorted, growling at Juthom.

What is your point of these words? Forgiveness? That will never happen!

Shaking his head slightly, Juthom looked up at the bronze dragon who was baring his teeth at him.

No. Dragons do not ask for forgiveness. I'm telling you about Stioks and how he thinks. How he brings about revenge. So settle down, young one, and listen.

Pammon growled, saliva dripping from his teeth.

Let it go. I made a promise like you did. When the moment comes, you can have your revenge.

Those golden eyes shifted to where Kaen was standing, and Pammon glared at him.

Their bond allowed Kaen to feel the extent of Pammon's rage and hatred for the dragon next to him. Here was one of the reasons his mother had died.

When that moment comes, he is mine.

Kaen nodded, turning his attention back to Juthom.

Continue.

Everything has been about an egg for generations. You see, Stioks suffers from a problem. Inside him is a power that will consume him. He tried to find a way to live forever, and the same death magic you have inside you, causing the rot you smell like, is from inside him. Elies died from it. You shall die from it. There is no escape that I know of.

Wait, how is Stioks able to survive if he has this magic in him?

Did I not tell you how he steals my power? He drains life from those around him. I cannot tell you the tens of thousands he has absorbed the life force from. His own family and so many others. What makes him strong is the amount of power he has stolen.

Rolling his head over, Juthom focused his black eyes on Kaen.

Your father was one of his greatest gains. Until that day, no other person had stood up to Stioks and survived the first strike. Their battle was a sight to behold. Hoste . . . Hoste was his name. He fought remarkably well for a man. His skill with every weapon he brought was worthy of a show for a king. Ultimately, he failed not because of his skill but because of the gap between the two.

Juthom stopped trying to keep eye contact with Kaen and rested his head on the ground again. Taking a deep breath, the black dragon let it out slowly.

One spell . . . one single spell brought your father to his knees. The fact you have resisted so many is a testament to your strength. Your father woke up, chained and bound in the dungeon Stioks had built so long ago in that mountain. He visited your father every day. Forcing him to eat and drink. Each day absorbing his life from him.

Kaen tried to imagine what Juthom was describing and shuddered. For so long, he had imagined a battle that must have ended with a single blow, or perhaps he died shortly after a well-fought one. Hearing that his father was tortured and his life drained from him opened a wound inside his soul.

How long?! How long did he suffer?

Over two years . . . for so long, Stioks tried to break him. Every day, he wanted your father to give in, to tell him where you were so he could torture his son. No matter what Stioks did to Hoste, that man fought with a heart greater than any I have seen. The day he died, I remember well . . . I suffered in his place. Stioks needed to take out his anger, and it fell upon me.

Kaen saw Juthom shudder, even though his body was broken and battered. Kaen could only imagine what Stioks must have done to make a dragon react like this.

Your father told him, 'No matter what you do, my son will never know you or be subject to you. He will grow up happy and with joy. While you rot until you are nothing but a memory people deem worthy of mentioning.' Those

words somehow made Stioks react in a way I hadn't seen before. He took all your father's remaining power and drained him dry.

Bowing his head, Kaen rubbed his eyes, trying to fight back tears that wanted to come. Rage and fury fought against the pain. Every emotion seemed to need a way to be expressed.

Let it go. Your father would not want you to be like this. Honor his name and his sacrifice by doing what we must. Getting stronger and ending Stioks once and for all.

Kaen felt his chest shudder as he listened to his dragon try to talk him down. He knew Pammon was right, but he felt an overwhelming need to act.

If you were healthy, I would fly now and take the fight to him. We could end this all right now.

But I am not, and you are not either. You do not have your bow or arrows. To go now would be folly, and you know it.

Kaen grumbled under his breath and knew that Pammon was right.

"Now what? What do you want from me now?!"

Juthom let out a sigh and looked up at Pammon.

I want to die. Promise me that you will not hold back the rage you feel if you defeat him. He has done things to me that I will never mention. Stioks will do far worse to you and your dragon if you fail.

Rubbing his finger in his ear, Kaen inspected the soot and dirt that came out of it.

"What about this new dragon?"

That wasn't part of the deal. You are supposed to end me.

Kaen laughed and shook his head.

"No, I swore I would if you told me what I wanted to know. This is something I want to know."

Juthom growled, but when Pammon put his front talons on the black dragon's neck near its skull, it stopped.

Tell him and let me end this. Tell Kaen what he asked.

Very well. The new dragon is weak. I almost regret that he is my offspring. Stioks treats him worse than he ever did me. He lies and tells stories of how you two bring death to the land. No doubt he is filling that eggling's mind with lies about how you two are responsible for my death and Upi's death. That desire for revenge will push the dragon to be like me . . . like Stioks. He won't stop till you two are dead.

A cough came, and Juthom trilled.

Kaen's eyebrows rose. "Why are you happy?"

Because no matter who wins, I have won. If Stioks wins, my offspring will carry my seed, and this land will fall under my legacy. If you and your dragon

defeat Stioks, I shall get my revenge, having aided in destroying the man who tortured me.

This is enough. Do not listen to this poor excuse of a dragon anymore. Let me end his life. Let me claim my kill and grow strong off his flesh.

Kaen considered what he knew and had heard from Juthom. Only one thing remained that he wondered about.

What is Stioks's weak point?

Juthom thrummed, coughing up blood.

That is the best question you have asked yet. Only his pride. Magic will not do much to him. He is resistant to most. Fire no longer touches him. He was surprised that my breath did nothing to you, blaming me for that. His physical power is above yours now that he has a dragon. The older the dragon gets . . . well, you know, the more powerful he will grow. Only his pride and his belief that he is invulnerable. Find a way to use that against him, and you might win. Otherwise, the only weak point he has right now is his dragon. Taerar is growing fast; from what I have seen and believe, you and Stioks share a similar lifestone. If that is true, Taerar will grow as fast as you have. Time is your enemy.

His head was bobbing, agreeing with the things Juthom was saying. Only one last thing remained.

Would two more Dragon Riders help in this fight against Stioks?

An army of dragons might be easier to summon than two more Dragon Riders. Even if you had them, I doubt their skill and power would be enough to stand against him. Could they survive a single hit from Stioks's spell? Even if you did find—

Juthom fought to lift his head, but Pammon still held it firmly in place. He thrashed a little bit, and then, after Kaen motioned to Pammon to let Juthom free, he held his head as high as possible, studying Kaen's stance.

Are you saying you have two dragon eggs?

Kaen shrugged, and Juthom began to thrum. It began to vibrate the area around Kaen, and for a moment, both rider and dragon weren't sure if Juthom would kill himself from laughing.

Exhaustion overtook the black dragon's desire to laugh, and his head and neck fell to the ground.

Do not throw them away so casually. They could be a great instrument if a battle comes, but you must protect them when they are revealed. Otherwise, you are just throwing away another life. I would instead recommend you give in to the power inside and command other dragons like you did me and Taerar. Fly to the island, command them to serve you. Become what you must to defeat Stioks.

Silence stretched as Juthom said nothing more, and Kaen considered his words.

I will never be like Stioks.

Then you have chosen a task that is impossible to win. If you do not defeat Stioks before his dragon is strong enough to fly across the sea, know that it will be a battle like you have never known.

Finish him. Eat, and then let's go.

Pammon didn't hesitate. His jaw opened and clamped down on the dragon's neck. Scales cracked and shattered as Pammon used every ounce of strength to sever the dragon's neck.

Juthom thrashed momentarily, groaning and wailing until a loud snap sounded, and the black dragon went still.

Pammon released his grip on the dragon's broken neck. Lifting his head into the sky, Pammon roared, the sound of it vibrating Kaen's entire body.

Frustrated at everything he had just learned, Kaen moved to search for his sword as Pammon began to eat the flesh of his fallen enemy.

31

Duty or Family

I'm fine. Eat. You need it. I cannot wait any longer, and Amaranth is willing to take me.

I will hurry and eat what I can. This will be here for at least another day.

Like I said, don't worry about me. I need to go meet Aldric. I can only imagine how Ava and the kingdom are doing.

I am not sure how long it will take to heal you of that disease you have, but it is different and yet the same as the one Elies had. When we return to the cave, I will do what I can.

Thank you, Amaranth. Thank you even more for going back to tell Ava I am ok.

Something like this happens whenever I think I have figured you out, and you surprise me.

Kaen sat against Amaranth's neck as she flew them toward the castle. Both of them worried about the state of the city. Her statement caught him off guard, taking his mind off the train of thought that had been plaguing him since Juthom told him what had happened to his father.

What do you mean by that?

The stories we have heard about Dragon Riders were not kind. Seeing what that man did tonight, how he tried to kill all of us, and how he even discarded the dragon that had lowered itself to work with him . . .

Amaranth turned and stared at him, her green eyes shining in the morning light.

I know you would never discard Pammon, Glynnis, or me as he did. Each time I meet more people, I realize how different and noble you are. The things Pammon says about you make more sense.

Kaen started to laugh and gave a slight nod to Amaranth as she turned and looked toward the walls of Ebonmount.

I am honored by your words and look forward to hearing what Pammon says behind my back.

As they flew, a slight thrum came from her, and when it stopped, Kaen realized she wasn't going to reply to his statement.

Every wall is guarded, and all of the siege weapons are loaded. It would appear they anticipate something other than our return.

Well, go slow and let them see me on your back. I would rather not risk you getting shot today.

Nor would I.

"Kaen!"

Aldric was rushing to where Amaranth had landed, running in his golden armor, followed by a small group of defenders.

Giving a small wave, Kaen slid off Amaranth's side and rubbed her scales.

Tell Ava I am sorry it took so long to get to her.

I already have. She is . . . well, I will not try to convey human emotions. Just know that when you get home, she is going to do many different things to you, she said.

Kaen chuckled and gave Amaranth one more gentle tap on her scales before moving to join Aldric, who was running faster than a king should have to.

"What is the news?! Pammon? Stioks?!"

Kaen frowned at Aldric's questions as they drew close in the open courtyard.

Amaranth turned and departed, leaving the two men and the half-dozen guards watching her fly away.

"All of our dragons are ok. Hurt but ok. Stioks is alive . . ." Kaen paused, shaking his head as he continued to frown. "He has a dragon. It is you—"

"A dragon?! When? How old?!" Aldric asked, firing off questions before realizing he had cut Kaen off. He finally noticed how Kaen looked, covered in blood, sweat, and grime and missing every part of his clothes except his damaged chest and leg piece. His shield was still on his arm, his sword clasped in his hand. "Sorry . . . forgive me. It has been a long night, and I am sure it doesn't compare to what you have endured. Continue."

"I can only imagine what you have had to deal with, Aldric. Do not worry about me. I will be fine in time." Kaen's statement caused Aldric's eyebrows to rise, but he kept quiet, waiting to hear what else there was to learn. "Stioks has a young brown dragon. I'm not sure how old he is, but it would appear he is at least old enough to fly with Stioks. Juthom is dead, as is the yellow dragon Upi. I . . . I lost in a fight against Stioks, and to say things are going to get worse would be a poor way to describe it."

Kaen glanced past the king and looked around the courtyard. "Is there a place we could sit, and perhaps I could get a drink and something to eat?"

Before Aldric had turned, one of the guards was off running toward a doorway, shouting and giving orders.

"It would appear that it will happen sooner rather than later. Would you like to get cleaned up, and I can bring Herb here in the meantime?"

Kaen glanced at his outfit and grimaced. "I will accept that offer. I'd like a pair of shoes and perhaps a shirt of some kind."

Two guards took off running, not waiting for Aldric to give instructions.

"If you will follow me, let us get you fed and cared for. It appears my people are taking care of what you need as we speak."

Kaen slipped out of his dragon-scale armor, looked in the polished metal mirror, and grimaced at the sight.

His skin was discolored, and sores were beginning to form. On his chest was a handprint, discolored and filled with pus and sores, where Stioks had put his hand.

Elies . . . I can only imagine what this was like for you . . .

Kaen put his foot in the steaming tub of water, moaning slightly as it felt amazing. He watched as the brown dirt caked on his feet and between his toes loosened and started to float.

"Better than nothing," he muttered, climbing in and sinking completely under the water.

After rising to the surface, Kaen picked up the bar of soap and started scrubbing his hair, beard, and skin with fervor. There was no time to enjoy this. He needed to get out there and plan what the kingdom and he would do.

Kaen pulled the shirt off, showing Aldric and Herb the mark on his chest and the sores on his body.

"By the spirits," Herb muttered as he leaned closer, looking at the pus pockets already appearing ready to burst. "Does it hurt?"

"No," Kaen replied. "I feel them but not like a pain or anything more than a simple discomfort. I have a diseased ailment as well as a weakness, but I'm not sure if both are from his spell or if one is due to something else."

Aldric snapped his fingers, and a servant came forward. He whispered something into the man's ear and then turned back to Kaen, who watched the servant run off.

"I know the elves did not seem able to help Elies, but I will still offer all the aid I can with healing or other readily available options. Does your dragon really think she can heal you?"

Kaen chuckled. "First, she isn't my dragon. I know it doesn't sound like an important detail, but after hearing how Stioks treated all the dragons he commanded, I want everyone to understand that. Glynnis and Amaranth are here because they choose to be here. They are a part of Pammon, and if we do not respect them and treat them right, they could choose to leave."

Aldric winced slightly and nodded.

"As far as healing me goes, Amaranth believes she can," Kaen said. "She will do everything in her power, and I have faith in her. She has never been one for false hope. Beyond that, we must consider a few things, and these next words will sound difficult."

Kaen paused, putting his shirt back on and moving to the chair he hadn't wanted to get out of a minute ago. Picking up his drink, he swallowed and looked at both men before setting the goblet down.

"Stioks is far more powerful than anything I have ever imagined. The older his dragon gets, the stronger he will get. I now understand what Herb and Hess meant when they talk about adamantine-ranked adventurers. The power he possesses and commands was difficult to imagine before he bonded with a dragon. Now . . ."

Kaen sighed. He knew the worst part was yet to be told.

"He also has a lifestone like mine."

"Surely not!" Aldric declared, standing up and almost knocking over his chair. "How is that possible?"

Aldric stumbled back a step, found his chair with his hand, and dropped into it. The look of shock and horror on his face as the king's mouth hung open and his eyes widened told Kaen volumes.

"Are you . . . certain?" Herb asked, his voice failing for a moment.

"There is no doubt in my mind it must be true . . ." Kaen shuddered as the fight from last night replayed in his mind. "He tortured and killed my father. He was going to do the same to me if Pammon hadn't done what he did."

Both men nodded slowly, and Aldric grabbed his goblet and drained it in a single go.

"So now what?"

Kaen looked at Herb and saw the question written all over the aging man's face. The role of leadership had taken its toll, and today, it appeared to be adding more lines and gray hair to Herb's head.

"Juthom shared that Stioks has mastered death magic but that it also consumes him. He drains life from others, using it to keep his sickness at bay. He did it with the dragons he controlled, and he . . . he did it to Hoste for two years . . ."

"Two years," Aldric muttered quietly, his voice sounding like he didn't believe that was possible.

"It gets worse . . . Many things will make what we must choose to do even more difficult," Kaen said. "If we do not win this soon enough, we will find ourselves facing a horde of dragons. Juthom is right, Stioks will have no problem enslaving the race of dragons. I, however, still do." Kaen shifted in his chair and closed his eyes for a moment as he laced his fingers together and rested his hands on his chest.

He felt his eyes twitching behind his eyelids as he considered what he was going to say. The quiet of the room sounded so loud as he thought.

When he opened his eyes, Kaen saw the other two men waiting, anxious to hear what he would say.

"I'm not sure we could win even if Pammon and I attacked Stioks right now. Even with his dragon wounded, the man is powerful. Worse yet, my bow . . ." Kaen took a deep breath and let it out. The pain of having lost it while fighting at night hurt more than he wanted to admit. "My bow was lost during the fight. I'm not sure if it survived the fall. I plan on having Hess send some students out looking for it."

Herb started to open his mouth, and Kaen shook his head. Nodding, Herb leaned back in his chair and waited.

"The arrows we have wanted to make are gone as well. They fell to the ground, and I hope they survived the fall, but again, I do not know. They could be in the trees or buried in the dirt. I hope that the students may be able to find some, and I am going to ask Glynnis if she will aid in searching from the sky. Her eyes are very good at picking out small details.

"With all those problems come the next ones. If my weakened status does not improve quickly, I will be even more crippled. There is no way I could hope to match Stioks now. Until Amaranth can figure out how to heal me, there is no real way for us to take the fight to him.

"Even if I were desperate enough to enslave a race of dragons, I couldn't undertake that journey for a while. If word got out that Pammon and I were gone, this kingdom would burn.

"Which leads me to our next thing to discuss. Soon, it will be time for both the eggs to hatch, and Phillip and Frederick are the two who will bond with them. This means a lot of other problems. I'll need to dig and build a few more caves for them as they will need their own place.

"We will need to build their rooms lower and with steps so that they and their dragons can climb them until both dragons can fly. The other problem is food. For the first few months, they are going to consume a lot of food and be limited to where they can travel. Pammon and the others will assist them, but we must focus on them."

When Kaen leaned over to get his drink, Aldric took that chance to interrupt. "So what you are telling us is that for at least half a year, we are going to be focused on raising a pair of dragons and getting you healthy?"

"And finding him a new bow and searching for ore to make new arrows," added Herb.

"Basically," Kaen replied, setting his cup down.

"I'm not sure how hard this will be," Aldric said with a slight chuckle. "Raising a kid is hard enough."

Kaen laughed and shook his head.

"There is one perk of having more dragons, though."

Aldric and Herb both raised an eyebrow at the same time.

"Our farmers are going to be getting a massive increase in dragon crap."

All three started laughing, a much-needed sound that filled the room.

32

What Makes One Strong

Kaen held Ava tight as she beat against his chest softly.

Tears still flowed down her face, and he could see how upset she was. It hurt to see Ava like this.

"I thought I had lost you . . . I cried all night long . . ."

"I'm sorry, I would have come but . . ."

Ava's sobs cut him off, and Kaen sighed as her hands finally moved to his waist and both arms surrounded him.

"I know . . . when Amaranth told me you were ok . . . I . . . I didn't know how to respond."

Ava sniffed, pulling her head back before leaning in and wiping her face against Kaen's now damp shirt. "I laughed and cried . . . this one hurt worse than any other time."

"I would have come if I could have . . . That is why I sent Amaranth."

Leaning as far back as she could while Kaen held her, Ava scowled. "You sent a dragon to tell me you were ok!" she snapped. "Instead of visiting me first! How could you—"

"Ava, stop!"

She looked at him, mouth open, as Kaen shook his head slowly and stared at her.

"Every other person in this city is worried about whether they are going to die! Aldric is still trying to get word out to everyone that we won. Right now, families and individuals are all cowering in their houses, afraid that a dragon might burn them to a crisp at any moment. While you had Amaranth here to tell you I was ok, no one else got that."

Kaen stopped, smiling softly as he watched the love of his life try to process his words.

A frown was replaced by a sigh and then a downcast look as Ava leaned her head against her husband's chest. "I'm sorry . . . I just . . . forgive me."

Kaen freed one of his arms, moved her head back, and tipped her face up. Gently, he kissed her on the lips. After their kiss, Kaen smiled. "I am not angry. I just wanted you to know why I did what I did. Had Glynnis taken me, you would have had to wait longer to hear from us."

Stroking her hair gently, Kaen moved his hand and rubbed his thumb gently against her cheek as she pressed into his touch.

"You are my everything. I would have come if I could have, so I sent the next best thing in my stead."

A thrum came from across the cave, and both of them turned to see Amaranth, Glynnis, and Pammon watching the two of them.

"Next best thing, huh? Amaranth says she didn't realize you thought more highly of her than Pammon."

Kaen started to laugh, and a trill came across the room, causing Ava to smile and squeeze Kaen tightly.

"Come, let's lie down briefly while we can. I know you are tired, and I have no doubt that you will be going in many different directions soon."

Kaen smiled and let his wife lead him to their side of the cavern.

Please remember to block anything you decide to do.

Oh, you know I am too tired for that, Kaen shot back, feeling the laughter in Pammon's tone.

A thrum that Kaen was all too familiar with echoed in their cave, and he felt his dragon's eyes on him.

We both know you are never that tired.

Almost three hours later, Kaen was leaving with Ava on Amaranth, letting Pammon and Glynnis fly back to the corpses and start eating again. Both dragons knew that an opportunity to consume a dragon shouldn't be wasted.

"Are you ok with going there?" Ava shouted into Kaen's ear over the wind. "I will understand if not!"

Kaen nodded and focused on the city beneath them.

Amaranth was flying low enough for people to see them on her back. Pammon and Glynnis had already set off to make a trip around the southern part of the city, hoping to encourage the citizens and show them that they still had dragons protecting them.

As the Hurem estate came into view, Kaen grumbled at what he knew needed to be done.

Don't forget to tell Hess that I need him to come here!

Why do you treat me like I'm some child who forgets things? We both know I'm not the one who makes those mistakes.

Ignoring the jab, Kaen knew exactly what Pammon was referring to, having once made the mistake of bringing back what Ava had requested and hearing about it for days.

I know . . . just make sure he hurries. Tell him also to tell Sulenda and Callie I love them.

A thread of disgust came through the bond.

Once again, I am nothing more than a messenger dragon for you . . . when do I get a turn to make you a messenger for me?

The moment I can speak to someone across a city or fly on my own, I'll gladly be that person.

Pammon laughed, and Kaen smiled, glad his dragon was slowly shaking the dread that had filled him that morning.

Lord Hurem had his special multi-lens glasses on and was peering at Kaen's chest and the boils and pus pockets while Ava held a lightstone close by.

"My boy, do you ever try not to get afflicted by the most interesting things? Poisoned, diseased by the orcs, and now this . . ." His father-in-law tapped with a metal probe and leaned back, lifting the lenses covering his eyes.

"Listen. I'm going to lance one of those pockets and put it in this jar as it drains. Hopefully, I can learn a few things about it, and I want to try one last test."

The lord of the house stood up and nodded at Amaranth. "I am grateful for letting me watch as you heal him. Thank you again for doing so."

He is not as bad as you describe him.

Kaen started to cough, and he saw Ava raise a questioning eyebrow when she heard what Amaranth had said.

I didn't say he was terrible . . . just overzealous regarding things like this.

Yet he is right. You apparently do have a knack for suffering horrible things.

Kaen winced as he felt the sharp tip pierce the pus pocket, and as the grayish-green ooze inside started to drip out, the smell hit them all simultaneously.

"That smells worse than a dwarf's ball sack!" Lord Hurem exclaimed.

Coughing, Kaen nodded and saw his wife pinching her nose.

"I can taste it," Ava muttered, her eyes watering.

Lord Hurem held the glass jar firmly, pressing on the wound and squirting more pus into the jar before feeling like he got it all and setting the glass container on the table.

Taking a few clean cloths, he dabbed the wound and ensured that no more would leak from it.

"Amaranth, if you don't mind, I am ready to watch!" the older man said excitedly, lowering his lenses back into place and leaning close to Kaen's chest. "Light, please!"

Ava coughed and held the lightstone closer with one hand while giving Kaen a look that told him how bad she thought it must smell.

A warm sensation came from Kaen's backside as a cold nose pressed up against his back and he felt the power of Amaranth's healing flooding his body.

"Interesting," Lord Hurem murmured as he shifted his head slightly, watching the skin and the sore start to heal some.

When Amaranth pulled back, Lord Hurem had a sharp knife in his hand.

"Kaen, do you mind if I cut off the sore I just lanced and see what is under it? I have my suspicions, but this might hurt."

"Go for it."

Lord Hurem wasted no time, deftly slicing under the skin of the boil he had lanced. Kaen hissed slightly yet never moved as the potion maker finished making his cut, grabbed the piece of skin with a pair of metal tongs, and moved it to a waiting jar.

"Amaranth . . . can you come look at this and tell Ava or Kaen what you see?"

Kaen turned slightly and watched as Amaranth brought her snout to his side. Her eyes shifted between gold and green as she inspected the area Lord Hurem had just cut off.

The area appears to be infected, but the centermost spot is not.

Kaen relayed her message, and the older man nodded. He dabbed the bleeding area and took a deep breath. "How open are you to seeing what we might be able to do to heal you?"

Kaen tried to read his father-in-law's face, but there was no expression. Just a pair of lips held together and cheeks that showed a slight clenching of the jaw.

"How bad is this going to hurt?"

Clucking a few times, Lord Hurem pulled a few more empty jars from a wooden carrier on the table. "I want to try five more things. Each one will require me to cut you. The last cut will be the worst."

A hand squeezed his shoulder, and Kaen saw Ava smiling at him. Her eyes told him she was there and would give him all the strength he needed.

"Well, I've never been one to shy away from pain. So let's get it done."

The older man smiled, flashing all his teeth.

"Just remember, what I'm doing is to heal you, not to torture you for taking my daughter away from us."

"Wait, you sai—"

A knife slipping under an unpopped boil cut Kaen's words off as tears formed on their own. He fought not to shake as the man gouged out a massive hole in his chest. Blood ran down, and Kaen watched as Lord Hurem quickly patted it and inspected the wound he had just made.

"Please heal him now if you would, Amaranth!"

* * *

An hour later, Kaen had been poked and prodded more than he had expected. The nasty taste of two different potions hadn't disappeared yet, even after he ate and drank.

"I should have some results in a day or two." His father-in-law's excited tone as he walked away, carefully carrying jars filled with pieces of his body, seemed way too cheerful to Kaen.

"He is a little weird, isn't he?" Kaen whispered in Ava's ear.

She nodded. "If you weren't here, I would be down there with him, watching and learning.

Kaen chuckled as he saw the truth of what she said in how Ava's eyes followed her dad. "You can go with him if you want. Amaranth and I will be fine. Besides, Hess is inside with your mother, and I need to talk to him."

Ava looked up at her husband and saw that he was telling the truth.

Rising on her toes, she kissed Kaen on his cheek before squeezing his hand and running after her father.

She is a weird one too.

And I love her for that. Besides, you like her.

That is because she is strong. A woman like her is a rare thing. This house produces strong women. The day you have a daughter, I expect you will find yourself losing to both of them.

She was right. If they had a daughter someday and she was anything like her mother, he would be in a far worse position than Hess was in with Callie.

That thought was almost like a summons as the doors opened on the far end of the courtyard and his dad's voice echoed from the room he was leaving.

Seeing Hess and Lady Hurem, Kaen moved to join them.

Be careful. That one is far worse than your wife.

Kaen couldn't contain his amusement at those words. As he walked, he allowed himself a moment to live, letting out a fit of laughter that left him feeling happy and content.

33

True Connections

Hess and Lady Hurem had been ok with just getting a glimpse of Kaen's chest before allowing him to pull down the new shirt he had received after his original one was covered in blood.

"I can't tell you how happy I am to know that you and the three dragons are alive," Hess repeated once more. "It was a long night, and there were tears from everyone but Callie. She never doubted Pammon would be ok."

"You mean Pammon and me?"

Hess snorted and shook his head. "Not once did she mention her older brother. Seems she might have had doubts."

Lady Hurem let out a laugh that had been well practiced over her lifetime, one that showed how much she appreciated the joke, yet with all the refinement a woman of her standard should show. "I have often mentioned to my husband how much your daughter reminds me of Sulenda. So strong and brave. If you two ever need a night by yourselves, we would gladly entertain her for a day or two."

Hess's eyes went wide, and Kaen saw that he was actually shocked at her offer.

"I . . . I will let my wife know. We would be grateful . . . I mean, I am certain that Callie would love a night with you two."

Lady Hurem waved his comment off with a flick of her hand. "Do not worry about being formal with me. I remember what it was like needing a night away with my husband and no child. In times like this, you probably need one even more."

Hess stood up and gave a slight bow. "I am grateful even still."

Lady Hurem stood up and smiled. "No need for that, please. We are family, and as such, we look after each other. Now, I will let you two discuss what you must do. I have things to attend to."

Hess nodded. "I hope you know how much the city appreciates what you are doing, Lady Hurem."

She cleared her throat and gave him a look. "Bridgette, please. We are not that far apart in age, and once again . . . we are family, so please call me Bridgette."

"I will try . . . habits, but thank you again, Bridgette."

Content with his using her real name, Lady Hurem moved next to Kaen and kept him from rising with a hand on his shoulder. She leaned over and kissed him on his forehead before whispering in his ear. "I am grateful to have you as a son. My daughter is doing better than I can hope. Just remember, she wants to be used and needed, just like you. So let her be."

She squeezed Kaen's shoulder and walked away with all the dignity and grace Kaen had ever seen.

"Boy . . . you're in over your head," Hess muttered once the door shut and they were alone.

Kaen cleared his throat. "Don't I know it."

Hess looked at the map where Kaen had drawn a square.

"That is a massive amount of land to search. If your promise of Glynnis hadn't come, I'm not certain we could find the bow or those arrows before it snows."

Kaen nodded and drew a few arrows on some other spots.

"We were totally outplayed. Stioks and his strategy were perfect. We showed our hand, believed he was where he wasn't, and fell into his trap."

Ignoring Kaen's complaint, Hess focused on the map, running his fingers slowly along the area Kaen had marked. After a moment, he took the pencil and marked a few more spots.

"Stop complaining. As with everything you know, fights never go the way you expect. Remember the cave or the orcs and even the bandits. No matter what, if you can come home"—Hess held up his stump and pointed to it with the pencil—"even if you are missing an appendage, it is still a win."

Kaen sighed and picked up his cup, rotating it slowly between his fingers.

"You still haven't commented on what I told you Juthom said about Hoste."

Grunting, Hess leaned back and closed his eyes for a second. When he opened them, he grimaced. "Holy dwarf balls, Kaen, what am I supposed to say? I mean . . . I don't think that damn dragon was lying. If what he says is true, the plan you have laid out is your best option. What else are you going to do?"

Kaen looked at the drink in his glass and then turned his attention back to Hess.

"I need your pickaxe."

"My pickaxe?"

"The one you used to work with when we were in Minoosh. I need to start getting stronger, and someone I know once showed me that the best way to do that is hard work. Besides, I need to start looking for more ore. If we can't find those arrows, we'll need to be able to make more."

"And the scales? Are you really going to send them to the dwarven kingdom?"

Kaen nodded, still turning his cup as he thought. "Aldric and the guild can have some since two corpses are so close, but Bosgreth owes me, and I am about to cash that favor in. That still leaves a bow."

Hess saw the look on Kaen's face and knew the answer before he told him.

"You're going to the wood elves, aren't you?"

"Always a step ahead," Kaen replied, chuckling softly. "No one else makes a bow like them. I'm going to also see if anyone has a rune for sale. Any places I could look?"

Hess grimaced, sucking in a breath through his teeth. "I'm out of the loop on that. Honestly, though, I know of one person who might, and she does owe you . . . otherwise, you would need to talk to Herb and ask him."

Kaen raised an eyebrow. "Owes me?"

"Yes . . . you saved her, and she owes you. Talk to Selmah. I'm certain she has something in her vault that might help you."

Kaen stopped turning his cup and looked at the ceiling, considering his dad's words. "I guess I could ask, but I would feel bad making her do something as a favor."

"Goblin shite, she would do it on her own, and knowing why would make her ten times more likely to help," exclaimed Hess. "You're fighting for this entire kingdom . . . no, the whole land out here. She will see that and do her part now that she is limited."

Wincing, Kaen nodded slowly. "Still, I will offer to pay."

"As you should! But do not play some role where you cannot accept charity if she offers it. Let her feel she is repaying you and contributing to this fight. That alone is more than some gold in her pocket will ever do."

Kaen exhaled before taking a long, deep breath. After letting it out slowly, he smiled. "I guess I sometimes forget that. Everyone plays a role. Even my one-armed dad."

Hess laughed and gave Kaen the finger with his one good hand. "It still works, as you can see. Now, I need to head back to the inn and update Sulenda and Callie before I go to the school and start searching for your lost stuff. Anything else?"

Kaen stood up and grabbed Hess in a bear hug.

"This is all I need."

Hess hugged him back, both laughing and grunting as they squeezed each other.

"Tell my sister I might have words with her when I see her next."

Hess snorted. "I'll make sure to tell her."

Kaen moved to where Amaranth had been dozing.

Studying the green dragon, he saw her eyes open and watch him.

You realize that you breathe loudly.

Unable to help it, Kaen laughed, holding his hand near her snout. She moved it to him, and he began to scratch the scales, working his way along her upper lip and down the base of her skull.

Trills rang out through the courtyard as he worked for ten minutes, scratching scales and moving to different areas he had learned over the years.

When he finally stopped, Amaranth snorted loudly, laying her head on the grass she was on, and groaned.

Your mate is correct. You can do amazing things with your fingers and hands.

Kaen broke out in a coughing fit, and he knew he was red even though no one else was around.

"Thank you . . . I think," he replied, watching the green dragon smile. "And thank you again for trying to help me get better."

I could say I am only doing this because it is in my best interest. If something happens to you, Pammon will no longer be the mate I desire. That would be a lie, though. I still owe you for my freedom even if you continue to say I don't.

Putting his hand on her snout, Kaen shook his head.

"You don't have to do anything because I did that. You have repaid any possible debt multiple times already."

Her eyes sparkled, the green color swirling until it almost went silver and back to green.

Have you ever been a . . . I believe the word you use is slave.

I have not.

Then, until you are, there is no way to express the gratitude and joy I feel every day. I wake up and know that if I wanted, you and Pammon would allow me to fly in any direction I desire. There is a part of me that is finally free without worry of choosing life over death if I say I don't want to do something. Having been oppressed and not being allowed to choose my own path, I know what it means to have one's will crushed by another.

Each time you make a request of me, it is precisely that. A request. You don't order me. You don't force me. Even though you have the power to bend my will and break me with just your words, you never do that. For that, I will always be grateful. And then there is . . . this thing you call family.

Amaranth shook her head as she snorted softly. There was a buildup of moisture around her eyes.

Pammon tried to describe it to Glynnis and me when we first arrived. Dragons don't have family. Even a mate is not family. At any moment, a male could leave his female, happy to pursue others that he might find a better fit. Pammon told me he would not be like that.

A slight thrum came from Amaranth as she watched Kaen's face.

It was funny to see one so big and large and as powerful as Pammon struggle with how dragons are. He made sure that both of us knew he wouldn't pick one over the other and that he wouldn't take another mate unless something required it, and we were both ok with it. Glynnis and I thought he was being foolish, but the longer I watched you and him and how you two treated each other, the more I understood this concept.

Shifting, Amaranth slid back slightly till she sat on all four legs, towering over Kaen, but bent her head low.

I realize now that you see me as family. You don't see me as a dragon to control or a tool. I hear how you talk about me, and Ava has shared with me how you defend us, telling me time and time again that the kingdom does not own us. That is why Glynnis and I are willing to trust you, and those you deem worthy, with our eggs. No greater gift can be given by a female dragon than her child.

Amaranth moved till her snout was on the ground, and her eyes looked directly into Kaen's.

Pammon's story tells that more than I think you may ever realize. His mother sacrificed her life for her child. She put him in a position where he would find a human, instead of hiding him somewhere he might hatch and grow strong enough to be free. She knew that it was better to have a human instead of being alone. She is undoubtedly looking down from the place where dragons go when we die and smiling to see the man her child has bonded with.

Kaen didn't realize as he watched tears slowly trickle from Amaranth's eyes that he was also crying.

Kaen Marshell, King of Dragons, rider of my mate, I owe you more than a dragon could ever know. You have given me a family. You are going to give my child a family. For that, I would fly you to the heavens and back. Since that is not required right now, I will pour out all of my magic every day until you are well because . . .

Amaranth began to shudder, huge tears flowing from her color-shifting eyes.

Because you are my family.

Kaen moved forward, brushing his hand along her snout and wiping away the tear that had just fallen, watching as it flowed along the scales.

"Thank you," Kaen whispered, putting his head against hers. "Thank you for being part of my family."

34

Family Time

The following two weeks passed as Kaen spent most of his time carving rock from the caves near the one Pammon and the other two dragons lived in.

Frederick and Phillip were constant companions, each earning their new homes by the sweat of their brow.

Teams had assisted in hauling off rock and stone while Hess spent more hours than he had initially intended overseeing part of the process.

"Looks like we are almost done," Kaen stated as he stood back and looked at the cavern they had carved out of the solid rock in the mountain. "You should be good for a while before we need to modify the amount of space in here."

Frederick had a grin that wouldn't go away as the last bit of stone they had broken free was taken to the massive opening at the edge of the mountain and pushed over.

"It's finally happening," he replied, his voice giddy with excitement. "How soon do we think till the eggs might hatch?"

"Hopefully, within two more weeks. Glynnis will be bringing hers here in a few days, and from that moment on, you must be here at all times. I'll have food and water brought for you and Hess will come to get some training in. For now, grab that broom and finish sweeping. I need to go check on Phillip's cave."

Frederick nodded and grabbed the broom leaning against a stone wall that they had carved out, more excited to sweep than Kaen could ever imagine was possible.

"Looks like you're about ready to move in," Kaen called out as he finished climbing the stairs that led into Phillip's new home. "What do you think?"

Standing there without his shirt on and covered with a thin layer of sweat, Phillip didn't look like the scrawny kid Kaen had met on the street so long ago. Scars covered a few parts of his dense, muscled body.

"They will have the bed up here in a few hours," Phillip replied, setting down a chest he had been moving to one of the sides. "I still can't believe it . . . a dragon."

Kaen saw his eyes light up with wonder at the thought of realizing a dream he had long since hoped for and never believed would actually occur.

"I'll remind you about that when your dragon craps in the cave for the first time. It's a smell . . . well, just know it's something you'll never forget."

Phillip laughed and shook his head. "I have smelled enough when I've visited the farms. Tell me it can't be worse than that."

Kaen chuckled. "It's worse . . . way worse."

Groaning, Phillip grabbed his shirt and put it on before moving to where Kaen stood with the pickaxe he had acquired from Hess.

"That thing is so insane. I watched you clear stone like it was nothing. Everyone commented that that pickaxe must be magical because you destroyed every bit of the mountain you touched."

Kaen smiled as he hefted the pickaxe up and ran his hand over its massive head. "I wish it were, but it's just a different breed. They don't make them like this anymore . . . kind of like Hess."

Phillip roared with laughter. "That man is something for sure. I can't imagine having grown up under him with two arms. It's hard enough to fight him when he only has one."

"He might argue against that statement," Kaen replied as he rested the pickaxe against the floor. "Every time we talk about you two, there is nothing but praise. Once again, I'll say this. You both have exceeded every hope I have ever had for you, and I'm looking forward to this next journey with you both."

Phillip smiled, but Kaen could see it was forced.

"What's wrong?"

Phillip shrugged. "What you told us about that fight with Stioks . . . to hear he is that strong . . . it's a bit intimidating, to say the least."

"And what is your fear?"

Phillip momentarily looked at the stone floor before returning his gaze to Kaen. "That I'll fail and something bad will happen because of it."

Kaen laughed, ignoring the confused look on Phillip's face.

"Listen, son," Kaen said, winking. That word meant something important was coming, as Kaen rarely used it. "Let me speak about failure . . . you've seen me fail repeatedly, and yet the only thing I regret more than anything is that I didn't act as I should have because I was afraid I would fail. Always do what you know is right, and don't worry about what happens from there. We can only control what we do."

Phillip took a deep breath and let it out. "I appreciate the advice, Uncle Kaen."

Both laughed, and Kaen waved as he walked toward the edge of the cavern, looking out over the city and watching the bronze dragon he knew was almost to him.

"Good luck, and tomorrow I look forward to seeing you with your egg."

Kaen rested the pickaxe against the wall before running and jumping off the cliff, landing on his feet on Pammon's massive back.

You're just showing off now . . .

Yet we both know you can't fit in his opening. Only Amaranth and Glynnis can.

A small thrum came from Pammon as he flapped his wings, waiting for Kaen to move to his new saddle.

Tell me, are you certain about the next few days?

There are things to do, and time is never guaranteed. As much as I would love to wait and see what happens here, there is no time.

Kaen clipped himself in, and as he patted Pammon's neck, he let out a groan he had held back from a minute ago.

I just told Phillip about the need to act and do what you knew was required. Shouldn't I take my own advice?

I'm not saying you are wrong; I'm just making sure you are aware of the problems it might cause. Amaranth said—

I know what she said, and I will be fine. Between her and Lord Hurem, I have no doubts they will find a cure.

Pammon snorted and continued toward Bren's training yard.

"Kaen!"

His little redheaded sister ran toward him, wrapping his leg with her arms.

"My gosh, what are they feeding you? Ogre steaks? How did you get so strong?"

Callie laughed and growled as she squeezed tighter and squealed when Kaen reached down and tickled her sides.

"Not fair!" she exclaimed during one of her attempts at speaking.

Laughing, Kaen grabbed and lifted her and hugged her before setting her back down on the inn's floor.

Looking around the room, Kaen frowned for a moment. Only a few patrons were there, and most were taking their time, enjoying the rare drink anyone got to experience anymore.

"Don't look like that," Eltina informed him. "I don't need another sad face in this place."

Smiling, Kaen held out his arms.

"Yer dumber than you look if you think I'm about to hug you," she stated as she crossed her arms and shook her head. "No way I will have people running their lips about me and you . . . imagine how that would tarnish my reputation."

Laughing, Kaen feinted at coming in for a hug as Eltina dodged backward and produced a rag, ready to pop him with it.

"How I've missed your wit and gentle soul," Kaen said as he sat down at the bar.

"About as much as I've missed your loose tongue and the way it attempted to seduce every woman that walked through those doors."

Chuckling, Kaen shook his head and ran his hand along the top of the bar. "Perhaps I should climb on top of the bar again. See if I can't liven this place up a little."

"Yer just saying that cuz there aren't that many people here to buy a round for. Besides, I ain't got enough drink to hand out when I know Sulenda won't make you pay."

"How bad is it?"

Picking at her teeth with a finger, Eltina shrugged. "We're doing better than most. Multiple inns have shut down because . . ."

"No food, alcohol, or a reason to celebrate?"

Nodding slowly, Eltina moved around the bar and climbed up on her raised area. "Want a drink?"

"You know what I want, and we both know there isn't a glass of milk to be had anymore. Last time I checked, it cost more than a cask of beer."

Snorting, Eltina pulled a mug out and filled it with a watered-down drink. "Once a week, we have a full house. Your mother-in-law makes that happen." Kaen saw the wetness around the crabby bartender's eyes, and she sniffed and used her rag to wipe them. "She's an amazing woman . . . buying food like that and giving it away here, all so I can make a few copper off the drinks we sell."

Nodding, Kaen rotated his mug a few times before lifting the drink to his lips. It had taken years, but he could finally manage to drink alcohol without any chance of getting drunk. Now, with that ability, there wasn't any decent stuff to enjoy.

"I'm blessed. Just as I know you are."

Eltina nodded and wiped a few cups out, letting Kaen enjoy his drink.

The back door swung open, and laughter and giggling made both of them look at the sight of Hess and Callie wrestling and tickling as they came toward the bar.

"Can't say I ever expected to see that side of that bastard," Eltina whispered. "Still . . . I guess I should be glad he's here. I'm unsure how Sulenda would be doing if it weren't for you and him."

Kaen stood up on his stool and reached across the bar, gently squeezing Eltina's arm before sitting down. "As I've told a few special people and dragons lately, you're family. Glad we can help."

Grunting, Eltina smirked and then moved off her block to check on the half-dozen patrons.

"Kaen! I brought Dad!"

Callie's cheer was one thing Kaen couldn't fight against. The way she could light up a room and dispel his frustration was hard to believe sometimes.

"Well, hopefully you didn't need to carry him. He's getting old and is awfully heavy."

Laughing, Callie rolled her eyes and ran back to the room where Sulenda was most likely working on the stacks of papers for her inn and the school.

"Booth?" Hess asked as he motioned to one with his head.

"Our usual?"

Smiling, Hess didn't wait for Kaen, moving to the booth they had sat in the first time they came.

"Only one arrow . . . that's all we can find so far. It's been two weeks, and the weather is going to be getting bad. Soon, I'll have to—"

"Stop searching," Kaen said, cutting his dad off. "One will have to do for now, and I'll make the most out of it. Besides, I got a plan when I visited the dwarves after the wood elves."

Hess grunted but nodded. "Sorry about the bow . . ."

"Don't be. It has done more than I could have imagined for a lifetime. The fact that it broke from that height proves it wasn't as indestructible as I thought. I'm sure Hoste will understand."

"Or he will haunt me until the day I die. Regardless, the caves are done?"

"Both are dug out, and Frederick is sweeping out his as we speak. Phillip will be done with all his furniture before the evening. Frederick should be finished completely by tomorrow. Then they will move the eggs."

Letting out a low whistle, Hess leaned against the back of the booth. "How long till they hatch?"

"That is the question everyone is asking," Kaen replied. "Maybe two weeks. You're still good to train them in their caves until the eggs hatch?"

"Gladly. I'm just thankful that Glynnis or Amaranth will take me there. I'm not sure I want to climb those stairs every day. Doing it four times was bad enough."

Laughing, Kaen slid his drink across the table to Hess. "Go ahead. Mom keeps you on a tight leash so you don't drink all the profits."

Smiling, Hess picked up the cup, draining it completely.

"I've missed this. Can't tell you how much I look forward to when this happens again."

"Soon . . . soon, Dad. We'll make it the way it was."

35

Finding Connections

"They look like kids," Ava whispered as she watched Frederick running his hand along the outer edge of the shell that Glynnis had just deposited on the bed of straw he had made for it. "Look at his face."

Kaen pulled Ava close as they stood side by side. "I'll never forget the day I found Pammon. It was hard to describe. Inside my mind and heart, I could hear his voice call to me." Kaen shook his head as he replayed that moment in his mind. "I remember Hess trying to pull me away, and he said I fought him like a bear. I can't recall that part, but all I could think of was being there for Pammon."

Ava nodded, watching Kaen as he shared that memory again with her. "What happens if they hatch while you are gone?"

"They have Glynnis and Amaranth. I've learned that when a rider bonds with a dragon, they can communicate with all dragons within a certain range if the dragon is willing and known. I can only imagine how they will handle two mothers telling them how to raise their young."

Ava chuckled as she glanced back at Glynnis, who was doing her best to stay back and give Frederick and the egg a little space. "She is anxious."

"Very . . . she mentioned it was harder than she had thought it would be," Kaen replied. "I can only imagine how hard it was on Pammon's mother."

Ava nodded. "While they are busy, let's return to our place."

Kaen looked at his wife and the way she was smiling. "Whatever you say, my love."

As they lay in bed beside each other, Kaen found breathing hard.

"You . . . you're sure?"

Ava nodded and gently ran her hand around the area on his chest that was constantly inflamed. The handprint was gone, but the flesh was constantly forming a boil or turning discolored compared to the rest of him.

"I'm sure. Amaranth told me three days ago. Somehow, she could tell. Are you still ok with me coming on this trip?"

Kaen nodded. His chest still felt tight at hearing that she was pregnant. "And Amaranth is certain it is twins?"

A giggle escaped Ava's lips as she sat up and smiled at him.

Kaen saw the light in her eyes, the hope. She was absolutely giddy.

"She is! I cannot wait to tell my parents, but I will until we return. If you are ok with that."

Sitting up, Kaen slid till he was against the back of the bedframe and then pulled her close. "I am completely ok with that. You know I will always allow you to lead when it comes to matters like this. Are you . . . do you feel fine?"

Ava took a deep breath and let it out, smiling the entire time. "I feel amazing, and I don't want you worried and acting like Glynnis or Amaranth is right now. There is no reason to be worried about me. Do you understand?"

Her tone had changed, and she glared at him even as she smiled.

Nodding, he moved so he could kiss her. "I will not act like either of those two, I promise."

"Good, because if you did, you might find your bed a little colder at night."

Chuckling, Kaen sighed and pulled her close. "I would never want that."

"You two behave," Kaen said as Ava took turns giving Amaranth and Glynnis scratches. "Remember, those boys will not survive if the two of you smother them too much. Both are extremely grateful and excited. Once they have bonded, do your best to allow them to fail a little. Nothing teaches the importance of doing things right better than having to shovel dragon crap."

Pammon thrummed at that comment, and both female dragons turned their attention to him.

"You can ask him later. Any questions?"

I'm so excited for you and Ava! Glynnis shouted in his head, making Kaen wince slightly. ***We look forward to the day your children come and we get to see them!***

Kaen smiled as Amaranth touched her nose against Ava's outstretched hand.

Watch over my sister. Do not let her become too tired. And make sure she eats. Those two children will need lots of food.

"I will ensure that Pammon brings us as much as she needs each night."

Satisfied with Kaen's answers, both female dragons came and touched their snouts against Pammon's before moving away and giving them space to climb on.

"Feels like we are leaving for a month with all this stuff," Ava groaned. "And these packages smell awful."

"Dragon scales . . . even when cleaned, they do have a scent. Maybe it's just the whole pregnancy thing."

Ava didn't say a word as she climbed up Pammon's side and moved to her spot on the saddle.

Once both of them were buckled in, Pammon gave a slight growl, and Kaen noticed that he smiled, sensing a wave of humor and something else through their bond.

What was that?

A groan came from his dragon as they leaped from the cave, and he began to beat his wings.

All this talk of babies has gotten those two worked up . . . each of them has "informed" me that when I get back, it may be time to spend some alone time with each of them.

Chuckling, Kaen squeezed Ava's arm as she leaned against his back, using him to shield her from the wind.

Just remember to shield me from those moments. I cannot handle enduring that while Ava is pregnant.

Don't worry . . . part of this is because Amaranth can sense what you and Ava did yesterday. She has bonded with her in a different way. It's not an actual Dragon Rider bond, but their emotions convey more than should be possible.

Do you . . . Kaen stopped, knowing that question was folly. *I suppose we shall one day learn how all this works. It is a shame Elies was not able to share more.*

He gave us all he had. Is she certain she can fly as long as we had initially planned?

Just go till she tells me we need to stop. And stay a little lower if you don't mind. I don't expect to encounter Stioks, but I also don't want to freeze her out.

I already intended on that.

Scratching his friend's neck, Kaen took a deep breath and let it out.

Moments like these made life worth fighting for.

"What happened?!"

Ava's shout was barely heard, but Kaen could only shrug as he looked at the carnage beneath them.

Can you communicate with her that we don't know? Hopefully, this will not go on forever.

I have already informed her of that. It is the work of ordinary fire, though. It doesn't look like a dragon did this.

Which would mean the orcs and goblins . . . How long has it been since we have been up here? Six months?

Longer . . . We may have to search for the wood elves. It may take longer than we expected. I will also need to fly to the west to try and find a place to camp for the night. Being in that mess below would not be good for either of you.

Kaen looked at the burnt remains of the forest below. As far as their eye could see was a black landscape, destroyed and burnt trees, and sections that had been knocked down completely. It stretched from the east and died out in the west, showing Kaen that it had to have come from near Luthaelia.

Let's head to the west a little and see how far this stretches. I would rather not have to fly so far later. Have you seen any animals?

Only a few, but for the most part, no. Not even a lot of birds are down there. This happened a while ago. At least a few months. I can tell by the greenery starting to sprout up in certain areas.

Months . . . I hope they are still alive.

Have no fear. Those elves are not going to stand and die. If I learned anything from our last visit, they are not foolish enough to fight as others, dying when there is a chance to flee and live elsewhere.

Yes . . . but if that is the case . . .

Finding them may prove to be extremely difficult.

Kaen watched as the forest slowly appeared in jagged sections where flames had not burned up all the trees. Some were charred, and then it was as if the forest said *no more* and the fire had just stopped.

Their path had taken them a bit off course from their intended direction, but Kaen knew it was necessary, especially when Ava squeezed his arm four times quickly.

We need to take a bathroom break. Are you ok with that?

Pammon thrummed and nodded.

She already asked me a few minutes ago. I told her I was looking for somewhere that would work for us to land. I'll take this, as she needs to go sooner rather than later.

As Ava and Pammon stayed together, Kaen moved to the east and reached the section that had burned out. Inspecting the ground, he noticed the greenery starting to overtake the burnt area. Grass and wildflowers created a new canvas of life over the dead ground.

I guess it is good that what happened wasn't a spell like the one used on Roccnari. Still, the question I have is how a fire could burn so far. These trees aren't dead. In fact, they look healthier than most trees I have seen in a long time.

My answer sounds weird, but perhaps the magic of the forest that the elder Queleth talks about is real. How many people consider dragons to be

a myth or thing of legend? Herb even told you that the wood elves have a special connection with the land.

Kaen nodded as he plucked a tender shoot from the soil and tasted it. It was sweet, and he could feel the life in it.

Then it hit him.

Closing his eyes, Kaen activated his lifestone and felt the power flowing through him. He opened himself to the view of the world he had learned while blind and held his hand over his eyes at the brightness of the green lights surrounding him.

Pammon . . . the land . . . it is full of magic . . .

Confusion came through their bond.

You're looking with your other sense, aren't you? What does it look like?

Kaen spun around slowly, seeing the power shifting as the tree closest to the spot where the fire stopped almost looked like a roaring fire of green lights running up and down its massive trunk.

Where the fire ended, the green lights danced all over, up and down every flower and blade of grass. Bending down, Kaen pinched off a flower and watched as the flow stopped coming into it but saw inside the flower a glow that pulsed.

There is a . . . give me a moment to think. Imagine a river that flows through the forest. Water rushes everywhere within the area it travels. These plants, trees, and blades of grass all have that flowing into them. They are saturated with it. Where the fire stops, I can see the same power pushing into those sections, forcing it back inside. The land that is completely burnt isn't devoid of this energy. It is just . . . like a dam is holding it back. Some still seeps out, but not the full extent of what they want to.

So is the forest alive? Is it magical?

Kaen moved to a tree and put his hand against the bark. He could see tiny insects climbing up the tree, their own lights against the one that the tree was bursting with. As he stood there, holding his hand against the trunk, he tried to think about how to see if Pammon was right.

He could sense and hear his dragon and Ava coming toward him, but he wanted to somehow tap into the power inside the tree.

Taking a few deep breaths, he watched as his own power in his hand pressed against the power of the tree.

Controlling his breathing, he relaxed, focusing on the point where his skin touched the bark. He willed the power in him to concentrate in his fingers. It gathered there, spinning and pooling in his hand as he tried to will it to somehow connect to the tree.

Moments passed, and time seemed to stretch as he tried to push it out of his hand.

Frustration took over as nothing he did seemed to work.

Yanking his hand from the bark, Kaen sighed and turned off his lifestone, letting his vision return to normal.

"That bad?" Ava asked.

Kaen snorted as she slowly turned, and he saw his dragon and wife watching him.

"I'm guessing I need to be a wood elf if I want to be a tree hugger."

Both of them groaned as he smiled.

"We ready to keep flying?"

"I should be good for a few more hours. Besides, Pammon promised me my own deer."

Kaen chuckled and helped her get up on Pammon's back.

"I'd like my own deer as well, if you please."

We shall see . . .

Thrumming, Pammon smiled, waited for them to finish getting situated, and buckled in. Once Kaen had tapped him on the neck, Pammon moved to the edge of the burnt land and snorted.

The cycle of life is complex. So often, something must die for a new life to begin.

With that deep thought, he took off, sending clouds of ash into the air, rising above a barren land while turning to fly above one filled with life.

36

Old Friends

I see it. Look and tell me if I am correct.

Kaen used Pammon's eyes and saw where his dragon was currently looking.

You appear to be correct. Those trees look like the others we had stopped at, but . . . this land is not where we had them on the map. For those trees to form here . . .

It would require magic . . .

Kaen nodded as Pammon seemed content with his answer.

You are starting to believe in this magical forest now, aren't you? Did Queleth say something or do something that has changed your mind from the first time?

Unfortunately, I have been spending too much time with you and others, and now I find myself thinking about things I would never have bothered with years ago. One of those things is what I heard you, Aldric, and Herb talking about. Combined with what Juthom said . . . It feels like a cycle of energy and power.

Pammon turned, adjusting his path toward the trees they were following.

Ava and I discussed it yesterday, as you know. Why were the elves so good at creating magical items? How did their people live so long even though their numbers were less as a race than the dwarves and you humans?

Have you considered that the land has some magical element, and they learned to tap into it? Think about that tree they lived in and the power it provided. Now we see the destruction that came upon their land once it died.

This is why Queleth had mentioned some of their problems with the elves . . . they wouldn't move and considered that one tree more sacred than anything else.

Why do the wood elves consider all the forest to be special? What if they use magic but in a different way?

Kaen wrestled with that same line of thought as he and Pammon watched the place where they now knew the wood elves were getting closer.

If Queleth finds out we are asking these questions, we might be given the honorary title of wood elf . . . or maybe a wood dragon.

Snorting, Pammon continued his descent, choosing not to respond to Kaen's joke.

"Welcome, Dragon Rider and Dragon!"

Kaen waved as a group of wood elves approached slowly, each waving and smiling but none he or Pammon recognized.

"You're tense. Is everything ok?"

Kaen nodded and squeezed her leg gently. "This is the usual greeting, but Pammon and I don't see any of the ones we recognize. If you look at them, they are also skinnier than usual."

Ava smiled and waved as she looked them up and down. "They are skinny, but are you sure?"

Kaen shrugged and undid their clips, climbing down from Pammon and then waiting to help Ava down.

A male elf with a brown braid down to his knees approached them and gave a deep bow, crossing both arms as he placed them against his chest.

"Welcome to the shade of our trees! I am Fenain. May I guide you to our tables?"

Kaen bowed and gave the same gesture. "I would be honored to sit at your tables. Tell me, is Elder Queleth here?"

A pained look crossed the elf's face, and he nodded slowly.

"Queleth is here, but he will soon rejoin the forest. We have a new elder, and she is looking forward to meeting you."

Kaen winced, saddened to hear that Queleth was not in good health.

"If you would follow me."

Kaen held out his hand and gently grasped Ava's when she put hers in his.

"Sorry," she whispered in his ear.

Kaen nodded, looking at those gathering around them and seeing that the number of wood elves also appeared to be fewer.

The tables were set up as they had been the last few times he had come: a long row of multiple tables with seats carved from trees in intricate designs. Flowers decorated the top, and some fruit and other snacks were set at the centerpiece. A woman he hadn't seen in years sat in the elder's chair.

"Dragon Rider Kaen! It is my honor to welcome you to our table!" She turned and looked at Ava and gave a bow. "You must be the wife, Ava, I have heard him talk about."

Ava smiled, bowed slightly, and elbowed Kaen ever so slightly.

"Please come sit and join me."

Kaen pulled out the chair as Ava sat down, and before sitting in his seat, Kaen couldn't help but bow and chuckle.

"How long has it been, Elder Sedel? How did they manage to convince you to take this seat?"

The woman sighed and waited until Kaen sat down before clapping her hands. A handful of elves came with a few cups of water and then moved away, standing nearby if needed.

"I wish my answer were that I desired it, but there was no other choice," Sedel stated as she sat in her chair. "When Queleth became sick, those worthy of the role were few. As you can see, many of our people are gone. The last year has not been kind to us."

Kaen nodded, took a drink from his cup, and smiled after setting it down. "Cold and sweet, just as I remembered."

"You are a very blessed woman to have a man like this," Sedel said, turning her attention to Ava. "After he won an archery contest against me, using all forms of trickery, he could have had his pick of any elf here."

Smiling, Ava reached over and put her hand on Kaen's. "I must say it is never a dull moment. I am also grateful that no one stole his heart from me."

Kaen groaned and rolled his eyes.

"Please eat," Sedel said in a quieter tone. "I know it isn't much, but now more than ever, your honor must be kept."

Leaning forward, Kaen plucked two small apples and handed one to Ava. As he took a bite, the juice ran down his lips and into his beard. It took great effort to hold back the moan he wanted to let out. "These taste better than anything I have experienced in a while."

Ava nodded as she chewed, smiling as she studied the bright red fruit.

Sedal watched as they ate, allowing the time required to provide what their customs expected to pass.

"I take it you want to speak elsewhere," Kaen asked, glancing around with his eyes at the elves nearby.

"When you are finished, I would enjoy showing you my residence and allowing you to see Queleth before he rejoins the land. He perked up when word reached him you had arrived."

Understanding the situation, Kaen finished consuming the last of his apples and washed them down with the water in his cup. Ava picked up on his lead, finishing only a moment after he did.

"My wife and I would be honored if you would let us see Queleth now before we are gifted with a tour of your home."

Sedel grinned and stood up, clapping her hands as elves rushed forward, taking the remains of their food and helping to pull out their chairs as they stood.

"If you would follow me. Please forgive the climb. I know it is not easy, and for a woman like yourself, anything while pregnant is not easy."

Ava released a startled gasp and glanced at Kaen, who shrugged.

"I will tell you how I know later, but for now, congratulations. Twins are an uncommon thing indeed."

Kaen began to laugh as he squeezed Ava's hand, trying to ignore her look of amazement.

Twenty minutes of climbing the stairs and bridges that ran up and to other trees brought them to a home cut inside the massive trunk of one of the side trees.

A cloth hung over the entrance, and Sedel smiled as she knocked gently against the tree.

"Queleth. If you are up to it, I have some visitors who would like to see you."

"Yes! Please come in! Send that young boy in quickly!"

Chuckling, Kaen smiled as Sedel pulled the cloth aside, and Kaen moved into the room. His heart broke as he saw Queleth sitting up in a bed, covered with a few blankets, and reduced to almost nothing but skin and bones.

The older elf smiled, his hands and head shaking as he lifted them, motioning Kaen to come to where he lay.

"Come! Come, my boy! Or I guess I should say a man! I have missed you and your dragon! Tell me, is this your wife?!"

The barrage of questions made Kaen forget the man's current state, glad to see he had never lost the enthusiasm he remembered.

"Yes. Ava, this is Queleth. Queleth, my wife Ava."

"It is my honor to meet you," Ava said with a bow. "Kaen has often mentioned his fondness for you and your people."

A glimmer of life shone in the man's eyes at her words. "It is my honor as well! Please sit!" Queleth glanced at Sedel and grinned as Ava and Kaen sat near him. "He came! He came like I told you he would!"

Kaen glanced at Sedel, who shrugged. She moved to sit in a chair across the small room.

"How did you know I was coming?" Kaen asked, looking at his friend.

"The forest told me! You touched it a few days ago, and I knew it meant you were coming! Sure enough, you have touched it daily, like a line pointing to here!"

Kaen knew his face looked confused as he glanced between Sedel and Queleth. "Sorry, I'm lost. What am I missing?"

"My boy," Queleth started before a series of coughs cut him off. Raising his hand, he waved away Sedel, who had stood. "I'm not dead yet. I am fine." The older elf turned and fixed his eyes on Kaen. "Now tell me, when did you learn to see life?"

Kaen took a deep breath, wondering what he meant, until his brain finally connected all the dots. "The green dots of magic?"

"Life . . . magic . . . power . . . call it what you will, but yes! When?"

"A month ago, I guess? Wait, how do you know I can see that?"

"You tried to impart yourself into the forest. You tried to connect and touch it. For that to happen, one must be able to see it. The forest is excited! A man has not done so in . . ." Queleth paused, scrunching up his eyes and face, making wrinkles appear like mountains. He looked at Sedel, and she could tell he needed help.

"The forest has never spoken to a man before," Sedel replied, smiling at Kaen and Ava's shocked expressions. "No man has ever opened himself up. Two women have in the history of our people, but those are stories for another day."

Queleth nodded, excited at what had happened.

"Kaen, your timing could not be better! The forest needs you! It needs your strength and to share things with you."

Kaen looked at Sedel, who was just smiling, and then back at his old friend, shaking his head. "I'm sorry, it needs my power and wants to talk to me?"

"Yes! Just like you and your dragon talk, it wants to talk!" He paused, shaking his head slightly. "Well, not exactly, but . . . you'll find out when it happens."

Kaen looked at his wife, who shrugged.

"Congratulations also," Queleth said, turning his attention to Ava. "Two children! They appear strong as well!"

"Ok, I can't take this," Ava said, her tone showing her frustration at how everyone seemed to know she was pregnant. "How do you all know this?"

"The gift . . . the gift shows me," Queleth replied as he held a shaky finger up to his eye. "I don't see you as you see. I see everything the way Kaen has seen it. I can see the tiny lives that are inside you."

Ava found her mouth open and looked at her husband, motioning to her stomach. "Can you see them?"

"I actually haven't tried," he stated as he looked at Queleth, who was beaming with joy. "Let me try."

Calming himself, Kaen felt his lifestone roar with power and closed his eyes, letting the world shift and again wincing as the light around him initially overwhelmed him.

"It is bright when you first glimpse it," Sedel said. "Give it a minute before you try to see your children."

Kaen nodded, trying to find a place to look that wasn't roaring with those green balls of energy or life that were everywhere.

Soon, the room settled down, and he could see the outlines of the walls and the tree they were inside taking shape. Against the wall, he saw Sedel sitting on a chair. Turning to where Queleth was, he saw the old man, his body and the light within it almost gone.

"Don't worry about me, boy! Focus on what matters!"

Kaen nodded, turned, and looked at Ava. He could see her, the shape of her face, her hair in some weird way, and then, as he looked at her stomach, he focused.

Power, energy, and light swirled within her core. Leaning forward, he tried to see through the lights, and slowly, it was as if a veil was pulled away. Two tiny lights appeared, different from all the others.

They flickered side by side, pulsating rapidly, so fast it almost made a solid light.

"Go touch her," Queleth whispered. "Watch as you do."

Moving around the bed, Kaen used his hands to guide him, never taking his eyes off the spot that he saw. When he got next to Ava, he fell on his knees and slowly reached out with his hands, putting them on her stomach.

Both lights flickered faster, pulsing with a brighter light.

"Kaen?"

Ava's voice was trembling, and Kaen couldn't answer.

He nodded, feeling tears running down his cheeks. "I can see them Ava . . . I can see our children."

37

Giving Everything

It had taken a few minutes for Kaen and Ava to regain their composure after that moment. Each of them cried and smiled, laughing and hugging at all of it.

"I won't lie, it's not fair," Ava stated as she wiped her face again.

"Many mothers have complained to me about that very thing," Queleth said, grinning the entire time. "They think I'm cheating, but it is a gift I am grateful the forest has given. Children are rare among us compared to you humans. We treasure every child, celebrating the life given to our community."

He coughed, and the three turned to see Sedel motioning at Kaen with her head.

"Ah yes, the next thing . . . I almost forgot," Queleth stated. "Kaen, I need to teach you how to do something . . . after I do, we will never get to speak again as we do now."

Kaen saw how Queleth's face changed, and his lips were drawn tight. "What do you mean? Teaching me will kill you?"

"Not like you think, but yes . . . I am . . . I am dying, Kaen. The forest has given me one last moment of joy before I go. Right now, I have more power and energy than I have had in months. That is because the forest has poured into me, and I must give it back. It is when I do so that you will learn what you must. It is then when you will be able to help Sedel and all my people."

Kaen started to speak when Queleth held up an unsteady hand.

"Don't argue. If you don't do this with me, learning what you must will be even more difficult, and I am afraid . . . more of my people will die. Do you understand?"

Sighing, Kaen nodded. He had been put in enough positions to understand when what needed to be done wasn't what he wanted to do. It was in those moments when the right thing required the strongest will. To push through when most would quit because it wasn't easy.

"What do I need to do?"

Leaning over, Queleth placed his hand on Kaen's knee and smiled.

"Just trust me, boy."

It had been a quiet moment with no words spoken as Kaen carried Queleth down the stairs and rope bridges. The older elf had smiled, enjoying the sun rays that somehow came through the canopy overhead.

Kaen wanted to ask, but it was as if the trees themselves had moved their branches to share the light with a protector of the forest.

"Here, set me down here and then come close," Queleth said when Sedel stopped at the base of the largest tree in the small town.

Bending down, Kaen set the elder against the bark, watching as Queleth reached out with his hand and gently stroked it, smiling as he did.

"Listen, my children." Queleth spoke in a voice that seemed louder and stronger than one in his condition should be capable of. "I am about to join our ancestors. Today, I will become one with our forest. This man, this Dragon Rider . . . my friend shall send me on my way."

A murmur and some voices were heard, and Kaen now noticed the gathering of what must be every wood elf inside the village.

"Do not argue and do not resist. The trees themselves have spoken about this, told me he was coming, and lent me the strength you can hear in my voice so that this moment can happen now."

Kaen stepped back as Queleth rose suddenly, his body which had shaken so much now steady as he slid his grip up the tree.

Gasps rang out, and Kaen saw tears in the entire village as they saw Queleth stand as he once had.

"My children, follow your new elder Sedel. She was chosen for this task, was trained, and is committed. It is no coincidence that she and Kaen are friends. We must trust the forest in its choosing. Now, each of you. Go home and wait. Soon you shall feel me."

Sobs rang out for a moment more before every elf turned as one, leaving just Kaen, Sedel, and Ava with Queleth.

A sound caught Kaen's attention, and he turned to see Queleth sliding down the tree, his legs going weak. He caught the man with a speed most wouldn't possess and gently lowered him to the ground.

"Thank you," whispered Queleth, his voice ragged and weak. "Now listen and do what I say. My time is almost over, and we must hurry."

Ava watched, tears in her eyes, as she reached out to Sedel to squeeze her hand. Sedel moved closer to Ava and smiled. "Thank you," she whispered as tears streamed from her eyes.

"Use the sight. See my life. See my power leaving me. Put your hand on mine and then focus and obey."

Kaen's heart ached, his lifestone surged, and as it did, he felt a presence drawing near. He had been so swept up in the moment that he hadn't noticed Pammon and that his dragon was so close.

Tell him I am here. Tell him I will help.

Help wi—

Just tell him . . . I can feel . . . I can sense what is about to happen . . . together we will help his people.

Kaen let the fire and power overwhelm him, feeling his vision shift and seeing the faint glow of the man he knew next to him.

Queleth's hand lay against the massive, bright, surging power of the tree, and Kaen placed his hand over his friend's.

"Pammon is here and says he will help."

Kaen could see the smile, a light forming across the elf's lips.

"Thank you . . ."

Trying to calm the shakes that were about to overtake him, Kaen heard how weak his friend's voice was.

"Listen . . . see the flow . . . the life leaving me and into the tree . . . match it . . . desire it . . . share yourself with it," Queleth said, taking deep breaths as he spoke. "Share your strength with my people . . ."

A sound he knew far too well came from Queleth's lips, and Kaen knew the elder had taken his last breath.

The last of the lights in his body were flowing to the tree, leaving quickly. Kaen ached, seeing his friend go but knowing what he had to do.

Power from Pammon filled him, and energy from his own life drove him.

His hand lit up brighter than the tree as he pressed against his friend's hand and willed what he had. Wanted what he controlled to be shared with the forest.

It felt like a wall pushing back, holding that exchange, testing to see if he was committed.

Something in his mind pressed against him, and Kaen realized what it was.

Without hesitating, he drew his knife at his waist and brought it to his hand, slicing the palm and then piercing the bark of the tree. He slammed his hand against the place he had cut and poured his desire out, drawing even more power to the point that he almost couldn't bear to gaze upon his hand.

And then the wall shattered.

The torrent of power that was raging inside him sprang like a river that had been held by a dam, now gone. It overflowed from every part of him, surging through the tree.

"It's happening," Sedel whispered, squeezing Ava's hand tightly. "It's actually happening!"

Ava watched, seeing nothing, but somehow, the hairs on her neck and arms began to rise as she felt something flowing through the forest.

More! I can give more!

Pammon's voice and strength surged through him, and the tree took it all, sending that power through its roots that ran under the ground and connected to a world Kaen slowly began to see.

He glanced down and saw a network of life and magic flowing beneath the surface. Beneath him was a sight he would struggle to describe as roots everywhere connected in a pattern he had never seen before.

Every part of him burned and hurt, yet Kaen had never felt more alive than he did in that moment. He realized what had happened and why the forest needed him. He had a purpose, and the promise he had made years ago was finally being fulfilled.

A little more! Finish this!

Kaen grunted as Pammon gave beyond what he should have. He groaned as he felt his own life pouring from him. At that moment, all he wanted was to fix one thing, to heal something he knew he could. To fight back the darkness that had plagued so much of these lands for so long.

As he grew weaker, feeling like nothing was left, a pair of hands caught him, catching him as he fell backward toward the ground.

"I've got you, my love."

Kaen smiled, hearing her voice and feeling her touch.

And then everything went dark, and he heard a loud thud before he passed out.

Opening his eyes, Kaen saw Ava watching him, sitting in a chair and smiling as she ran her fingers slowly over her stomach.

"Hey," Kaen said, his voice a little raspy.

She chuckled and sat up, grabbing a cup of water and bringing it to his lips. "Hey yourself. How are you feeling?"

Kaen took a drink and then sat up, cracking his neck and feeling out his body.

"I feel . . . good. How long have I slept?"

"Oh . . . almost a full day. You and Pammon were out after whatever it is you did."

"A day?!" Kaen exclaimed, disbelieving that it was true. "How?"

"That I can't answer, but what I can say is just when I think I have figured you out, you and Pammon do something like this and surprise me."

You're awake, finally. I guess I should have expected you to take longer to recover.

Kaen started to laugh, and Ava raised an eyebrow at him.

"Pammon . . ."

She nodded, setting the cup down from where she had taken it.

How are you feeling, and what did we do?

I feel remarkably well after giving all of my power and strength yesterday and even better after eating a few deer earlier today. As for what we have done, you will have to see that for yourself.

Kaen looked at Ava, who had a smirk on her face.

"What am I missing?"

"Besides being a hero to these people? Go outside when you are ready. Pammon and I agree you must see for yourself."

Throwing back the blanket that had covered him, Kaen took the boots Ava held out and quickly put them on.

"Come with me?" he asked, holding his hand out to her.

"Always!"

They moved toward the cloth that covered the doorway of the room he was in, and when Kaen stepped through and got his first glimpse of the forest beyond, he stumbled and stopped moving.

"Impossible," Kaen whispered as Ava came up next to him. "The forest, it's . . ."

"Alive. Alive and well, thanks to whatever you did."

Glancing down, Kaen realized they were in the highest part of the tallest tree. He could see out over the entire forest, and the colors of the leaves were now a bright green. The air smelled better, and looking at the bark behind him, Kaen could tell it was improved, too.

"Let's go down. There are so many waiting to see you."

The trip from the top had taken thirty minutes, as every elf they saw and passed ran over, bowing and giving him their thanks.

Kaen immediately saw the difference in each of them. No longer did they look starving and weak; now they looked as he remembered, strong and alive.

"How is this possible?"

"Sedel said she would tell you, and if you pay attention, she is waiting for you at the table below."

Kaen glanced over the edge and saw that a large group was approaching the table; this time, it was filled with food and fruits.

Looking at his wife, who smiled at him, Kaen leaned over and kissed her, wrapping his arms around her and pressing his lips against her. He felt her hands rubbing up and down his back.

PLEASE STOP OR BLOCK THAT!

Kaen pulled back, wincing for a moment before laughing. He saw Ava also chuckling, and both couldn't help laughing the rest of the trip down.

Sorry, I got a little carried away.

I know . . . trust me, I know . . .

38

Payment for a Bow

"We are honored by what you and your dragon have done for us," Sedel shouted.

A chorus of shouts and cheers came as Kaen watched those at the table clap and whistle.

"Please! Feast upon what the land has given us!"

Kaen couldn't believe how much food was there. All sorts of berries, fruits, nuts, and more, as well as a cooked deer, awaited him and the others.

After scarfing down more food than he realized was possible, Kaen sat back and looked at Sedel.

She smiled and nodded, knowing he had questions.

"This is wonderful," Ava said. "This is totally different than the day we arrived. Tell me how you did this."

Shrugging, Kaen just smiled. "I wish I knew . . . the forest was dying, its power or life or whatever was weak. Those fires . . ."

Kaen sat back and cocked his head.

"You ok?"

"How do I suddenly know the fires did so much damage to the forest and its life force? We didn't talk about that, did we?"

Ava shook her head slowly from side to side. "Not while I was around."

It's the forest. I know the answer as you do.

Kaen sat up and closed his eyes. Activating his lifestone, he saw the power of the forest and all the life in everyone around him.

Pammon was off to the side, near one of the tables, and Kaen looked at his friend.

It's inside you . . . the power in you is different than before. I mean . . .

Kaen glanced at himself, looking at his body and then at the wood elves around him.

The color, the lights, the way it moves . . . we are like them somehow.

A thrum came from Pammon, and Kaen turned to see his friend looking at him.

Ask the forest what you did. I can hear it trying to talk through you.

Kaen calmed himself, taking breaths and letting the sounds of those near him fade away.

Quietly, a tiny thread of something touched him. Through his feet, the connection to the ground, he felt the power of the forest there.

Words didn't come, like he had expected, but just knowledge. A feeling.

The land was cleansed from the death that had tried to consume it. He realized now why Queleth had died so suddenly. He had given his life force to save the forest. It had been too much for one elf to heal, and it would be too much for one man to mend.

Kaen could sense that, but he also knew the forest had required Pammon. Together, they had done what was needed.

Then, a thread of something entered his mind.

Struggling to understand it, Kaen finally realized what it was. He had been cleansed.

Changing his vision, Kaen looked like a fool at the table as he undid the laces on his shirt and yanked it off, startling those around him as he stared at his chest, touching it.

"Kaen . . . your skin . . ." Ava's voice broke as she saw what he was looking at. She stood up, reaching out with a trembling hand and touching his skin as he smiled, nodded, and laughed. Both of them began to cry as they hugged each other.

After a moment, they turned and saw everyone trying not to stare politely but wondering what had just transpired before their eyes.

Coughing, Kaen quickly put his shirt back on and wiped his face.

"The forest cleansed me from an injury I could not find healing for."

Sedel nodded. "I had heard you were cleansed. I was not certain about what, but now we all know." She motioned to the elves, who were smiling and nodding as they watched him. "Again, I say it is good you have a wife because some might be willing to share if you desired another."

Ava's face turned red, and Kaen shook his head, rolling his eyes as Sedel laughed, content with her actions.

"Feast, eat, and relax. Later, we need to talk."

The celebration continued for some time, and Kaen was grateful when it was time for Sedel, Ava, and him to be alone. Pammon was sleeping soundly on the forest floor, having partaken of more animals than he usually would, somehow knowing, he said, that the forest did not mind.

"So tell me . . . why did you come?"

Sedel's question seemed obvious, but Kaen hadn't been expecting it.

"I need a bow. I lost mine in a fight with Stioks. There are no better archers or bow makers than the wood elves."

Sedel nodded. "That is true. What kind of bow do you need?"

"I would prefer one similar to the one you used. It was larger than mine and had more power. Its quality was exceptional. I also have two runes if you can use them in the bow's crafting."

Leaning forward, Sedel's eyes sparkled at Kaen's words.

"Runes? For a bow? This must be some exceptional work you are hoping for. I guess the next question would be when do you need it by?"

"You already know that answer."

She shrugged. "Yet when you tell me now, it makes me feel better when I say no."

Ava laughed, poking Kaen as she leaned against him, enjoying his arm around her. "I told you she would say something like that."

"You were right . . . but the truth is I need something better than my regular bow now. Even its slight magical power cannot allow me to use all of my strength. I have broken a few bows trying to see how far I could push my power through them, and what I now know is that the bow has to use my blood."

Leaning back in her seat, Sedel quietly clapped her hands together before rubbing them a few times. "You seem well informed in things most humans shouldn't know, but I guess none of this should surprise me. I'll ask one last question and then give you an answer. How much are you willing to pay for such a weapon?"

"I'll assume gold doesn't matter."

Sedel shook her head.

Kaen scratched his chin as he thought and knew precisely what she would need.

"I can't promise I can do what I did the other day, but I will give all I can."

"Then we shall make for you the finest bow you have ever held," Sedel answered, leaning forward, wearing a smile larger than any Kaen had ever seen her display before.

Kaen waited and watched as Sedel took the two runes he had gotten from the packs on Pammon's back.

Remind me how I committed to sharing my power again . . .

Kaen chuckled, knowing Pammon was not upset or bothered.

Unless you want me to get into a sword fight again, I need a bow that doesn't shatter when I infuse my power into the arrows . . . so tell me what you want to do . . .

We can do a portion of what we did last time. I'm still not completely recovered.

She understands. Now, what I really want to see is how she does this.

Sedel was carving out a section in the village's main tree. Once she felt the space was deep enough, she placed one of the runes in it. Measuring with her hands, she repeated the process lower in the tree but in the same line.

"Kaen, come here and cut yourself like you did last time. Place your hand above the top rune. When you are done, I will take care of the next part."

Moving to the spot where Sedel waited, Kaen cut his hand again, amazed at how fast it had healed and that there was no scar. Placing it on the hole with the first rune, Kaen closed his eyes, concentrating as before.

This time, there was no wall to break. The forest gladly accepted him, welcoming Pammon and him back as if they had lived here their whole life.

Kaen could feel its desire as they poured their power into the tree. He could sense that it was sending the energy he gave farther out into the areas that still needed help to recover and grow.

Then he felt himself drawn to the tree. Glancing down, he followed a single root that ran straight down. Deep within the soil was a basin, like an underground water area. Instead, it was slowly filling up with the power he and Pammon gave.

Kaen could hear the forest asking for as much as they would spare, knowing that this well needed to be full.

I can . . . still give . . .

Pammon was straining just as hard as he was, yet Kaen felt amazing. The amount of energy and life flowing from Pammon was like a tidal wave channeled through his hand.

It flowed down into the place below, and when he struggled to stay standing, the forest thanked him, cutting their flow.

Stumbling a little, Kaen took a few deep breaths and glanced over at Pammon. He could see that his energy had drained drastically. He was no longer the immense light that he had so often been.

You know this isn't the last time we will do this, don't you?

Kaen nodded as his lifestone went cold and his vision returned.

"When do you leave?" Sedel asked, her tone back to the one she had the day they competed in shooting arrows.

"Maybe tomorrow," Kaen replied, knowing they needed to sleep tonight at least.

"Good. When you return, it will be ready."

Kaen glanced at the tree where his hand had been and saw that it had sealed itself up.

"You're not going to let me watch, are you?"

She smirked and shook her head. "There are some things that may one day be revealed to you, but the forest must say that it is allowed . . . I think it has set a price, and you know how much that will cost."

Grunting, Kaen nodded and looked at Ava, who was waiting a few steps away.

"I don't suppose you have a room we could use that isn't at the top of the trees?"

Laughing, Sedel needed a moment before she could respond. Her complexion had turned red from laughing so hard and long. "I do. Are you ready to turn in?"

"More than ready," he replied, motioning to Pammon, who was already gently snoring.

"Then come, allow me to escort you both personally."

"What was it like?" Ava asked as they lay there, Kaen fighting off the sleep he desperately desired.

"How does one describe seeing the forest through its roots and every tiny aspect of it? The leaves shine and shimmer like all the stars at night. Insects have their own light, and underneath us is a maze of roots that seem to run forever in every direction."

Ava ran her hand over the spot that was no longer diseased. "And it was able to do this? How powerful or what is . . . I don't even know how to ask about it."

Kaen leaned over, kissing her on the head.

"I wish I could answer those questions, as I have them as well. I may never know, but what I do know is this. The forest is fighting in its own way, and it has cleansed me of something I wasn't sure even Amaranth or your father could heal. I feel amazing. Even though I am worn out and tired, I am at peace."

Ava ran her fingers through his beard and then gently tugged on it, pulling his lips closer to hers. "Then go to sleep, and perhaps you can show me how amazing you feel in the morning."

Kaen smiled and laid his head back, making a mental note to block his presence from Pammon in the morning.

39

A Return to Tanulivar

Kaen stared at the spot on the tree where he had bled and fed the forest the night before.

That spot looks different, doesn't it?

Nodding and not answering Pammon, Kaen ran his hand along the area and felt his skin rise up in goose bumps, every hair on his arm standing up.

"What is it?" Ava asked after he shuddered upon touching it.

"I'm not sure, but it's like . . . like I can feel part of me inside the tree right here," Kaen responded, slowly pulling his hand away.

"Five days, I need five days," Sedel said, smiling as she watched Kaen and Ava from a few feet away. "Do not show up before then, or I will send you off for a few more."

Kaen looked at Ava as she gently elbowed him in the side.

"If he tries, I'll make sure to stop him. Sometimes, he acts like a child who can't contain themself," Ava replied.

Sedel motioned to the people who were working around the village. "This place is alive again because of you and your dragon. We will never forget that the forest and our lives will always be connected to you."

She bowed and then clapped her hands. Two servants came forward, each with a small wooden box. They gave one each to Kaen and Ava.

"Do not open those yet, but once you return to Ebonmount, talk with the king and find two places within his border where he will allow you to plant those seeds. Once you plant them, do with them what you did here. It will create a connection through the earth to us. If ever the forest is in such peril as before, you will be able to sense it through your connection with those."

Kaen looked at the smooth, dark brown box that was barely bigger than the palm of his hand. He wanted to open it, curious about what was inside, but he resisted, instead bowing to Sedel. "We are honored by this gift."

"Queleth was right when he told me you were different," Sedel replied, a slight smirk on her lips. "He knew I was furious about how you beat me back then, but you still showed honor and grace. Those are not traits most humans or Dragon Riders have been known for. Combined with your youth . . . Just remember, we need five days to craft this bow. Until then, may your journey be successful."

Tell me, is everything going to be like this?

Kaen chewed on his lip as he looked at the forest below.

I'm not certain, but we have both talked many times about fate. You and I do not believe our lives are scripted out for us, yet when things like that happen . . . it is hard not to wonder why.

Your wife agrees with us but even she has been struggling to deal with everything that seems to keep coming against us. Are we strong enough to weather all these storms, or will we eventually break from the constant beating?

Kaen chuckled, rolling his eyes even though no one could see his expression.

If you talk like that, you have been having it out with Aldric or Bren way too much. That sounds like something one of them might say.

It was what Bren said a few years back, and I now understand it better. How many times have we endured impossible storms and yet risen above them? Sure, we come away bruised, battered, and beaten, but still, we are stronger on the other side. Look at Hess. Even though he lost an arm and is weaker physically, his mind and will are stronger than ever. I'm not sure he would be the family man he is today if he had both arms.

Scratching his beard, Kaen knew the truth of that statement. Hess had some dark moments, but his will and outlook on life changed once he rose above them. That man lived as if every day was a blessing, and it had taken a while for Kaen to understand that.

My question is, when is the next storm coming?

Probably in a week. The clouds are forming already.

Groaning, Kaen ignored Pammon's joke and looked east, seeing the clouds Pammon had just pointed out.

Soon enough, winter will be here.

It had taken effort for Pammon to fly slow and take his time as he carried Ava and Kaen toward Tanulivar.

The land beneath them was bleak, as most of the forest had been cleared miles from the farms that still operated.

Only the dwarves needed to manage the fields were out there, protected by a small company of warriors in case an attack came.

Rows of orc and goblin corpses were lined up a few hundred yards from the tree line—a reminder to all those who came that their people would die as well.

Ava says she never realized how sad this place looked.

I'm afraid of what it might look like on the inside. It does not appear there are many dwarves living outside anymore. I can see a few fields that have not been used in a year.

War is an awful thing. Primarily when it serves no purpose but to remove an obstacle in the way of tyranny.

Groaning, Kaen punched Pammon's neck gently.

That was Aldric from two years ago. I'll never forget that line.

Thrumming, Pammon made his way toward the landing area they used on their last visit.

Once I drop you two off and we get unloaded, I must find something to eat. The few animals I see would probably get us both in trouble if I consumed them.

Through Pammon's eyes, Kaen saw the land as his dragon did. Fields that had once had hundreds of sheep or cows now only had a few dozen. The walls that surrounded them looked in worse shape than he remembered.

"Dragon Rider Kaen!" the short dwarf shouted, approaching him and Ava as they climbed off Pammon. "We were not expecting you!"

"I had not decided to come until a few days ago!" replied Kaen. "How many dwarves do you have with you?"

Kaen recognized Brabrel, Elnidith's second-in-command when she was here before she left for Ebonmount. He had aged, and a few silver hairs were noticeable in his beard.

"Maybe eight total. Do you need help with those packs?" Brabrel asked as he looked at the bundles tied on Pammon's back.

"I do. Dragon scales. Black dragon scales, in fact."

The dwarf's eyes became wider than a saucer as he looked at Kaen and then at the bundles. Joy and hope began to appear on the dwarf's face.

"Stioks?"

Kaen shook his head, seeing Brabrel scowl at learning the man was still alive.

"It's a long story, one best told inside and out of the cold. Also, this is my wife, Ava. Ava, this is Brabrel, the guardian of the house."

"Protector," Brabrel shot back. "'Tis a pleasure to meet you, Miss Ava. Please come inside and enjoy our fire. If you want to sleep here tonight, I can offer a small snack and perhaps something else to eat."

"I would prefer that," Kaen answered as he went with Ava and Brabrel toward the two-story building. "Let's get this unloaded, and then I can pester you about what has happened since last time I was here."

Brabrel groaned as he heard Kaen's words, tugging his beard slightly. "I'll need some ale if we are talking like that."

Kaen watched Ava sit by the fire in her chair, a small blanket draped over her legs as she sipped on a mug of dwarven ale.

"She's a good-looking one, even if she doesn't have a beard," Brabrel teased. "Should I ask how in the world you managed to marry her?"

"We don't have enough time for that—years of planning and trickery. Besides, since it's just you and me, I need to know the status of your kingdom. Both of us know that Bosgreth always holds back when he and I talk."

Taking a swig from his tankard, Brabrel nodded as he wiped the foam from his beard. "Aye, we both know that. What can I say . . . life isn't all that great. Dwarves were meant to live in the mountains. Never coming out or feeling the sun on your face, hold some fresh dirt up to your nose. That isn't living. It's a wonder the people haven't revolted sometimes."

"How are the other dwarves? Still staying strong?"

Brabrel scratched his head as he scrunched his weathered nose. "We are a strong race. A little ale and some coins make most happy. The food we eat doesn't taste the same. What is growing in the mountains makes an awful drink. The bread doesn't taste much better. Even the animals are having a hard time dealing with the changes. The only ones that have done well are those damn goats."

Kaen pointed at the table where some dried jerky was still lying on it. "Goat meat?"

"Goat meat!" exclaimed Brabrel. "I'm glad I can have some meat, but after a few years of just goat meat, I'm saying I would do a few crazy things to taste beef or mutton again. And the price of a chicken . . . you can almost buy a piece of land. Those things are worth more than men now, I reckon."

A small snort came from Ava, who was trying not to eavesdrop.

"It's ok, lass. You can laugh. That is the one thing we still have even when things get tough. We laugh and sing songs."

"How long since the last time the orcs came?" Kaen asked, picking up a piece of the jerky and trying it again.

"In force or at all?"

"Both."

Brabrel set his tankard on the table and leaned back in his chair. Closing his eyes, he put his hand behind his head and tapped a foot on the floor for a few seconds.

"Two weeks ago a small raiding party came through. About one hundred. Killed over half before they ran away. Seems like a waste on their part. Especially since it was mainly goblins and a few orcs."

Opening his eyes, Brabrel looked at Kaen. "Since a full attack? Over two years. They easily lost twenty thousand plus. They never made it past the first section of the bridge. Upset a lot of the engineers hoping to show off the breakaway points and drop an army into the ravine."

"So why are you all still in there?"

Snorting, Brabrel glanced around the room and then sat up straight. "You know why. Until the day Stioks is dead, I doubt we will ever come outside those walls again."

Ava said, "Can I ask a question?"

Brabrel smiled. "Ask anything you want, ma'am."

"What do the dwarves want? Do they want to stay in the mountain, or do they want to come outside?"

"No one knows for certain. Some want to stay safe, especially those with younger children. A few are upset they missed the chance to travel to Ebonmount, live outside, and work there. Many, however, have heard how bad things are in your area and are grateful they don't have to deal with that fear. And then there is the news of Roccnari . . ."

Kaen watched as Brabrel swished his tongue around in his mouth. Suddenly, the dwarf leaned over and spat on the ground.

"A whole nation . . . gone . . ." Brabrel said, looking at Ava. "That is why most don't mind hiding behind the wall and stone. No one wants to imagine that happening here. So if you ask a dwarf now what they want to do, almost every single one will say live in the mountain."

"But why are you out here, then?"

Tapping the table with his stubby fingers, Brabrel sighed. "Honestly . . . I'm a bit of a dreamer. Elnidith caused that problem. She gave me a vision of a different world. That means I understand death could come every day. I might wake up and trip, breaking my neck and dying next to my bed. I could die in the field, tripping in a hole. An orc or ogre might get lucky and bash my head in. Even better, a dragon might swoop down and eat me. Since I learned these things, I haven't wanted to live in a mountain. I want to fight and liberate my people so we can again be free."

Ava smiled and then looked back at the fire. "Now I know why Kaen likes you. You two are a lot alike."

40

A Different Welcome

Kaen and Ava stood near the bridge. Looking over the side, they saw a cluster of bodies.

"So many," she said in a hushed tone.

"Aye," Dagan replied. His voice carried more joy in that statement than Kaen could ever remember hearing from the king's dwarf. "They were foolish to think they could ever cross this bridge. You already saw the fortifications before they could even make it here."

Ava looked at Kaen, who was studying one of the joining pieces of the bridge. "And this bridge actually can break apart?"

A smug smile now rested on Dagan's lips as the dwarf gently stroked his brown beard. "That it does. We would have drawn them into the next pillar if they'd managed to get past the first section. Once there, the chains would have been freed, and this entire piece would pivot, depositing their foul bodies to the chasm below."

Kaen coughed, tapping a few sections of the bridge Dagan had just discussed. "When was the last time you tested those and this hinge?"

The dwarf's eyebrows danced as he raised them up and down while moving to where Kaen was. "It's been . . . I think . . ." He turned and looked at one of the guards waiting for them. "Grombdul! When did we test these last?"

The plate-wearing dwarf he had just called out sputtered for a moment and then shrugged. "Sir! I'm not certain, but I believe it was at least within the last two decades!"

Kaen started making some noises as he sucked wind through his teeth. Pulling his dagger from its sheath, he slipped it between the joints and pried up some packed sediments.

"What are you doing?" Dagan asked, barely stopping himself before pushing Kaen away.

"Look," Kaen replied, not looking up as he pounded and forced his dagger into the almost cementlike layer. "It's so hard it might not actually hinge like you want it to. The weight might make it happen, but if it didn't . . ."

Dagan's eyes widened as he snorted, his mustache moving from the amount of air he was blowing out. "Why . . . how can you think to know more than a dwarf? This is our bridge. Of course it will work!"

Kaen stood up, cleaning off his dagger against his pants and slipping it into his sheath. Afterward, he grabbed the backpack he was carrying. "I hear you . . . but I'm just saying you might want to test the bridge or have a crew clean this entire thing out. Imagine how bad things might get if you needed it to work, and it didn't. Especially if Bosgreth found out later you had been warned."

The two of them stared each other down. Dagan was utterly beside himself to be told by a human that a dwarven marvel of technology might not work, while Kaen was frustrated at the constant way the dwarves never believed he knew anything.

Dagan gave in first, snapping his fingers as he shouted. "Grombdul, get a pair of engineers to inspect this point immediately. Have them report to me directly what they find!"

The sound of plate boots running across the bridge rang out, and Kaen gave a slight nod to Dagan, who dismissed it as he moved farther along the bridge.

"We need to go inside. The king is anxious to talk with you about certain things."

Ava rolled her eyes as she fell in step with Kaen, who mimicked her reaction and shrugged.

"You warned me," she whispered.

"And you didn't believe me," Kaen replied quietly.

The sounds of the castle echoed through the halls as an entire race was packed together, trying to manage the daily chores.

Ava stared in awe as they traversed the walkways, which encircled a huge open section that had been dug out. Within it was a park with trees and grass being cared for by workers.

"They are actually still alive," Kaen stated.

"You didn't believe we could keep them alive, did you?" Dagan asked when he saw Kaen's expression.

"I had my doubts," Kaen admitted as he pointed to a few places for Ava. "Part of me wants to know how much dirt you all moved into here to make that and the farms happen. I noticed the huge sections of ground off to the west last time that were gone. The manpower . . ."

"You mean dwarven power," Dagan corrected him with a grunt. "You seem to forget the willpower we have. Perhaps I can find someone to show you and your wife the levels we have dedicated completely to supplying food."

Moving closer to Dagan, Ava put on her best smile and pointed at one of the massive lightstones hanging on a pole near the park below them. "Forgive me if this is a foolish question, but those lightstones, how long can they last?"

Huffing, Dagan tried to reduce his unpleasant demeanor and smiled for Ava. "Those eight lightstones are only found here," he replied with a grin. "Our workers are making extra because they only last a few weeks. The energy required to charge and make those uses a fair amount of our available magic power."

"And similar ones are at the farming grounds?"

Dagan nodded as he motioned to the stairs leading down. "I think I may have a little time to show you the park before we go and see Bosgreth."

"Oh, I would love that!" exclaimed Ava as she gently touched the dwarf's shoulder before moving back to Kaen with a slight spring in her step.

She missed the dwarf's cheeks and forehead turning red, but Kaen did not.

Without another word, Dagan almost skipped down the stairs.

"As you can see, only a few dwarves are allowed in the park simultaneously. There is a drawing from all the people, which allows them a turn. Every name is in the pot, and trading your spot is prohibited."

"That seems like a great idea," Ava said as she and Dagan walked around the edge of the grass. She had taken the dwarf's arm in hers and led him like a puppy with a treat.

Kaen strolled behind them, chuckling to himself at hearing Dagan speaking more today than he could remember in all their other visits combined.

Bending down at the edge, Kaen felt the grass with his fingertips.

When he had done that, a few grunts came from the guards behind him.

Dagan turned and looked at Kaen with a frown.

"We aren't supposed to touch the grass if it's not our turn. The caretakers have mentioned how easily we could damage the grass if everyone did that."

Kaen stood up. "I understand. Forgive me."

A gentle squeeze on Dagan's arm drew his attention to Ava and that smile she had mastered, earning Kaen nothing more than a nod as the two began their walk again.

Hours after they should have arrived at the golden doors that led to Bosgreth's throne room, Kaen smiled as his wife moved back to him, letting Dagan prepare himself before they entered.

"You should be an emissary with how well you handled all of that," Kaen whispered, earning a playful tongue extended in his direction.

"You're just jealous that he likes me and not you."

Shrugging, Kaen pointed at the massive golden door that was opening.

The noise of shouting and yelling from inside reached their ears, now explaining why the doors had been shut in the first place.

Once those engaged in the shouting match finally noticed the small procession approaching them and King Bosgreth, they quieted down and moved to opposite sides of the long carpet leading to the throne.

"Dragon Warrior Kaen!" Bosgreth exclaimed, his look of relief washing away the frustrated one he'd had a few seconds ago. "Welcome, and thank you for your timely appearance."

Dagan winced at those last words, even though his king had never looked at him.

"King Bosgreth, I am honored as always to be allowed to see you," Kaen replied, giving a slight bow as he continued moving toward the king and through the pack of dwarves focused on him and Ava.

"Allow me, if you would, to introduce my wife. Ava Marshell."

Bosgreth moved off his throne and down the few steps. Even with all the white hair and wrinkles that marked him as older than dirt, his movement did not affect his age.

Ignoring protocols and the whispers that could be heard, Bosgreth approached Ava and gave her a slight nod. Holding out his hand, he waited, and once she put hers in his, the old dwarf leaned forward and kissed it gently.

"Lady Marshell, meeting the one person who could bind this man is an honor."

Kaen and Bosgreth started to laugh, and Ava looked at the two of them for a moment before realizing the joke.

"I'm not sure who has bonded who, but I am grateful every day I get to wake up next to him."

A brief moment of pain flashed across Bosgreth's face as he grimaced momentarily, replacing it with a smile that had been mastered over a lifetime. "To have someone you love like that and be able to wake up next to them is a gift greater than anything else. Cherish it always."

Ava nodded, and Kaen squeezed her hand as she stood beside him.

"Now then, since you two are finally here, let us move to a room off to the side where we can discuss things privately." After he finished talking, Bosgreth gave both groups about to protest a glare, cutting off any words they might say.

"Dagan, please ensure that our advisors are led back to the duties they are expected to fulfill. Afterward, if you can make it in time, come join us."

Dagan gave a very stiff bow and turned, his facial expression hidden from Kaen and Ava but not from the dwarves, who immediately began to hurry toward the golden doors across the throne room.

After the gaggle of dwarves was halfway across the room, Bosgreth sighed.

"I will probably pay for calling him out like that, but he knew how quickly I wanted to see you both."

"That is my fault," Ava blurted out. "I may have used my feminine charms and gotten a tour of the park and a few other areas."

Sighing, Bosgreth nodded and motioned to the door at the side of the hall they were going to go through. "I had no doubts . . . that one can be swayed by a woman's voice and hand. Much has changed since you last were here, and I am interested in all the news you bring. So let's move to the room I have prepared and talk there."

Without waiting for a response, Bosgreth moved toward the room, a slight limp showing up after the first few steps.

Kaen and Ava moved quickly to catch up, Ava looking and pointing at different decorations within the throne room. The entire time, Kaen kept one eye on the dwarven king. He could see what Bosgreth was trying to hide.

The king was dying.

41

Gift Given

Kaen watched as Bosgreth slumped into his padded chair and waved away the only attendant in the room.

In the moments since he descended from the throne to this new chair behind closed doors, the dwarf had significantly aged.

Bosgreth looked up and saw Kaen studying him and let out a sigh. "I'll assume your watchful eye has noticed what I try to hide from the others. You two come and sit next to me. We need to talk."

Kaen nodded and moved to the chair Bosgreth indicated next to him. After helping Ava sit, he turned and saw those watchful eyes studying him.

"You've changed, Kaen, since the last we talked. Something is different. Tell me."

Unable to resist a smile, Kaen shared with Bosgreth everything that had happened since the last time they talked.

Stroking his white beard, which had become thinner, Bosgreth still wore the frown he had acquired once Kaen shared the news of Stioks's new dragon.

"Yet you managed to slay the black dragon and one of his mates. That must be a feat indeed."

"I'd like to say I played a role in that, but everything is due to Pammon. He won that fight for us. I was far outclassed and outmatched."

The king leaned over, grabbed his cup, and took a drink slowly. He watched Ava and Kaen and chuckled after a moment. "Twins . . . that is a fortunate thing indeed. I will pray that the spirits watch over you and them both. May they enjoy the success you will bring for all of us."

Ava smiled and slightly bowed her head. "I am grateful for your kindness to Kaen all these years. I know he has shared many stories about how you always try to send him away under the effects of a certain beverage."

Bosgreth choked on his drink and started coughing. Pounding his chest a few times, the king smirked at Kaen. "I'm surprised you told her about those times. I remember you always commenting about wanting to keep them a secret."

"A secret with my wife is not something I want to keep. I don't hold anything back from her."

"As it should be . . . I miss the companionship and friendship of my wife, but soon I will see her again, as you can tell." Having spoken, Bosgreth shifted in his chair and winced. "I may only have a year more at best. Those who have spent years helping me stay strong are certain there is little more they can do to help me anymore and . . . I'm tired. Tired of how this has all taken place. Daily, I fight against my own people and an enemy that seems bent on destroying us."

Bosgreth snapped a finger, and his attendant came and bent his ear to the king. After they had exchanged a private whisper, the dwarf moved to a side room and shut the door.

"I have already set things in motion. Dagan will be the next king. It will draw some ire, but he is the only one I can trust with this task. Are you willing to support him?"

Kaen could feel those eyes reading him again. Even without strength in his body, the king had no lack of willpower and mental fortitude. "I know that Dagan is committed to the dwarves and their safety. While he is a bit young . . . I can see how, in time, he will be a great king."

Laughing, Bosgreth nodded. "'Young' would be a nice way to put it. That dwarf is barely a hundred years old. Meanwhile, I am pushing three hundred and have outlived what most considered I was capable of. If you can help guide him . . . I know that we can once again enjoy the time of prosperity with men and dragons that the legends tell of."

Ava had let her normally composed face show the shock when she heard how old Bosgreth was, and the king smiled at her. "Do not worry about how old I am. If what I hear about Dragon Riders is true, your husband will live longer than most dwarves."

Nodding, Ava winced a little, and Bosgreth realized what his words had done. "Forgive me . . . I had forgotten what that would mean."

"No apologies are needed, King Bosgreth. It is a truth everyone who loves a Dragon Rider must endure. Hopefully, things will change in the coming years, and we can solve that issue."

Bosgreth looked at Kaen and gave him a forced smile. "So, what do you need from me?" he asked. "We both know you aren't here for a friendly visit."

"I need armor crafted from those scales and quickly. My current armor is damaged and . . ."

"You still haven't found a way to open the case that houses the armor in Ebonmount?"

"Not yet," Kaen replied. "I have tried everything I can think of, and nothing has worked. Not even using my blood like some of the boxes I thought the case might resemble."

Grunting, Bosgreth turned when he heard the door open and saw his attendant come in with a small box. He motioned to Ava and smiled when his dwarven helper stopped before her.

"Mrs. Marshell, I would like to offer you a gift. I had hoped to give one to my child one day, but as life sometimes happens, that never worked out."

Her blue eyes gazed at the golden box the size of a small pack; she looked at Kaen and then back at Bosgreth. "I'm not sure I—"

"Nonsense, you wouldn't deny a dying king's request, would you?"

Kaen smirked as he watched Ava look at him. "Don't ruin your perfect record as an emissary," he teased.

Sighing, Ava reached for the golden box, her hands trembling slightly as she lifted the lid and leaned forward to look inside.

"Oh!"

Her voice and pitch made Kaen lean forward in his chair. He tried to see what was inside, but he couldn't because of the angle and depth of the box.

"I can't," Ava gasped as she looked at Bosgreth. Her face flushed as she glanced at the item inside the golden box. "It's too much."

"Please," Bosgreth replied, his voice low and pleading. "That has sat by my bed for so long. Seeing you and Kaen together and hearing what you both have been through, I cannot think of a better person to wear that now. It was made for a queen, so why not the wife of our only hope in the coming days?"

Unable to take it any longer, Kaen stood up and moved to where he could see what was in the box. Inside was a single necklace. The metal was pure gold, crafted in a technique he had never seen. In the middle of it was a massive ruby, so red and bright it almost looked like there was a light inside it.

"Bosgreth . . . that is—"

"This is a gift for your wife. Now help me here and put it on her," the king said, interrupting Kaen, who had started to protest.

Kaen turned and looked at his dwarven friend, seeing how his eyes pleaded with him. He reached inside, running his fingers along the edge of the chain until he felt the clasp. It came apart so quickly when he pushed a small piece, yet he knew it wouldn't just open on its own.

Lifting it slowly from the box, he moved toward Ava, who was struggling to accept the gift. As he got behind her, he leaned forward and draped it around her neck. She lifted her hair, and Kaen closed the clasp and let the necklace rest against her skin.

"Just how I remember it," Bosgreth sighed. "I know my love would be ok with this decision."

"Thank you," Ava gushed as she stood up and approached Bosgreth. Hesitating a moment, she ignored any potential breach of decorum and bent over, kissing the king on the forehead.

Bosgreth blushed, wiping a tear from his eye.

"What about me?" Kaen asked jokingly. "Surely there has to be something sparkly for me."

Ava and Bosgreth laughed, and Kaen kissed his wife on the cheek, getting an eye roll for his comment.

"I'll give you armor instead," Bosgreth replied. "The books and helmet are done, but I wasn't sure when we could get them to you. Not something one just sends off in a cart across this world during this time."

Kaen sat back down. "How long will it take to make what I asked from the scales I dropped off yesterday?"

Sensing the change in mood, Bosgreth shifted and winced again from the pain of the movement. "We understand the processes and have made a few chest pieces for some of our dwarves from the leftover ones you first gave. Sadly, we cannot modify those to fit you, but we can now make them much faster. Do you still want four suits?"

Kaen nodded and saw Ava's face.

"Four?"

Bosgreth looked at Kaen and saw the smirk the young man wore. "You haven't told her?"

"I was planning on it after they were done."

"You're making me a suit?" Ava asked. She looked confused at his decision. "Why?"

"Well . . ." Kaen turned to face her. "I was thinking that when the time came to fight, you and Amaranth could fly together and use your spells to help. You're one of the stronger mages I know, and your knowledge and power would be useful on the battlefield."

Touching her stomach, Ava moved her hand softly. "What about the babies?"

"That is a choice for you, but if you decide to join us, then I can think of no better protection than the armor Bosgreth would make for you."

"I would be honored to do so," Bosgreth chimed in. "It has been a long time since I have overseen the process, but I might find some joy in going down to the forge and checking on the process for your suit."

Ava looked at both men, shocked that they might consider such a thing acceptable. "A pregnant woman on the battlefield? That seems . . ."

"Dwarven women do it all the time. Some say it makes them the fiercest warriors. Knowing they fight not only for those who are alive and next to them but also for the life inside them." Bosgreth shook his head as he looked up at the ceiling, lost in his thoughts. "It's been a hundred years at least, but we had a group of dwarven women, seven of them pregnant, leading a charge against orcs . . . they tore through those beasts as if they were nothing, spurring on every man near them. One of their children is the one I have suggested to be king."

"Dagan?" Kaen asked.

"Yes. His mother was a powerful woman. I remember her and my wife, Gradnulla, spending many nights laughing together."

Bosgreth turned and looked at Ava, who was still gently rubbing her belly. "Perhaps your children will be just as great, not just because of the blood that they come from but because of the commitment of their mother."

"You think too highly of me," Ava replied. "We have barely met!"

"Yet I see how your husband looks at you and has grown because of you. There is something to be said about a man with a wife like you."

42

Giving a Gift Back

Bosgreth's serious look caught Kaen and Ava off guard. "You two are adventurers, and I have spent enough time and effort to research a few things. Your children are going to be like both of you. Strong and capable. With you both raising them, they would be humans my people will accept—just as I have made that happen."

The attendant came forward, pulled a rolled-up piece of paper from his vest, and handed it to Bosgreth.

"Inside here is a document that names Kaen an honorary dwarf."

Kaen couldn't help but chuckle, and even Ava snorted at that comment.

"Don't laugh, even though I see the humor in that statement," Bosgreth continued. "Your status as a Dragon Rider carries many things, but this changes everything. You can go anywhere without needing an escort. Your presence will be treated as one of our own. You can even have a place built within the mountain for you." Leaning forward and ignoring the obvious effort it took, Bosgreth motioned to the map that hung on the wall across the room. "Every dwarf has the ability to own land. No human or elf can ever own land in our domain. You, Kaen Marshell, can be the first human to have that privilege. Upon my passing, a portion of my family's estate has been willed to you. Some have not taken kindly to this gesture of mine. The act of giving you the dwarven title was one thing. Giving you land told them how serious I am about this."

Bosgreth held out the paper to Kaen and waited. Kaen accepted it and opened it quickly to avoid making the king wait longer.

Reading the document, Kaen felt a warm feeling inside him growing. "Bosgreth . . . this is too much."

"No, it's not!" exclaimed the dwarf as he slammed his hand onto the rail of his chair. "You and your dragon fight for something you don't have to. Every report I have ever heard from our people in Ebonmount is how you have treated them as your own. As such, today, I have adopted you as my own. You shall carry on a part of my name, and I cannot be happier hearing that it shall have two children with it."

Ava had a few tears forming in her eyes as she moved to read what Kaen was holding.

Kaen pointed to a paragraph, and both read it multiple times.

Dragon Rider Kaen Marshell is formally added to the bloodline of Bosgreth, King of the Dwarves. They shall be granted a tomb upon the day they require it, buried with the royal family. All spouses and children shall bear the name and receive the same privilege for a thousand years.

Kaen gave the paper to Ava, knelt, and bowed to the dwarf. "Thank you," he whispered. His chest shook slightly from the strain of what he felt inside. His lifestone was raging on its own, and his mind was trying to comprehend all that this would change.

"What does all this mean?" Ava asked as she motioned at a few other lines on the sheet.

"I'm assuming you are looking at the lines about war?" Bosgreth asked.

"Yes."

The dwarf raised his white eyebrows and shrugged. "When he finally feels that it is time for a battle that will end all battles, the dwarves will follow him. Not even Dagan can deny that request if I am not here to honor it."

"I will do what I can to earn this," Kaen said, rising to stand beside Ava. "There is something I want to do if you are willing to allow it."

Bosgreth's eyes narrowed, and he studied Kaen's face and the grin his now-adopted family member proudly displayed. "I may regret this, but what is this request?"

Sighing, Bosgreth felt the grass beneath his bare feet and smiled as they moved through the park. A crowd of dwarves had gathered around the edges, spreading word that their king was in the garden, walking with the Dragon Rider and his wife.

"This is a feeling I have not felt in a very long time," Bosgreth said as he grimaced a little, feeling blades of grass slide between his stubby toes. "It has been far too long since I have allowed myself to feel the earth against my skin."

Kaen smiled, and they all slowly walked toward the tree in the center, choosing a path through the grass rather than the stone one most used. "I want to give something to you all, and I am starting to see a pattern. Things are given for a reason. I believe that is true for what I was given for this moment as well."

The murmurs of the dwarves, who watched as the three finally stood next to the tree, rose to a clamor when Kaen pulled out a knife. The sounds of a few armored guards on the edge made Bosgreth turn and hold up his hand.

"Are you really going to try and do that?"

Kaen nodded. "I feel I need to, to show my people that I am willing to give them a part of me."

The king's face now showed a smile that Kaen had only seen a few times, and he nodded as Kaen sliced a piece of bark off the tree. The bark was brittle and weak, and even with the dirt that had been brought in and the stones they used to give it light, the roots were unable to acquire the nutrients they needed.

You ready?

I am, though I must say the guards were not very excited when I landed close to the bridge. It is good that you had some guards come and warn them this would happen.

I did mention what was in the letter: a flock of animals for you to always enjoy when the dwarves are once again no longer forced to hide inside.

When that day comes, I hope they are prepared for the meal I shall enjoy. Let's get on with this.

Kaen motioned to Ava, who came close.

"Hold my hand if you would."

Ava nodded, giving Kaen an expression he had seen countless times when she wasn't sure what would happen but trusted him with every part of her.

Kaen cut his palm with the knife, putting it away and then pushing his bleeding hand against the cut he had made in the tree. Reaching out, he grasped Ava's hand.

"I love you," he whispered and then closed his eyes, opening his lifestone to the power that raged inside him. His heart was overwhelmed at what Bosgreth had done. It showed an acceptance that Kaen had never considered possible. Now he wanted to give back to those he might one day be able to dwell among for short moments.

The tree heard him, and pain filled Kaen's soul as he saw the lack of energy and life within it. It was so dull compared to what he had seen in the forest with the wood elves. How it was even alive surprised him.

Thank you again, Pammon.

We do this for family. Which I am learning is growing daily.

Kaen couldn't help but chuckle at Pammon's joke until the power of his friend—and in this moment, he realized, his closest family member—flooded him.

The tree drank from him and Pammon. Power flowed through their bond and into the tree. Kaen saw it pour through the tree, and the power spread through the entire park in an instant. Branches extended, leaves grew, the trunk became stronger, and a crack echoed in his ears.

Grunts and then sounds of people murmuring and then cheering rang out through the mountain.

Ava's hand squeezed his, and he felt her through that connection. A small flicker of power came from her hand into his, and even with all the noise of the dwarves around them, he heard her gasp.

His mind went back to the tree. Roots grew and burrowed through the rock, somehow forcing their way through their stone prison. Deeper and deeper they went, finding weak points in the stone and following a path to a place they somehow knew.

How much will we give?

I will give everything I can. They need this.

Pammon didn't reply, but a surge of power came from Pammon, and Kaen matched it, willing his lifestone to burn hot. From his hand clasped with Ava's, he felt her lending power, not the storm that surged from his dragon but a reminder that she wanted to be a part of this.

The root burrowing through the rock expanded, growing thicker, and drove like a spear through leather, easily penetrating the stone prison.

Kaen could see and feel it as it plunged through the mountain, amazed at how much life and power was flowing through the tree. He could sense it spreading around him, and it was connected to the rest of the park. His focus was on the root that was doing what seemed impossible.

And then it stopped, branching out from where it had broken through the stone into an area filled with water. Those roots surged toward the water, filling the space with tiny roots that soaked up the water that it desperately needed.

Exhaustion hit as the tree cut the connection between them. Kaen leaned against the tree, using its weight to support him, and felt Ava collapse against him.

You always seem to give in ways I cannot imagine possible. Open your eyes.

Kaen turned off the view he had been using and saw the park that had once seemed barely alive, now lush green and having spilled out past the original borders erected for it. All around him, the grass had extended almost fifty yards in every direction, springing up and growing under the feet of the dwarves who had been standing and watching.

The tree he was leaning against was now strong, its bark no longer dry and brittle; instead, a canopy of branches and lively leaves covered the area. The other smaller trees that had been planted were also thriving, their limbs having grown some and leaves covering them in thick foliage.

Turn left.

Kaen paused, wondering why Pammon had said that.

Turning to the left, he felt wonder and awe through their link.

That is a marvelous sight. Now I see what the world looks like through your eyes.

Shock hit Kaen as he heard those words from Pammon, and something happened in their connection.

[Two Souls Become One]
[Bond of a Single Being - Unlocked]

Kaen's legs went weak and became stronger at the same moment. For half a heartbeat, he felt ready to collapse, and for the next half, he felt he could climb the tallest mountain without pause.

What was that?!

Pammon said nothing, but Kaen felt everything his dragon felt. All the fears and concerns that Pammon had been holding back, keeping secrets from Kaen, were no longer blocked by the wall that had been built. The fear of losing Glynnis or Amaranth, the death of his rider. An ache from hearing Juthom talking about what Stioks did to his mother. Like a flood, it rushed through Kaen's mind and heart.

Are you . . . crying?

Pammon felt everything Kaen had been hiding as well. All his doubts, fears, and the overwhelming regret and pain of his decisions. Knowing that Ava was pregnant with twins scared him more than he would ever admit. Neither could hide anything at that moment, and the emotions swirled between them.

I am so sorry . . . I didn't know . . .

How could you? We both have hid our pain from each other, trying not to burden each other with what we feel.

Time stopped as they saw each other for a moment without any pretending.

Two beings who were scared about people and a dragon they loved and never knew if the next day might be their last with them.

You need to forgive me. I am sorry for not being honest.

And I you . . . I am sorry for what I hid.

No more. I am not certain we can hide those feelings ever again.

I don't want to. You mean so much to me.

You need to answer Ava. She is talking to you and looks worried.

Kaen blinked and saw Ava staring at him.

"Are you ok? What's wrong?"

Reaching up with his free hand, Kaen felt his cheeks. They were wet.

"Sorry . . . I . . . Pammon and I . . . we are different now. Our bond has changed."

Ava's face scrunched, and her eyebrows narrowed as she looked at her husband. "We will talk later. Right now, we need to deal with Bosgreth.

Turning around, Kaen saw the dwarven king on his knees. Tears had washed down his wrinkling face, yet a smile greater than one Kaen had ever witnessed was plastered on his face.

"My boy . . . thank you."

43

A New Forest

The celebration that night and the next day had been the first moment the dwarves had remembered to live in a very long time.

Every dwarf came and saw the new park, getting a chance to walk on the grass and feel it under their feet. Each of them was in awe of the change and how the air seemed alive and refreshing near it.

Food and beer flowed as King Bosgreth opened the stores and had a celebration marking what Kaen, Ava, and Pammon had done for their people. He also announced to all the proclamation, granting Kaen and Ava dwarf status.

Pammon received a rare treat of a cow, brought out to him for what he had done to aid the tree's growth.

That night, Kaen and Ava met their new family and celebrated life coming back to the dwarves.

"I know you must leave, but we have a few things to discuss," Bosgreth said as Dagan joined them in his private room. "We must reveal some changes the two of us have agreed on."

Kaen and Ava sat in their chairs, watching the pair as both dwarves smiled.

"I will step down in the coming weeks, aiding Dagan's transition to king. After hearing your praises the other night, none shall go against him. Thank you for that."

Kaen smiled at Dagan, who seemed giddy with the news he and Bosgreth planned to share.

"We have also decided it is time for us to move back to the world outside the mountain and not hide in here as we have."

Kaen felt his jaw drop at that news, seeing both dwarves excited about that announcement.

"It will come slowly and in stages," Dagan said, taking over from where Bosgreth had stopped. "We will need to select specific groups to help strengthen different areas, but we must remember that we will not be scared into hiding. If the orcs attack, they will find us ready to meet them on our land, using their blood as the fertilizer for our plants."

"I don't know what to say, but wow. I'm sure that news will be well accepted."

"It will be my first act as king," Dagan replied. "With Bosgreth standing next to me and the two of us announcing our agreement, it will help secure the support of all the dwarves. Now, on to another thing. I will have our smiths working as quickly as possible on your armor. It will probably take us four months to complete all the sets."

"Would it be faster if you only did one?"

Shaking his head, Dagan tapped his chest. "It's faster if we make each of the four pieces simultaneously. Making one chest and then starting the greaves would be longer than making one and then making the other three. Only one forge in our mountain can actually heat and shape them. It would be best if we gave you all four at the same time, or you are welcome to come and pick up the pieces that are done every month."

"Don't forget," Bosgreth cut in. "When your children are born, I want to know right away. I want to personally oversee the etching of their names under yours in my family quarters. I have our artisans working on that right now, adding a branch for the Marshells."

Ava bowed slightly. "I am grateful for that. I cannot wait to see that one day."

"Now, is there anything else we can do to help the two of you before you leave us?"

Kaen stood and looked at Dagan. "How about you hug me before you become too stuffy and act like Bosgreth, unable to show emotion."

Roaring, Dagan rose to his feet, and both men grasped each other's forearms and embraced. "I am grateful for you, Kaen Marshell. Forgive me if I have been a bit gruff with you."

Laughing, Kaen shrugged. "You wouldn't be a dwarf if you weren't a little gruff."

Bosgreth choked from laughing at Kaen's comment, and Dagan winked. "Spoken like a true dwarf."

As the air whipped through their hair, Ava squeezed Kaen tightly as they flew through the sky. They were sad to see the kingdom of Tanulivar fading from view but excited to hear about the change coming to their people.

Things are changing. I can smell it in the air.

I would ask if that was yourself you were smelling, but we are flying too fast. Life does seem different. Everything seems different.

Pammon nodded, and Kaen felt an itch he needed to scratch.

Go ahead. I know that you want to.

You really can sense everything I am thinking, can't you?

It's like the walls we try to hide behind, or the feelings we were too scared to be honest about are no longer there. I feel what you feel for Ava; it isn't like before. I don't feel overwhelmed or controlled by it. The love is different than the way you sometimes think.

Pammon's thoughts flowed through their bond, and the confusion that came through them echoed in Kaen's mind.

What is that? Those feelings?

Amaranth told me something before we left. Realizing what made dragons and humans worth bonding. Only now do I finally see what makes the bond worthwhile to a dragon. Family. My family includes you, Ava, Hess, Sulenda, Callie, and many more.

It goes beyond desiring gold, land, or countless mates. There is a connection that satisfies me more than all those things. The power I gain from you is not enough to make this worthwhile for most dragons, but the joy I feel surpasses everything else.

I belong. I have a home. I even have a purpose that brings me a sense of peace.

Laughter came through their bond.

So go ahead and see what your growth looks like. I can feel it eating away inside.

Chuckling, Kaen couldn't help but agree with Pammon.

[Simple Status Check]
Kaen Marshell - Adult
Dragon Bond - One Soul 30%
Age - 23
HP - 3405/3405 (33%)
MP - 758/758 (33%)
STR - 53 (33%)
CON - 60 (33%)
DEX - 57 (33%)
INT - 53 (33%)
WIS - 47 (33%)

Pammon snorted. He could feel the numbers as Kaen gazed upon them.

Those numbers . . . are they—

Good enough to actually fight against Stioks? I'm not sure . . . still, that is hard to imagine. Are there any more bonds after this?

Pammon began to thrum.

I was surprised to find out about this one. How can I have any idea about

that? Your wife would like to know what we are talking about. May I share your stats with her?

You know you can.

Kaen felt Ava squeeze him tightly a few seconds later and started to laugh.

She is very . . . jealous.

Well, I have no doubt that I will never hear the end of it now.

Having spent one more day camping out in the woods, Kaen felt a tingle of excitement as the tree he knew Sedel was near came into view.

I could feel it calling to us. I'm not sure how I feel about that.

It is like a part of us is there. As we get closer, it calls to me, telling me more about the forest and how it is doing.

Do you realize that Sedel knows we are on our way?

Kaen smirked as he rubbed Pammon's neck.

I thought I could feel that as well. Almost as if I could see her turning and smiling in the direction we are coming from.

Sounds of laughter and cheers rang out through the forest as they landed in a clearing near the trees that seemed to sing to them.

Ava pointed at a few children dancing and carrying necklaces made of flowers, waiting just a few yards from Pammon.

"It appears they are no longer afraid of Pammon."

"You are correct, my love," Kaen replied, unhooking them both and starting to climb down. "Then again, we both know he is really a soft and gentle creature underneath this hard outer exterior."

Pammon snorted and glared at Kaen, who laughed as he dropped to the ground, waiting to help his wife dismount.

I shall find a way to repay that comment later. Have no doubt it will come in time.

Rubbing Pammon's side as Ava climbed down, Kaen just smiled. He felt alive, and the forest seemed to recharge him.

As they stepped away from Pammon the children rushed forward, bowing and giving each of them two necklaces of white flowers. After Ava and Kaen acquired their gifts, they couldn't help but let the children grab their hands and draw them closer to the rest of the wood elves, waiting for them in the center of the trees.

Glancing back at Pammon, he saw two men bringing him two deer.

Seems everyone gets a little treat.

Pammon said nothing, but Kaen could feel how happy the gesture made his dragon.

"Kaen and Ava Marshell! Welcome back!" Sedel called out as the people clapped and cheered. "Join us at the table we have set for you!"

More tables were lined up, and Kaen realized there were at least thirty more wood elves than he had seen last time.

"When did—"

"After you and Pammon healed the forest, it brought home some of the elves who were out there, trying to find a new path. They returned because of you," Sedel said, cutting Kaen off. "Now, please, let's sit so we can celebrate as creatures of the forest!"

Leaning back in his chair, Kaen watched Ava play with the children. They had brought her various flowers, each one a different color and type.

"The children are excited about the news of your offspring. It will be a great day when they are born. Now tell me, what did you do in the dwarven kingdom? I can feel the faint touch of a tree there even though the distance is so great."

Sighing, Kaen put his elbows on the table and leaned against it. "You can feel it from here? How?"

"If a tree fell somewhere in the woods, but you were not there to hear it, would it make a sound?"

Kaen felt his face scrunch as he considered Sedel's words. "I mean . . . I guess even if I wasn't there to hear it. What does that have to do with anything?"

"I can hear it because the forest would tell me it fell. The magic that flows within you and your dragon and slightly within your wife tells me what you did. I had not expected it, but it seems that the forest feels it was a great act and is excited about it. In so little time, you have done things never achieved in our history. One day, when this land is no longer at war, the forest has a request of you, but do not ask. For now, focus on the path before you."

Kaen's head was swirling from everything Sedel had said. "So does that mean you have finished my bow?"

"You're always so straightforward . . . no time to sit back and enjoy good company," Sedel teased before standing up and raising her hands.

The wood elves all went silent. Even the children hushed and looked at her with anticipation.

"My people, today we shall give our savior the greatest bow the tree has created in a millennium. We pray that it serves him well as he fights to protect us and all who inhabit this land and seek peace."

Kaen had almost expected applause, but instead, it was so silent that only the wind and the sounds of the forest could be heard.

"Bring forth our gift," Sedel said, clapping her hands.

Men rushed off in two directions as Sedel stepped down from her seat.

"Kaen Marshell, please follow me. It is time to give back to you as you gave to us."

44

The Gift from the Forest

Kaen and Ava followed Sedel, and the wood elves gathered at a place with special memories.

"The archery tournament," Kaen said with a slight chuckle, getting a nod and grin from Sedel.

"What better way to receive the bow than to fire it? I would offer to challenge you to a contest, but we both know that is a waste of arrows and time."

"Maybe not time," replied Kaen as he squeezed Ava's hand. "I always enjoyed watching you set up a field designed to let you win."

Sedel snorted, breaking her carefully maintained appearance as she recalled the contest they had first competed in. "I must admit I was frustrated for a while after you snatched that victory from me. Queleth told me it was a good lesson that life always has surprises even when we think there are none." Slowing her step slightly, Sedel turned and focused her eyes on Ava. "I'm sure you will agree that your husband brings many surprises."

Ava laughed as she leaned into Kaen. "He does have a way of doing that. Even when I don't think anything else is possible, he somehow heals a forest and is granted the status of a dwarf."

Sedel tripped, barely catching her step at Ava's last statement, and her face betrayed her. "A dwarf?!" she exclaimed. "They have given him the actual title of a dwarf?!"

Eyes turned as every wood elf within the sound of Sedel's voice waited to hear what reply might come.

"Well, actually, it is Kaen and me, as well as any of our descendants, for two hundred years," Ava replied playfully. "Supposedly, there is a stone tree that they have already added our names to. Bosgreth is excited about when we will bring both children so he can see their names added to his tree."

Choking on nothing but air and her own spit, Sedel rubbed her face as she shook her head. "Impossible," she muttered. "A dwarf and not just any dwarf but kin to the king."

Kaen sighed. "Forgive Ava, she is just showing off. I was just as surprised and confused about the whole ordeal until I learned why Bosgreth did it."

"And why is that?" asked Sedel, doing her best to regain her composure.

"So that when the time comes, and I call for their help, the dwarven army will have to heed my summons and fight."

Sedel's eyelids looked like a bird's wings flapping. She had blinked so many times so fast that Kaen wasn't sure if he should say something.

"Queleth, you are a thorn in my side," Sedel growled as she finally gained her composure. "You do realize we are obligated to do the same thing when you call?"

Kaen's head cocked to the side slightly, and he looked at Sedel and then at the wood elves standing around, watching them talk. "I . . . do now . . ." Kaen replied slowly. "Do you really think Queleth knew this would happen?"

"I have no idea," Sedel stated as she motioned for them to continue toward the archery area. "I can say that he often held things back because he found it humorous when the rest of us learned about them eventually."

Kaen nodded and saw Ava motion to Pammon, who was already lounging near the archery area. "How did he get here already?"

Tapping his head with one finger, Kaen smiled. "He left as soon as I knew where we were going. Said he wanted to get a good view."

Ava groaned and rolled her eyes. "Not like he can't see above all of us."

"Have I ever mentioned how much I like your wife?" Sedel asked as they drew closer. "She is like me, annoyed with common things like a dragon who takes up prime viewing space when he can easily see above us."

"Then ask him to move," Kaen replied, grinning like a fool. "I'm sure he will listen to you."

Shaking her head, Sedel copied Ava and rolled her eyes. "There is no need. For now, follow me."

Kaen stood where he had fired his bow that his father had given him. As he and Ava waited for the elves to finish setting up the course, he leaned over and kissed his wife.

"I love you," he whispered, staring into her blue eyes.

"You'd better," she answered, smiling at him. "The stuff I put up with as you fly around everywhere, treated like a king. Our children will be difficult to rein in if this is a common thing."

Chuckling, Kaen watched Sedel approaching with two wood elves walking behind her. Standing up a little straighter, he saw that each of them carried an item wrapped in forest green cloth.

Sedel stopped a few yards before Kaen and turned to face the crowd.

"Brothers and sisters! Today, we bear witness to the forest and the gift it has given our friend, protector, and brother. May we revel in the knowledge that we will play a role in the coming battle through the bow that Kaen Marshell uses."

Cheers and applause echoed through the forest as everyone turned their eyes toward Kaen and Ava, giving a slight bow before returning to silence.

Sedel nodded and turned to the woman who carried what Kaen knew was the bow. She lifted the cloth that hid what was underneath and draped it around the woman's shoulders. In her hands was a dark brown bow, easily four feet long, and it took Kaen's breath away.

Bowing slightly at the woman, she lifted the weapon up with both hands and held it out toward all the wood elves for them to see. The people murmured approval, yet Kaen couldn't take his eyes off the bow.

It felt like Sedel was taking her time as she lowered her hands and the bow and turned toward him. She had a playful grin, but Kaen didn't see it, focused only on the weapon the forest had given him in the fight he needed to win.

The bow was unstrung, but he saw a brown string wrapped around it and following the curves of the wood, where he knew the rune had to be inside. Even from a few feet away, Kaen saw the power that the back and the belly would provide, their gentle slope that led from the grip and string notch.

"It's beautiful," Ava whispered, and Kaen nodded.

Sedel held the bow out with both hands. "This has yet to be shot or even strung because no one here has the strength to string it. It would appear the forest has high expectations for you, Dragon Rider Marshell. Now take your bow and show us what the forest has gifted you."

Kaen hesitated, and Sedel gently moved her hands closer.

His hands trembled for the briefest moment until his fingers touched the wood, and Kaen could feel the magic and power inside the bow. It called out to him, and he quickly took it from Sedel, holding it and admiring its beauty. The grain pattern was impossible to believe—so tight and all running in the same direction. Turning it around, he ran his hands over its curves and shook his head in disbelief.

I agree. I do not believe there has ever been a bow like that one.

Kaen grinned and couldn't help but nod.

It seems weird still that you can read my mind.

It doesn't take a mind reader or someone with my gift to see how you feel. It is obvious by your face and how you touch it that you believe that. One should caution you to ensure that Ava knows you find her more attractive than that bow.

Kaen glanced up and saw his wife smiling at him.

He grinned and then put the bottom of the bow with the string already cinched around the notched area. Wrapping a leg around it, he applied pressure, easily pulling the other end down and placing the string along the notch.

"Amazing," Sedel whispered, as Kaen had done with so little effort what none of them could do.

Looking at his friend, Kaen shrugged. He held the bow by the grip and gently touched the string as he pretended to pull it back.

[Inspect Weapon]
Heart of the Forest
Bound to Kaen Marshell
10 to Dexterity
30% Damage
Piercing Shots
Unbreakable

Kaen almost dropped the bow when he saw the stats on it. His hand began to tremble, and he looked at Sedel in shock.

"Do you know?"

Her lips drew tight, and she shook her head. "The forest did not allow any of us to know what it is capable of. I think perhaps it is better that way."

She is right . . . that is something none should know but you and your wife.

And you . . .

Well, that's obvious. Now stop standing there like an eggling and show these people what that bow can do.

"Thank you," Kaen said as he bowed deeply. "I am honored that the forest and you have created this for me."

"Does that mean you are ready to show us what it can do?"

Smiling from ear to ear, Kaen nodded. "I would be happy to."

Applause and cheers rang out through the forest as Kaen fired the last arrow. It pierced four targets before finally coming to rest in the fifth. Even when the targets were set ten yards apart, the bow's power sent the arrows flying so fast it was hard to see them as they traveled.

"That was impressive," Sedel declared. "Had you had that bow when we first met, I wouldn't have offered to shoot against you."

Laughing, Kaen put the bow around his body as he pulled an arrow from the quiver they had given him.

"I'm going to have to redo all of my arrows . . . the extra pull distance would be impossible with the ones I use now."

She pointed at a place near a tree. "There are three hundred arrows just like the ones you used, ready to be taken."

"You all have been so gracious to us. How can I repay this debt?"

Sedel laughed and shook her head. "We still owe you more than we can ever repay. Now tell me, when will you leave?" Kaen smirked and Sedel shrugged. "We both know you are anxious to go. You were never one to stay in a place unless there was a reason, and now . . . there is no reason to stay here. I can hear the trees whispering goodbye to you. Just remember what you have been given, and when the time comes, call. We will come."

Kaen nodded and looked at Ava standing nearby, chatting with some elves and laughing.

"Would it be wrong if I offered to hug you goodbye?" Kaen asked with a sheepish look.

"It would be ok this one time," she replied, holding her hands out as Kaen laughed and came in to give her a gentle hug.

"Thank you again for this," he whispered before he pulled back.

"The same goes for you. Thank you for showing the honor and grace that men have long been accused of no longer having. Do what you were born for. Lead this land to a new age."

Her words reverberated in Kaen's heart and mind as he wrestled with a thought he had wondered for so long.

Have we been born for this purpose and task?

You know I have no answer for that, but I will always do what I must to ensure that my family is safe. If I was born to do that, then I will be thankful that I can.

45

Two Egglings

Kaen started to smile the moment he knew what Pammon had found out.

The eggs, they . . . you already know . . .

Laughing, Kaen felt frustrated at Pammon for not being able to share that news.

Sorry, I could feel it and knew the moment you did. Tell both Glynnis and Amaranth I said congratulations.

We need to find a way to hide or surprise the other, at least at first. This will be difficult at times.

I doubt that. Since you already ignore most of what I think or feel, what will be different?

Snorting, Pammon turned his head and looked back at Kaen and Ava. They were slowly creeping up in altitude so they could go above the mountains an hour away. Seeing Pammon's massive bronze body with those peaks in the background made Pammon look larger than usual.

I choose not to reply to or respond to most of what you think. If I did, I would never get a moment of peace. Why does your mind wander so much? Ava also wants to know the names, but I was told even I would have to wait to meet the egglings.

Two days ago. I guess they came sooner than expected. A silver and a red dragon.

There is a boy and a girl. I am not certain how I feel about dealing with two egglings.

I'm sure you'll do fine. One look at you and they will probably not bother you at all.

Kaen felt the pain and worry of that statement from Pammon.

You want them to! Bah, I knew you were a softy!

Thrumming slightly, Pammon turned his head back toward the mountains.

Ava's hands tightened around Kaen, and he groaned as he grabbed tighter on the leather strap.

[Flight Burst Activated]

Don't deny you are excited, just as I and Ava are.

I will not deny it. You know, I couldn't hide it even if I wanted to. Having children before you feels weird, though.

That statement hurt both of them, as Pammon said it. Each knew the struggle of how it affected them both.

You are fine. I understand. It will give me time to spoil them just as I know you will spoil mine.

As they sped through the sky, Pammon thrummed, joyful at what awaited them back in Ebonmount.

Kaen and Ava were laughing as they saw the scene unfolding beneath them.

At the base of the mountain they had carved a home into, within the walls of Ebonmount, were two tiny dragons running around and playing with Phillip and Frederick.

"They are so tiny!" Ava yelled as they approached the four dragons on the ground.

Kaen nodded and smiled as he saw all four dragons lift their heads and watch as Pammon's body filled the sky above them.

"Amaranth says the silver dragon is hers!" Ava exclaimed. "She is very excited from how she is yelling in my head."

Your wife has no idea how excited they both are. The two of them will not stop talking and bragging about their egglings.

From what I can see, they look like strong dragons. I honestly think they are larger than you were two days after hatching.

Pammon snorted, and Kaen smiled.

That is not true. You must have forgotten.

Rubbing his friend's neck, Kaen smiled, ready to meet the newest members of their family.

"Phillip! Frederick!" Kaen shouted before he turned and helped Ava dismount from Pammon.

Both young men were waiting a little off to the side, their dragons each with them. Phillip was scratching the scales of his silver dragon, and Frederick and his red dragon were wrestling as they waited to introduce their newest friends.

Amaranth and Glynnis did not worry about waiting, as the boys and their dragon had. Each of them was alongside Pammon, rubbing their necks and snouts against his.

Kaen smiled as he sensed his friend's joy when the two dragons greeted him.

Moving a few yards away from Pammon, Kaen and Ava stood side by side, waiting as Phillip and Frederick approached. Their dragons came alongside them, each watching Pammon with their eyes. Kaen noticed that the silver male dragon had gold eyes like Pammon and the female red dragon had green eyes like both mothers.

Amaranth's child is the silver one, which means Glynnis's is the red one.

Thank you for the reminder.

"Kaen! Ava!"

Both boys quickened their pace and waved, smiling from ear to ear.

"Foros, come say hi to Kaen and Ava!" Phillip exclaimed.

The silver dragon came forward first, holding his head high and seeming unafraid of being close to Kaen or Pammon.

Holding his hand out, Kaen smiled. "It is a pleasure to finally meet you and welcome you to our family, Foros."

The male dragon, almost seeming to move and act how Pammon did, quickly pressed the top of his head into Kaen's raised hand. He trilled as Kaen began to scratch the scales between his eyes.

"Just like your sire," Kaen said, motioning for Ava to come closer. "This is my wife, Ava."

Ava held her hand out, and Foros looked at her. His golden eyes were bright and almost shining in the light from the sun overhead. Without hesitation, he again put his head against Ava's hand and trilled as she started to scratch his scales.

"Congratulations," Kaen said to Phillip, who had a proud expression on his face.

Both men shook hands and hugged as Kaen patted the young man on the back.

Turning to face Frederick, Kaen saw the red dragon watching him, her green eyes studying him.

"Tazorath, come and meet Kaen," Frederick said as he moved closer to Kaen. The two of them embraced for a moment.

With her head slightly lower, she approached slower. After looking once more at Frederick, who smiled and nodded, she thrust the top of her head into Kaen's hand. Her trill was higher than her brother's as Kaen moved his fingers, took a small step forward, and began to scratch under her jaw.

"You are a beautiful dragon, Tazorath," Kaen said. "You are strong and sleek like your mother."

Kaen's words seemed to embolden her, and Tazorath rose up from the ground.

"Good, never be afraid of me or my wife. We are your family and are here to help you grow and be the greatest dragon you can be."

Ava moved away from Foros, came to stand next to Kaen, and held out her hand as before. Tazorath hesitated only a second before pressing the top of her head into Ava's hand, trilling again as Ava scratched the female dragon.

"You have some beautiful egglings," Kaen said loudly as he turned and looked at Amaranth and Glynnis. Are they giving you four any trouble?"

Mine is like his sire: stubborn and believing that he already knows everything.

Kaen snorted, as did Pammon at Amaranth's words.

Tazorath will be an amazing flyer and strong like her mother and sire. She will shed the shadow her brother tries to exude.

Pammon approached his children.

Kaen saw both take a step back slightly, Tazorath a few more while Foros held his ground.

Lowering his massive head, Pammon brought his snout almost against the ground.

Come, my children. There is nothing to fear. I will do whatever I must to protect you and help you both grow to be great.

Foros moved forward quickly, almost knocking Ava and Kaen down as he rushed past them.

Phillip started to object, but Kaen cut him off with a shake of his head.

The silver dragon slowly approached, his gold eyes watching and studying his sire's eyes of the same color. As he got closer, Pammon began to thrum, watching as the silver dragon, so small, came up next to him and stopped just a foot from his snout.

Foros lowered his head, and Kaen felt his eyes widen as the dragon spoke.

Sire.

That one word tore through Pammon like a fire through a dry forest. So many feelings and emotions that the fearsome dragon had held back and locked away flooded through their bond, and Kaen saw a single tear forming.

Pammon brushed his snout gently against Foros's neck and body.

My son . . . never be afraid to approach.

A trill came from Foros as he rubbed back against Pammon, and Kaen felt Ava squeezing him, her arm having encircled his waist.

Seeing the safety of the moment, Tazorath joined her brother, not pausing as he had done.

Sire.

Her voice was so sweet, and a higher pitch than Glynnis's.

Pammon's heart leaped as the red dragon brushed against the bottom of his jaw.

Daughter . . . I will always be here to protect you.

He began to alternate between the two egglings, scratching both gently with his massive snout as each of them trilled with delight.

"Not what I expected," Frederick said. "Of course, nothing has been like I expected."

Phillip laughed. "By the way, your warning about the smell of their crap . . . it did not prepare me at all."

All three men laughed at that truth.

"No, not much can prepare you for that. I'm assuming they understand why they cannot do that inside?"

"They do now. Amaranth and Glynnis have been exceptionally helpful, especially since they only speak a few words," Frederick replied.

"I do remember those days," Kaen sighed, feeling Pammon's gaze shift to him as his friend knew exactly what he was talking about. "How has the food situation been?"

"So far, so good. We have a few deer in cold storage. Glynnis and Amaranth have gone hunting, each returning with food. I'm not sure what to expect as I see how much each of them eats," Phillip answered. "Foros is only two days old and acts like a single deer isn't enough."

Laughing, Kaen nodded. "That won't change for a while. Do either of you need anything?"

Both boys shook their heads even though Kaen could see they looked a little tired.

Frederick shrugged. "King Aldric has graciously sent helpers to feed and clean the dragons. Hess came by and told us both that we are spoiled."

"Hess told us that you might be jealous," Phillip added. "From what I heard, you were forced to hunt for the food you fed Pammon."

"I about cleared out a forest trying to keep him from complaining."

"Everything go as you hoped?" Phillip asked, switching the conversation.

"Better. There is a lot to discuss with both of you, but I also need to make sure my wife and our two children can rest."

"That sounds like . . . Two children!" Phillip exclaimed.

Frederick stood with his mouth open, and both of the egglings turned to look at what had excited their riders so much.

Ava laughed and nodded. "Yes. I am carrying twins. We haven't told anyone, but since the dwarves and wood elves know, I guess we can share this news with you."

"Dwarves and wood elves?!" exclaimed Frederick. He then groaned and looked at Phillip, who was shaking his head.

"How long till we can fly and visit their homes?" Phillip asked.

Kaen shrugged. "Honestly, I have no idea. I hear that each dragon is different, but if they eat and train, it will hopefully only be a few months. In the meantime, we have a lot of training to do."

Kaen's face changed as he gazed at both boys. "You need to know that how we have trained before will be nothing like it. Everything you think you know about pain and suffering, forget it. I need to prepare you both to be as strong as possible. War is coming soon enough, and you two may be the key to helping win it."

Both boys nodded, their smiles and excitement gone in a moment. Instead, their expressions were replaced with a look Kaen knew too well: those of soldiers obeying orders. Gone were the young men in a moment.

Before him now stood two new Dragon Riders.

46

The Problem with Power

"You look tired," Aldric said with a chuckle. "Not in a bad way, just one I recognize. I'm assuming you have been playing with the talk of the town."

Kaen nodded and groaned as he sat in his chair, watching Herb and Aldric grin like fools.

"Aldric is right. Every person in town is gobbling up any tidbits of information that leak out. When you returned, it was a frenzy of excitement."

"See, that's funny," replied Kaen, "because all I can think of right now is how the next thirty days will go. Those two are going to eat a ton, and right now, the only place to get food is on the other side of the mountains. Pammon, Amaranth, and Glynnis will get tired of playing the role of food delivery."

"How much food are they going to eat?" Aldric asked as he shifted in his chair, and his foot started to tap against the floor.

"You remember how much Pammon ate before the war?" Kaen asked, smirking the entire time.

"I do . . . please tell me they both won't eat like that."

"Not at first, but there will come a time when both of them will easily eat four or five deer daily. You already have three dragons forging for themselves. The distance they will have to travel will make things harder, but hopefully I can help with some of that tomorrow."

Aldric raised an eyebrow, and Kaen heard Herb's chair scrape across the floor.

"How do you plan on doing that?"

Kaen gave a slight shrug and picked up his cup, draining it in one go.

Rolling his eyes, Herb waited until Kaen set his cup down. "So what news did you promise we would want to hear?"

"Let me start at the beginning," Kaen said with a slight sigh. It may take a while, but I promise it's worth it."

Herb and Aldric sat in their chairs, staring at each other as Kaen stood up and stretched.

"I would have thought both of you would be jumping for joy at that news," Kaen said once he sat back down. "The dwarves and wood elves are ready to fight when the time is right. What else is there?"

Herb shook his head. "He doesn't realize, does he?"

Aldric chuckled and shook his head as well. "Kaen, do you know that no human has ever been accepted as you have by the wood elves or the dwarves? To hear what you can now do with the forest . . . it's a bit too much to comprehend."

Kaen frowned. Both men had gone quiet again after their brief comments.

"Why does any of that matter? We are united against one threat, except for the kingdom of Golden Edge, but I don't think anyone expected any less."

"Kaen, I would have to ask my historians to check, but I do not believe that at any time during the history of our lands, a man has united the races as you have," Herb replied. "Then, when you consider what you are as a Dragon Rider . . . it's a bit overwhelming."

Standing up, Aldric turned and stared across the courtyard as he clasped his hands behind his back. He stood there humming a tune for a moment before turning around. He gazed at Kaen, lips drawn tight for a moment. "Kaen, if I were a weak man, I would be concerned for my throne. Everything about you is drawing power to you, putting every kingdom in a difficult position. If you fall, we are lost. There is no way we can defeat Stioks. We have known that for a while now. Without you to lead us and be at the front of the line, we would fold in a moment.

"If you win this fight as we hope, many might call for you to become king of Ebonmount or of Luthaelia. That would—"

"But I wouldn't want that!" Kaen protested.

Aldric closed his eyes for a moment and let out a deep breath. "I know that, but just because we both feel that way doesn't mean the people will understand. This then puts us in a difficult position on how to progress. Do you stay here? Where could you and the other dragons go? How would the people respond if you left?"

The king paused and watched as Kaen considered each of those questions, realizing the problems and the lack of easy solutions.

"Then you have the dwarves. It may not seem like a power play, but they have given you something no man has ever been granted. A place in the mountain. Imagine if a Dragon Rider takes up residence there. Especially one whose dragon has two females that are laying eggs . . . what kind of power shift could take place there? In one moment, I am torn; I believe this act was meant to be sincere and not political, yet I cannot help but see the potential problems it might cause."

"I had enough problems with the adventurers' guild when you were no longer to be one," Herb said as Aldric paused again. "You can only imagine the possible issues that may arise soon as Phillip and Frederick are no longer allowed to be part of the guild. Will they vote to change the rules? How will that impact ranks and positions of power? Imagine being a lowly bronze adventurer and knowing you'll never match the power of you and your two newest riders."

Kaen's mouth opened, but he said nothing, caught off guard by the line of thinking the other two men were considering.

"I know it is a lot and probably upsets you, but as a king, I must always look at all the angles regarding political power. You know you are free to go anytime, and I will never attempt to do what the others did, but that doesn't mean I can be unmindful to what may occur."

"Even if I don't want to be a part of any of those things?" Kaen asked, already knowing the answer.

"Thus lies the true problem with Dragon Riders," answered Aldric. "Now you know why there was a separate group that they belonged to. No king could ever use their power for his own purpose lest the land suffer. When the Dragon Riders became corrupt, pursuing power as humans often do, the kingdoms suffered under it. As you can see, many will fear another time like that."

"That is why Golden Edge treats dragons as they do," Herb interjected. "Knowing they can limit the number who make it safely to our shore helps to ensure they do not have to worry about a dragon or his rider causing problems in their kingdom. The last time I heard from my spies in the capital, none seemed concerned about Stioks at all. There was more concern about you and the women with you."

"Don't worry about these things, though," Aldric said. "This is something I will deal with, and make sure to keep you informed. Just know that if rumblings happen, we will need to act quickly and make sure that we are on the same page."

Kaen nodded and saw that Aldric seemed a little more relaxed after voicing his concerns.

"Should I worry about anything else?" Kaen asked as he looked between both men.

"Nothing that you cannot handle," Herb said with a chuckle. "You will have to deal with the excitement of the people in the city and wanting to see the new dragons. We are doing our best from the adventurer side, with Aldric's help, to release information slowly. We want to prevent possible problems from those who are already infatuated with dragons and limit knowledge that will get back to Stioks."

"Herb is right. You handle the dragon stuff. We will deal with the rest. Besides, it sounds like you have enough problems with food coming up for the next few weeks."

Sighing, Kaen nodded. “I might wish we could trade. Anything else?”

Aldric shook his head, and Herb did the same.

“Then, if you don’t mind, Pammon is almost here, and I need to head back to my growing family. I’ll be here tomorrow evening. Bring your family, and I will bring mine.”

Both men nodded, each with a raised eyebrow as they saw Kaen grinning.

“Tomorrow, I take it, will be a surprise?” Herb asked.

“You have no idea,” Kaen replied as he stood up and walked toward the other end of the massive courtyard.

At that end was Pammon and his massive body, his bronze scales reflected in the fading sun.

Their words are valid, and you know it. We need to consider what to do after we win this war.

You say that like the solution is simple. Can you imagine living elsewhere? What about Callie, Hess, and Sulenda? Can we take Foros and Tazorath with us?

Finding a place where we can be free to live as we should while also being able to help the people of this land will be challenging. You must remember that wherever we go, we go as a family.

You seem . . . softer since meeting your children.

Pammon’s emotions betrayed him, leaving no chance of denying it.

I wasn’t certain how I would feel, but once I saw those two, I could sense a part of me in them. The moment we touched was impossible to describe. It was far greater than any joy I ever felt when Callie would touch and play with me, only outdone by the bond I have with you.

I can only imagine . . .

Soon. Soon, you will hold your children, and then we shall see who is more emotional about their children.

Kaen laughed and scratched Pammon’s neck as they flew to where the other four dragons were waiting.

Just remember. You’ll have to help teach them what it means not to be an eggling . . .

Thrumming, Pammon turned back and looked at Kaen. He smiled, showing his teeth.

Why do you think I’m finally going to understand how it was when I was an eggling?

You don’t remember how much trouble you gave me, do you? The constant begging to eat, not wanting to crap where I told you to, chasing after rabbits and other animals . . . and then the chicken . . .

That foul beast is surely dead by now . . . my only sorrow is that some orc probably ended its life instead of me.

Kaen and Pammon laughed as they descended to where their growing family waited.

"Are you sure you're ok with staying here tonight?"

Ava nodded, taking her small blanket and snuggled down against Pammon. "I couldn't think of a better place to spend our first night back."

Grinning, Kaen settled in down next to her.

Pammon lay in the middle, with Glynnis and Amaranth each on one side. Between them were Foros and Tazorath, each with their rider.

"It seems weird to have five dragons all snuggled together, but I am certain I wouldn't have it any other way," Kaen said as he lifted his arm and let Ava settle in against him.

"I can't wait until our two can join us for a night like this," Ava whispered, closing her eyes and laying her head against Kaen's side. "Imagine a child in each of our arms."

That would be difficult to imagine . . . two children whining about being hungry and crapping everywhere.

Kaen started to laugh, and Ava looked up at him.

"Sorry, Pammon said he can't wait to deal with the crap our children have."

Pammon lifted his head to look at Kaen and Ava, his golden eyes almost glowing in the dim light of the few fires near them. A snort came, sending a little mucus that missed both of them completely but still made them jump.

"Pammon," Ava said, her eyes narrowed and her voice sounding a lot like her mother's. "Please don't do that. Just ask Amaranth. Nothing is worse than upsetting a woman."

Amaranth and Glynnis both started to thrum, and Pammon groaned, laying his head back on the ground.

What have we gotten ourselves into?

Kaen coughed, trying to keep from laughing and getting in trouble again.

Something I know we both wouldn't trade for the world.

47

Mending a Broken Alliance

Food!

Foros took off after the rabbit he'd spotted, and Kaen started to laugh as Phillip watched his silver dragon tear off into the trees.

"He's not going to catch that, is he?"

Shaking his head, Kaen smiled. "Not at all. See how he waddles? It will take at least a week before he can possibly catch one. Even then . . . After about two weeks, he should be ok with the task on his own. The problem is those creatures won't fill him up. And I doubt he can fly over the mountain for a few months."

Pammon thrummed as he watched his son trying to catch a rabbit that had disappeared so quickly into the trees.

Come back, my child. You need to be more stealthy to get close. It heard you and saw you coming from too far away.

Ignoring Pammon's advice, Foros continued to chase through the woods for a bit, trying to accomplish what was not going to happen.

"When should I tell him to come back?" Phillip asked, with a slight look of concern as Foros disappeared behind trees.

"Give him a few more seconds, and then call out to him. You still haven't managed to talk to him without using your words?"

Shaking his head, Phillip kept his eyes on the forest, tracking his dragon even though he couldn't see him. "I try, but it feels like I'm just thinking, and he hasn't responded at all. Was Pammon this stubborn?"

Pammon turned to look at the two Dragon Riders, and Kaen laughed.

"I would say he was worse, but Pammon might argue I was wrong," Kaen replied, keeping an eye on his dragon. "All I can say is that both of you need to learn to work together. Let him be the dragon that he is. You be the rider you want to be. Thankfully, I never crushed Pammon's spirit, and he never resented me for being bossy. We learned together without a real teacher."

Phillip nodded and raised his hands to his mouth. "Foros! Come back!"

He frowned, and Kaen could see that Foros had ignored Phillip.

You were asked to come back. You need to return to your rider and listen to him.

But the rabbit! It is so close and—

I said come back.

Pammon's tone echoed through Kaen's mind as he listened to the two of them talk. A moment after Pammon had finished instructing his son, they heard a noise quickly coming through the trees.

Phillip smiled, and Kaen snorted, not sharing the knowledge of what had taken place.

A few more seconds passed, and a silver shape waddled briskly from the woods.

"You'll get the next one," Phillip said as he moved toward his dragon, who slinked slightly as Foros moved past Pammon.

He is your rider, and you are his dragon. You need to trust that he cares for you and wants the best for you. Sometimes that means you must abandon a meal. Do you understand?

Kaen watched as the two dragons locked eyes, and Kaen felt a little tinge of sorrow for Foros, who bowed his head and let Phillip console him with some scratches.

Yes, sire.

Pammon leaned over, gently took his snout, and nuzzled Foros's side, bringing a trill from the silver dragon.

I do not want to be harsh, but you must learn some things, and it will be hard. Just as your rider will have to train and practice, your mother and I have much to teach you. There is a threat, and we must fight together. One day, you will fly beside me and prove how strong you are.

Kaen watched as Foros raised his head and his chest puffed out.

Now apologize to Phillip and then get ready. We need to return to home.

Foros turned to his rider and rubbed his head against Phillip's chest.

Forgive me for not coming when you called.

"You're forgiven!" exclaimed Phillip. "I'm not mad, just concerned. I want you to be safe."

Foros trilled as Phillip scratched his dragon's head, and soon both were playing and wrestling for a moment.

Why do I feel you are going to say I was worse than that?

Kaen smiled and moved up next to Pammon and scratched his side.

You were an eggling with a boy who had no clue how to help you be the dragon you needed to be. I wouldn't trade a day or how they turned out.

Pammon bent his head and nudged Kaen playfully as they wrestled, laughing and thrumming as Pammon lifted Kaen off the ground and Kaen grabbed two horns along his snout.

After Pammon set Kaen down, both turned and saw Phillip and Foros watching the two of them.

"One day, you will be like that," Phillip whispered.

Soon, I hope.

Pammon beat his wings as he carefully lowered Foros to the ground, letting him out from his talons. Flying through the sky with his son perched between his massive claws was a thrill for Pammon and Foros.

After Foros and Phillip were deposited, Kaen and Pammon repeated the process with Frederick and Tazorath.

She is much easier than her brother. Why is that?

Kaen shrugged as he watched Frederick and Tazorath laugh and play after being returned from their outing.

I think it is because her mother is not as strong-willed as Foros's.

Pammon thrummed and ignored when the other dragons turned to look at the two of them.

Are you sure about bringing them tonight? It will be their first time around that many humans.

I have faith you can manage them. Besides, they need to meet Callie, Hess, and Sulenda, who will be there tonight as well.

You are a brave man . . . that girl is going to be challenging to manage with two new dragons.

Kaen chuckled.

The good news is that it falls to Hess and Sulenda to manage their child.

Pammon's sides vibrated as he thrummed louder; both of them were thankful that Callie was not their responsibility.

Ten minutes after Kaen had planned on starting what they would do, Callie had given in to the truth that she would not spend time with Foros or Tazorath. Both had been anxious as the little girl almost charged them.

Phillip and Frederick laughed at how each dragon seemed nervous when she raced toward them.

I remember that voice . . . there were moments I remember it outside my shell . . . it seemed to go on forever, Tazorath said as she peeked her red head from behind Frederick's side.

"That was because she spent a lot of time in the cave when you were an egg," Frederick said, scratching Tazorath's chin. "She was upset that you couldn't be her dragon."

But she doesn't have . . . the thing inside your chest. How could I be her dragon without one?

Frederick shrugged. "I'm just glad you are mine."

Holding the box that Sedel had given him, Kaen stood in the center of the massive garden of the keep. Kaen smiled as he gazed at everyone gathered, nodding as he acknowledged everyone he knew. Ava stood next to him, holding a small knife, ignoring the glances she received from those wondering what was about to happen.

"King Aldric and other esteemed guests and members of my family, I have a gift from the wood elves, and tonight, I am honored to be able to share it with you. It may not seem like much now, but know that what you are about to receive will prove itself over time."

Opening the box, Kaen took out a seed as large as his palm and held it between his fingers.

He cleared his throat and did his best imitation of Aldric when he spoke in the throne room. "This is a seed from the tree that the wood elves live in and call their own. I am not allowed to say the tree's name, but you have heard it mentioned in stories and legends. This kingdom will have a treasure today because of the wood elves and their desire to mend bonds long lost."

Kaen nodded at Ava, who handed him the knife after pulling it from the sheath. He cut an X on the outer part of the seed and then sliced open his palm. As he squeezed the seed gently, his blood dripped out of his hand and onto the ground near his feet.

Some sounds of surprise and shock came from those watching, but Kaen ignored them, bending to his knees and then punching his fist into the ground.

His arm went deeper than his elbow, and he turned to Ava and smiled.

She leaned down and put her hand on the arm, holding the seed in the ground.

Ready?

You ask as if you cannot feel the power inside me.

I still like to ask.

Pammon thrummed softly as Kaen smiled.

Igniting his lifestone, Kaen closed his eyes and saw the world shift around him.

Power from Pammon flowed into him through their bond. Kaen felt the love and gift of Ava's power coming through his arm.

All of it coursed inside him and then flowed through his arm into his palm. The seed shuddered and flexed, his hand flying open as the magic was sucked into the seed, thirsty for a power that would allow it to become what it was meant to be.

Roots grew and formed, seeking the nutrients in the soil and a place to dig deep. Water was close, and like a spider's web, it went out searching for everything it needed to be what it was destined to become.

Kaen's hand was pushed up from the ground as the tree trunk grew, seeking the air and space needed to live. He did not allow his hand to leave contact as the earth shuddered and a trunk pushed up and out.

In a minute, a seed had turned into a tree, standing over twenty feet tall, its branches spreading quickly as leaves sprouted.

Kaen couldn't hear the sound of those watching, unable to believe their eyes at the sight before them.

His arm shook from the power it felt like the seed had demanded, and his legs felt weak, but with Ava and Pammon lending their respective strengths, Kaen continued to pour more from his lifestone.

A torrent of blue fury blazed inside him, causing the tree to shudder as it grew again, its trunk stretching and expanding, the sound of bark shifting and evolving.

We need to stop! You cannot do what you are doing!

Kaen heard Pammon, yet his life seemed to ignore his friend as it burned. His body was giving out, and as the world started to spin, Pammon roared. Ava grabbed his arm with both hands, yanking him from contact with the trunk of the tree.

Falling to the ground, Kaen drew deep breaths, and he could hear Ava also panting.

What were you thinking? Why were you giving your life for that?

Pammon's words and worry flowed through his mind, but something else existed. A connection that seemed to reach out to him.

Lying there in the grass, the tree and its canopy above him, Kaen saw the magic flowing through each branch and leaf. He could see Ava and the magic that flowed inside her. His two children and the spark of life moved within.

Can't you hear it?

Pammon said nothing. Kaen felt the acknowledgment from his friend a moment later.

Is that really the forest? Is that really Sedel?

It is . . . somehow we have connected . . . The tree! They are connected.

You are foolish, but I can think of no other man I could imagine being my rider. Somehow, you have done what I doubt anyone else could do before.

"My love, are you ok?"

Kaen nodded, turning his lifestone off and being overwhelmed by the exhaustion it had held back. "I'm a little tired . . . thank you for stopping me," he whispered.

Groaning, Ava leaned over and kissed him on his forehead. "Thank Pammon. He told me you were being an eggling."

Kaen laughed. Finally, he opened his eyes and saw with his normal vision what had taken place.

"It's beautiful," he said, sitting up with Ava's help.

She looked up and nodded.

There in the courtyard stood a tree that most would have thought was over fifty years old. Its four-foot-wide trunk stretched upward, covered in white bark. Its white branches stretched outward, covered with leaves, the brightest green most would ever see.

Kaen turned and looked at everyone in the courtyard. No one was looking at him, not even the dragons, as each stared at what he had just created.

48

Bonding While Training

"I'm not sure how this is possible," Aldric said for the hundredth time. "You are going to make life interesting."

Hess nodded. "I have said that since the day I took him in. That's my son."

A groan came as Sulenda shook her head. "Stop taking credit for what isn't yours to take."

Everyone laughed, and Kaen kissed Ava's hand as she stood beside him. His legs were weak, and no one seemed to care that he sat in a chair while the rest stood.

"This is what the wood elves wanted you to have. It connects us to them."

"I just wish Kaen would listen when Pammon or I tell him to listen," Ava teased. "Sadly, he did learn to be stubborn like his father."

"What will this tree do?" Herb asked as he continued to stare at the tree. "I mean, I have heard the rumors and reports of the hall."

"Our land will heal faster. Soon the forest and the fields will produce as they should, and if I am right, creatures will return," Kaen replied. "I'm not sure how quickly, but it will happen faster than normal."

Kaen glanced at Pammon, sitting near the tree as Foros and Tazorath continued to circle the tree with Phillip and Frederick.

Life is returning . . . thank you for helping with that again.

Pammon's contentment was like a steady stream that never seemed to end. As Glynnis and Amaranth lay near him and watched two egglings and two young men laugh and play, they saw what none had believed would ever happen.

We need to train them to be strong. I will not risk them, but I will gladly die for them.

Kaen nodded, even though no one would know why he did.

Even though my children are not born yet, I feel the same way.

Two days later, Kaen and Pammon were still recovering from the energy they had expended, watching both dragons search the woods for game.

Foros was beside himself, having learned that Tazorath had already caught a rabbit.

Phillip and Frederick were sweating, both men pulling the plows across the open field that Kaen had them preparing for the farmers.

They do not enjoy this kind of training as much. Did they expect a different type of workout?

They had, but you and I both know that there is much to be done, and a fall crop still has time to grow, especially with the crap they are producing daily.

You know what will happen in the coming weeks. What will you do then?

I will do nothing; you will do all the work. Training them to fly is your realm. Their two riders, however, may wish I had picked someone else.

Pammon thrummed slightly and turned to see Foros exit the trees with a rabbit in his mouth. The silver dragon swallowed the trophy and roared. Twenty seconds later, his sister burst from the tree line, her red scales reflecting the light.

Kaen saw her grin as she dropped two rabbits on the ground, roared briefly, and then snatched them both up, swallowing them whole.

Seconds later, Foros was racing back into the woods while his sister dashed back in the way she had come from.

Imagine if you had a sibling to compete with . . .

There would not have been a single deer in the entire woods.

Kaen laughed loudly, shaking his head as he knew Pammon was correct.

I am grateful that did not happen.

"How was the training?" Ava asked as Kaen finished wiping himself dry after bathing. "Amaranth says that the dragons and their riders are passed out in their caves."

Kaen nodded. "They found out that Pammon and I are serious about training them. In the coming weeks, things will ramp up and get harder."

"Just remember they are boys and young dragons. Do not push them too hard. An injury would not be good for one of them to suffer."

"I guess I shouldn't mention that Amaranth could heal any injury they suffered," Kaen replied, realizing that wasn't a wise choice.

Ava shook her head and glared at him. "There are worse injuries than just physical ones. You may break their spirit. Then what?"

"They're Dragon Riders now and our best warriors in the kingdom. How am I going to break their spirit?" Kaen asked, confused by Ava's temperament.

"Do you remember how Hess treated you and Pammon? Were there ever days that you two could play and laugh, or was every day as hard as the one you put those four through?"

A slight thrum came across the cave where Pammon, Amaranth, and Glynnis lay coiled together.

She is right. Hess pushed us for a day or two and then always made sure we had fun.

Groaning, Kaen looked at Pammon and the half-peering golden eye that watched him before he turned to look at his wife.

"You're right . . . I guess . . . I just don't want them to not be ready when the time comes."

"When will that be? Three months? Six months? A year?" Ava fired back. "Do you know exactly when you were ready to fight Stioks? Is there any chance you believe those boys will be ready before our children are the same age as Callie?"

Three dragons thrummed, and Kaen growled softly as he exhaled through his nose. "Fine, I will make sure to add some fun and games to what we do," Kaen said, relenting.

Flashing a grin, Ava kissed Kaen on his cheek. "Good, now finish drying off, and let's head to bed. All of us are tired."

I think you got it way worse than I do.

Frowning at Pammon, Kaen held out a hand and gave his dragon the finger.

Pammon thrummed for a few more seconds before settling down and closing his eyelid completely.

"Leave Pammon alone," Ava called out over her shoulder. "No one likes it when you act like an eggling."

Sighing, Kaen quickly finished drying off and ran to catch up with his wife, ignoring the satisfaction Pammon was expressing through their bond.

Kaen smiled and watched as the boys and dragons waited for him to say go.

They had been training and playing different games for the last three weeks, and today would be a new challenge.

Foros bristled at having lost to his sister. His silver scales rose and fell rapidly as he took deep breaths, preparing to launch into the air and start flying.

Tazorath snorted and gazed at her brother, her green eyes watching him.

Remember, brother, when I win again, I eat first.

Foros snorted and shook his head, not risking a glance to the side.

You will not win today. That, I guarantee.

Phillip and Frederick both laughed as they heard their dragons arguing. Each boy held a bow in his hand and an arrow ready.

"Remember, your dragon spots the prey. You shoot the prey. Stay on your own side," Kaen called out. "The winner gets the coveted prize of a trip into town. Rumor has it Sulenda is making a special stew tomorrow."

Both boys laughed as they grimaced. That was not the prize, but getting into town for a few hours was.

"Go!" Kaen shouted, not bothering to count down.

A flash of silver and red scales leaped into the air, wings beating rapidly as the two took off for their side of the forest. After a few seconds, both boys rushed in, letting their dragons gain a little bit of height before trying to track the prey they found.

"Let's go watch the fun," Kaen said as he patted Pammon's neck.

Thrumming, Pammon took a few strides before launching himself into the air, his massive wings causing the trees to sway as great billows of air were sent their way with each stroke.

You enjoy this game almost as much as they do. Makes me wish we had a dragon back then to compete against.

You are correct, Kaen said as he saw both dragons circling as they continued to climb, trying to spot either a rabbit or a deer. *I was always amazed at how well your eyes could see things.*

In a few moments, Pammon was higher than his children, his wings propelling him at a speed Foros and Tazorath quickly learned they could not achieve.

Kaen shifted his eyes to Pammon's and watched the game beneath them unfold.

Tazorath has found one first. It appears she is as gifted as her mother when it comes to this.

She does fly faster than her brother, but he is committed. Like you, he doesn't like to lose.

Pammon thrummed and watched as his son's silver frame moved beneath him in the sky. Those silver wings reflected the sun, and Kaen considered how hard it would be for Foros to hide except on moonless nights.

It's not something I would have expected you to be concerned about. Remember what Ava said. Do not make everything they do about fighting.

Taking a deep breath and letting it out, Kaen scratched his beard absently as he saw Foros find a rabbit.

He has found one, and Phillip is closer than Frederick is to the one Tazorath has located.

You ignored my statement.

Only because that is harder than it sounds. Every day, I carry my bow and the one arrow that will work with this for Stioks and his dragon. I still need to scout that mine Herb reported a few days ago and see if I can find more ore.

Then go. Let them be like we were. Let them play and have fun in the forest. Make them sleep out in the woods. Stop being so protective.

Kaen felt Pammon's scales on his neck and scratched them. He could sense that Pammon meant those words.

When did you learn to let go? At first, I thought you wouldn't let them out from under your wing.

When Amaranth and Glynnis informed me that treating a dragon like that did not create a strong dragon. Those who were coddled were weak. They know that I love them. Right now, that is enough. Let them be the strength each other needs.

Somehow, you have become wise; I'm not sure when this happened. Has my wife been talking with you?

Pammon thrummed and then stopped.

Look! Phillip got his rabbit, and Foros has already located another!

Kaen laughed as he felt pride pour through their bond.

Are you ever going to tell me which one is your favorite?

Pammon snorted loudly.

Bah, you and that stupid question. I have no favorite!

And yet I see you give Tazorath more nuzzling than Foros.

Pammon's vision shifted to where his daughter was, and Kaen smiled as Frederick retrieved the rabbit he had shot.

She has found a deer!

Oh, that will not go well for Phillip and Foros . . . still, it is a good half mile away, and Frederick isn't that stealthy.

That boy could wake a dead dragon with his running through the forest.

You're ignoring my question about why you give Tazorath more physical touches.

Because my son feels that getting too many is a sign of weakness; I do not know where he got that idea. He is stubborn, like his mother.

Choking, Kaen thumped his chest a few times with his fist.

Yes . . . because his father isn't stubborn at all . . .

Pammon snorted and tucked his wings on the right side, flying upside down for a moment before righting himself.

You know I hate when you do that . . .

Yes . . . yes, I do.

49

Sharing Burdens

"Frederick seemed pretty excited with the win," Ava said as she helped Kaen cut up some of the vegetables he had acquired. "Winning by one point, all because of a deer."

Chuckling, Kaen nodded and finished chopping a carrot, depositing the tiny pieces in the bowls with the other vegetables. "I think he scared away all the other game because Phillip had five rabbits, and had we not run out of time, they would have probably won," he replied. "Besides, seeing how Tazorath struts around after she wins is pretty funny. She knows it bothers her brother a lot."

Groaning, Ava rubbed her belly gently and then poked it twice. "You two better not be like that. I'm not sure I could handle that kind of competition."

Kaen leaned over and kissed her on the cheek while rubbing his hand softly on her stomach. "Ignore your mother. She doesn't want to have any fun."

Laughing as the flat side of the knife slapped his backside, Kaen held up his hands in surrender.

"Go get that pot and bring it here so I can put these into it. I'm afraid it's mostly vegetables and not a lot of meat."

Shrugging, Kaen fetched the pot from the cooking fire and brought it over to her. He studied the exhaust that Herb had had some tradesmen come and build for them. How it managed to carry the smoke so far always amazed him.

"I'll be fine without meat. I've had my fair share of it. You need to eat it. You're eating for three."

"Please don't remind me," Ava said as she frowned. "None of my pants fit anymore, and I'm stuck wearing these dresses and skirts."

Having set the pot down, Kaen helped Ava as they transferred the vegetables in, and she added a few spices. Motioning to him to take it back, Kaen pretended with a few grunts and groans that it was now too heavy to carry.

"You know I love you, Kaen Marshell," Ava said with a sigh. "Even if you act like those boys out there with their dragons."

Frederick and Phillip sat at the Dragon Rider Inn's bar and slowly sipped their one cup of alcohol. When word had reached the townspeople that they were there, it wasn't long before the place was packed with people just coming to see them.

Each did his best to talk and acknowledge those who wished them well, telling stories of when they were kids and more.

"So, what is it like having a dragon?"

Frederick motioned to Phillip that it was his turn to respond to that question for the thousandth time.

Not losing his cool, Phillip leaned down and ruffled the hair of the young boy brave enough to ask. "It's hard to compare it to anything because there is nothing better I have experienced than that. Getting to train from when Dragon Rider Kaen paid for everything was special. When I got my lifestone was one of the greatest days of my life, but when Foros spoke to me, and I knew he was my dragon . . . it was ten times better than all of that combined."

"Woah . . ."

Frederick chuckled as the little boy stood there with his mouth open, shaking his head in disbelief.

"Do you think I can have a dragon one day?"

Phillip winced slightly. No matter how many times he heard that question, it did not have an easy answer.

"Maybe," he replied with a smile and a shrug. "I never expected to get a dragon, yet here I am. All I can say is to work hard and obey your parents. Who knows what will happen in the coming years."

The boy nodded, eyes as wide as their cups, and bounced on his feet. "Thank you again, sirs!"

Phillip winked as the boy's parents led him away, watching the child whisper, "One day, I'll have a dragon like them."

"Are you sure Kaen sent you two here to relax?" Eltina asked as she leaned over the counter. "From the looks of it, he sent you two here to deal with all the questions he doesn't want to answer."

"Maybe," Frederick replied as he looked at his half-empty mug. "I'll gladly take a night away to relax. Kaen wasn't lying when he said we would train harder than before."

Snorting, Eltina motioned to the people in the room. "I will say this, that boy always makes my life harder. I had to bring out two casks because of how many people had come in. I won't have alcohol for a week if more people keep coming in. Doesn't he know how hard it is to get alcohol?"

Phillip leaned forward and motioned to Eltina to come close.

The dwarf leaned in, moving her beard out of the way as she got on her tiptoes to get close.

"He did mention something about wanting you to suffer . . . something about getting you back for all those times you made him buy rounds for the whole inn."

"Goblin nuts," Eltina cursed as she stood upright and scowled at Phillip and Frederick, both boys laughing at her expression. "You're both about to find out what that feels like if you want to play like that."

"I yield!" Frederick declared. "We both know I don't have any money."

Rolling her eyes, Eltina focused them on Phillip, who picked up his mug and turned to look around the room, ignoring her gaze.

"Bah, you two are just like him. Spirits help us, just what we need. Two Kaen Juniors . . ."

"You don't have to worry about that," Frederick said. "With Ava having twins, we won't be—"

"TWINS?! Ava is having twins?!"

Frederick's face went white as he realized that Eltina had not heard the news yet, and now, in one moment, it would appear the entire town was about to find out.

"I'm going back," Phillip said with a sigh as he put his cup on the counter. "Good luck with this one!"

Frederick watched Phillip bolt for the door as people began to come to where Eltina was leaning over the counter and trying to grab Frederick by his vest.

"Uh . . . I gotta go, too!" Frederick exclaimed, setting his mug down so hard it spilled over the bar and knocking down his stool as he jumped off.

"Come back here, you fool!" Eltina shouted as both boys ran out the door, leaving a throng of people asking Eltina what she was talking about.

"I swear I'm going to murder those boys," she growled under her breath as she prepared to deal with the chaos unfolding in her inn.

"Rule number one, make sure what you say is common knowledge or be very careful when you say it," Kaen said as he walked along with Frederick and Phillip.

Both boys were loaded down with chains and dragging them across the field they had already cleared of rocks and rubble.

"Now, I personally think it was funny, but my wife . . . well, she told me I needed to make sure you both understood the rules about sharing that a woman was pregnant."

"Sorry . . ." gasped Frederick as he labored under the weight. "It . . . wasn't . . . Phillip's . . . fault."

"I know," Kaen replied, seeing Phillip not saying a word but toiling silently. "That's why his weight is slightly less. But you two have been attached at the hip since I can remember. You have always done everything together. One day, you may live apart, responsible for a kingdom, and as I have learned the hard way, the words of a Dragon Rider carry a lot of weight. So today, you two will also learn to carry that weight."

Two grunts came as the boys dragged more weight than most men could ever imagine moving at once across the field.

I want you to know their dragons are upset.

Because you are punishing them for what their riders did? That was your choice.

No . . . they want to help their riders. Flying will only do so much to wear them out. They cannot do too much as they continue to get stronger. So I was thinking . . .

That might be a good idea. Why not let them carry that burden together? It would also help the boys to see that their dragons suffer because of their actions.

Exactly. If you look closely, you can still see the scar from that arrow the goblin shot me with in the cave.

Kaen began to curse, and both boys risked a glance to see if it was something they caused. Seeing that Kaen was looking at the sky, they put their head down and kept walking.

You're going to make me suffer for that one mistake my entire life, aren't you?

I'm just proving a point. One mistake can cost a rider or a dragon considerably.

Grumbling, Kaen caught up with Phillip and Frederick.

"Ok, boys. Drop the weights and rest. In a moment, we'll move to lesson number two, courtesy of Pammon."

Kaen and Pammon watched as both boys and their dragons worked together to pull the heavy chains and weights across the fields. It had taken time for Phillip and Frederick to figure out the best way to get the chains to stay without hurting their dragons' wings or neck.

I know they are complaining to each other slightly, but I can also feel a sense of bonding from this. It is a good thing that you listened to me.

Yes . . . now, how long do we want to make them do this? I'm getting bored watching the four of them lug those things back and forth.

There is one more trip. After that, they should be ready to return home and eat. Amaranth and Glynnis both went and found food for them. Apparently, their mothers wanted to make sure they would eat well when they found out what we had planned for today.

No one got you anything, did they?

Pammon snorted as he lounged on the ground next to Kaen.

No, they did not. I voiced my feelings about that, and neither seemed concerned with my problem.

Laughing, Kaen shrugged as he held his hands up to his mouth. "One more lap, and then you four are done! Rumor has it there is some fresh venison back at your place."

A few whoops and hollers, along with some trills, broke out briefly, and Kaen couldn't help but grin when he saw the four of them work harder, anxious to finish the task and go home and eat.

You really are a brutal trainer. We should ask Hess to help.

I already sent him a letter. That is his task for next week. We have other things to do.

"So how many days should I expect you to be gone?"

Kaen scratched his chin, feeling the thickness of his beard. "Two days, maybe three. If the mine is what Herb says, I'll do some work inside it. Without that ore . . . well, I need more arrows, and I'd feel a lot better having an extra one or two."

Ava said, "I'll be fine. Glynnis and Amaranth have told me they will help me with anything I need. Besides, my mother will be bringing a few things up here. Now that we are living here, she feels we are lacking in being ready for a baby . . . or two."

"Are you ever ready for a baby? Even Aldric said that it turned out he was not ready for his child. With two, I can only imagine how unprepared we will be. Have you considered your mother's offer?"

Groaning, Ava shot daggers at Kaen with her eyes. "I would prefer not to live with my mother or have her here. She would be into everything and want to do it her way."

Kaen crossed his arms and bit his lip for a moment as he watched his wife complain.

"What?" she asked, frustrated at how he looked at her.

"It seems odd . . . the woman I know doesn't let herself get bossed around and almost always ensures things are done her way. Are you saying you cannot handle your mother?"

Ava's mouth flew open so fast that Kaen was concerned she might pull a muscle in her jaw. Yet no words came out as she forced it shut and wagged a finger at him.

Finally, she groaned and raised her hands in the air as she turned and walked away.

If she could have breathed fire . . . well, it is good you can't be burned by it.

Kaen started to laugh and regretted it the moment Ava spun on her heel and strode back to him. She pressed a finger in his chest before grabbing his shirt and pulling him toward her.

"You're a stupid man to tease a pregnant woman . . . especially one who always gets her way. Now, why don't you be helpful and take care of dinner? I'm going to go rest. Understood?"

Kaen nodded, resisting the urge to smile and draw even more ire from his wife.

Now we both know for certain I was correct. You have the harder mate.

I would never agree with that statement.

Why?

If I did and Ava ever found out that I said that, breathing fire would be the least of my concerns for a long time. You and I might end up living in the woods again, in a shed I'd have to build with my own hands.

How do you always know what to say that will keep me from ever sharing our secrets with her? I still have nightmares believing I'm going to die as an eggling, crushed by your terrible shed-building skills.

50

An Honest Day's Work

Kaen glanced at the map as Pammon descended along the mountainside. A multitude of tunnels had been dug out on the west side, south of the keep, and none had yet produced the ore they hoped was there.

These are the mines that your friend died in . . . I can feel the sadness in your heart.

They are. It seems so long ago. Over five years ago . . . maybe almost six?

I remember how you talked about them. They were full of life and wanted the life of an adventurer. They died doing what they wanted to do: protecting the people of this land.

Kaen patted Pammon's neck, feeling its rough scales against his calloused hand, and just nodded. Every day, something seemed to remind him that there was a battle looming, that death was always a possibility, and that death was risked because of what it meant. Others would be able to live a full life.

That one down there, the eighth one from that set of carts, is the one we need to go in.

Turning his lifestone off and allowing his own vision to return, Kaen reached back and felt the handle of Hess's pickaxe strapped to his back. The worn wood and leather on it had seen countless swings. Secretly, he prayed that the next few days might give him some success.

"Uh . . . Dragon Rider Kaen, we can send a few men in there with you if you want with some lanterns. The sketch you have shows where we think there might be some of the ore you're looking for," the foreman said as he watched Pammon fly off. "We'll need to also build supports depending on how far you dig. Just tell me what you want us to do, and it's yours."

Kaen nodded and looked at the twenty or so miners watching him now that his dragon was almost out of sight.

"Well, the truth is I don't need the lanterns or lightstones to see," Kaen replied, seeing the looks he received for that comment. "I plan on digging at a rather fast pace. If I'm correct, two tunnels nearby have a chance of the ore I'm looking for."

"That be true, but surely you would need some rest, and I'm not certain you know just how hard mining might be, beggin' yer pardon," the foreman said, scratching his chin. "It ain't like fighting."

Kaen nodded and removed the pickaxe from his back, taking the leather cover off its head.

Most of the men and a few women who were there whistled, their eyes focused on the metal tip.

"Let's just say it's not my first time swinging a pickaxe. I'm afraid I might actually move faster than your support team can keep up."

A few chuckles came from the crew, and the foreman looked at Kaen and then at his pickaxe. A sly grin appeared, revealing the few of the man's teeth that still remained. "That sounds like a bet we might want to take. Are you interested in wagering?"

Smiling, Kaen held out his hand. "I'll wager your support team runs dry before I do. Either way, I'll ask my dragon if he can bring back a deer for us all. Two though if you win."

Some whistles and yells of joy came from the crew, and everyone was nodding with excitement.

Shaking Kaen's hand, the man smiled. "Ready whenever you are."

Kaen lost himself in the simple task of swinging the pickaxe. His night vision made work in the tunnel a breeze, and the men behind him worked quickly, making sure that timbers were set up and safe.

He cleared out a section, waiting for the men to haul off the stone in the carts. The workers laid more tracks, and then, once the rubble was gone, the support team came in, erecting the braces and getting things in place while Kaen moved to the other tunnel, repeating the process.

His muscles ached in a good way, and the sweat that fell was replaced by the water he drank continuously. A young boy and girl brought a bucket of water, standing in awe as he drank most of it before dumping it over his head.

Men watched, amazed at the body he displayed. There was no fat, just a mountain of muscle that showed he was not soft and lived up to the legends they had heard about Kaen.

Every time he walked by or saw one of the miners, Kaen would laugh and joke, ask questions about their families, and engage them in conversation. He even joined in with a few of the songs, singing the words to the ones he knew and making them up for the ones he didn't.

Between the ringing of his pickaxe on stone, the noise of rocks breaking, and the work of men, Kaen heard something he had missed: the sound of life in everyday work.

"Mr. Marshell." A voice came from behind, getting Kaen's attention as he attacked the stone before him.

Finishing his swing and letting the rock fall, Kaen turned to see the foreman, Mr. Brumbledon, holding a lantern and looking at him with awe.

"Everything ok, sir?"

"It is . . . it's just we are out of timbers. We hadn't planned on you doing so much in one day, and well, it is time to stop for us in a bit anyway. We can get some timbers cut tomorrow and be ready to do some more support work, but would you be ok if we stopped for the day?"

Kaen hefted the pickaxe up and put it over his shoulder, feeling the grime of stone and sweat sliding under the wood and against his skin. "I think that would be ok. Besides, my dragon is waiting for us to finish. He has some gifts for us."

Kaen saw Mr. Brumbledon's eyes widen. "Gifts, you say?"

Kaen nodded and motioned toward the tunnel they had entered through. "Let's go outside and wash up. I'm looking forward to Pammon's gift."

They are an interesting group. They remind me of the people from Minoosh. They are hardworking but enjoy what they do.

They are the people we fight for. Hearing them sing, seeing them laugh. Knowing they were doing everything they could to keep up with me. I know many will go home and wake up sore tomorrow.

Don't worry about me until it is time to turn it in. I am full and content. I cannot believe I found a herd of deer over the mountain.

Kaen smiled as the people he was sitting around a massive bonfire with laughed and celebrated, consuming the two deer that Pammon had brought back. He couldn't help but remember when he had been at a campfire like this at the quarry. Those memories solidified his commitment to what he was doing.

"Rumor has it you have two children on the way," a voice called out, getting Kaen's attention.

"It is true. Twins. I'm not sure what will be harder, raising two children or our two new dragons."

A younger man with reddish hair raised his hand, and Kaen chuckled, nodding for him to speak.

"Is it true that Stioks has a dragon like yours?"

Grumbles and people shushing the young man turned the night silent, with nothing but the sound of the flames consuming the wood they surrounded.

Kaen took a deep breath. "He does. Things have changed, and I would like to say that the coming battle will be easy since we have two new Dragon Riders, but I won't lie to you. Stioks is strong. He has had at least sixty years or more to hone his strength and power, and I've only been doing this for about five years, but let me tell you why I'm certain we will win."

As he paused, Kaen shifted his gaze to everyone around the fire.

"This isn't a battle that just dragons and Dragon Riders fight. How many here were on the walls defending against the orcs and goblins?"

Hands shot up, and only two young boys who looked less than fourteen years old sat there, frowning that they couldn't raise their hands.

"It wasn't me who defended the walls. It was the people of Ebonmount. It was you defending your families and fighting for the life you want. Seeing you all working today, hearing you sing and laugh, and getting to share a dinner with you tonight has done more good for me and my commitment to fight. It is because of you all that I am willing to fight."

Some of the people clapped each other on their backs and smiled. The same young man raised his hand again without pause, and people groaned, telling him to put his hand down.

"What's your name?" Kaen asked.

"Kevin, sir."

"Ok, Kevin, what is your question?"

"Well . . . I was wondering . . ." Kevin stammered, looking at the expressions everyone was giving him. "When do you think you might win?"

More groans came, and a few threw small stones at Kevin until Kaen raised his hands and stood up.

"No, let him ask it. I would rather he ask the hard questions because he wants to know when life might return to normal. He is brave enough to ask what I'm sure many of you want to but aren't willing."

Some feet shuffled against the dirt as people didn't look at Kaen.

Kaen turned his attention to Kevin and saw the boy's small smile at the praise. "I wish I had an answer, but I don't. I plan to train the riders and find the ore I seek. That ore is pretty special to me and will help in the battle. When I fight Stioks next, I believe we will win once and for all. I would like to say there won't be any deaths on our side, but every one of us knows there is a cost for war. Battles are hard and require a commitment that most aren't willing to give."

Kaen held up his right hand. "This hand can do a lot of things. I can swing a pickaxe, as you all found out."

The group laughed and nodded as Kaen waited for them to go silent again.

"I can wield a sword or a bow and try to strike down my enemies. I can also hopefully hold my children one day and guide them to be people who try to help others. Each of you has that same hand. You get to choose what you want to do with it, how you want to live. I choose to live with one goal, with one purpose."

Kaen turned his gaze toward the fire that burned near him and felt his own lifestone begin to burn.

"I fight so that families will never know the pain of a lost father or mother. I lost my dad as a child because he risked his life to kill Stioks. He sacrificed everything so that I might have a future." Kaen's gaze moved back to the people around him, shifting from person to person as he continued to speak. "I will do the same. I will fight so that no one else will have to endure what I did. So that you can return home to your families each night."

The fire crackled and popped after Kaen finished speaking. He saw the people staring at him, tears forming on many faces. The sounds of rocks under boots made Kaen turn to his right, and he saw an older man moving toward him.

"Thank you, Dragon Rider Kaen. Thank you for your sacrifice," the older man said, tears rolling down his wrinkled and leathery face.

As others got in line, each one came to offer Kaen their thanks before moving back to their seat.

After they had all finished, Kaen stood there with a few tears running down his cheeks, yet with a smile.

"It is my honor to fight for you all. Now, please, let's laugh and sing some more. I would rather not cry anymore!"

Everyone clapped and started to laugh. In a moment, the celebration of life began again.

51

Mining with Purpose

"I'm thinking you need to consider focusing on this shaft," Brumbledon said as he pointed at the crude map of the mines. "I've studied the rocks we have been hauling out and I can see a few trace minerals that might point to what yer looking for."

Kaen nodded as he devoured the lunch they had for him. Rice, beans, and some hard bread might not seem like much to most people, but after a morning of working, it was filling.

"If we focus on that section, your team can keep up?"

Shaking his head, Brumbledon frowned. "Honestly, I don't think anyone can keep up with you, but we'll do our best to limit yer downtime. You can either rest or go back to the other shaft but truth be told, yer just too strong."

Laughing, Kaen pointed at the pickaxe near him. "Part of it is that beast. My dad used it, and I can see how it helped him be the man he is."

"I wouldn't wanna wrestle either of you," Brumbledon said with a chuckle. "That feat you did with the log about made half my team want to sign up to be Dragon Riders."

Kaen shrugged, swallowed the last of his water, and grabbed his pickaxe. "Well, let me get to work on that tunnel, then. I saw the support team come out a few minutes ago."

Frustration began to set in as Kaen helped with every task possible so he could get back to the tunnel they were mining, helping with the supports and carting out rocks.

He stopped working only when he drank water or moved between jobs.

You need to realize that you may not find anything. Just because you desire to find something doesn't mean it will be found.

Kaen grunted internally as he broke off another piece of rock.

I'm trying . . . I really am. Just for once, I wish something would go right.

Pammon began to laugh through their bond, and Kaen rested the shaft of his pickaxe on his shoulders.

Why are you laughing? I'm serious!

Kaen, you are being an eggling. Stop and think about everything that is going right. You can see, your wife is pregnant with twins, you have two new Dragon Riders who are growing, and there is far more than just those few things. If your wife were here and heard you say those things, she would probably dunk you in a trough.

Sighing, Kaen realized Pammon was right.

I guess I am being an eggling. Sometimes I get so focused on what is before me.

Your problem is how you view the world. Unlike everyone else, you can see it in so many different ways, yet you often choose to look at it as a normal man. You aren't one. You are a king, a husband, a Dragon Rider, a son, and more. You helped grow back a forest, convinced the dwarves to leave their mountain, and last night gave those people outside hope.

Scratching his neck, Kaen considered Pammon's words. His friend and dragon was right.

You're right. I forgot that I can look down from your neck almost every day and see the world beneath me. I can also use your eyes to see the world in a whole different way, and now I can—

Kaen?

Pammon wondered why Kaen had gone silent as he tried to sift through the thoughts in his riders' heads.

I can see different! Kaen exclaimed, his internal shout ringing loudly inside Pammon's head.

Pammon groaned, but Kaen ignored it, having been on the opposite side of that feeling before. Instead, he closed his eyes and willed his lifestone to burn. As power flooded through him, Kaen shifted his vision, letting the world of magic and things flow through his eyes. He turned, studying the mountain he was inside.

The stone wall had faint traces of magic, so tiny but enough to make out the walls and floors. He could see the pieces on the ground and the dying light of power inside them.

Reaching out with his free hand, Kaen touched the walls and tried to peer past the outer stone. He remembered what he had seen with his children inside Ava and looked beyond.

The end of the tunnel showed nothing, just an empty space stretching as far as his vision would allow. There were tiny cracks in the stone, but nothing showed up as he hoped.

He grunted loud enough that it echoed in the area of the tunnel where he stood. Kaen almost jumped when he heard a voice behind him.

"Are you ok, sir?"

Spinning around, Kaen saw the young boy with the water bucket, life energy outlining him in the tunnel.

As his gaze traveled toward the boy and beyond, a bright light off on the right down the tunnel caught his eye.

"Excuse me, son," Kaen said as he moved past the boy, dragging his right hand on the stone wall as he walked back down the tunnel and toward what he saw.

He continued for about five yards and stopped, facing the wall and peering at the glowing vein he saw deep within the rock. It was brighter now that he was closer, but there was something different within the stone, at least a dozen yards before him.

"Boy!" Kaen shouted, turning quickly to see the child running toward him with the water bucket.

"Yes, sir! Need a drink?"

Kaen laughed, nodded, and took the entire bucket from the child, drinking a few massive gulps before handing it back.

"I need you to do me a favor. Go and get Mr. Brumbledon and tell him to hurry!"

The boy nodded, and Kaen saw a smile on his face before the boy took off.

Do you really see some?

Touching the wall with his hand once more, Kaen smiled.

I believe I do. Something other than rock is here.

Then get to work. And Kaen, it's good to feel you like this.

Kaen realized he wasn't just smiling; the way he felt was pouring through his bond. Hope, joy, and excitement—they all came because Pammon helped him realize how fortunate he really was.

Grabbing the shaft with both hands, Kaen planted his feet and began to attack the wall with a purpose. His lifestone roared inside him, and his only focus was the glowing spiderweb of a vein he saw within the rock.

"You're certain?" Brumbledon asked for a second time. "I don't mean to disrespect you, but you're telling me you can see the vein?"

Kaen nodded and watched as men brought timbers in to support the area he had just cleared.

"We still have about seven yards before I think I will be there, but yes. It looks like a bunched-up spiderweb, with some thick spots and lots of little trails that run off before ending."

Brumbledon shook his head in disbelief. "If you really have that gift or ability, I'd love to keep you here longer, but what you just described sounds exactly what they look like. They're never as large as you wish those veins would be, either."

"Well then, I've asked my dragon to gather some more deer for everyone tonight. It may take a bit, but I want to hit it by tonight."

Nodding, Brumbledon whistled, and everyone in the mine stopped working or talking.

"Listen up! We'll work till Dragon Rider Kaen says we're done! It will be a few hours at least, but he's promised you all some more meat!"

Cheers and shouts echoed through the tunnels and stopped after Brumbledon gave a long, sharp whistle.

"Now! Get to work and be smart! We got a mine to dig!"

The sounds of miners getting back to business sprang up immediately as Brumbledon turned to look at the supports that were almost done being installed.

"Lead on, sir. We are your team!"

Kaen nodded, put a hand out, and gently squeezed Brumbledon's shoulder. "I couldn't ask for a better group to work with either."

Four hours had passed, and Kaen was practically bursting with excitement. He wanted to finish the last of the rock between him and the dazzling display of magical energy pulsing only about four feet away. The men were finishing up the last set of support beams and would soon be done.

"You sure you don't want no more water?"

Kaen turned, noticing that his faithful water hauler was back again. "I'm good, but in a little bit, I might. I think I've had to piss more times than I can remember and have sweated enough to start my own stream."

The boy smiled as he nodded and went to ask some of the other miners.

You must be close. It feels like you are about to come out of your own skin.

I haven't been this excited in a while! You should see what I see.

A few moments passed, and Kaen could feel Pammon's mind as it took in what he saw.

That is . . . hard to describe. I have seen this view before, but nothing like that.

Laughing, Kaen turned his head to let Pammon see the difference between the tunnel and the walls. As he looked up slowly, he saw a faint glow off to the left and above him, almost out of the range of his vision.

Is that more?

It would appear that it is. Had you not glanced through my eyes, I doubt I would have bothered looking so high.

As always, I am the bringer of good things.

Kaen groaned as Pammon laughed through their bond.

"It's ready, sir!" one of the men on the support crew shouted.

Keeping his eye focused on the spot they had just located, Kaen held out a hand. "Who has some chalk? I need to mark a wall."

He felt someone put a small piece in his hand, unwilling to tear his eyes off the second vein it appeared they had found. Drawing on the wall where it was, Kaen shifted a few steps and made another mark. Once more, he repeated the process and marked the wall a few steps again.

Turning around, Kaen saw the man's mouth open. "Thanks. I marked another vein and gave you three points of reference. It's up in that direction, so after I'm gone, you all can have the honor of finding it."

"Thank . . . thank you," the man replied with a stutter.

Ready to finish what he had come for, Kaen gave a quick nod and moved to the stone that was between him and his prize.

Forgive me if I get a little bit excited.

Pammon was almost as excited as Kaen, their minds and emotions mixing.

"Three!"

Kaen swung the pickaxe, grateful for all those years he had spent working with Hess in the quarry. He had already gained seven points today, bringing his skill up to twenty-eight.

A chunk of rock fell, and the sound of men cheering slightly behind him urged him on.

"Two!"

As he gave everything he had in his body, Hess's pickaxe slammed into the stone, digging deep, and Kaen ignored the fact that it shouldn't be able to. Kaen's strength was propelling it hard enough that he wondered if it would shatter a dragon scale.

Cheers erupted as Kaen wrenched the pickaxe free, taking a large chunk of stone with it and letting it fall away.

His eyes were fixed on the glow, which he saw was a fingertip away. He could read the vein, the crack between it and the rock. He had surgically attacked the stone, preparing everything for this one last blow. All those years had led to this moment, and he knew what the next swing would bring.

"One!" Kaen roared, his words filling the mine as he drove the tip of the pickaxe into the last joint that held the stone in place and prevented the world from seeing the treasure behind it.

The stone cracked, breaking free from its purchase, and a massive section fell toward the ground.

Jumping back quickly, Kaen dodged the falling stone and stared at the ore he could see. As he let his lifestone fade, the light of the light orbs filled the dark tunnel, and the men behind him were quiet.

A gleaming section of ore lay glistening in the rock, waiting to be freed from its prison of stone.

Smiling, Kaen turned around and looked at the men.

Raising the pickaxe over his head and almost hitting the low ceiling, he shouted, and everyone joined in with him.

In the sky, Pammon smiled, his entire body flooded with the joy his rider felt at this victory.

Well done! Now collect that ore, and let's eat!

Pammon felt Kaen laugh but knew he was carried away by the moment's celebration.

Angling toward the ground, Pammon glanced at the three deer in his claws.

Perhaps I should celebrate as well . . .

52

An Evil Taskmaster

It never ceases to amaze me how you can cause the common people to celebrate. Look at them. They are like that because of you.

Kaen was still wearing the same smile that he had worn since the first piece of ore broke free. The men were ecstatic when he held it in the air, celebrating as if he had found gold or gems. Looking at the dancing and laughing workers, all stuffed from the two deer Pammon had brought them, Kaen absently patted the bag under his arm.

I'm glad everything turned out. Thank you again for helping me with all this.

Snorting, Pammon shifted his head a little and gazed at Kaen with his golden eyes.

Please write that down.

Write what down?

That once again I have done what was required and brought forth success when the world seemed bleak and dark. You were lost, caught in the embrace of hopelessness, till I rescued you.

Kaen groaned and reached up, scratching Pammon's side.

Who has been teaching you that stuff? I mean, seriously, that is horrible.

When you leave me alone with Aldric and Herb to use the restroom, they start talking like that and act out stuff. I've not figured out why.

They're mocking me . . . Hess and Herb did that a few years ago, but to my face.

Pammon started to thrum, realizing that was what the two grown men had been doing.

Seems you have a group of fans.

Nodding, Kaen closed his eyes and relaxed.

I'm going to sleep. It was a pretty long day. Tomorrow, we go home. I have a wife and some dragons to see.

Pammon's mood changed, and Kaen could sense that his dragon was also looking forward to seeing their family.

"Damn, son, this is a pretty big find!" Hess exclaimed as Kaen gave him the bag of ore. "And you could see through the mountain? That seems unfair!"

"Blame it on the wood elves. But with that and Pammon's help," Kaen said loudly, earning a slight thrum from his ever-present friend, "we managed to succeed. How many arrows will this make?"

Making a few faces as he lifted the bag up and down, trying to judge the weight, Hess clucked his tongue for a moment. "Two."

"What? Only two?" Kaen asked. The look of puzzlement on his face made Hess shrug.

"We'll need to purify it, and by the time we make it fit the new bow you got, there will only be enough for two. I doubt we'll have much left over either."

Groaning, Kaen nodded. "I don't think the vein I pointed them in the direction of will be enough for one, then. It wasn't as bright as this one was. I just wish I could have seen more."

"Hairy dwarf balls, son, you're complaining about not being able to find ore like no one else has in generations. The last time I remember hearing someone do something like that was a dwarf who supposedly had a nose that could smell it. I found it hard to believe, but knowing what you did, who knows."

Giving Hess a slap on his gimpy arm, Kaen winked and then headed toward Pammon, who was standing up in Bren's courtyard. "I need to go see my wife. Tell Sulenda and Callie we love them. Maybe in a week or two, she can come torture Foros and Tazorath for a bit."

Pammon started to thrum again, this time loud enough that it echoed off the walls.

They did not seem to enjoy her attempts at charming them.

I heard. Apparently, Callie was upset they wouldn't let her ride them.

"You be safe! I'll have these in a week or so!" Hess shouted as he waved his stump.

Kaen stood there, enjoying how Ava felt in his arms and her lips against his. Even though he had only been gone a few days, something had made him miss her more than usual.

"Don't say it," she said quietly after they broke their embrace.

"Say what?"

Ava glared at him, smiling slightly, letting Kaen know she was playing. "My stomach . . . it's huge! These two children are already starting to grow!"

Rolling his eyes, Kaen shook his head, ignoring Ava's attempt at pulling her top tight over her stomach to make it even more pronounced.

"Please . . . you can barely tell. I mean, besides how much you are eating and how you walk," Kaen teased, backing away quickly to avoid the fist she was already starting to send toward him.

"You better be careful," she howled as they darted around the cave. "You might find yourself sleeping on the floor!"

A thrum came from Pammon as he watched the two play.

You seem in excellent spirits. Should I ask what happened?

Turning his head toward Amaranth, Pammon ran his jaw against her neck, bringing a trill from her.

Sometimes our riders learn how fortunate we are. I am grateful every day that you and Glynnis decided to come with us across the sea. Imagining my life without you two now seems difficult.

A thrum came from next to him, and Pammon swung his neck around, looking at Glynnis, who stared at him with her silver eyes.

You are growing up if you have realized how fortunate you are to have the two of us. Perhaps you would like to go out in the coming days and fly together.

Pammon felt Glynnis's intent, and a scent he knew far too well began to appear.

Amaranth growled playfully, and Pammon turned to see her eyes changing colors as she watched him.

Perhaps that can happen. I will ensure that Kaen does not need me and let you know when.

The scent grew stronger, and Pammon snorted, shaking his head before laying it on the stone floor and closing his eyes.

You can sense that, and you know what they want.

Kaen laughed from across the cavern, and Ava glanced at him before turning to stare at Amaranth.

"Stop that!" Ava said, poking Kaen in the side. "Why would you laugh at them like that?"

Kaen shook his head and smiled. "I'm not laughing at them. I'm laughing at Pammon."

Ava looked at Pammon, who ignored her question, his eyes closed, trying to sleep.

Turning back to see her husband sneaking away, Ava ran after him, embracing him from the side as they made their way to the small dinner she had prepared.

"You're going to have to tell me what was so funny about that," Ava declared. "Amaranth wants to know as well."

Shaking his head, Kaen smirked. "Sorry, my love, but Pammon would not appreciate it if I told you or his mates. Some things are best kept between Dragon Rider and dragon."

She groaned and rolled her eyes, letting him pull her toward the table.

* * *

"Faster! You need to be faster!"

Phillip and Frederick raced by Kaen, each covered in sweat from the multiple times they had run the obstacle course, which was now part of their weekly training.

As they slowed down and prepared to join Kaen where he was standing, a roar in the sky mimicked Kaen's shouting.

You two are letting your riders win! You are dragons who can fly! Do not let them win again!

Kaen chuckled as Pammon's voice resonated through him.

Neither Foros nor Tazorath replied. Both simply slowed down and landed near Kaen, knowing that their riders would soon be there.

"You two look tired," Kaen said after the silver and red dragons had come near him and plopped to the ground. Their wings and tails were spread out, the extent of having run this gauntlet over a dozen times and its effect on them on display.

Think we should give them a break? We have run them pretty hard.

Are you trying to be the nice one and make me out to be the mean one?

Pammon's question made Kaen chuckle, and he watched as his dragon started to land in the field they were constantly training in.

I mean, they're your kids, so they have to love you even if you're mean. I'm just the fun uncle who tells them their sire is mean and always breathes fire.

Pammon growled as he landed, causing Foros and Tazorath to quickly rise up from the ground.

You would do that. Just wait till your children come. I will make sure they love me more.

Kaen burst out in laughter, getting looks from both dragons and riders as he shook his head at Pammon.

I have no doubt they will say your name long before they say mine.

Frederick and Phillip made it to where Kaen was standing, each going to his dragon and scratching their heads and necks.

"You four have done well. So Pammon and I decided that you deserve a break."

Both boys smiled, and the dragons let out a trill.

"You will camp out here tonight. Find yourself some food and cook it. There is water in the well at the far end of the field. Tomorrow, we will start after the sun is up. Do you have any questions?"

"So, no more training today?" Phillip asked, his tone not hiding his disbelief.

"No more training. I know you have been busy while Pammon and I were mining. Tomorrow we will go elsewhere for some training. I'll pick up some clothes and supplies. You're going to be roughing it for the next few nights."

Both boys exchanged glances with each other and eventually shrugged and nodded.

"Beats running this thing over and over," Frederick replied.

Pammon began to thrum, already knowing what Kaen was thinking.

"Uh . . . it has to be better than this . . . right?" Phillip asked after hearing Pammon laugh.

"Sure . . . believe that," Kaen answered. "Just be ready when the sun is up. We'll be here."

Phillip and Frederick let out a groan for a moment before starting to discuss what possible pain Kaen might have in store for them.

You really are evil. I like it.

I just tried to think what you would do, and the idea came to me. Undoubtedly, your children are strong enough for what I'm thinking.

Pammon thrummed.

If not, they will be.

"Listen up, I want all these stones broken to about this size. Once that is done, Foros and Tazorath will take turns carrying the stones a quarter of a mile toward town. Eventually, you will bring them into town for the people to use. If they are broken from dropping, then they won't count."

Phillip and Frederick looked at the quarry they were standing in. The ogres and goblins had destroyed it when they came through the land, but there were still plenty of stones to be hewn, and each boy was strong enough to move them.

"How many do we need to get to town?" Phillip asked, his expression not hiding his concern about what Kaen would say.

Kaen looked up at Pammon, who was sitting at the top of the quarry, reviewing the task with his two children.

"Fifty stones, larger than three feet. Make sure they are the length of the pickaxe handle. Once all fifty are inside the outer walls of the kingdom's defense, you can return home. Until then, you need to find food and water here. While I don't expect orcs or goblins to bother you, a wise person once told me to always carry a weapon."

Both boys looked around the quarry once more and saw stones that might be large enough to count and others that would need to be broken.

Dropping the sack of various tools he had been carrying on the ground, Kaen walked toward the ramp leading to the top.

"That's it?" Frederick shouted after him. "Just fifty?"

Kaen didn't look back but just nodded and waved, a massive grin across his face.

This is going to take longer than you expect.

Oh . . . I don't plan on seeing them for a week. Learning to cut a stone to the correct size is more complex than it looks. Either they make the stone too big, and Foros and Tazorath will struggle to carry it, or they may end up making it too small. Trust me, all four of them will beg to run the course again.

Pammon thrummed as he watched Kaen coming up the ramp, his smile even larger than before.

53

Long Plans

They finally have figured out how to get the sizes they want. That's much sooner than you believed.

Kaen smiled as he patted Pammon's neck, using his friend's eyes to watch the two boys working on rocks and the dragons doing their best to move the stones.

It's been two days, and they only have fifteen rocks to show for it. They still have to transfer all those stones at least ten more miles before getting to the walls. Don't forget, the dragons have to swap every quarter mile. That means forty-plus exchanges.

Pammon started thrumming as he watched Foros and Tazorath struggle with a stone.

You really are evil. I'm glad Hess never made us do anything like this. How in the world did you come up with this?

The capital needs stone. People need jobs. They need to get stronger and work together. The other day, it came to me in that mine. They can have all that while helping out the city.

Well, at least you are letting Amaranth and Glynnis bring them food every other day. I can't imagine them being able to keep going without it.

They would be fine hunting their food if the forest was in better shape. There is another perk as well. All that dragon crap will help where they are at.

Which is near Minoosh . . . two dragons with a lot of stones . . .

Kaen groaned and gave one of Pammon's scales a gentle thump.

That isn't how it goes, but yes. Now, let's go home. I need to meet with Aldric and Herb.

The three men looked at the map, and occasionally one moved some tokens around, yet they had not spoken for almost ten minutes since they had started.

"I think that is the best option based on current intel," Herb stated after no one touched anything for almost a minute. "We know where their allies and troops are. The one thing we aren't sure of is whether the orcs and goblins will come or are already present."

"This depends on many factors, though," Aldric said as he tapped the northwest part of the map. "We don't know how many warriors from Pensworth will answer Stioks's call. If they come out in force, their warriors would be formidable for our people to fight."

"But what if we wait till Foros and Tazorath are old enough to help?" Kaen said, pointing at the five tokens he had sitting on the edge of the map. "If we send a pair with each army, Pammon and I can draw Stioks out alone. Then our armies would have dragons to help with whatever resistance is there."

Grunting, Herb slid a piece of paper on the edge of the table closer. "Based on the last report, the armies are growing each month. How many months are you planning to wait?"

Both men stared at Kaen, who frowned as he considered what he and Pammon had discussed.

"At least four months would be best. That gives us time to build our armies and prepare with the dwarves and the wood elves. Foros and Tazorath should be a decent size by then. If correct, that would give them twenty seconds or so of their breath."

Taking the two tokens representing Glynnis and Tazorath, Kaen set them over by the army from Ebonmount.

"If both of them are here, it would give our troops a massive boost in damage and also help against the potential orcs and goblins."

"Why does everyone always talk about orcs and goblins?" Aldric asked. "The ogres are the real problems. I mean, yes, the ten thousand or more troops cause a problem, but those ogres, especially the one you mentioned fighting in the cave, can decimate most armies on their own."

"That is why I want us to wait until the dragons are old enough to help," replied Kaen. "Just having Amaranth and Glynnis isn't enough. Especially since Amaranth doesn't have a breath weapon."

Herb nodded as Aldric grunted. The king picked up the other two tokens, representing the silver and green dragons, and put them next to the dwarf and wood elf armies.

"So we wait four months?"

"At least," Kaen replied. "I would prefer seven, but you know why I want to wait that long."

Chuckling, Aldric nodded. "I'm assuming you're actually planning on having Ava on the battlefield even though she just gave birth to your twin children?"

"It was her request. She and Amaranth want to be together. They have a . . . weird bond. Sometimes I'm unsure what it is, but it differs from what Pammon and I share. It's not a true bond, or I don't believe it can be."

"Didn't Stioks and Juthom have a bond?" Herb asked, his eyes staring up at the ceiling as he racked his brain about what they knew.

"Juthom said they had something but not like ours. Stioks wasn't resistant to the cold or heat from their bond, and he couldn't fly as high as Pammon or I could. He also didn't get the bonus to his stats from the bond. Still, they could communicate, and there was something about it."

"Ava is a strong mage. Having her above the armies would be very helpful," Herb chimed in. "I do miss having her within the adventurers' guild, especially with the skirmishes that have been taking place north of the mountain pass."

"Show me where you are having problems," Kaen said as he took a pencil and handed it to Herb. "I have plans next week to take Foros and Tazorath out with Phillip and Frederick to train in those forests while also bringing back some wood for the kingdom."

Herb shook his head and put a few marks along the woods north of the kingdom pass. "Unless you plan on going way up here, out where that quest you first took was, you should be fine. We are running into packs of goblins, orcs, and the occasional ogre in the area east of there. I would venture to say they are not as organized as the ones we faced south of us."

"We're getting off track," Aldric said as he tapped the map where the tokens were placed. "Seven months. You want us to wait seven months and then launch an all-out assault on Stioks and his kingdom. Do you really believe that he will not invade before then?"

Crossing his arms, Kaen ran his tongue over his teeth, waiting for what he knew was coming.

Stioks won't attack until his dragon is older. Based on the size we saw and the knowledge that he has a lifestone like yours, that puny thing will be about the size of Amaranth or Glynnis in seven or eight months.

That means what? Do you think his dragon will be weak?

Pammon's mind was filled with different thoughts, and Kaen picked up on the one that bothered him the most.

It's still Stioks. You're more concerned with him and what he might be doing right now.

We know that he has been creating wands and harnessing his and Juthom's power. With Juthom gone and the last of the female dragons they had, he will slow down, but I don't want to underestimate the power of those tools.

You three forget that we are not sure how many more he might have, and if he gives those to someone in charge of the armies you face, do you expect

to win those battles easily? Even with two dragons leading each of those armies, we are hoping that it will be enough.

Pammon was searching for food on the other side of the mountain, and Kaen could feel the frustration at the unknowns and variables they would face when the armies and kingdoms finally attacked.

What happens if the ogres, orcs, goblins, and whatever other creatures come and attack? Can Tazorath and Glynnis stop them? I would like to think so, but my child won't be that strong, even with eight months of life coursing through her body. She is also underfed and lacks the experience you and I have.

And Phillip and Frederick will most likely be on the ground when the battle comes.

I believe they can ride earlier since we know how to make the harnesses, so we are pushing Toros and Tazorath to get stronger. Their lack of experience and fighting creatures of that caliber will be our biggest problem, even if that happens.

Kaen saw the other two men watching him, knowing he was conversing with Pammon.

"Another minute, if you don't mind."

Both nodded and turned back to the map, studying it some more and whispering between themselves while waiting for Kaen to be finished.

What if we go and practice against the kobolds? It would be a better fight for the four of them. The boys could practice a variety of weapons and hopefully gain a few more skills. Their dragons would be able to get some practice in fighting against armies.

Pammon said nothing, but Kaen knew his dragon agreed with that option.

I would rather attempt that than return to the castle of the orcs and goblins.

As would I. So seven months? Eight at the latest, depending on Ava?

That is the best option. Anything beyond that puts us in a position where we must consider that Stioks might begin to attack randomly.

Nodding to himself, Kaen frowned, knowing that Pammon was right. If Stioks attacked, the biggest issue would be the man's ability to plan and his experience fighting. Almost dying once was a lesson he didn't want to have to learn a second time.

"Ok," Kaen said, getting Aldric's and Herb's attention. "Pammon agrees. We need seven or eight months. Anything beyond that is too long. So knowing that, what is our plan?"

Herb sighed and rubbed his chin while Aldric moved to a table a few feet away.

"Let me grab something," Aldric said.

Both men watched as the king dug through a few drawers, finally pulling out a stack of papers and returning to them with his notes.

"I have only two thousand men I would call truly battle-ready. Another thousand, maybe, who would be there for support and minor incursions. I cannot promise more than that with my limited number of mages and healers."

Aldric paused, putting two of the papers he had brought back down side by side on the table. "This is the armor and weapons I have available. The second sheet shows the number of troops we can conscript from those who fought on the walls and are willing to fight. If we pull everyone from the defense of the walls and trust that no orcs or ogres will come, we can have another ten thousand max. Their armor will be limited and their weapons even more limited."

"But seven months," Herb interrupted. "If we have seven months, surely we can—"

"No," Aldric replied, cutting Herb off. "There is not enough ore coming in. We haven't had a chance until recently to start mining again. Unless we change that, there is no way I can begin to hope to even get there."

Kaen started to chuckle, and both men turned to see what was so funny about their predicament.

"You two seem to not realize what my plan with Frederick and Phillip has been this whole time. Didn't you hear what I asked about those trees to the north?"

Herb's eyes narrowed at Kaen, and then they widened as realization set in. "You're using those two to help prepare for the coming battle!"

Smiling, Kaen nodded.

"Right now, they are bringing over fifty rocks from the quarry where Minoosh was. They will have the materials needed to start building forges. Next, we will be headed north to start gathering wood, usable for both weapons and fueling those forges. After that comes the mines I was just at. They and their dragons will be training nonstop, but if I learned anything from Hess, some of the best training comes from swinging a pickaxe and an axe."

Aldric smiled. "That would actually work. If you can help with that, I'm sure I can get others to participate."

"Consider it done!" exclaimed Kaen as he held out his hand toward his friend.

Both men shook, and the atmosphere in the room finally began to break. Hope was starting to build.

54

Growing Stronger Isn't Easy

Kaen and Pammon were waiting in the area where Foros and Tazorath had been setting the stones inside the outer walls of the capital.

I'm impressed. Seems they realized sooner than later the number of stones that might be too small.

"And there are at least sixty stones here. I guess they didn't want to go back and start again."

Both dragon and rider laughed, watching as Foros and Tazorath each came with a large stone in their claws.

They have grown, even with less food than I know they would prefer. I can see the muscles that I did not have at their age.

That's because you spent more time playing.

Pammon huffed, and Kaen chuckled, feeling the acknowledgment but frustration at his statement.

"Kaen!"

Phillip and Frederick were coming from the wall, looking a bit worn out but also displaying a few extra muscles than a week ago.

They have grown as well. Perhaps you do know a thing or two about training people.

"Hey, boys!" Kaen shouted back, watching as both of them started to race toward him, pickaxes swinging in each hand as they ran.

One of them will figure out that running like that isn't intelligent.

I agree. Now tell me, how many days do we want them to rest before I break their spirits again?

Pammon thrummed and considered what both groups would need to recover. Foros and Tazorath started to descend only a hundred yards from the ground, each displaying their teeth in a smile, knowing the task was finally complete.

You two have done well, Pammon said, praising his children. **I am proud to see that you made good choices and are getting stronger.**

We owe our mothers for the food they brought us. I haven't seen anything beyond a rabbit in the last few days.

Pammon smiled and looked at Foros. His golden eyes watched his sire as he spoke.

You, Tazorath, look to be getting stronger as well. Your mother will be very excited to hear how much you have grown.

A trill came from his daughter as she gently set the rock on the ground.

I am grateful for your instruction. I can tell the difference now in how long I can fly and what I can carry.

Kaen shook both young men's hands as they arrived, dropping the tools on the ground and panting from their race.

"I almost had you," Phillip said between breaths. "That stupid series of holes slowed me down."

Frederick stretched, looking at his dragon as Tazorath flew toward him.

"Tell me we are going to get at least a day off," Frederick asked, returning his attention to Kaen.

"I'm still waiting on Pammon to decide how many days you need before we start the next part of training."

Both groaned at Kaen's choice of words.

"How many will we need?" Phillip said, repeating the words they knew held their next stage of training. "Do we want to know what is coming next?"

Kaen shook his head and grinned. "Nope, but just enjoy the time you get. You deserve it. I would make sure you eat and sleep."

Reaching out and scratching a few scales on Pammon's leg, he turned and saw his dragon watching him.

Three days. You four have three days until you must meet us at the pass to the north. I suggest you prepare a little more this time. Bring some extra food and clothes.

Pammon leaned down and put his head near Phillip and Frederick.

You two also need to make sure to bring rope. Lots of rope.

Both boys nodded, refusing to allow their bodies to step back from Pammon's presence like they wanted to.

"Understood."

Pammon nodded, turned back to his children, and gave each of them a few gentle rubs with his chin before returning to his original spot.

"You heard Pammon," Kaen said, shifting his gaze between boys and dragons. "Phillip and Frederick, get on Pammon. Foros and Tazorath, go wherever you want."

Both dragons turned to their riders, each spending a moment with a little scratching of scales before the red- and silver-scaled dragons took flight and made a beeline toward their caves.

"Can you drop us off at Hess and Sulenda's inn?" Frederick asked. "I know we smell, but we can get some food there and see our parents before heading back to our place."

Kaen nodded and watched as the two boys grabbed their tools and moved toward Pammon.

Three days. You're very generous.

Pammon thrummed, ignoring the glances the two boys gave him.

I have no doubt that may not be enough for what is coming. Just exactly how many trees are you planning on cutting down?

Kaen smiled and shrugged.

A large part of the forest . . . enough for you to teach your children to fly.

Thrumming louder, Pammon smiled, his massive teeth on display as both boys groaned.

"We're totally getting screwed," Phillip declared.

Nodding, Frederick sighed.

Pammon hovered above the forest, shock and awe coming through their bond as they looked down at what the two boys had done over the last two weeks.

If you had told me this plan and we had bet on it two weeks ago, I would have lost. You really do know them better than I can believe.

Rubbing Pammon's neck, Kaen took the compliment and smiled. He was looking through Pammon's eyes and saw what amazed his dragon.

That is wide enough, correct? You can use Glynnis and teach them to fly through that run. It isn't as good as the one we had back in Roccnari, but it was the best we could do in only two weeks.

Pammon thrummed and shook his head.

Only two weeks . . . It took us a few months, with the help of the elves, to build our course. I'm not confident they would like to know you were able to accomplish what you did with those boys.

I agree . . . now let's go down there and see how the transportation of those logs is going.

Kaen watched as Phillip and Frederick finished cutting two trees into more manageable sections. Each had his shirt off and wore only pants and boots.

Their hands were covered in calluses from the labor they had done over the last three weeks. Their muscles looked ready to burst through their skin. Food had been plenty, but the amount of work they put in every day had stripped their bodies of any ounce of fat. Nothing about them looked like a boy about to be seventeen years old.

You definitely did not look like that at seventeen.

Kaen nodded and said nothing. Pammon was correct. Had Hess tried to push him like this, there was no doubt in Kaen's mind that he would have fought and complained about it every day. Yet every moment these boys trained, Kaen knew their commitment and trust in him. They were a totally different class of worker.

I'm going to go help them. I could probably use a little exercise also.

Groaning, Pammon watched as Kaen jogged to the area with the axes.

Turning his neck, Pammon looked at his two children, who were waiting for their riders to attach the ropes to the harnesses they had created for them to help drag logs.

Tell me, are you two ok with what this training has required of you?

Tazorath took a deep breath and let it out before she chose to speak.

While I would prefer not to be turned into a mule or some other common animal, it is hard to argue with the results. Look at Foros and his back legs. They have grown as mine have from the work we have done.

Foros trilled at the comment from his sister for a brief moment.

We both have grown stronger. Tazorath has gained more size than I thought she might. Mother warned me that she would not be as large as me, but it appears she will eventually outgrow Mother.

Pammon thrummed and moved to give an affectionate touch to his children.

You both are correct. This training may seem beneath you, but Kaen has years of seeing what worked for us and is making sure you two are prepared for what is coming. I told you that we have only half a year before you must show the world how strong you are.

Snorting, Foros shook his head and bent backward, adjusting one of the ropes with his snout.

Should I ask what is coming up after this?

Pammon grinned and gazed at both of his children. Pride and love overwhelmed him.

You two will be spending a few weeks with me and Glynnis.

Foros and Tazorath glanced at each other, locking eyes for a moment before looking at their sire.

I'm unsure if I should be afraid or excited, Tazorath said as a shiver ran through her spine.

Thrumming, Pammon gave each of them another moment of physical affection before sensing Kaen coming toward him.

"Push, and I'll pull!" Kaen shouted.

The rope he had slung over his shoulders was tight, and Phillip stood next to Frederick, hands outstretched as they pressed against the tree trunk they had hacked into a smaller section.

All three worked together, dragging the thirty-foot section of wood toward the dragons, moving quickly through the dirt that had been packed from all the other trees that had been dragged and rolled over it.

Pammon backed up, watching both boys smile as Kaen showed off, doing far more work than they were.

Yes, boys, he is showing off.

Laughter came as the two stopped pushing, watching the tree continue, albeit slightly slower, in the same direction Kaen was moving.

The rope strained under the weight, but Kaen never missed a step. His legs continued to drive power with each step, moving a weight that most would never imagine was possible.

You two realize he can most likely lift that if he wants to.

That's not possible! Is it?

Pammon turned and looked at Foros, who was watching Kaen intently.

He has done it before.

Kaen stopped dragging the log and stood up, sighing as he looked at Pammon. "You're ruining the moment. I'm not here to show off, just to help!"

Frederick and Phillip caught up with Kaen and held their hands out, waiting on the rope.

"We'll take over. Something tells me we both need to get a little stronger," Frederick said.

Smiling, Kaen handed both boys the ropes. "I've got years on both of you, but I have no doubt if you two keep doing what you have been doing, there will be a day that nothing will be impossible.

Each of them smiled and got set, pulling together with practice, and the log moved again.

"Once you get these last four trees to the road, you're done," Kaen announced. "After that, we'll head back to town."

"Where you two going?" Phillip asked, glancing over his shoulder at Kaen.

"I want to scout with Pammon. We should be back in a few hours. I'm assuming you will be done by then?"

We would be done faster if they played less.

Kaen chuckled and looked at Foros.

"I'm ok with them playing. I'm also glad that you are being kinder to your sister."

That statement caused Foros to shift his head.

I have never been—

A gentle growl from Pammon cut Foros off.

"You haven't always been kind. While not mean, I do not mind your confidence. Just know your sister has talents that make her just as special as you are. Rejoice that you have someone to help push you to be better. If Pammon had

had a brother or sister like you do, something tells me he would be stronger than I can imagine."

Pammon thrummed and shifted lower.

We need to go. Otherwise, they will not finish, and I will not get my dinner tonight.

55

A Moment of Relaxation

Pammon roared gently as Amaranth and Ava tried to pass him and Kaen.

They seem intent on cheating.

I don't think you said they couldn't use their Flight Burst skill. If you wanted to, you could use your skills as well.

I would not do that. If I did, Amaranth would accuse me of cheating.

Kaen sighed, smiling as the wind whipped past him and his wife, and Amaranth surged ahead.

What is good for the goose isn't good for the gander . . .

I have no idea what that means . . .

Laughing, Kaen leaned against Pammon's massive neck and urged his friend on.

Let's not worry about it. For now, let's focus on where we are going.

Kaen slowly inserted the piece of meat into Ava's mouth as she lay on the blanket, her head on his leg.

"It's hot," he stated again, ignoring her scowl as he made it dance in his fingers a few inches from her lips.

Grabbing his wrist, Ava pulled his hand down and took the strip of meat from his fingers, getting awfully close to the tips that held it.

"You almost bit me!" Kaen exclaimed, watching as Ava and chewed the venison they were about to enjoy. "I was trying not to burn your tongue."

"More like starve a pregnant woman," Ava said between bites. "I was hungry."

Laughing, Kaen wiped his fingers on his pants and then ran his thumb against his wife's cheek as she chewed.

"I love you. More than anything," he said, watching her smile.

After she finally swallowed her bite, Ava winked at him. "I love you as well, my love. Just know, though, that next time, I'll bite your fingers if you do that again."

Nodding, Kaen grabbed a fork, stuck it in another piece of meat on a platter near him, and handed it to Ava. "In that case, you can feed yourself," he teased.

She playfully snatched the fork from his hand and smiled, gladly feeding herself as he watched her eat.

Looking up and out toward the west, Kaen stared even though he couldn't see Pammon or Amaranth.

"Why are you smiling so much?"

"Please, you know why. Amaranth didn't hide her excitement about coming out here today."

Shaking her head, Ava finished her food and shrugged. "She might have mentioned that some alone time with Pammon was on the list."

"Alone time," Kaen said, mocking her slightly. "Even with him doing his best to block what they are doing, it's impossible now. I'm just glad they took it a bit away from us."

"Is it weird? Feeling that?"

Kaen shrugged as he ran his finger through Ava's hair. "It's hard to describe. You knew what it was like that night we returned from across the sea."

Groaning, Ava nodded and rolled over so she could sit up and face her husband. "Don't I know it . . . that was not nice of Pammon at all."

Kaen nodded, smirking as he recalled that night very well. "I might have earned that, as I mentioned before, but now it's not as . . . animalistic? Is that a word?"

"I think I know what you mean," Ava replied as she moved closer to Kaen. "Amaranth had also commented on that, and I think we both know the difference in those moments. Sometimes you really want that connection, and other times it is because you show your love for the other through it."

Kaen nodded and shuffled closer to his wife, grabbing the log he had been leaning against and shifting it slightly to provide support for his back. She leaned backward against his chest, and Kaen wrapped his arms around her, putting his hands on her growing belly.

Ava rested her hands on top of his and smiled. "No movement yet but I'll tell you when I feel something."

"I can't wait," he replied, closing his eyes and leaning against her.

Sitting there quietly, both fell asleep in each other's arms.

Pammon watched as Kaen helped Ava onto Amaranth.

Each was smiling, and Kaen could tell that Pammon was frustrated. He knew that the woman and the female dragon were talking, yet he couldn't hear what they were saying.

Look at your wife. She almost laughed about something. Indeed, Amaranth wouldn't say anything about me or my performance that would draw such a reaction.

Kaen couldn't help but chuckle, earning a backward glance from Ava as she finished climbing up into the saddle.

"Should I ask?"

Kaen shook his head. "Not unless you want to share with Pammon and me what you two are talking about."

Ava's cheeks turned a slight shade of red, but she said nothing.

I would prefer to have some secrets. We shall refrain from being so obvious that we are talking in the future.

Pammon snorted and shook his head.

Do not make promises we all know that you two won't keep.

Trilling, Amaranth turned after Ava had clipped herself in and took a few steps before becoming airborne, not waiting for Kaen or Pammon to be ready.

She is cheating again . . . why does she do that?

Because she knows it bothers you. She can tell how much it affects you, and in a small way, it is because she cares.

Grumbling, Pammon lowered himself as Kaen jogged and jumped almost to where his saddle was, easily getting onto it in one go. Pammon didn't wait for him to clip in, already moving and going airborne before Kaen wrapped both legs around his neck.

One of these days I'm going to fall and then what?

It won't be that big a fall; besides, you're strong enough to handle it.

Groaning, Kaen got set and clipped in, laughing as Pammon did his best to catch up with Ava and Amaranth.

Kaen held Ava in his arms, watching her as she stood back a few feet from the clear stone that marked their child's grave. She said nothing, just staring at it, holding the small flowers she had picked earlier.

The wind whipped around them and the sound of the air over the rocks made a melody that sounded almost calming.

"It's perfect," Ava said quietly. "I still owe Pammon."

"As he said before, it was his honor. This was his gift and an expression of his love. Besides, you have no cows to give."

Chuckling, Ava sniffed back a few possible tears and leaned her head against Kaen's chest. "Thank you for coming with me."

"You know I'll always come with you whenever you want if I can. Now let me see the flowers, and I'll take care of them."

She handed the flowers to Kaen, who moved the last few steps and wedged them into the crack where he had put the previous bunch. Eventually, they would dry out and be swept away by the wind, but for a day or two, they would stay, hopefully bringing joy to their child's spirit.

Kaen turned, sensing Amaranth already coming to land on the small ledge.

"So soon?"

Ava nodded and smiled. "I don't require as much time now. Besides, I have been gifted with two children, and I know they need their mother to stop freezing her backside off on the top of this mountain."

Kaen moved and embraced Ava, holding her close as he watched Amaranth approaching them.

"Pammon is dying, by the way. He was concerned she might have said something humorous about his performance to you based on how you were giggling and smiling."

Looking up at Kaen, Ava winked. "What could a female dragon possibly tell me about a male dragon and them having sex that could make me laugh."

Rolling his eyes, Kaen shook his head before shuddering. "Forget that I asked . . . not the image I want in my head."

Ava nodded and reached up, taking her husband's head in her hand. She pulled him close and kissed him on the lips.

"Just like you don't need or want that image, she doesn't need or want the image of us. That is why there is now a barrier in the cave."

Kaen realized his mouth was open, and Ava began to laugh, turning to see Amaranth finally settled on the ledge.

"I didn't realize—"

"She and I know . . . as I said, not everyone wants to see that."

Moving quickly, Kaen hurried to help Ava onto Amaranth and saw the green dragon watching him, her eyes having turned silver for now.

He felt his cheeks turning warm and realized he was embarrassed at the thought of Amaranth and Glynnis being uncomfortable with what they had done. He had never considered it until now.

I wondered if I should have said something a while ago, but you seemed not to realize it, and I wasn't sure how you would respond to that news.

Groaning, Kaen shook his head as he helped finish getting Ava into position.

If it was that bad, someone should have said something to me!

We just did. Amaranth said she would handle it and she did. Your wife took care of that problem without embarrassing you because, apparently, she was right. I can feel how you regret all that now.

Sighing, Kaen moved back, letting Amaranth fall off the ledge and toward the ground before her wings caught the air and she swooped back up into the sky.

Next time, tell me . . . I'm assuming this is why Ava has told me to make sure I'm always wearing pants.

Kaen could hear Pammon's thrumming as he approached the ledge. The laughter and humor in that statement flooded their bond.

I did threaten once to bite off the worm . . . As a male, I understand the desire one might have to flaunt his appendage, but even I do not desire to see that again.

Clearing his throat, Kaen smacked his mouth a few times before he started to run.

I swear . . . why is it everyone tells me important stuff way later than they should?

Swooping by the ledge as Kaen jumped off it, Pammon arrived at the right speed and height for Kaen to land on both feet against his shoulder.

Pammon continued to thrum as he flew, glancing back at Kaen, who wore a scowl.

I'll try to let you know sooner next time. That means pay attention to why Ava has your boots closer to the cave's opening. The smell is pretty awful.

Plopping down into his saddle, Kaen clipped himself in and grunted.

Anything else?

The tone of his question hid none of the frustration Kaen felt at realizing he had been oblivious to so many things in his own home.

Why don't you ask Ava when we get back? I'm sure she has a list and would be happy to know you are prepared to learn how long it is.

Pammon's enjoyment of the moment bled through their bond, and after a minute, Kaen couldn't help but smile and eventually laugh. He knew he was fortunate enough to have those who loved him and did what they did while trying not to embarrass him.

Never mind. I'll just live in the joy of blissful ignorance.

Pammon groaned and turned his head to look at Kaen once more.

For our sanity, please talk to your wife.

Kaen leaned back and laughed, ignoring the glare Pammon gave him.

56

Pushing Past Our Limits

Foros, focus on that turn! Your angle is off, and the speed isn't right! If you don't fix it, you'll—

The sounds of limbs snapping as the silver body crashed through some branches of the nearby trees echoed through the forest.

I've got him . . .

Pammon didn't come down this time, keeping his position in the air as Amaranth moved to where Foros was, now on the ground and in obvious pain from the impact.

Alright, daughter. You saw what your brother did wrong. That turn requires you to slow into it and then explode out of it. Make sure the angle is right, or you will end up like him.

Tazorath said nothing, dropping down toward the forest and the start of the path they had cut through the woods last week.

Pammon studied it again, still impressed with what Kaen had created. Kaen had marked every tree Phillip and Frederick had cut down. The man had somehow designed a path in his head while they scouted out this area.

How is he?

Amaranth had reached Foros, and the green glow of healing was visible from where Pammon soared.

He will be fine. He has a few minor scrapes and a broken bone, but in a few minutes, he will be ready to go again. Have you tried this course yet?

Pammon grinned, knowing full well that question was now asked for the third time, and Kaen would lose the bet they had made.

I have. Multiple times. Though I am not the fastest, I would say I did rather well, considering my size.

Perhaps I should give it a try later and see if I can do better.

Pammon could sense her attempt at humor, a tone as she spoke that had become more assertive since bonding with Ava.

Maybe you can show our two children later if they don't figure it out.

Amaranth finished healing Foros, and both dragons left the ground, getting airborne again and moving into position to watch Tazorath as she attempted her first full run.

You may go!

Thank you, sire!

Pammon smiled as he saw his daughter spin and dive, gaining speed as she approached the opening near the road. Unlike her brother, she had a natural flying ability like her mother. She could see the spot she needed to line up with on the first straight part and took off like a predator after a meal.

Tazorath knew the next turn was coming, a sharp one to the right that would quickly turn left after only fifty yards. She used her red-scaled wings to angle and catch some air, slowing quickly before banking around the turn and flapping them to gain back some of the speed.

The trees were at most fifty yards tall, and staying within them was hard for maintaining speed in the narrow path. Pammon had struggled with how his wings almost touched the edges, knowing Kaen had also intentionally done that for him.

Watch that side!

Tazorath reacted instantly, shifting her entire body and leaning into the left turn, following the wide arc.

You need more speed. You're dropping!

Pammon saw his daughter's body began to slide down toward the ground.

Once she had completed the turn and reached the straight area again, her body leveled out, only thirty feet or so above the ground, and she started trying to gain as much speed as possible for the next series of turns.

Tazorath had seen where Foros had messed up and knew she had to at least beat him. It was only two turns in that he collided with the tree branches sticking out. Eight turns back to back like a snake moving across the ground were designed to pinch them in tighter at each turn, making going fast harder as there was less room to beat their wings as they shifted side to side.

Moving to the top of the trees as she gained all the speed she could, Tazorath banked to the right, going as far wide as possible toward the trees before cutting into the turn.

Nice work! Now, roll for the next turn!

Tazorath focused on the angle she knew she needed, rolling as her father instructed.

Her speed as she came around the turn pushed her toward the same branches her brother had just knocked off, but she was able to tilt her wings slightly to slow down, making the turn.

You're dropping! Prepare for the next turn.

Her move and change of her wings had sent her downward, requiring some height for more speed as she approached the next turn, rolling again to angle for it.

Move! You're too close to the branches! Fix the—

Pammon sighed, seeing his daughter clip two branches. Knowing her run was over, she slowed down and came to a stop on the ground.

I've got her. She should be fine, but that was good for the first run.

She learns fast; I think she almost figured out that next part. Thank you for checking on her.

Pammon saw that Tazorath was holding her left wing a little differently and knew she probably had injured it when the branches had clipped her.

Foros, are you almost ready?

His son looked up at him from where he was flying beneath.

I am. I'm not sure I can make that turn . . . It is too narrow and—

Stop.

Pammon's words cut off his son, and Pammon began to move toward the entrance to the course they were trying to learn.

I know what you want to say, but do not doubt yourself or make excuses. Size matters for some things, but what is more important is pushing yourself and finding out what is possible. You can do this, and you will do this. We will focus on this course and other things for the next few weeks. When we are done, your mother will praise you for how well you accomplished this feat.

Pammon didn't need to see Foros to sense the waves of pleasure from him after that praise. It always struck Pammon as something weird. He could sense how his children were feeling when they were close.

Amaranth, please let me know when you are done. I want you two to go up into the sky and watch me with Foros.

Pammon raced through the last straightaway, his massive body barely fitting between the trees as his wings stretched just enough to flap and gain the altitude needed for the last part.

Kaen, you are an evil man for what you did here . . .

Pammon's thoughts made him thrum as the last thirty yards quickly approached.

The last two movements required flying sideways and rolling completely upside down to maintain the speed necessary for a fast drop in altitude.

Pammon pulled his wings in, rotated his body, and flared them slightly at the top. They dropped downward as he angled toward the almost ninety-degree turn.

A few yards from the top, he came out of his roll, having picked up the speed required, and his wings stretched halfway out, letting him finish the back turn that angled almost ninety degrees.

Having cleared the last turn, he saw the end of the straight path zooming toward him and began to beat his wings quickly, rising toward the tops of the trees.

As he flew past the trees at the end of the course, his talons and tail almost clipped them.

Breathing heavily, he extended his wings completely and flew till he was circling the air with his family.

That was incredible . . .

Pammon smiled at Tazorath, who was watching him. Her green eyes sparkled as she watched her father approach them.

You two can do the same. Remember, you are young, but you are gifted. Inside, you are the blood of your mothers and me. Right now, it feels like we are pushing you harder than you desire, but it is for one purpose: to win a battle that will end a war and allow you to live with your rider in a new age—an age where you can travel this land, find new things to eat, and see places.

I'm ready to go again.

Pammon smiled and turned to where Foros was preparing to dive toward the course entrance.

I'm sure you are. Now, show me what you have learned.

That sounds like a good first day. I shouldn't have doubted you showing off for the three of them.

Pammon groaned and forced his side out, pushing Kaen some as his rider leaned against him.

They will get there. I can see what improvements they need. Glynnis and Amaranth will train them until we get back. Are you ready to go in the morning?

Stretching, Kaen nodded.

Look at those two. They are gone. I don't think they were prepared for today at all.

Pammon nodded. He had already seen Phillip and Frederick asleep a little away from where he and Kaen were.

Any luck today?

There is actually a lot. I scouted all the mines in the area and marked half a dozen or more spots where there was ore. It's not what we want, but I found the ore for the weapons and armor we need. One mineshaft actually opened to a rather large cavern, and there were lots of areas in there with some potential. I doubt they will have it all done before we return, but Aldric said they are already preparing the forges. Wagons will come tomorrow and start hauling off everything.

Pammon glanced around the camp where buildings were set up. The shacks they had erected didn't look sturdy, but Pammon knew all this had been done in only a few days.

Are they going to build a place for Phillip and Frederick? Seems unfair they are sleeping outside.

Kaen chuckled.

You seem to forget we slept outside most of the time as well. For a Dragon Rider, it's not that big a deal, especially if their dragon can spend the night with them.

I did mention that to Amaranth and Glynnis. They will try not to wear them out as much as I did so that both Foros and Tazorath can make it here at night. A dragon and a rider need to be close.

You're right . . . That is why I had them do the first two tasks together. The mine isn't a place they can help out. Besides, I have no doubt that in a few weeks, the lessons those two will learn when it comes to flying will be greater than anything you have ever had.

Pammon thrummed once before stopping, realizing it would wake everyone up if he continued.

Do you remember what Tharnok told me the day he tested my flying skills?

Kaen began to laugh, holding his hand over his mouth.

You move like a bird with only one wing that is about to die or something like that . . . right?

Yes . . . Pammon answered, sighing as he laid his head on the ground facing Kaen. **He had told me on many occasions that I flew about as well as a moth or other creatures who fluttered around, not doing anything. It hurt, but now I realize why he pushed me so much. Imagine if he hadn't. We would have never made it to the land of the dragons if he hadn't. I'm not sure we would have survived that first encounter with Stioks.**

Kaen stared at Pammon, those massive golden eyes almost glowing in the night.

I'm grateful for them every day as well. I pray that Elies and Tharnok are finally at peace.

As do I.

Both closed their eyes, knowing the next week would be important in the training.

57

Remembering It's a Team

Kaen and Pammon swept over the desert area, scouring the land for the kobolds they could see still moving in groups of hundreds and even up to a thousand.

It would appear they have fractured off from the large army they once had. We may have done more damage than we believed.

Nodding, Kaen mulled over the possible implications that might mean as they finished their second day of scouting.

Are there still at least fifteen thousand of them? None of the groups was more than two thousand at best. It also appears they are moving to different areas and breaking up into smaller groups. Do you believe they feel they won or lost?

Pammon thrummed as he considered Kaen's words.

I have no doubt that we won that battle. They lost a significant part of their forces, and now it appears they are headed home. You saw that none of them were near where we fought.

Yes, but if they are like this and the orcs are weakened as much as we both believe they are, what is the chance that either could be a threat in the coming months? I can't imagine the kobolds making that kind of trek, knowing they would have to come through the pass of Ebonmount. That would be a slaughter for them.

If they try and come through the swamps, I'm not sure how their bodies would handle those changes. And if all the caves are sealed up from the swamp side, they would be trapped on the southern end of the mountains. That would then require an army not prepared for the marshes and swamps to cross all the way to the southeast side of the bowl and then head north into Luthaelia. That march alone would cost them countless troops.

Kaen felt Pammon's agreement with his assessment. As his dragon shifted slightly to the south, Kaen's mind wandered to Ava and the twins she was carrying.

How easily your mind wanders. What will you do if we are in battle and it does that?

Scratching Pammon's neck, Kaen couldn't help but smile at the talking-to Pammon was giving him.

I'll try to be better and not think about my wife and children. I'm pretty confident you didn't do the same thing yesterday.

I did think of my children and my mates, but that was not while we were discussing something. You changed your thoughts while we were talking about armies. I was simply flying.

The wind carried the laughter away, but Kaen knew Pammon had won that battle.

You are correct. I was just considering how the upcoming battle would impact everything. If we can wait until after our children are born, Ava will ask her mother and Sulenda to watch them.

Pammon snorted, and Kaen knew how he felt about that decision.

How hard have we become? Both of us are willing to go to war with our mates, knowing what may befall either of them.

There was nothing he could do but frown. Their options were limited. Soon they would have to fight while they had an advantage. Waiting any longer would have given Stioks time to prepare for another attack and his dragon time to grow.

Then let us head back home. We have all the information we need for now, and there are many more things to do before we are ready to bring your children and their riders here for the next lesson in war.

Pammon immediately changed directions without waiting, preparing to head back to Ebonmount.

Through their bond, Kaen felt Pammon's excitement. He couldn't wait to watch his children fight the kobolds.

A grin appeared as Kaen imagined what the kobolds they would fight would think, seeing a silver and red dragon coming at them while two young men tore through their ranks.

"It's unbelievable," Aldric exclaimed as he waited for Kaen to finish reading the report he had given him. "Those two boys . . . Dragon Riders have managed to spur on that entire mining operation, and if we can keep even half of the ore they have procured in this last week coming in, we should be able to outfit most of the army with at least a decent weapon."

"And those trees your group brought for our workers have already been moved to the mills," added Herb. "If I wanted your head to be any bigger, I would say you are a masterful leader and planner."

Kaen groaned as he finished reading the numbers on Aldric's paper. "That is impressive. Almost a ton of ore . . . how?"

"That vein you found turned out to run for almost ten yards and was at least three feet wide in some sections. The entire company began working in shifts once they found it. Rumor has it there were a lot of bets on if it would ever end."

Aldric chuckled, and Herb was grinning like a guy who had just gotten his first kiss.

"Well, they have one more week of mining, and then I need to shift their training again. Their bodies should be ready for what comes next. After that, I've planned a month of solid training before we leave to pick a fight with the kobolds."

"You're certain that is still the best choice?"

Kaen nodded at Herb as he held the report out for Aldric to take back. "How many actual fights are your adventurers getting into now with orcs and ogres?"

"Not enough that if your two showed up, it would provide any real training," Herb admitted. "And even with you there, do you really want to toss them up against ogres?"

"They did fine in the cave, but part of a war is being surrounded and fighting against large numbers," Kaen replied. "There may be a chance they cannot be on their dragons during the battle. Riding from the safety of a dragon is one thing, but being on the front line and leading an army is totally different."

Aldric nodded as he placed the mining report back on his stack of papers. "Not many get that kind of training because war is usually the only way it happens. What is your plan?"

Kaen laughed and shook his head. "If I shared that, someone might let it slip, and I don't want that to happen," he said. "Just ensure that what I asked for is there in three weeks."

Aldric's smirk had grown into a full smile as the king believed he had figured out what Kaen intended to do. "Would it be ok if I came on that day?"

"By all means, it would be a great thing," Kaen replied, and then his eyes went a little wider. "I may have something even better for you in the coming days after that."

Aldric saw the gleam in Kaen's eyes and shrugged. "Always here to help when I can."

Kaen turned to Herb. "Make sure the healers are there also. I'm going to need some help with that day."

Sighing, Herb bobbed his head, less excited about Kaen's plan.

"Alright, I need to head back to my wife. If you two will excuse me."

Both men nodded, and after shaking hands, Kaen went to where Pammon had just landed, noticing the smile his dragon was sporting.

You are being devious, but I like that new idea. Aldric should be a fine addition to that training.

Those two boys are going to either love it or hate me. Either way, they will be the best warriors I can imagine this kingdom has seen in a long time.

Not counting you, of course.

Kaen groaned. Pammon's sarcasm was evident from the tone of his voice in his head.

Exactly. Now, let's head home. I need to go love on my wife a little.

Thrumming, Pammon took off into the air, still smiling about the devious nature of his rider.

"Why are you always leaving me?" Ava asked, frustration dripping from her voice. "Don't you care about me and the babies?"

Kaen's eyes glanced around the cave where all three dragons were watching him.

"Of course I care, my love, why would you—"

"Because you're always going and leaving me here!" she exclaimed. "I miss you! It isn't easy, and my mother . . . oh dear spirits, my mother keeps trying to come here and help pass the time. Every day, it's something else she wants to talk about. And then Amaranth wouldn't take me where I wanted to go! She said she needed to help you! So I was left here with Glynnis!"

Ava continued to talk, her voice rising and lowering faster than Kaen could keep track of.

What am I missing?!

Amaranth's eyes were now yellow and glaring at him.

Your wife has been like this for the last few days. All of a sudden, her mood changes, and I cannot keep up with it. It wears me out just—

"Are you ignoring me?" Ava asked, getting between Kaen and Amaranth, standing on her toes. "What is Amaranth telling you?!"

"She said you have been a little stressed lately with how much I have been gone, and I need to take you with me on some of the things I am doing. I'm sorry, my love," Kaen replied, slowly putting his arms around her and drawing her close.

Ava nodded against his chest and started to cry for a moment before forcing herself to stop.

"I'm sorry," she groaned. "I'm all over the place. One moment, I'm fine; the next, I feel like I need to throw or break something!"

"Don't apologize to me, my love. I didn't want to bother you with riding nonstop for a week, but perhaps I should have at least asked. Don't worry, I'll be here for the next month or so. I would love to spend any time you want together."

Squeezing him tightly, Ava nodded. "Thank you. I love you."

Kaen kissed her forehead and smiled.

That was well done. I remember when Amaranth and Glynnis were like that for a time. They were not as easy to comfort as Ava is.

Perhaps it is because I only have to keep one woman happy.

Pammon's thrum echoed through the cave, and Ava's head snapped quickly at Pammon, glaring at the dragon.

"Why is Pammon laughing?" she asked, a hint of anger noticeable in her voice.

"He mentioned that it surprised him that I was smart enough to know that all you want is to be with me. Usually, I act like an eggling."

Ava snorted and then gave a curt nod, glaring at Pammon once more before turning back to Kaen and smiling. "He's right, you know. Usually, I have to be specific about what you need to do."

Not saying a word, Kaen simply smiled.

You owe me . . .

She may not breathe fire, but for a moment, I feared a little for my safety.

It took Kaen a lot of willpower to keep from laughing. It appeared the next few months would be even more of an adventure.

58

Bashing Each Other's Brains In

Your smirk makes you look diabolical. Perhaps you should have told Ava no when she asked you to shave.

Kaen felt his chin and the skin that was now not protected. Why Ava had wanted him to shave it a few days ago didn't make sense, but Kaen simply said yes and cut it off. The wind against it felt weird, but he didn't care about that.

Hess seemed to enjoy making fun of my baby face. Regardless, we are about to witness something fun.

Pammon thrummed as they watched the two sides gather and finish getting into position.

Phillip and Frederick were on Kaen's left, each with command of ten students of their choice.

Across the field were one hundred seasoned guards, along with a very special commander. King Aldric was in his gold armor, wearing a flowing cape and holding a shield and wooden sword. He would serve as the ogre for the match, directing and leading his troops against the outnumbered students. His troops' weapons were wooden clubs, spears, swords, and axes, while each of Phillip's and Frederick's squads had spears, shields, and swords.

"This is going to be fun," Hess said as the two sides got ready. "How did you come up with this?"

"I tried to imagine something you would do to make me get better, and this was about as awful a thing as I could come up with," replied Kaen as he motioned to the judge across the field.

The woman ran back to the edge of the field and, once on the boundary, pulled out a horn and blew it three times. The last blast was long, and the moment it ended, Aldric's team began shouting and charging.

"They're not moving," Hess said, pointing out the obvious. "Defending? Against ten to one? That's a bad decision!"

Kaen said nothing, simply watching as the group of students, none older than seventeen, moved to a wedge position as the last thirty yards between them lessened.

The students held their position as the grown men thundered toward them. When the shout came from both boys, they surged in unison, aiming for the middle of the group coming at them. With the army only two deep, the wedge could easily push through them, and only a few yards past them was Aldric.

"This is going to hurt," Kaen said, chuckling as he saw Aldric react.

With movement that only came from drills and practice, the men shifted based on Aldric's call. The lines barely separated while the troops shuffled into position, suddenly becoming four soldiers deep.

A small falter came, the lines collided as the tip ran into the now thicker part, and the sides collapsed upon them.

Frederick was right behind the tip and bent down, holding his shield over his head, while Phillip ran and jumped up on it. This gave him a boost and thrust that propelled him over the men who were still running forward.

"Hairy dwarf balls, Kaen!" exclaimed Hess.

It was a brave and ballsy move for sure, but as Phillip came down on the ground and prepared to roll, Aldric was already there, catching him midroll with his shield.

Like running into a wall, Phillip stopped immediately, not getting up from the collision.

A horn blew, and both sides stopped fighting at once. Healers ran out onto the field and started checking the fighters. Even though they wore padded armor and helmets, injuries would occur, and there was no time to wait for one to recover.

Pammon had started thrumming once Aldric put Phillip onto the ground and was still laughing.

Part of me wishes their dragons were here right now to have seen that. Foros would be anxious.

Which is why they are still at the course. They need to complete it before they can come here.

We may not see them here then for a week. It is still hard on their bodies.

Kaen said nothing but nodded, moving down the steps of the small tower he had built to oversee the battles.

He moved with a purpose toward Phillip and motioned to Frederick to join him. Aldric stood by, saying something as a healer attended to the downed Dragon Rider.

"What went wrong?" Kaen called out. "Why didn't you win?"

Frederick motioned at the group of warriors with Aldric. "We are outnumbered ten to one."

Shaking his head, Kaen finally arrived where Phillip was and snorted as he looked down at the rider.

"That's not the reason. Phillip, you figure it out yet?"

Groaning, Phillip took Aldric's hand and shook his head. "No, but I now know not to do that against the king or an ogre. You made it look so simple."

Aldric laughed at those words and saw Kaen roll his eyes.

"I'm also much stronger, faster, and more experienced than you," Kaen reminded him. "I need a better reason. If not, you can try again."

Both boys looked at the other, and each finally gave in to not knowing the answer.

"King Aldric, do you know what they did wrong?"

Smirking, the king glanced at both boys and then at Kaen. "Do you want me to give them the answer or are you just making sure I know?"

"Don't give them the answer yet, but I want Phillip and Frederick to know that it isn't some secret I'm holding on to."

"Wait, King Aldric already knows the answer after one fight?" Phillip asked.

"I knew before we ever fought," replied the king. "Remember, I'm older than Kaen and have had to learn battle strategy all my life. Now, get set again. There's nothing like a bit of fun and bashing each other's brains in."

"Especially when there is a healer," Frederick pointed out.

Kaen and Aldric laughed and nodded, each moving back to his position.

"Again!" Kaen shouted as he walked toward his lookout tower where Hess was waiting.

Laughter and some cheers from both sides came as they returned into position.

How long till they figure it out?

Glancing up at Pammon, Kaen shrugged.

I hope sooner rather than later.

Stretching and groaning, Kaen walked across the field toward the carnage before him.

Over forty of Aldric's men were dead, and all of the students and both Phillip and Frederick were down as well. The horn sounded, and everyone who was not dead took a knee, gladly waiting on the water brought to them by some of the younger students.

As Kaen looked at the crowd of students who had cheered while they watched the last two skirmishes, his heart broke.

The knowledge that many of them might die weighs heavily upon your mind. Since the founding of this school, you knew it would happen. When

the first child died defending the walls, her death spurred the defenders on. It lit a fire in their hearts, and that day, news of her taking down four orcs before dying spread along the wall like a blaze.

Would you deny every warrior a chance to see someone so brave risking their life for the same thing you claim to defend?

The lump in his throat grew, and Kaen knew that Pammon was right. It didn't make the truth easier, but so many of the children had told him before that they were fighting to protect their parents or siblings. They all shared the same goal and purpose.

I just thought, what if my children were in that group? As a parent, could I stand by and let them sacrifice themselves?

What about my children?

Pammon's question pierced his heart like a knife. Kaen immediately wrestled with the knowledge that he had not considered that as he should have.

Pammon, I'm sorry . . . I . . . I never asked.

Kaen had turned to look at his dragon. Both of them held the other's gaze, ignoring the spectacle behind Kaen.

I know. It would be a lie if I did not mention that at one point. It hurt in a way that was hard to describe. While they were eggs, it bothered me that we naturally assumed they would fight. There was no doubt in my mind that they should have riders, and yet . . .

Pammon paused, moving from where he had been resting and coming close to Kaen. He lowered his head, gazing down at his rider, his snout a few yards away.

Kaen felt the breath of his dragon each time he breathed out. The pain that was no longer able to be hidden was there for him to feel as if it were his own.

It is different now that I feel for them, as I know you will feel for your children. I push them to become strong because I want . . . no, I need them to survive. There is no telling how their death might impact me. Having witnessed how it hurt you and Ava when you lost your first one . . . I'm scared.

Kaen reached out with his hand and blinked multiple times as his dragon bared his heart to him. Pammon put the tip of his jaw into Kaen's hand and closed his eyes, breathing deeply and slowly letting it out.

You know I am scared as well. I have acted foolishly because I let fear control me. Yet at no point did I ever ask you how my fearsome dragon felt . . . for that, I am sorry. What can I do to make this right?

Pammon shifted his head so that his gold eye could take in Kaen after he opened it.

Win. We finish this once and for all. No matter what happens, we create a place where your children and I can live without the fear we have now.

Nodding, Kaen did his best to try to hug Pammon's massive jaw.

No matter what, we will kill Stioks and end the threat he presents.

Even if it means our own lives.

Kaen wanted to respond in agreement, yet his voice failed him. He had almost died once at Stioks's hand, and the fear of it happening again still gave him nightmares.

Even if it means our own lives. We will do what we must for our family.

Pammon nodded and nudged Kaen with his jaw, pushing him back a few steps.

Good, now turn around. Everyone is watching us.

Shock filled Kaen's face as he remembered where he was and, turning on his heel, saw that Pammon was right. Everyone was watching the two of them.

Taking a deep breath, Kaen smiled and moved closer to the two armies and all of the students.

"Alright, listen up!" Kaen shouted, making sure everyone was watching. "Take a knee or sit on the ground; I need a few moments, and I know most of you are exhausted."

A sigh of relief came as soldiers and students promptly knelt or sat down on the field, which had been torn up by the day's fighting.

"You all did exceptionally well today. Know that each of you appeared to improve, and part of this practice isn't just for Phillip and Frederick to become better fighters but for all of you to excel as warriors. Follow your leaders, trust their wisdom, and see how you might help your brother or sister grow."

Kaen motioned to one of the students from Frederick's squad. She rose and moved quickly to where Kaen waited for her.

"Angela here is only sixteen, but I'm sure if you ask any of the guards who came with King Aldric today, she doesn't fight like a sixteen-year-old should," Kaen said as he put a hand on her shoulder, keeping her face turned toward the crowd.

Some nods and cheers came from the guards, causing her to smile.

"However, even as good as she is now, she can become better. If you watch her, you will notice she takes in everything. She rarely repeats the same mistake twice. Today, she got better between each fight because the men across from her didn't hesitate to attack. They didn't see a sixteen-year-old girl; instead, they saw a warrior with a spear and a sword ready to end their lives."

Kaen gave her a nod, and she quickly moved back to her group, smiling and receiving a few slaps on the back and shoulder.

"Now listen when I say this next part and bear it in mind."

The noise died down, and for a moment, the only sound was the wind gently blowing across the field.

"We are training like this because a day will come when the fight doesn't end at the blowing of a trumpet. A battle will take place where the only way it ends is when one side is completely killed or flees from the battleground. So train to be the side that wins. Train to be the side that gets to come home and celebrate with their friends and family that peace will finally happen, and we can go back to living with those we love!"

Kaen's last words were so loud it almost surprised him.

Aldric didn't wait a moment when he knew Kaen had finished his speech.

"For the peace of Ebonmount!" he cried.

As one, every person jumped to their feet and cried out the same thing.

"For the peace of Ebonmount!"

"For the peace of Ebonmount!"

"For the peace of Ebonmount!"

It would appear Stioks and his armies should be afraid.

Kaen smiled, cheering with those gathered.

The day is coming when his body will be either on the ground with my sword through his chest or in your stomach.

Pammon thrummed loudly, causing the crowd to roar and cheer again.

Perhaps we should make a bet on who wins.

59

Breaking Limits

The days passed, and with each one, Phillip and Frederick began to realize their mistakes.

Countless formations had been tested, and some proved to be more successful than others. One led to their defeating over half of Aldric's men.

The king had been replaced, and Hess was now commanding them. He was still moving with grace and power as he directed the rotating group of guards.

Half the group rotated out every two days, giving new recruits a chance to get experience while having those with them to guide and teach.

Phillip and Frederick also began to experiment with different students, finding that some worked better with one formation than another.

It was on the eighth day when everything fell into place.

Phillip and Frederick had outfitted themselves with two swords, forgoing the shields they often carried. It was the third skirmish of the day, and for the first time, they stood side by side, using their students as a shield behind them and to their side.

When Kaen saw the formation they took, he grinned and turned to Pammon, who nodded slightly.

How many do you think they will defeat?

At least three fourths. Much will depend upon how they figure out their strengths and weaknesses, but I feel for those guards who meet them first.

As the horn blew, both groups charged each other this time.

Hess called for a change of formation, stacking his troops in sets of five, two deep and in an X pattern. Gaps were formed, and Kaen groaned as the shift happened quickly.

Maybe not three fourths . . .

Pammon thrummed once.

Too late to take it back.

The sound of the collision that came as both groups collided was impressive, but the number of guards cut down within the first moments was even more so.

Phillip and Frederick used a skill, not waiting as they sometimes did.

In the first few seconds, ten men fell to the ground, struck by their swords and now dead for all intents and purposes.

Kaen winced from the power of those strikes, knowing the healers would have their hands full in a moment.

The students followed quickly, keeping the pockets of other troops at bay as the two Dragon Riders cut through the men who came at them with ease. They had stood about five feet apart, which gave them enough room to cover the middle between them while also covering their own sides and front.

In moments, the guard section faded fast as the outer groups tried to collapse from the side and back.

Unfortunately, it left Hess unprotected, and both boys dashed toward him.

Frederick spun as they got close, cutting off the rush of four men and giving Phillip a few seconds of uninterrupted time against Hess.

Neither wore a smile as they sometimes did when they had practiced or dueled.

Both had grim looks and as Phillip came at Hess, the older man didn't hesitate.

Hess activated his shield bash, and Phillip rolled from the attack he knew was coming. He had feinted for a quick assault, trying to draw out the attack.

Kaen couldn't help but grin as he saw Hess scowl, but his dad wasn't out of tricks yet.

The shield had pressed forward so fast, and even though Kaen constantly teased Hess about being beyond his prime, a single shift in position led to Hess activating the shield charge.

Phillip stood as he saw Hess barreling at him and held up both swords, preparing to block what he knew would most likely knock him out of the fight or at least stun him.

Hess had trusted the men too much with his back, however. Phillip's roll had put Hess between Frederick and himself. As Hess drove forward, Phillip whistled, and even though Kaen couldn't see his dad's face, he could only imagine his expression.

Frederick was on Hess's unprotected back side in a blink, landing two strikes against him as his shield barreled over Phillip.

Both were down and out, falling to the ground together as Hess cursed.

Frederick spun and blocked and parried the two guards coming at him.

Ok, maybe I was right, three fourths!

Pammon groaned, and they watched with smiles as the fight continued.

* * *

Frederick groaned as he lay on the ground, panting from the exertion but still smiling.

"Seventy-eight . . . we got seventy-eight!"

Phillip laughed and nodded. "Nice work on Hess."

"It was your plan . . . you knew what Hess would do," replied Frederick between breaths.

"You two have improved more than I realized," Hess said as he stood near the boys. "I guess I have also gotten a little soft in my own way, being too predictable."

Kaen stood near them, letting them talk about how things went. The students were ecstatic at how well they had done, and the guards discussed what they could do to avoid that again.

After the healers were finished, Kaen got their attention with a simple whistle.

"Good work! Now comes the hard part," Kaen declared, a massive smile on his face. "Now, both sides know what these two need to do to win. I expect Frederick and Phillip to improve on what they just did, just as I anticipate their squads finding better ways to support them."

Kaen turned toward most of the guards. "You know this and must find out how to make it harder on them. When your turn is up, tell the next group and warn them. I don't want you making it easy on our two Dragon Riders."

Everyone laughed and nodded.

"Good, thirty-minute break, and then we go again. We will keep going until both riders are alive and every guard is defeated."

Kaen gave a quick nod and turned to move back to his position.

"Son!"

Stopping midturn, Kaen smiled at Hess, who was coming to join him.

"Walk with me a moment, I want to ask a question."

Kaen raised an eyebrow but nodded and walked back to the tower with Hess.

"How long do you expect this to last?"

Kaen sighed and bit his lip for a moment as they walked. "Less than a week, hopefully, no more than three days. After that happens, I have something else then."

Hess laughed and gave his son a gentle hit to the arm. "I was never this much of a bastard, but maybe I should have been. You're pushing these kids and men just right. It amazes me how much they don't get too frustrated with the same thing. Are you intentionally giving those speeches when you do, or is it pure luck?"

Scratching his face, Kaen didn't say anything for a few steps. Finally, he stopped and turned to look back at the group that had been behind them. "Look at them."

Hess saw that everyone was laughing and talking, both groups mingling and having animated conversations.

"It's easy to see right now they don't need me telling them anything. A little praise or a simple correction, and that is all they require. When things were not like this a few days ago, you remember what I did?"

Hess groaned and nodded. "Kicked my arse in front of every one of them."

"Hey, I let you win a few times."

Groaning still, Hess nodded. "That you did because we both know I can't win on my own."

"While that might be true," Kaen replied, "they needed a distraction. We showed them different techniques and attacks. They got a break and also got to learn. I'm sure you saw both sides using the stuff we showed them since then."

"That intelligence and wisdom stat of yours must be getting too high now. That's some fine thinking from a boy who couldn't tie a proper knot for so long."

Kaen laughed as he recalled the frustration of the memory Hess mentioned.

"You know my plans. Five or six months is all we can afford. I already sent word to the wood elves and dwarves. They will be ready when the time comes."

"What about here? How long will you do this?"

Kaen looked at Hess. His smile had vanished. "Until they finish one last task. Don't tell anyone, but after they are ready here, we will go with our dragons and fight some kobolds."

"What? Why would you do that?" asked Hess, his voice louder than he had intended.

"I remember that some of my best training was done in a goblin cave, fighting an attack on Minoosh and going up against a pack of bandits."

"What about those orcs?"

Kaen winced at the memory of Luca. "Pammon and I learned more than I ever knew I needed from that fight . . . These boys have seen fighting and been on the front line, but now they need to learn what a Dragon Rider can do. You've felt their hits; even when they are not giving everything, it hurts."

Hess nodded, reaching behind with one arm and rubbing his lower back. "They do hit a lot harder than I remember."

Chuckling, Kaen motioned to Pammon. "Ask him. He will tell you how his children are doing. Foros and Tazorath are both growing stronger every day. When we are ready here, the six of us will head to the desert, and there, dragons and their riders will find out why armies fear us."

Kaen paused, leaned over, and grabbed Hess, pulling him close. "They will also have someone like I had who could easily solo everything to ensure nothing goes wrong."

Hess roared with laughter and embraced Kaen. "Good luck, then. I'll do what I can to make sure they are ready."

Kaen patted him on the shoulder and then motioned to the tower. "Now, if you'll excuse me, I need to go talk with Pammon some more."

* * *

Four days later, cheering filled the air, and Kaen stood on the tower smiling as Pammon thrummed.

They finally did it. That was impressive.

And two of their squad members are alive as well. Even better than I had initially believed.

Some might say that was luck, but they really are impressive.

Kaen glanced up at the sky and then at the group celebrating below.

I'm going to call it a day. Would you like to go and check on Amaranth and your children early? They can be done for the day as well. Go hunting or whatever you four want.

Pammon leaned over to Kaen and nudged him gently with his snout.

I would very much enjoy that. Your wife and Glynnis should be back anytime as well.

Kaen nodded and began descending the steps of his tower.

Could you believe how excited she was to go with Glynnis to visit Bosgreth? When I first asked, I wasn't sure if she was going to kill me or say yes. Still, it helps us because we don't have to go and get the armor they should have done by now.

She is excited to show off her belly to Bosgreth and Dagan. Still, it was good for both of them. Glynnis felt left out with how Amaranth and Ava get along. Perhaps they will be able to forge a new relationship.

Kaen nodded and was almost upon the celebration of students and guards, who seemed to not care that they had just been destroyed by two boys.

Waving and smiling, Kaen moved to where Phillip and Frederick stood, grinning like they had just killed the largest deer in the kingdom's history.

"Congratulations, you two!"

"I can't believe it!" exclaimed Frederick. "I almost thought we were going lose near the middle, but thankfully, our squad kept them off our backs!"

Some cheers came from their group, and Kaen nodded, raising a hand for silence.

"Ok, now comes the good news!"

Phillip and Frederick both groaned.

"You all get to celebrate. Head to town, stop by the Dragon Rider's Inn, and food and drink are on me!"

Cheers broke out, and Kaen gave them a few moments to celebrate before raising his hands again.

"One more good piece of news! Tomorrow is a rest day. Sleep, stretch, eat, do whatever you want, or what your king tells you to do."

Some laughter and groans came as the guards knew how true his last words were.

"After that, we start here again, and trust me, it's going to be even harder then."

"And there's the bad news," muttered Phillip.

A few groans came, but no one seemed to care too much. Dinner, drinks, and a day off were worth celebrating.

"Now get cleaned up and get a move on!"

Kaen turned and stared at Pammon.

Why haven't you left yet?

You don't want a ride back?

No, I'll walk with everyone else. You go see your family. Tomorrow is all yours as well. Enjoy it.

Pammon thrummed, and as he leaped off the ground, he gazed at Kaen.

Glynnis is going to be very upset to learn she missed out.

Then we better pray she gets back tomorrow.

As Pammon flew over their heads, his thrumming continued for a while.

Kaen could sense his joy and excitement.

"What was that?" Hess asked, having snuck up next to Kaen.

"Just a happy dragon about to go spend time with his family. Care if I join you and Sulenda?"

Putting his arm around Kaen's shoulders, Hess smiled and tugged him back toward town. "We'd love it."

60

What a Dragon Rider Can Do

"Thank you for trusting me with that task. Glynnis and I needed some girl time together."

Kaen smiled and kissed Ava on her neck as he rested his hands on her stomach.

Leaning her head against his chest, Ava kissed his cheek and smiled. "Dagan was excited to see me, and the dwarves seem to be making amazing progress in getting their land in order again. They hope to have a winter crop ready before next month hits."

Sighing, Kaen began to hum gently and slowly swing his hips as if they were dancing.

"You're not listening to me . . . you and I both know nothing is going to happen anytime soon."

"I wasn't planning on that," Kaen replied, kissing her once more before turning her around and holding her in a more formal dancing pose. He brought her close and smiled. "Can't a husband just want to dance with his wife because he missed her and not want to jump in bed?"

Ava frowned and looked at Pammon, who lounged with Glynnis in the cave.

"Huh . . . Pammon says you really aren't thinking that."

Laughing, Kaen did a quick little twirl with her and brought her back to him. "No, I honestly missed you. Pammon and I figured out how much our family means to us, and I wanted to ensure that I was spending time with you. I don't want you worried that I care more about the coming battle than the woman I married."

Ava cocked an eyebrow before shaking her head and shifting so she could lean her head against his chest. "I'm not sure who you've been talking to, but you owe them a dinner. You'll never get in trouble if you keep talking like this."

Kaen rested his head against hers, and they danced to the tune that he hummed for a while.

* * *

"This is amazing!" Frederick declared as he sported the tunic and pants the dwarves had made him from the scales. "Though it is already a little tight in some spots . . . perhaps we should stop cutting trees and hauling rocks."

Kaen groaned and shook his head. "No, we'll fire out a fix, but I wanted to ensure that those fit. Now take them off and get dressed. It's time for round two."

Phillip mimicked Kaen, groaning as he began to walk toward the stairs that would take him to the cave he and Foros shared. "We're screwed," Phillip muttered. "Remember what I said."

Frederick sighed and moved to the area to change. "Be gentle, please," he begged playfully. "I don't want to get hurt again."

Laughing, Kaen waved as he moved to take the stairs to the ground where Pammon was waiting. "Just remember, you both wanted to be a Dragon Rider. It comes with all this."

Kaen smiled at the guards and students as they stood on the field after a day off.

"You all look well rested. Anyone here not ready for today's fun?"

Some groans and chuckles came, but no one raised their hand. Everyone wanted a spot to learn and grow. The guards required a sign-up list because of how successfully it had been received.

"Alright, now comes round two of my training, and today is going to suck for the Dragon Riders and their squads."

Groans came from the students as they began to wonder what Kaen had in mind.

"Guards, I need your best. Don't give in. This is where we really make them suffer."

The guards gave a few cheers and jokes, but it was easy to see in their eyes that everyone wanted to grow and would do their best against each other.

"Alright, here is what is about to happen. Each Dragon Rider and their squad will face fifty guards alone."

There were a few whispers and some things were said between a few people, but most looked at Kaen like he was half-drunk.

"The only way we progress is after the Dragon Rider survives and defeats the leader of the guards and all the support troops. After that, we will add ten more. We are done here once the Dragon Rider can defeat all one hundred troops and the leader."

Nobody said a word after Kaen stopped talking, but there were many side glances and looks of concern.

"Not to doubt you, sir," one guard called out, "but can that really be done?"

Kaen smiled and nodded.

You're so evil! You paid that man to ask that question!

And you know why . . .

Pammon began to thrum, and everyone looked past Kaen at the massive bronze dragon laughing near the tower.

"That is a perfect question that will only be answered by demonstrating that truth! All of the guards and Hess will face me."

Hess groaned and let out a curse as he spat on the ground. A few guards turned and looked at him. "Get yer weapons, boys, and let's get set up. We're about to get our arses kicked in a spectacular way."

Kaen smiled, approached Phillip, and held out both hands. "May I borrow your swords, please?"

Sighing, Phillip relinquished them as he shook his head. "You're going to show off . . ."

"No, I'm going to prove a point that you and Frederick must figure out. You're stronger and faster, but you don't trust yourself. Only Hess can actually do anything to you both. You will easily accomplish this task once you realize that and learn how to deal with that problem."

Kaen moved to the section where the two boys usually started and waited as Hess got his group together.

The guards started to form a tight circle with Hess in the middle. One hundred men surrounded their leader, and Kaen could see that none of them looked excited about what they imagined might come.

"Whenever you're ready!" Kaen shouted.

"Let's do this!"

The guards began to move toward Kaen, jogging slightly so that none tripped in the formation they held.

Kaen glanced at Pammon, who was shaking his head.

Don't kill anyone . . . that would not go well.

Please, you and I both know I will barely hit anyone.

Pammon groaned as Kaen dashed forward, becoming a blur on the field.

A few groans and a lot of moaning were the only sounds coming from the guards as Hess spat on the ground.

"You did that intentionally, whittling them all down until it was just me so you could make me look old and slow."

"Please," Kaen replied as he winked at Hess. "I would never make you look how you are. Besides, it was a lesson, and I think I taught it well."

Turning to Phillip and Frederick, Kaen returned the swords he had borrowed.

"Learn from what I did. I've got faith in you two."

This is going to be fun to watch every day. Are you sure you don't mind if I'm not here?

Scratching Pammon's neck as his dragon stood near the tower, Kaen smiled.

Go. I don't mind walking into town, and it's good for their morale. Besides, you and your family need each other also.

I take back a few of the things I said about you being evil. Perhaps you're just slightly chaotic with a side of good sprinkled in.

Groaning, Kaen patted Pammon's neck.

Tell your family I said hi and that I'm not mean. Perhaps one day, they'll believe me.

Thrumming, Pammon turned and was in the air a few seconds later, sending up a cloud of dust across the field.

Kaen smiled as he saw Pammon fly away and then turned his attention back to the spectacle about to start.

"Alright, protectors of Hess, listen up!" Kaen shouted. Once everyone was watching, he found himself grinning, knowing what was about to take place in this next round. "Every guard alive gets a free drink on me! If Hess lives, then it doesn't matter how many of you die. I'll buy drinks for you all!"

A massive cheer erupted from Hess's side, and Kaen put his hands against the tower's edge, leaning against it as he prepared for the carnage.

You're really going to miss this next fight.

Yet I'm watching even as I go.

The horn sounded, and Kaen and Pammon laughed as Frederick and his squad prepared for the rushing horde.

"Why do I feel you are intentionally trying to ruin us?" Phillip asked as Frederick and Kaen walked with him back to town. "Every day, I have a glimmer of hope, and then you squash it like a bug under your thumb."

Frederick started laughing, and Kaen smiled as Phillip groaned.

"You want me to answer what you already have heard again? I don't mind repeating myself," Kaen replied as he gave Phillip a playful punch to the arm.

"No, I know it . . . I'm just thinking I was an idiot all those years ago when we found you on the street. We should have known to run away after we smelled you, but alas, we did not."

"Damn, we were stupid kids," Frederick chimed in.

After a minute of walking in silence, Phillip turned to Kaen and replaced his smile with a serious expression. "When the battle does come, do you believe we'll be on the ground?"

Kaen took a deep breath and slowly let it out as he considered the thing he had discussed with Pammon at least a hundred times now.

"You're stronger on the ground than in the air. Both of you aren't bad with a bow, but the truth is if you lead those armies, they will follow you, and when you can do what I'm training you for, the monsters you face will flee."

"Kind of like in the mountain?" Frederick asked.

Shaking his head from side to side, Kaen finally nodded. "I don't think they wanted to risk it anymore. They were trapped, and they saw what I had done to their wall breaker or siege, whatever ogre they called them. The real question is, what would you do if you faced me on the battlefield?"

Both boys looked at each other, their eyebrows almost touching their hair as they shook their heads.

"I'd like to say run, but I know that wouldn't matter much," Phillip declared.

"Exactly," Kaen replied. "When you stand on that battlefield wearing a full set of black dragon-scale armor and start killing everything you fight, what is going to happen to the morale of those people and orcs? In order for that to be possible, you need to learn how to make that happen. That is what we are learning."

Both boys said nothing for a few minutes, absorbing what Kaen had just said.

As they were about to enter the town, Frederick started to laugh, and the other two looked to see what was so funny.

"I forgot to do what I promised I would," Frederick said. "Eltina told me she was going to cut your tongue out the next time she saw you. Something about ruining her life and making it impossible to keep anything in stock."

Kaen laughed. "I'm so in trouble . . . Hess is walking in there tonight with one hundred guards, and each of them is going to get a drink from me. I don't think I can ever return there."

All three started to laugh and forgot about the stress that had been trying to keep them down.

Tomorrow would have its own problems, but for tonight, Kaen knew he was about to get destroyed by a short, dwarven woman who ran a bar.

61

Big Moments

Last two! You can do it! Get your altitude quickly!

Pammon was beside himself as Tazorath closed in on the last two turns of the course. He couldn't believe how fast she had progressed in her flying skills, but each day, her mother would set a path before both of his children, helping them follow her as much as possible.

I told you she would get it before Foros.

Pammon thrummed. Glynnis was dripping with excitement, and waves of satisfaction at how her daughter was flying seemed to radiate from her.

Tazorath came to the last turn, banking hard to the right, starting the drop, and diving into the ninety-degree turn.

Her wings almost clipped the trees as she turned at the wrong angle, but Tazorath managed to clear the branches by less than a yard.

Pammon and Glynnis were anxious as they watched their daughter start the barrel roll that would set her up for the next part.

They had spent weeks practicing the move higher in the sky, and doing it from this height provided a greater chance of risk and injury if they hit the ground.

Tazorath rolled out, her body giving the slightest stall in the air as her wings adjusted to point her in the right direction.

She finished the turn, claws almost brushing the limbs, and managed to divert her direction to the middle of the last long stretch of open space. Beating her wings as fast as she could, Tazorath was running out of room as the trees at the end of the clearing drew closer, every second risking a crash that would require Amaranth's assistance.

Faster, daughter! Faster!

Pammon watched as Glynnis dropped in altitude, getting closer to Tazorath, trying to will her to rise faster.

Tazorath fought for every foot of altitude, her body angled as she had learned from her mother countless times. As she rose toward the treetops, Pammon heard his daughter's roar.

The trees shook as she raced above the tops, so close that the wind of her passing shook them.

Pride filled Pammon's heart as he saw his daughter and her beautiful red-scaled body flying over the tops of the trees.

Well done, my child, well done!

Thank you, father and mother!

The joy in Tazorath's voice came through their connection as her words reverberated in their mind.

Come, let us land and celebrate this accomplishment for a moment.

They began to turn as one, changing direction to land in the one clearing that would hold all three of them.

You're as skilled a flyer as your mother, Pammon said while nuzzling Tazorath with his neck and chin.

She trilled as both parents doled love on her.

I wasn't sure I would make it after I messed up that first turn, but I wasn't going to stop. Either I would clear it or crash.

Glynnis thrummed, giving a few extra touches with her snout.

I had no doubt you would do it. You have learned well.

Trilling still, Tazorath watched as Foros and Amaranth joined the three of them.

Well done, sister. I am glad you succeeded.

Foros moved between the gap Pammon created and touched his head with his sisters.

Thank you, brother. I am still upset that you beat the challenge before I did.

Thrumming, Foros turned and looked at Pammon, who was showing his teeth. His smile was so wide that it was evident how happy he was at this moment.

Our sire was very persuasive after his last talk . . .

All four of the dragons began to thrum as Pammon groaned.

I do not believe you appreciated what I really said. The good news is that we still have plenty of light in the day, and there is abundant food in the forest. After that, we can surprise your riders with the good news.

Tazorath's and Foros's roaring filled the trees, and Pammon couldn't help but laugh as his children celebrated their success after so much training.

You are a great father to them. Glynnis and I are grateful for how you treat them compared to the other dragons from where we come. Once again, I am thankful that you have shown us all why having a rider is not what we have been told.

Pammon shifted slightly, hoping to draw Amaranth closer with his neck and wing.

The council fears being controlled, yet they have no idea how much that fear holds them. Imagine living one's life for centuries as they have. They will never know the love that we do. The joy we share right now is a treasure outside their realm of understanding.

Amaranth and Glynnis came over and forced their way under Pammon's wings, each trilling as he drew them close and took turns rubbing each of them with his snout.

Let us hunt together and then share the good news.

Foros and Tazorath raced off, each excited that this part of their training was done and ready to share their success with Phillip and Frederick.

Kaen noticed the five dragons approaching them as he stood on the tower, watching the battle wind down.

Frederick was closing in on defeating seventy guards with just his squad, yet Hess was harassing him as the guards still alive shifted tactics, picking up spears and creating distance between themselves and the Dragon Rider.

I have felt the joy and pride rolling off you like that water on the island. I will not share the surprise your children have, but I am happy for you.

Thank you. Inside, I feel like I am filled with gas, not in a bad way that hurts but one that makes me feel at peace.

Kaen started to laugh so hard that he began coughing at Pammon's attempt to describe his feelings.

You mock . . . no . . . that was not a good way to describe it . . . Perhaps if I said—

No . . . that won't work either. I understand, and by no means do I want to hear what you were about to say. Now tell me what you think of this fight.

Pammon watched as Frederick struggled against the last fourteen guards and Hess. Unable to close the gap and reduce the number of guards, he was getting pressed closer to the boundary as Hess continued to defend against his attacks.

Maybe he will kill a few more guards, but he will lose. His head is moving too much, and he is trying to focus on too many men. If he would commit to one side and clear out a portion of them, he could use the space to—

Pammon stopped talking as Frederick did just what he had described. The rider rushed toward three guards with spears, tossing a sword at two of them that struck them in the head while grabbing the spear of the one thrusting it toward him, hoping to stop Frederick.

Yanking the guard forward with his own spear, Frederick knocked the man down with a fist to the guard's chest.

He moved fast, trying to get free of the circle around him, and as he broke through the three he had knocked down, the horn sounded when a spear slammed into his back.

Hess was very dirty with that attack. It was good, however.

Kaen snorted and nodded as he started his descent down from the tower.

That boy might have won if Hess hadn't hit Frederick with that spear toss.

Kaen was going over the fight's details when all of them turned to watch the dragons landing near the tower.

Frederick and Phillip were smiling, each having felt his dragon and the joy they were exuding.

"Alright, everyone take thirty minutes. We need to see what our dragons need."

The warriors nodded, moving to the food and water waiting for them off to the side.

"Why are all five of them here?" Frederick asked. "And why is Tazorath like she is?"

Kaen shrugged, keeping a straight face. "Ask them yourselves, but me trying to figure out what is going on isn't worth the time. If Pammon doesn't want to tell me something, no complaining is going to make it happen."

Both boys laughed, each having already learned that lesson from their dragons.

They took off jogging to where Foros and Tazorath sat, both almost bouncing from the excitement of their news.

Kaen stayed back a few yards, giving them a chance to enjoy their moment.

They are bigger and stronger than I remember you being at their age. The muscles along their back make their scales look tight.

Pammon snorted, shaking his head as he watched his children tell their riders the good news.

I would say the same about them being more muscular than you, but I know how you humans like to compare size, so I won't.

A cacophony of whoops and hollering came as both boys learned that their dragons had finally conquered the course. Trilling came as each dragon received a lot of scratches and hugs.

Waiting patiently, Kaen finally joined the group after the celebration among Tazorath, Foros, Frederick, and Phillip died down.

"Congratulations, you two, on completing the course!" Kaen exclaimed, smiling and nodding at the silver and red dragons. "The good news is you get to be here for the next stage of training, and hopefully, with your help, your riders will finish their training soon."

Kaen couldn't help but grin as he saw the four look at him with confused looks on their faces.

"Are they going to fight with us?"

Kaen and Pammon both began to laugh.

"That would not be fair, but they are going to help in a different way. They will play the role you practiced months ago. Unlike rabbits, they will give you information about your enemies. They will watch your back and sides better than you can," Kaen informed them. "The trick will be learning how much information to give and when. Too much, and it will overload your rider. Too late and well . . . they die."

Both boys groaned but never stopped scratching their dragons' necks.

"I'm assuming we will go again even though it's getting a little late," Frederick asked.

Nodding, Kaen motioned to the field. "We can go one time, and then we will break. It will be a good chance to try it, and then you four can discuss tonight what worked and what didn't."

As Kaen spoke, Pammon moved around the group until he was standing beside Kaen. His massive size shadowed his rider. Had the bronze dragon stepped wrong, he could have easily crushed Kaen. Yet Kaen did not shift as his dragon settled next to him.

"You've seen me and Pammon together for over five years. We have had countless opportunities to practice in ways you are just now getting to learn. There will be battles you cannot fight alone, and you need to learn how to communicate."

Kaen turned and stared at Foros, who shifted slightly under his gaze. "Foros, you are very much like your sire. I know you think highly of yourself, which is a strength, but remember that Phillip depends on you. Embrace your strength, but also learn to trust Phillip's. He is smart and steady. You two will do amazing things if you learn to depend upon the other."

Ignoring the smile both Phillip and Foros gave, Kaen turned and looked at Tazorath and Frederick.

"You two are quite the same pair," he said with a chuckle. "You both get excited, and often you start talking faster than I imagine is possible, but it is because you believe anything is possible. Tazorath, learn to breathe and slow down a little. Be direct and specific with your instructions, and don't overload Frederick with them. You have a great eye for things and notice lots of tiny details others might miss. Use that to help Frederick in those battles. Frederick, you need to trust her and find a way to encourage her to speak up. Sometimes she allows you to take too much of the lead. Learn to see that she is smart and crafty."

After giving a few words of advice and encouragement, Kaen put his hand on Pammon's scales near his feet. "One day soon, I hope to teach you two how to use your dragons' eyes to see. It will take some time and require a change in your bond, but when you learn it, you will finally understand how they view the world."

Both of you riders need to always remember: Dragons are not pawns to be moved on a board. My children are part of you. Treat them as your own body. Never see them as anything less than family. When you do that, the bond you two have will change, and you both will grow stronger because of it.

Phillip and Frederick both gave a bow to Pammon.

"We will, and thank you again for trusting us with your children," Phillip said.

Pammon nodded slightly before turning his head to look at the field behind him.

"Pammon is right. It's time to see how you four do. Phillip, you're up first!"

A trill came from Foros as Phillip scratched his silver dragon's neck, and they touched heads.

"Let's do this!"

62

Fighting Kobolds

"This is going to be the big test!" Kaen exclaimed as Frederick and Phillip finished getting ready.

When they looked far away, the dry dirt of the desert and the heat were already starting to cause ripples across the ground.

"You both know what to do. After all, it only took a week for you both to finally defeat one hundred guards after your dragons helped."

Frederick smiled when he lifted his belt and checked the weapons strapped across his back.

"Let me ask a question for the hundredth time. How much are you planning on actually doing in these fights?"

Kaen shrugged, wearing the same grin he had worn every time the boys had tried to get a specific answer from him.

"I'm here to assist as I see fit. Don't get overwhelmed; work together. Your dragons will provide support from the sky. If this fight goes well, we will find a bigger group, and I will help more."

Kaen crossed his arms and stared at the two Dragon Riders, each wearing a black dragon-scale tunic and pants. Their arms, hands, feet, and helmets were standard chain mail but would provide plenty of protection against what they would face.

"You two are much stronger than when we were in the cave. If you had been this strong back then, we would have killed every orc, goblin, and ogre in there."

They smiled and poked each other playfully before Kaen's grunt made them get serious again.

"Today, you could die," Kaen stated, pausing afterward to prove the seriousness of his words. "Yes, Amaranth is here, and I have two potions, but we are not planning on needing them. Is that understood?"

Both nodded, each rechecking their outfit and weapons.

"Good. Now, we have about two miles to cover before we find the group Pammon has found. We won't run, but a good jog should help loosen us up. Any last questions?"

Both boys shook their heads.

Nodding, Kaen started to jog toward Pammon.

We are coming.

I know . . . there are about four hundred here, by my current count. Foros and Tazorath are anxious, but from what I see, this should be a pretty easy fight. There are no mages and only a few archers.

Time to see how these young men do. Tell Amaranth to be ready, just in case.

Pammon's laughter came through their bond, and Kaen groaned a little as he ran.

So much for complete confidence, but she is ready if needed.

Phillip and Frederick didn't slow down as the massive gathering of kobolds came into view. They were moving away at a steady pace and were only a quarter of a mile away when the kobolds at the back of the army noticed them.

They are changing directions. They see you.

"Foros says they see us! Let's go!" Phillip shouted, picking up the pace. Frederick moved a few yards away, keeping a distance both felt comfortable having.

Kaen followed from behind, glad the boys had first gone with a shield and sword. He might have recommended the spear had they asked, but each had over a thirty already in their sword skill and wanted to use what they felt strongest with.

The kobold army shifted, trying to protect those at the back, who were weaker than the group at the front. They had not expected trouble from behind, and none of them had realized yet the real strength of the enemy at their flanks.

Both boys reached them before the enemy could respond. In less than forty seconds, they were cutting through the scales of the creatures, shrieks and shouts coming as every strike cut down a kobold.

Get closer to Phillip. You're drifting away! Go left!

Kaen watched as Frederick adjusted himself in the midst of battle, aware of the information their dragons were relaying. Both Foros and Tazorath kept their minds open as they spoke so that Kaen would be aware and could assist if needed.

Three larger armored ones on your left!

Kaen knew that Foros had worked hard to do what Pammon instructed worked best. His short directions made Phillip a beast on the practice field.

Phillip shouted something, and Kaen couldn't hear it as he stayed behind about twenty yards, only killing a kobold when one was foolish enough to come at him.

Frederick shifted, following Phillip's change in direction. Both boys had soon cut through the thin layer of protective defenses the army had at the back of their line and were now in the archers and smaller troops with limited weapons, if any.

There is a group of fifty heavily armored warriors pushing through their ranks. You have about one minute before they get there!

Frederick shouted something, and Kaen heard "One minute" over the sounds of the dying enemy. Both men drew closer to each other, tightening up their defenses.

Occasionally a few kobolds attempted to flank them, and both would pivot, allowing the one to clear their flanks while the other kept their front direction clear.

Over a hundred are dead already.

Kaen grunted as Pammon relayed how they were doing.

That is impressive. How big is this group coming at them?

Stay close, but they should be ok if they don't get surrounded.

Kaen moved closer, killing two kobolds foolish enough to run at him, their heads falling off with a single slash of his sword.

He could see the group of kobolds that Pammon and Tazorath had mentioned. They were like the ones he had seen when Pammon and he had helped Glynnis. Standing taller than the rest, they wore a mixture of chain mail and plate armor. It appeared that most were wielding a buckler or larger shield, and spears pointed upward as they moved through the ranks.

Communicate with them what's coming and the weapons used!

Heavy warriors with spears and shields! Some with swords and a few with clubs!

Kaen smiled as Foros immediately responded.

Both Frederick and Phillip could see the advancing heavily armored kobolds. With time ticking down before the group reached them, both boys started backing up quickly. They began to sheathe their swords and pull the spears off their backs.

After killing a few of the standard kobolds in range, the boys set up side by side, preparing to deal with the first real threat of the day.

You have moved closer to them. Do I need to come or send Amaranth?

Not yet. I can help if need be, but this is their first real test since the walls. I don't expect trouble, but it would be foolish not to be prepared.

As they spoke, the first seven heavily armored kobolds rushed at the two Dragon Riders, not yet understanding the caliber of warriors they were about to engage with.

Each boy moved faster than the warriors had anticipated, and in the first few seconds of fighting, four were dead and two were injured.

Kaen couldn't help but smile as the boys rushed forward as one, their spears moving so fast that they would be a blur to most people.

As the second row of armored kobolds made their way into the foray, Frederick and Phillip were finishing off the first line of attackers.

The choice to switch to a spear had been the best move. They did not allow themselves to be outranged by the weapon, and combined with their speed and strength, every blow was a killing one.

Stabs to the warriors struck their faces or necks with such consistency that Kaen made a mental note to ask the two what their skill was.

In less than a minute, the group of armored warriors were on the ground, dead or dying, as the boys broke apart slightly and began to hunt down those who had yet to start running.

The chaos of the army turning on itself to flee, and being unable to when the front of the army had come back trying to help, created rows of kobolds unable to move.

Faster than Kaen had hoped, all but a few of the army were dead, as a few had managed to run away.

I've got these. Foros, you get those.

Kaen watched as the two dragons approached, their bodies glistening in the sun's rays as they reflected off their scales. Two arrows of death, one silver and one red, came at the creatures, who had no idea what was about to befall them.

"Tell me your thoughts on how this went."

Both boys finished drinking the waterskin Kaen had given them and looked at the other, waiting to see who might go first.

Sighing, Frederick decided it would fall on him as he lowered his skin first.

"Overall, it felt easy . . . am I allowed to say that?"

Nodding, Kaen watched, his arms still crossed across his chest.

"Their warriors in the back were not a threat, and at first, I know Phillip and I were anxious about the armored warriors, but with how few could come at one time, it wasn't that bad. I'm not sure I would say the kobolds are any different than an orc."

Nodding, Phillip wiped his arm across his lips. "Be honest with us. How was this fight compared to what the army will be like?"

Kaen laughed and pointed at the bodies behind them. "A battle like you two will face will be different. There will be countless men and fights taking place all around you. Bodies will be everywhere, and your hardest problem will be which man is on your side. You won't be certain without something to mark someone as an ally. Based on how you two appear to be skilled right now and the strength and speed you both have, the big test will be once you are surrounded."

Kaen moved back, took his sword, put the tip into the cracked ground, and spun it around, creating a circle.

"This is my range with my sword. Anything or anyone who comes within this gets attacked unless I'm certain they are an ally. Even with that armor you wear and hopefully the full set you have, weapons can pierce it if they are wielded by a strong enough foe. Even a goblin, if he gets lucky, might slip a spear or sword into a spot that isn't protected. I doubt it would kill you unless it was an eye or your throat, but it will hurt and make fighting harder."

Pammon started to thrum as he gobbled down another kobold, the dragons all filling their stomachs with their fallen foes.

"Phillip, stand here, and Frederick over here."

Both young men moved to the opposite sides of the circle Kaen had made.

"Do what I did, and now draw a circle, but don't move from where you are standing."

Each of them repeated Kaen's movements, and their circles almost met precisely in the middle of his.

"In a battle, one of the problems fighting side to side is your circle overlaps. While that is good, fighting with swords is hard, which is why the front lines often have shields and spears. Thrusting is easier and can press against those charging. If both sides have that style, then it often becomes who can push back the other while injuring them. What you two need to be is someone who destroys their formation and takes out those leading them."

Kaen moved from where both the boys stood and smiled. "Do me a favor and watch what I'm about to do."

A few yards from both boys, Kaen put his weapon away and flashed a grin."

"Watching?"

The second both Frederick and Phillip nodded, Kaen moved.

Each held his spear still in his hand, pointed at the ground. They tried to react as Kaen went from a resting position to in each of their faces, yanking the spears from their clenched fists.

"What the—"

In less than four seconds, Kaen was back where he had started, holding both spears.

"This is what you need to become," Kaen said, his smile gone. "You need to learn to move faster than everyone else and attack with such speed that there is no time to react." He tossed both boys their spears and then sighed. "People and monsters move at one speed, but weapons move much faster. Learn to be faster than the weapon."

Frederick rubbed his face with his hand and groaned. "All it takes is five more years."

Shrugging, Kaen motioned to Pammon. "And a dragon like mine. Don't worry, though. You two are becoming more than I could have ever hoped for at this stage of training. Now, get some food and use the restroom if you need to. We've got more kobolds to hunt."

63

Pammon Shares a Secret

"Enjoy the food!" Ava said, smiling at the child who took the bowl from her.

"Thank you, miss!" the girl who couldn't be more than nine called out as she ran toward the table where her parents waited.

"Feels good to be helping the people of the city together," Kaen whispered, nudging Ava gently with his shoulder. "Almost wish I could convince someone to play some music so I could dance with you here before everyone."

Laughing, Ava rolled her eyes and shook her head as she ladled out more soup into a bowl and handed it to another child who had been waiting in line. "These kids aren't ready for that kind of fun yet."

"True. I'm just glad your mother asked us to help. I hadn't expected this many people to show up."

"You do realize you're the Dragon Rider?" Ava asked. "I mean soup and food is good, but getting it from Kaen and his wife beat anything else, I think. Still feel like you are on track with your plans?"

Kaen nodded as he took a tray of bread someone had just brought for him to hand out. The days seemed to run together as they trained almost nonstop. Realizing how much time they had been doing this, he knew he needed to point out why he was a cting this way. "We're into month four of training, and things are only going to get harder on all of them. Hess is working on making the harnesses. I honestly believe that next month, both will be able to attempt riding their dragons."

Ava chuckled and shook her head gently. "None of them have attempted it yet?"

Rolling his eyes even though Ava couldn't see it, Kaen sighed. "Thankfully, not yet. Phillip and Foros discussed it the other day, but I would prefer to be safe . . . unlike Pammon and I were."

Kaen gave a few pieces of bread to a father with two children and nodded in response of the man's silent *Thank you*. "You two obey your dad!"

"Yes, sir!" the older boy almost shouted.

The younger sister clung to her father and stared at Kaen and Ava as if unsure if she would be safe from the pair.

As the family walked off and another group made their way toward them, Ava gave Kaen a kiss on the shoulder. "I'm just glad you are better. It's nice having the man I fell in love with back."

Kissing her on the forehead, Kaen couldn't help but smile. "It's weird. Even with a battle that will determine so many things only a few months away, I haven't been this happy in ages. Even Pammon seems to be doing well with all this."

Ava nodded as she turned back to help a family with six kids.

As tired as he was, Kaen couldn't help but feel content. Sleep would have been great, but seeing the people he fought for daily like this reminded him what it was all about. It had been too long since he had felt this way.

"We have begun making armor, and the smiths are producing it as quickly as we can smelt the ore. The dwarves who are experienced in this have been a boon with some of the processes. They made things more efficient, and it has resulted in less waste."

Kaen nodded as he read the reports Aldric had given him. The king was staring at the map they occasionally modified with tokens for troops. "With the armor and weapons, I think we can finish up in the coming months, and these two groups here can be listed as a medium-armored group."

Herb tapped one of the tokens he had placed a month ago. "I've got a group here that will be ready to help also. These adventurers have been getting a lot of practice with some of our older and more experienced ones. The mentoring has gone amazing."

Glancing up from the report, Kaen looked at Herb even though the guild master wasn't looking at him. "I'll tell Selmah you called her older the next time I see her."

Herb groaned and turned to see Kaen grinning. "She'd probably pretend to be upset because you told her that. Still, she has been instrumental in helping our mages get stronger. I only wish . . ."

Kaen nodded, knowing what Herb had hoped for. Amaranth had inspected Selmah and agreed she could do nothing to help the woman with her injury. The lines in a person's body controlling their mana had been damaged beyond repair. The fact that she could still cast spells and possessed the magical power she did surprised the green dragon.

"That will be a great support group. Would you rather keep them bundled up or spread out?" Aldric asked as he picked up the small note card on the table that matched the token. "Forty mages spread out would do wonders and present less of a target for the enemy to focus on."

Herb nodded. "I planned on it, but it's easier to list them all together. My real goal is to help outfit each of your groups with adventurers. A healer and warrior together can keep the lines strong. My archers and scouts, with yours, will help create chaos against any enemy we encounter."

"And two dragons supporting each army along with a Dragon Rider," Aldric added. He turned and saw Kaen looking at the two of them. "Did you three really kill that many kobolds?"

"At least four thousand. It took a few days, but they cleared out enough to hurt their ranks for a while. Only one of them suffered a slight injury, and I'm glad it happened," Kaen replied. "Had they walked away unscathed from the battle, I feel it might have led to them being too overconfident."

"We don't need any more Dragon Riders with that problem," teased Herb.

"You're right," Kaen said as he stood to join the men at the map. "I've suffered for it, as have others. Right now, my plan is simple: help them grow and get stronger. We have three months, maybe four max before we attack."

"Especially since winter is here."

Putting his hand on Aldric's shoulder, Kaen squeezed and nodded. "Our food supplies are fine. The crops growing in the mountains have finally started producing. The winter crops will survive, and for the first time in a while, it appears the animals are starting to reproduce faster than we have eaten them."

"And we got those two loads of dried fish in two weeks ago," Herb said.

Sighing, Aldric scratched his chin as he looked at the map again. "Do you really think the dwarves and wood elves can be in place when we want to attack? The snow might not all be melted by then."

"Dagan said they will be there. In the next six weeks, I will know how much more time we need until the attack. Once that date is set, there is no turning back."

Aldric and Herb both nodded at Kaen's words. They had six weeks to decide, and once they committed to the fight, Stioks would find out. There were spies in the capital, but nothing could be done about it.

"Well, I guess that completes our business here. Any plans?" asked Aldric.

Kaen groaned and then sighed. "I always have plans, but right now, I'm going to see my wife and spend some time with her before we get back to work."

Aldric reached out, shook Kaen's hand, and smiled. "As always, I am grateful for your commitment to this task. May the spirits watch over you."

Herb shook Kaen's hand and grinned. "I only wish Fiola were still here to see you. I don't think she would be surprised at how much you have grown."

The mention of Fiola brought back a few memories, and Kaen smiled. Some were good, and some were bad, but he knew that Fiola had done what she thought was best for the adventurers' guild and the kingdom.

"You two stay warm, and thank you for trusting my judgment."

"You're sure you don't want to come with us?"

Ava scowled and shook her head at him. "If it wouldn't be un-ladylike, I'd give you the hand gesture I always catch you and Hess sharing. No, I'm not getting on the back of a dragon and flying to the south side of this land in the snow. Unlike you, some of us would be frozen to the bone. Besides, your children are kicking me constantly."

"My children? Why are they my children when they are kicking you?" Kaen teased as he moved over and put his hand on Ava's stomach. He could feel that they were indeed kicking more often.

"Two more months, maybe three max," Ava sighed. "Mom and Dad said they will be ready when the time comes since it is twins."

As will I.

Ava turned and smiled, nodding at Amaranth, who was watching them. Her eyes were changing colors as they had a lot in the last while.

Kaen got down on one knee and kept his hand on Ava's belly. Closing his eyes, he willed his lifestone to flood him with power and saw his two children larger now, each growing and moving inside her. He could see their arms and legs pushing and shoving as the two of them were pressed against each other. Their heads had small features, and he could make out their eyes, noses, and mouths.

"They are beautiful," he whispered as he watched them.

"You know that's not fair," Ava groaned, jealous of whenever he did this.

A thrumming noise came behind them, and Kaen and Ava turned toward Amaranth.

Kaen marveled at the power that outlined the green dragon as his eyes moved past Ava to Amaranth. She was always so bright, and her scales seemed filled with their own magical power and life.

Then he froze as he stared at the green dragon, and Pammon, who had been relaxing next to Amaranth, stood up quickly and began to trill.

"What in the world just happened?" Ava asked. "Did you two tell a joke or something?"

A grin broke out on Kaen's face, and he stared at Amaranth and saw her eyes and the light of them swirling.

Do you know?

Do I know what?

Pammon was almost giddy, if one could call a dragon that, as he shifted from side to side.

She doesn't know! I know, and she doesn't know!

Glynnis had moved because of how Pammon had stood up, and the yellow dragon was staring at him.

Kaen turned his eyes and looked at Glynnis, wondering if he might find something similar. After looking for a bit, he realized that there was not the same thing inside her as inside Amaranth.

"Kaen!" Ava said loudly, trying to get his attention. "What is going on?"

"One second, my love," Kaen said, turning his eyes back to Ava. After standing, he kissed her on the head. He grabbed her hand and led her slowly to where Amaranth was. The green dragon was shifting around, no longer lying down but instead nervous at why Kaen was coming toward her and why Pammon seemed ready to explode.

"Amaranth, lie back down if you will. I promise I'll tell you in a moment."

The green dragon grumbled, but she lay down, folding her wings against her.

Kaen got next to her and smiled. Looking up at the green dragon, she could see her eyelids pulled down halfway as she watched Kaen and Ava.

"Do me a favor and lift your wings and hold them up for a moment. I want to show Ava something."

PLEASE HURRY! I'm dying over here!

Kaen tried to not wince or laugh as he felt Pammon's excitement about to burst. He tried to remember a time Pammon had acted this excited and knew there hadn't been one.

"Kaen?"

"Trust me, my love. Here, let me guide you."

Kaen moved behind Ava, held out both hands, angling them a little apart, and moved her to where he knew was the right spot.

"Can you feel it?"

"Feel wha—"

Ava stopped talking, and Kaen felt her tense up in his hands.

"Are you serious?" she whispered.

Someone best tell me what is going on!

It had taken every ounce of Kaen's power to control what he had not said or revealed. Pammon had sensed it immediately and was about to give away the secret he knew.

"Pammon, would you like to tell her?"

YOU ARE PREGNANT!

Amaranth began to move, and Kaen gently took Ava in his grasp and pulled her back as the green dragon shifted. He looked at Pammon, who was smiling, every tooth he still had showing.

You are pregnant! He can see the egg! He can see—

Kaen started to laugh and then felt Pammon using his eyes.

Impossible! How did you?!

What?! What can he see?!

Amaranth's voice was trembling, confusion and excitement flooding her words in both Kaen's and Ava's heads.

His wife was trembling in his arms as she reached out and touched Amaranth's side now that she had stopped moving around so much.

Two . . . there are two eggs.

Pammon's words seemed to be quiet as he spoke. Disbelief in what he was seeing through Kaen's eyes.

How did you hide that from me? How could I not know?

Kaen smiled and looked up at Pammon, letting his dragon see himself through the view Sedel used to see the world.

It took everything I had, and I was almost unable to . . . but . . . congratulations! You're going to be a father again.

Pammon sat down harder on the stone floor than he had intended, and the noise of it echoed through the cave.

Glynnis came over and nuzzled against Amaranth.

Congratulations, sister! One dragon has not had two eggs in over five hundred years!

Amaranth said nothing, her body sagging against the ground next to Pammon as the words she had heard still ran through her mind.

"Congratulations!" Ava exclaimed. "Aren't you excited?"

Amaranth nodded and turned her head toward Ava.

I am, and yet I do not know how to feel. I had hoped, but it often takes a while between eggs . . . and two eggs . . .

Turning her head toward Pammon, Amaranth touched him with her snout.

What shall we do?

Pammon laughed, his thrumming echoing through the cavern.

We shall welcome two new children and build a bigger cave.

Kaen laughed and turned his lifestone off. Opening his eyes, he turned his wife around and kissed her.

"I guess you really are rubbing off on Amaranth after all."

64

Snow Days

The last month had been filled with lots of private celebrations at the news of two more eggs coming in a year or two. None of the dragons knew how long it would take for them to be strong enough to be laid. Still, Aldric and Herb had been excited at the prospect of such a rare thing.

Phillip and Frederick had been excited at the news also, but their two weeks spent in the mines had taken a lot of their excitement out of them.

Kaen spent time with Hess and Bren discussing tactics and plans, and both men worked hard to get the students old enough for battle trained. Even with snow on the ground, they worked them through the basic formations and taught commands. Time was not an ally, and bad weather or not meant nothing when one's life depended on it.

Five months had passed since they had started this plan, and as Kaen went over his list of things to do at the dinner table, Pammon was moving toward the cave opening again.

"Cold?"

Ava nodded, and Kaen smiled as Pammon released a steady stream of fire that turned the rocks near the entrance orange. After he stopped and they continued to burn for a few minutes, the air that came into the cavern began to warm up.

Sighing, Ava smiled and looked over Kaen's shoulder. "Pregnant and freezing is not what I had planned on. It feels really cold this year."

Kaen joined his wife and sighed as she had. "It is, and things are slowing down because of it. The snow is deeper than we had expected. If it weren't for Pammon and Glynnis, I'm not sure we could get some of the supplies we have back and forth between the mines and the forges."

We both knew it wouldn't happen.

Kaen smiled, ignoring the fact that Pammon was bragging again. He had started doing that more since the news of twin eggs.

"The good news is that no movement has been spotted at the caves to the south. Pammon checked those out the other day, and it appears that the orcs and goblins, if they are still in the caves, are done coming out for now. After the snow melts . . ."

Ava leaned over and tapped a line on his papers. "Still think they can learn flying by then?"

"Ask Pammon, it's his call."

Ava turned and smiled at the bronze dragon, looking over the partition at the two of them.

They are almost strong enough. I believe it will be safe to try again in a few weeks. The loads they are helping to carry are what they need. They are still far away from being able to fly how I would like them to with a rider.

"We have time . . . not much, but we do."

Pammon nodded and turned, moving back to Amaranth and Glynnis.

You still need to decide when we attack. If I remember the last meeting with Aldric and Herb correctly, it was two weeks. No matter what you decide, we will be ready.

You seem to forget what is holding me back.

Pammon paused his step and turned his head to gaze at Kaen.

Kaen felt his dragon's eyes upon him and shifted in his chair so he could peer at them.

Then we go without her. Perhaps it is for the best, but you cannot delay everyone and everything for her sake. Just as I would prefer Amaranth not to be involved in this fight, you and I both know it would be foolish to send your wife into battle pregnant.

Pammon bent his neck and moved his head closer to Kaen. His massive snout hung over the partition, and Kaen felt his friend's warm breath.

Do not delay what must happen for the safety of your wife and child. Remember that everyone has someone they love who is going to fight. Many will not come home. More than either of us wants to acknowledge. Be the leader you must be and make the decision only you can. The longer you hold off, the worse things will get for everyone.

Kaen began to nod. Closing his eyes, he covered his mouth with his hand and let Pammon's words help him with what he had been struggling with.

You are right. Let us go and tell Aldric right now that we will attack in two months. I will not wait any longer.

Pammon angled his head slightly and snorted, sending out a well-aimed blast of mucus that almost hit Kaen but completely missed Ava.

After staring at the mess on the floor, Ava began to groan and glared at Pammon. "One of you better clean that up, or so help me, I will make both of your lives miserable."

Kaen slid the table across the floor and stood, making sure to avoid the spot on the ground. "I guess I will take care of it, even though it wasn't my mess."

Pammon thrummed and started to move to where Amaranth and Glynnis were. He froze a few steps as the words came from them both as one.

Clean that up, or don't come over here.

Pammon looked at both of his mates and saw that their eyes reflected the tone in which they had just spoken to him.

Grunting, Pammon turned, approached the partition, and leaned over.

Kaen had taken a few steps to go get some towels when he heard a sound and turned to see Pammon scraping his claw along the ground, collecting most of his mucus on it. His bronze dragon then walked awkwardly to the front entrance and flicked it off the edge.

That was a little disgusting, but uh . . . thanks . . . I think.

As Pammon glared at Kaen, the dragon's eyelids became tiny slits.

We need to go. A breath of fresh air is what we both need.

Kaen saw the look Ava was giving him and nodded.

Let me finish up this last bit, and then we can go.

In the town below, the snow that accumulated in some places painted a beautiful picture in the gray light of the day.

The places where forges were roaring nonstop had no snow on the roofs or even around parts of the buildings. They could see the paths that had been made on the streets, and Kaen watched as men scooped snow and put it in carts, taking it elsewhere to drop before repeating the task again.

Kids were playing in the snow, throwing snowballs, and building snowmen.

Even in the coldest times, those children love to play.

The snow that attacked his face slid off, and Kaen nodded.

Aldric seemed relieved at the news. It was time to commit.

It was. Now, we must finish what we started.

Kaen rubbed the scales on his friend and stared up at the clouds, which continued to gently release snow upon the land.

It is . . . now let's return home and see if our wives are no longer upset with us.

Pammon laughed as he slowly changed directions in the sky.

I don't think that will ever happen completely.

"You're sure about this?" Hess asked as he cinched the harness a little tighter around Glynnis.

"Who else can I send?" Kaen asked. "Phillip and Frederick aren't ready for a trip like this, but I cannot leave the capital undefended. If I had to think of a time Stioks might attack, this would be it. I could send one of them with Glynnis, but then I'm left with the problem of not being able to have them practice flying."

Hess nodded, grumbling as he did. "I'm just saying I'm going to freeze my balls off, and we both know it."

Kaen laughed. "Good thing you don't use them anymore, then, I guess."

They embraced, and Hess sighed. "You're a good man and a leader. Hoste would be proud of you."

Kaen smiled, giving Hess a gentle punch on one of his arms.

"He would say the same about you. Now go be safe and return quickly."

Kaen turned to Glynnis and scratched her neck as she patiently waited.

I owe you this, and I will try to find some way to repay it. Thank you, as always, for doing what I ask of you.

Glynnis playfully pushed against him with her neck.

You have always shown me kindness and favor, and as we have mentioned before, you always ask. I am grateful for how you treat my child and my mate. Anything I can do to help keep them safe is no problem at all. How quickly do you want me to get to these places?

Kaen glanced at Hess, who was slowly making his way onto Glynnis's neck.

The man wore more clothes than Kaen imagined possible. The cloak he had around his face and head would hopefully keep him warm. He even had a cloth mask that would help protect his mouth and nose.

"Hess, remember to let her know if you need a break. Otherwise, she will keep going as fast as she can."

Hess nodded, slipping a glove on with his teeth. "I'll manage."

Kaen gave Glynnis another scratch or two before backing up.

"Be safe, both of you. If something happens or comes at you, fly away. There is no one faster than Glynnis."

After waving, Hess pulled up his mask and yanked his head covering as far as he could over his head. He gave three taps on Glynnis's neck and then grabbed onto the rope even though he was buckled in.

In a moment, the yellow dragon was airborne, already speeding quickly through the air and getting altitude faster than Kaen could imagine.

How come you aren't that fast? Kaen teased.

A groan came from behind him, and a massive amount of snow suddenly slammed into Kaen's back.

"Seriously?!"

Kaen spun and saw Pammon grinning. Another claw full of snow was already on its way. Diving to the side, Kaen barely avoided the snow that could have easily filled a wagon.

Perhaps you should instead ask yourself, why am I not smart enough to realize that keeping my back turned to a dragon with this much snow around isn't a good thing?

Pammon thrummed as Kaen grabbed a handful of snow and tossed it at the massive dragon. The tiny ball of snow hit a scale and fell to the ground.

Groaning, Kaen held both hands up in surrender.

"Fine, you win! Now, let's get back to work. We have too much stuff to do, and I don't want to be completely wet."

Still thrumming, Pammon moved closer so Kaen could climb on.

On a side note, snow down one's backside, even if the cold doesn't bother you, isn't a pleasant feeling.

Pammon leaped into the air, unable to stop laughing as Kaen shifted multiple times on his saddle.

65

Sharing Knowledge

Do not drop that low! You are risking both of your lives when you do that!

Pammon shouted louder than he intended as Foros dove toward the target that Phillip was waiting to try shooting at with his bow. The silver dragon kept forgetting how differently he flew with a person's weight on him. A week of flying with the harness and saddle had helped prepare him for those changes, but Phillip was over two hundred pounds of solid muscle, and it was still a new experience for both of them.

Phillip took his shot and missed by a dozen yards. Kaen could see the young man's frustration.

Tell him to relax. When Foros is anxious and tight, it makes it harder on both of them. Let his legs and the clips deal with keeping him in the saddle. Focus on taking the shot when it feels right.

Pammon relayed the information as the rider and dragon moved back up into the sky.

Tazorath and Frederick started their turn, and Kaen smiled as the female dragon, though not as strong as her brother, had a better grasp on how to fly with the extra weight on her back.

Her angles were almost always perfect, and when it came time to turn or dive, each wing was in the precise position to keep her from getting off balance.

The same dive that had gotten Foros and Phillip came up, and the red dragon came down over the treetops and into the straight path of cleared trees. Frederick waited, keeping his core tight and the bow ready. He drew back and let it go only when he was almost on the target.

He missed by only a few yards, and Kaen saw him smile. He also gave Tazorath a few pats as they began their climb out of the straightaway.

Tell them both to land. We've been at this for a while, and I want to talk for a few minutes instead of relaying the same information repeatedly.

Pammon thrummed and watched as his children turned to where Kaen always held these conversations.

"Phillip, tell me what you think Foros is doing wrong."

Kaen watched as Phillip opened his mouth and then closed it, choosing to consider his words for a moment. Foros's eyelids closed halfway as he stared at his rider.

"That's not really fair . . . I mean, we already heard what Pammon has said."

Kaen shrugged and shook his head. "Do you think Pammon and I agree on everything? We fight all the time. I say and do things he doesn't like, and he says and does things I don't like. You two, however," Kaen said as he pointed a finger between the two, "can't seem to stop fighting and trust each other. Now listen and pay attention."

Kaen moved to where Foros was, holding out his hand and waiting on the silver dragon. After a moment, he put his head against Kaen's hand. A change in the dragon's attitude began as Kaen stood there momentarily.

Listen to me, Foros. Tell me what is wrong.

The gold eyes stared at him, and Kaen could feel the frustration flowing through the silver dragon's body.

I . . . I'm afraid I can't do what I need to, and it will get us both killed.

Kaen nodded and began to scratch Foros's scales.

Listen to me and know that what I'm about to say is true. I have those same fears, as does your sire.

Foros looked at Kaen before turning his gaze to Pammon, who nodded.

Part of this bond is fearing for the other person's or dragon's life. I felt guilty for a long time after my actions got your sire shot early in our bonding. It pained me more than you can know that when I chose to tell him to do something, it could have possibly ruined his chances of flying for some time.

He likewise can tell you stories of when he feared I would die because of his actions or my own. The difference, though, is we don't hold it back. We share it with each other. You and Phillip have to be honest with one another, and I can see that you aren't.

Kaen turned to Phillip, who was getting only one side of the conversation. He could see how Phillip handled the fear of his dragon.

"Listen to me, Phillip. I've known you a long time, and I know how brave you are and can be. But tell Foros what you're afraid of."

Looking down at the ground, Phillip breathed heavily for a moment. "I also fear that I will cause Foros to get injured or . . . killed."

The silver dragon moved his head from Kaen's hand and shifted to where his rider was. He nudged Phillip with his snout, and the young rider embraced his dragon. Kaen stood there watching the two of them.

They're close.

I know, but we can't force it. It has to be them.

"Phillip, look at me."

The young man scratched his dragon for a moment and then turned to see what Kaen would say next.

"He is your friend and partner for life. If you die, he will die. If he dies, you will die. Do you understand this?"

Phillip took a massive breath and let it out slowly as he nodded. "I do."

"Then both of you need to take some time and figure out what your bond really means to each other. Remember what it was like when you first heard each other and touched one another, those first scratches and times you played together. Remember how you felt the first time you saw him get hurt."

Kaen motioned to Foros to come closer to him. After the dragon did so, Kaen again reached out and gave him a gentle scratch along the jaw.

"Foros, remember how you felt when you saw the two of them surrounded by those kobolds. The panic that was in your heart at the injury. How you couldn't be stopped no matter what we said and dove down to help him, even if it meant you might injure yourself."

Phillip started to chuckle, and a gentle thrum came from Foros.

I remember that feeling . . . and the talking-to I got from my father later.

Kaen grinned and nodded.

"Now, go farther down the field and spend a little bit of time being honest. Stop being brave for the other and stop trying to hide how you feel. Remember how it hurts when you are apart. I'll call you both back in a bit, and we can give this another go."

Are we not in trouble?

Kaen shook his head. "Not at all. Remember, most of what you're going through I have been through. Your father and I have had many hard moments, and now we can feel each other to the point that it is almost impossible to hide anything from one another. That is because we are committed more than anything else."

Foros tilted his head, and his eyelids went completely wide momentarily.

Even more than your mate?

Kaen groaned, and Pammon started to thrum.

Do not make him answer that question, my son. The answer he gives, no matter how painful, will not help his mate or me. I know how he feels, and I can tell you this. He cares about everyone so much that he is risking his life, yet if it came down to the world or me, I would win.

Pammon leaned close, bringing his snout down to where it touched the top of Foros's head.

The difference is I am just as committed to him. I would not allow him to sacrifice who he is for me. If it meant the world or my life, I would give my own because of what the pain of losing this world would cost him.

Kaen reached out and touched Pammon. "As he has said . . . you will know the other and how you feel, but only after you are honest—really honest. Now go."

Phillip and Foros started walking in the direction Kaen had pointed, and Kaen shook his head as he looked up at Pammon.

"It's a good thing I love you, or I'd punch you."

Pammon groaned and took a few steps back, giving Kaen room with Tazorath and Frederick.

"As for you two," Kaen said as he turned to face them. "When did your bond change?"

Frederick's mouth opened slightly, and Kaen was certain that if Tazorath hadn't had red scales, she would have blushed.

"How did you know?" Frederick asked, stammering as he did.

"It's not my first time. I can tell by how you two act and treat each other."

It was two days ago. After that crash we had.

Kaen started to laugh; his eyebrows rose as he remembered that moment. "It was a pretty bad crash. I could tell you both were scared for the other."

"After it happened and Amaranth healed us, we just shared that fear and . . ." Frederick paused, turning his head toward Phillip and Foros. "You're trying to get them to figure out what we did."

"I am. Tazorath, how do you feel since the change in the bond?" Kaen asked.

It is different in a good way. I can understand better how he feels and even start to know what he wants to do. He also knows what I am feeling, and he anticipates my movements better when we are flying.

Holding his hand out as he did for Foros, Kaen waited for Tazorath to come to him. She didn't hesitate and moved quickly, putting her snout against his hand. She trilled as Kaen began to scratch her scales.

"You two have reached the first step. There are many more steps in your bond, and that will take time for you two to figure out," Kaen said. "Let me share one last bit of advice."

Taking his hand down from Tazorath's snout, Kaen spoke to Frederick. "You must figure out what drives you and makes you do this. Figure out what will keep you fighting even when nothing else is left. Whoever or whatever that is, once you are committed to it, and once Tazorath knows it, things will change again."

Frederick nodded as he glanced off to the side somewhere, obviously lost in his thoughts.

Pammon moved close to his daughter and nuzzled against her a little.

Little one, you must also help your rider find his purpose, and it must be one you can agree with. If you do not, your bond will not change. It will stay as it is now. Both of you will be weaker, and there is a closeness you won't know.

Pammon pulled his head back and looked down at his daughter.

Trust me when I say these next words; I mean them with my entire being. There is no joy greater, not even the joy I have watching you grow and become a strong dragon like what I have with being Kaen's dragon. Even your mother or Amaranth cannot match how I feel. You know how special you are to me because you feel my love for you. I hope you and your rider can achieve the bond Kaen and I share one day. Nothing else, no matter how great or amazing it is, will matter when you do. Not even yourself.

Tazorath stared at her father and slowly nodded. Turning her head toward Frederick, she moved closer and pressed against him.

Frederick started laughing and scratched her neck repeatedly as she trilled.

Kaen sighed and looked at Pammon, seeing his best friend and partner staring at him.

Perhaps we should take the rest of the day off. You and I need a moment to talk.

Kaen looked down at the land beneath him. The few clouds below where he and Pammon were flying hid portions of the land, but there were gaps that seemed like little pockets of treasure. Clumps of trees, a road, life.

What are you thinking? I can feel your mind and heart wandering.

You really meant what you said to Tazorath, and I know it. I needed a moment up here to say those same things to you. Even more, I need to say one last thing.

Kaen undid his harness and began to walk along Pammon's neck even as the air rushed against him.

Pammon did what he could to glide, making sure not to shift too much.

Every day, I'm grateful for you and how you love me. I know we don't use those words enough, and sometimes you don't like them, but I keep hearing them appear as time goes by.

Kaen began to crouch down as he made his way to Pammon's skull, using his hands and feet to crouch along the ridges and spikes on the upper part of his friend's neck. Finally, he reached the two horns on the back of his friend's massive head and grabbed onto both of them, standing between them and letting the wind blast against his body.

What are you doing, you eggling?

Kaen laughed, and even though the wind carried it away immediately, he didn't try to stop it. Staring out this way was a whole different view and one he had not enjoyed enough.

Bending down, Kaen kept one hand on a horn and began to scratch the scales near the outer part of the other horn.

Trills and a controlled cough came from Pammon, and Kaen smiled as he felt his friend sigh.

I know you won't promise me to not sacrifice yourself if you believe doing so would save me or anyone else. Just know that I would never want to trade you for anything. You're part of me.

Kaen tapped his chest with his free hand.

As much as my lifestone is part of me, so are you. So do not throw yourself away for me.

Pammon said nothing, knowing Kaen wasn't done as the words and emotions inside his friend wrestled in his heart.

There is a reason why the bond said what it said. We are one soul. For that reason, I will destroy Stioks and anyone else who tries to take you or anyone else in our family away. I promise you this.

Pammon continued to fly, slowing down some so the wind wasn't as strong against them. After a few minutes, Kaen felt his friend and the thoughts he had.

Soon we shall do what we made a pact for a long time ago. To give everything so that others can have a family and never lose another loved one.

Kaen smiled and leaned against his friend's skull, gently scratching the scales as they flew above the world.

66

Battle Plans Discussed

"The ground is too wet and muddy to continue. We are done for the day."

All of the guards and the students who had been practicing for the last hour nodded, no one complaining about not having to be covered in mud or soaked through their clothes anymore.

Kaen watched the students start to file away, moving toward their dorms so they could clean up while the guards began marching toward the city.

"Three weeks," Phillip said.

Kaen didn't reply for a few seconds, considering what that timeline meant. The dwarves and wood elves would be preparing to march soon. Their journey would be much harder, but if his numbers were correct, ten thousand dwarven warriors were going to combine with one hundred wood elves.

"Kaen?"

"I heard Phillip. I'm just considering a few things. Your army will be moving soon, and I will send you out there in two weeks to meet with them," Kaen replied. He finally turned and saw Phillip and the young man's confident look.

"I'm ready, or as ready as I can be. Frederick and I still can't believe our stats or the gear we have been given. It feels like it's too much."

"I wish it were more . . . I really do, Phillip. I can't prepare for what is coming. The news we got last week only made it worse."

Grunting, Phillip nodded and glanced at the kids he had grown up with the last few years. Every week, he went over the names of the ones he knew who had died while they defended the walls. The thought of how many more he was going to add hurt.

"One more fight, one more battle. Even if they know we are coming, we will end this."

Turning, Kaen nodded and held out his hand.

Phillip grabbed it and pulled Kaen close, giving him a quick embrace before stepping back.

"I know you never wanted to be my father, but often I see you as the brother I wished I had," Phillip said. "You have pushed me and Frederick to be the best we can be, and trusting us with our dragons was the greatest gift either of us could imagine . . .

"Helping us bond," Phillip continued, his voice now lower, "helped Foros and me to get past some of the issues we were having. Things are better now, and I know we will both do what we must."

Grinning, Kaen reached over and ruffled the short hair on Phillip's head. "I guess if you're my younger brother, I need to beat you up more often," he teased. "Just know you both exceeded any dreams I had over five years ago when you two ran up to me. You've earned everything you have."

Phillip nodded and then moved to where Racha, the headmistress, stood.

Kaen watched as he snuck up behind her and grabbed her, spinning her around while laughing.

They have grown up, and the time for us to go is now. We have much to do.

One day, I will answer for all our actions, and I pray the world sees what we did as necessary. Knowing how many will die still weighs heavy on my heart.

Pammon moved closer, and Kaen turned, letting Phillip and Racha have a moment to remember all the times she had caught him misbehaving and everything else.

Let's go. Aldric is waiting for us.

Pammon looked through Kaen's eyes, as they had moved the map indoors. The constant rain and cold weather threatened to ruin it, and finally, they gave up. Both Aldric and Herb were glad to know Pammon could still be an asset in planning.

"Only two of my spies made it back. That means the other eighteen must be dead."

Aldric grunted at Herb's words, and both men knew the cost those spies had paid.

"As you can see, the final information we have from over a week ago suggests they are preparing to engage here. It's a smart decision."

Kaen studied the map, feeling Pammon's desire for him to occasionally shift his eyes.

"That slight incline will make it hard on our troops, and if the fortifications the spies mentioned are finished in the coming weeks, getting through them will be difficult," Aldric stated as he ran his finger near markers they had placed last week. "I'm not sure dragons will be that helpful against them. We can't attack from a different side unless we want to end up in a forest, which would be even more dangerous for our troops."

Kaen grunted as he bobbed his head.

We still need to try to engage Stioks as the battle starts, which means we are deeper into his territory. Surely, he would defend his own castle.

I'm not certain . . . that man doesn't think like we do.

Pammon knew Kaen was correct, but the thought tasted bad in both of their mouths.

"Should I ask?" Aldric asked as Kaen's eyes flickered across the map.

"Pammon and I are dealing with our problem of Stioks. Drawing him out is going to be hard. I'm not certain we can, and with two armies, we're left trying to guess the direction he might come."

"If you do fight, what is the plan?"

"Win at all costs," replied Kaen.

Herb scoffed at the answer to his question, but Kaen just shrugged.

"Even if it means Pammon and I die, we will not let that man get away. In three weeks, this ends no matter what."

Both men saw the fire in Kaen's eyes and knew he was not joking.

"Surely you and Pammon—"

"No," Kaen said, cutting off Aldric. He turned his attention to the king, a man he had come to call a friend, and frowned. "You know there are times when the only choice is the hardest. I will not make this battle for naught. If it takes my life so that your children, my children, and Pammon's children can live and grow, then if left with no other option, we will take it."

Herb and Aldric stood there quietly. Both weighed the words, and each knew the mantle of leadership and its costs.

"Fiola understood that."

Wincing, Herb nodded. "She did, and you're an arse for using that to prove a point, Kaen Marshell. Have you told Ava yet?"

Crossing his arms and filling his lungs with air, Kaen let it out slowly and shook his head.

"She knows my commitment, but I have not said those words. I'm not even certain she will be able to help in this fight, and a part of me is thankful for that. Unless she has the children soon, she will not be ready in time."

That is a lie, and you know it. Amaranth will do what Ava asks, and unless you command my mate not to help, Ava will be there.

Growling, Kaen turned his attention back to the map.

"Here! This is where the armies of Ebonmount must attack. I'll have Frederick lead the middle, but put your best fighters on the edges. We must overtake one of their sides and crush them from the back."

"What if they do that to us?" Herb asked, tapping the number of tokens on the board. "They outnumber us three to one."

"Three to one and with defenses and elevation. It feels like suicide," Aldric muttered.

Kaen picked up the two dragon tokens and set them between where Frederick's army would be and Stioks's main army. "I'm giving everything I can with these two. Together, you have the fastest dragons with lightning attacks that will arc between their armies. While it won't scorch the earth, they may be able to destroy the fortifications without leaving a burning patch of land that we can't cross either."

Scratching his chin, Aldric slowly nodded. "That is good. What about the dwarves, though? They have a limited range, and while I expect them to build some siege weapons, can a hundred archers really do that much?"

"If you saw them shoot as I have, you'll come to appreciate the power of their archers. Most of them have abilities that allow for multiple targets. If Sedel fights like I hope she will, she alone can cut an army down as long as she is protected."

"I wish I could send some mages to help up there, but the distance is too far, and the dragons couldn't support them all."

"Herb, you're fine," Kaen replied. We've done everything we can. Our armies are leaving in a little over a week, and we will march toward Stioks's kingdom. Pammon, Glynnis, and Tazorath will stay to protect the army as you move. Once you are in place, if I haven't seen Stioks, we will search for him."

"With only two arrows?"

"There was no more ore, so each army shall only get one. Sedel will get the one for the northern army, and you two can pick your best archer to have it. If Stioks appears, they will call for Pammon and me, and we will come."

Each of them turned their attention once more to the map.

What if we got there early and tried to take out their defenses?

Kaen understood what Pammon was thinking, but getting that close and not knowing what Stioks might have planned left Kaen worried about the unknown.

It is an option, but the real question is, at what risk? If we fly in low and do that, and Stioks comes in from above . . .

Pammon was groaning, and Kaen knew it.

Everything depends on where Stioks is . . . even when we are attacking. I can snap his dragon in half with one bite, but if he hits me again with that spell like last time, it will be harder to fight and stay with them.

How strong were you a year after you hatched? Can you even remember that time?

The walls vibrated slightly, and Kaen sighed as both men looked at him.

"Yes . . . Pammon is laughing."

They chuckled and nodded, paying attention to the map and leaving Kaen alone.

That seems like a lifetime ago. I was stronger than my children by quite a bit, yet that was due to your lifestone. I'm not certain we can know how strong that whelp is now. Even if Stioks used magic of some sort, there is no chance he could match me one-on-one.

And yet it isn't one-on-one . . . I'd like to think I've grown, as have you. Stioks, as always, will be the greatest test.

Together, we shall end this.

". . .at least with their armor, those two should be safe."

Kaen caught the last part of the conversation Herb and Aldric had been having. His mind wandered back to the suit of armor in the guild hall.

"Herb, can you take me to the guild vault tomorrow?"

The shorter man turned and nodded, raising his eyebrows. "Have you figured something out?"

"No, but I just realized there might be a clue I'm unaware of now that I can see that I couldn't before."

Do you really think that will work?!

Kaen could sense the excitement Pammon felt at his idea.

Maybe, but let me finish talking here.

"I can do that first thing in the morning if you want. Just meet me inside the hall, and we can go down to it."

Kaen nodded, stretched, and then let out a yawn. "I don't want to be rude, but as you both can attest, it's been a long six months. I need to go check on my wife, who looks ready to give birth."

Both laughed and nodded, turning toward the map so Kaen could leave.

As he walked toward the door, Kaen wondered what tomorrow might bring.

Perhaps . . . Tomorrow, we shall see.

67

Pursuing Chances

"Don't stop, my love," Ava moaned.

Kaen smiled and continued pressing his thumbs into the bottoms of her feet as he massaged them.

"You don't know how good that feels . . . I could melt right here."

"It can't be that good," Kaen said as his wife opened her eyes and leaned back in the padded chair her father had bought her.

"I'd say something ugly, but I won't because you are willing to do this. Just know one's feet get exceptionally sore after carrying these two children of yours that don't seem to ever sleep."

Slowly, he worked his way up her foot and to her ankle, eliciting more groans and moans.

"Can you two please stop that?"

Ava started to laugh, and Kaen couldn't help but chuckle as they looked at her parents, who were sitting a few yards away on a couch Pammon had brought to the cave.

"I'm sorry, Mother, but surely you know how amazing this feels."

Lady Hurem sighed, closing the book she was reading. "While I know how that feels, I try not to make everyone and every dragon in the room feel uncomfortable as I enjoy it."

Lord Hurem chuckled, but he quickly went quiet when his wife turned to see what was so funny.

"Care to comment?" she asked.

"I do not, but I remember someone perhaps letting a few of those slip once or twice when they were pregnant."

Ava's mother scowled, and she opened her book, pretending to read so she could ignore everyone's snickers.

"You could be a little quieter," Kaen teased as he switched ankles and calves.

"And you can stop pausing . . . especially since you plan on doing this whole war thing with or without me."

"I doubt our troops would like to see my wife on a dragon and giving birth in the air," Kaen replied. "Even with Amaranth there to help, I'm not open to that discussion. If I had to, I would command Glynnis or Amaranth not to let you come if they ignore reason and bring you."

Ava glared at Kaen, seeing that her husband shot back the same look. "You wouldn't!"

"My love, there are many things I would prefer not to do, but if one of them was making sure that you and our children were safe from foolish ideas, then yes, I would."

A growl came from the back of the cave, and a louder one Kaen recognized drowned it out.

"Pammon!" Ava shouted, pulling her feet off Kaen's lap and trying to stand up. "Do not be mean to Amaranth!"

How did I get involved in this fight? I simply told Amaranth she was being foolish if she didn't believe your statement about forcing her to leave Ava here.

Kaen started to laugh and held out a hand to assist Ava, who was still struggling to get up. Her stomach not only had grown in size but also was sticking out very far. Her simple dress had gotten Kaen in trouble for a comment he had made when describing how it looked on her.

"My love, please settle down unless your actions are meant to make the children come sooner."

Groaning, Ava finally took Kaen's hand and let him help her stand. "I would not give you that pleasure." She moved to where her mother was sitting and held out a hand. "Would you care to walk around the cave with me?"

Smiling, Lady Hurem closed her book and took the hand Ava had offered. "I would love to walk with you. These men seem to forget we are not weak."

Ava groaned and shook her head.

Kaen looked at Lord Hurem, who kept his eyes on the pages he was reading, not giving anyone a chance to drag him into the current problem.

Sleep had come in spurts. Ava tossed and turned all night, unable to sleep well, and Kaen did whatever he could to help her get comfortable. Eventually, she ended up in the chair her mother had brought for her.

Kaen was getting ready to leave as the sun crept into the cave when his father-in-law approached him and Pammon.

"Can I bother you two for one moment?" Lord Hurem asked.

"You know I'm always here if I can help. What do you need?"

His father-in-law glanced around the cave, acting very suspiciously, and Kaen began to wonder what the man might say.

"I have a request, and my wife had made me promise I wouldn't make it, but since she isn't here, I will ask. Would Pammon and you be willing to give a little blood again? I think I have figured out what has been wrong with the potions we have attempted for the last few years. With the battle only weeks away, I would like a chance to see if I can finally get it right."

That would mean getting jabbed in my gums again . . . Since I know what it is for, I will do it again.

Grinning, Kaen nodded. "Pammon said he would be happy to help because the reason is a good one. When would you like to do it?"

"Now, please!" Lord Hurem exclaimed. "I need to escape . . . I mean, work on a few things back at our estate where it is a little quieter and less intense."

Kaen and Pammon both laughed, the thrums of his dragon echoing quickly around the room.

"Sure thing. Come climb on, and we can drop you off first and let you take our blood. We still have plenty of time before I need to meet Herb."

"Splendid!"

Kaen smiled as the man, who usually tried to act regal all the time, climbed up Pammon's scales like a child climbing a tree.

He is more intelligent than I have given him credit for. No man wants to stay here if they will talk to him like that.

It will pass. I remember two female dragons who became very difficult to deal with a few weeks before they finally laid their eggs.

The term you are looking for is nesting. Dragons do not lay eggs like those fowl chickens who must all die.

Kaen laughed at Pammon's joke and climbed up after his father-in-law.

True. Perhaps we can find a chicken, and you can see if you can scare an egg out of it.

"What was wrong with Pammon?

Kaen chuckled at Herb's question as he put the disk in the door and watched it spin.

"Oh, he got jabbed in the gums by Lord Hurem and acts like an eggling. I know it hurts, but I didn't cry when the man cut me."

"How big was the needle he used on Pammon?"

As the door began to unlock and open, Kaen stretched out his arm and tapped his shoulder. "From my fingers to here. The worst part was it was about as thick as a piece of corn and had to be hammered in. Guess who got that awful job."

Herb winced, his face looking like he had eaten something sour. "That sounds horrible."

"I know, having to listen to Pammon cry as I hit that thing twice was awful."

Groaning, Herb waited for Kaen to go inside. "I'll stay out here unless you think it's worth me coming in," he said.

"No, I'm not sure what will happen. Just give me a few minutes."

Kaen felt Pammon still pouting through their bond, but it was worse now.

I didn't mean it like that. You know I was just messing with Herb.

How about you let me pound that rod into your leg and see how you do.

Ignoring Pammon's comment, Kaen walked across the empty room toward the only thing still in it.

As he approached it, he sensed Pammon using his eyes to see.

So many dragons gave for that outfit. I can only imagine what it must offer.

I'm hoping we find out.

Coming to a stop a few feet from the case, Kaen ran his hands along the glass and realized what it was.

This is dragon glass!

Impossible! It is like a solid sheet. How could one make it do that?

Dragging his fingers along it, Kaen moved to the sides, checking both the side panes.

This is all dragon glass . . . How they made this . . .

We have lost so much with the fall of dragons and their riders. Imagine if we could use something like that to defend with. I'm not even confident I can shatter it.

Kaen nodded as he listened to Pammon, running his hands along the edges and corners. He resisted the temptation to try to pull it up or move it again. The last time he tried, that had not gone well.

Let's see what we can see.

Closing his eyes and igniting his lifestone, Kaen saw the world shift as his vision changed. The box that was clear with his normal eyes was a swirling vortex of two colors, a deep red and a lighter red, constantly shifting and moving. They intertwined and shimmered up and down where the box was. The wall, floor, and ceiling had the normal magical energy that outlined where they were.

What is that? None of the rest of the world looks anything like that, does it?

Not that I can remember seeing. This is new.

Running his hand against the glass, Kaen saw the swirling shapes move and congregate near his hand, almost creating a barrier.

It is like it is blocking me from being able to get through.

When he used two hands on the same glass, the colors shifted and moved, again creating a flat surface that met his hands.

Try hitting your head against it.

Kaen chuckled as Pammon attempted to joke at their inability to still make it through.

I don't understand, but something here is powerful enough to be different. Perhaps we should visit the dragon glass you made and see if it looks the same?

We have time, and that would be our best course of action. Ask Herb his thoughts.

Opening his eyes and letting his lifestone go quiet, Kaen ran his hand across the glass again, releasing a sigh at being denied once more.

"I've heard of dragon glass, of course, but that stuff is from legends. Are you certain that is what it was?" Herb asked as Kaen took the disk from the door lock.

Flipping the key around in his hands, Kaen shrugged. "You'll be like 'of course he did' when I tell you that Pammon made some."

Groaning, Herb shook his head as he rubbed his eyes. "Well, of course he did . . ."

Both of them chuckled, and Kaen gave his friend a gentle shove.

"Know any way to get rid of it?"

"I don't believe anyone does. That is what makes it so special. That stuff made some of the best weapons imaginable. If Pammon could make some, and we could find a way to actually craft with it . . ." Herb's voice trailed off as he considered his words. "Bah, goblin nuts! If I had known we could have made some in the dwarven kingdom, they could have probably figured it out by now."

Kaen winced at Herb's words. "Seriously? You think they could have?"

Herb shrugged. "They have always been the best weapon and armor makers in history. It would be them if anyone knew how to or could figure it out."

There is no time, so stop that foolish thought. It would be too late even if I flew straight, draining myself dry of mana. You also are forgetting your wife, who would probably kill you for possibly missing the birth of your twins.

Groaning, Kaen stretched his neck from side to side as they arrived at the first of many sets of stairs.

"It is what it is. Let's get out of here. Pammon and I have something we need to check on."

Herb said nothing, leading the way through the maze of stairs as they moved upward toward the surface.

It's different. There is no color or even an element of magic in that.

Kaen ran his hand over where the dragon glass was, unable to see it unless he used his normal vision.

How? I mean . . . it's as if nothing is there, but we know it is.

Like it is absent of all life and magic.

Tapping his finger against the glass, Kaen could see his finger and the magic inside it smashing into the edge of the glass, but it was as if an invisible wall were there, stopping his finger and pushing back the skin and flesh.

Well, this doesn't help us at all. Sorry, now I feel like we wasted time.

Don't do that. We are seeking every chance we have to do what only we can do. There is no wasting of time if we are intentional in what we do.

His lifestone went cold and Kaen opened his eyes.

Rubbing the glass once more with his hand, Kaen moved toward the edge of the shelf.

Let's go. We have a lot of stuff to get done. Time is running out.

68
Exciting News

"Be safe and remember your training. We all have faith in you."

Frederick nodded as he sat on Tazorath's neck, clipped into the saddle. He looked like a Dragon Rider, covered in a full suit of armor except for the boots, which were leather ones he would swap out later for chain ones. The shield on his back and sword on his hip came from Aldric, a gift from the king. Baskets of arrows were strapped to Glynnis, and every other weapon the boy would need was on her to help with the weight.

"Thank you again for believing in us," Frederick replied as he waved. "We shall see you in a few weeks, flying over the land after defeating those who seek to do terrible things."

"Spoken like a true Dragon Rider!" Kaen exclaimed. "Now go and tell Bosgreth I am summoning the dwarves to war."

Tazorath roared, her mother joining in a moment later. Kaen felt chills as their cry carried across the courtyard of the adventurers' guild.

Both dragons leaped into the sky, the sun reflecting off the red and yellow dragons' scales.

"That makes me want to head out," Phillip declared as he watched his lifelong friend fly off. "Waiting isn't going to be fun."

Kaen shook his head and gave Phillip a side punch. "There won't be any waiting. We've got a lot of stuff to do, and according to my mother-in-law, my wife is due to give birth any day."

"You're certain about sending them with the dwarves and elves, not me?"

Putting his hand on Phillip's shoulder, Kaen nodded. "We discussed things, and in the end, it all rested upon Ava not having the children yet. She wants to be able to go, and if I sent you, Amaranth wouldn't be able to come. It's just too many variables."

The young man nodded, glad to know that the reason wasn't a lack of faith in him.

"Congratulations, by the way," Phillip said, digging into his pocket and pulling out a small item wrapped in cloth and tied with a red string. "It's from Frederick and me."

Kaen moved the package around in his hand, feeling that two items were inside. "Should I ask?"

Laughing, Phillip shook his head. "Just open it already."

Kaen undid the knot and carefully unfolded the layers of cloth after the string was removed. When he reached the gift inside, his fingers fumbled momentarily.

"Phillip . . . I . . ."

"We thought your children might one day want them, and we owe a debt we cannot repay. Hopefully, this will go toward showing you our gratitude. Those things changed our lives just as you did. Know that we are committed to whatever path you ask us to take."

Kaen blinked and sniffed as a few tears welled in his eyes. Slowly he picked up one of the lifestones and held it up to his face. The stone was clear, and Kaen couldn't help but smile at what it represented.

"Thank you, Phillip, for everything."

"Just promise us not to tell us if you get ones like yours. I won't lie. They were difficult to come by, but Aldric understood our request."

"He gave these to you?" Kaen asked, impressed that the king still had some.

"No, we paid for them. Aldric offered to give them, but Frederick and I couldn't accept. You have paid so much for us and this kingdom. We needed to pay that back somehow."

Carefully wrapping the stones back in the cloth, Kaen slid it into his pouch and then grabbed Phillip, hugging the boy tightly.

A few moments passed as each said more in that moment of embrace, and when they both gave three taps on each other's back, they separated, smiling and laughing at the tears each had shared.

"I'll go and show these to Ava right now. She will love them."

"Should I ask what that means for me?" Phillip asked, groaning after asking the question.

"Go find Hess. He is at the inn. Bren has the training ground ready for you to land."

Phillip nodded and slapped Kaen's arm before jogging to where Foros waited.

Thank you for giving him to me.

Kaen nodded in acknowledgment at the silver dragon staring at him with his golden eyes.

"Take care of each other. I'll see you both soon."

Before Foros took off, he roared like his sister, causing Phillip to laugh as they flew toward the town.

While I may not be old, they make me feel old. The weight of responsibility isn't heavy yet on their shoulders. Getting to enjoy life like that brings back many fond memories.

Turning, Kaen smiled at Pammon.

If only the council knew what dragons were missing out on by not having a rider, they might start to fight to get one.

Pammon thrummed and shook his head as Kaen started climbing his scales.

I doubt that day will ever come, but one day, when we revisit them, I cannot wait to see how they cower. Perhaps you can make more than one piss themselves again.

I'm trying to climb. Stop trying to make me laugh.

Pammon continued to thrum, his chest vibrating as Kaen cursed his dragon for a moment.

Come on. We need to see our mates.

Ava began to sob, and Kaen regretted showing her the lifestones the boys had given them.

"I . . . I didn't know," he whispered to Lady Hurem, who was giving him a disapproving glare.

"You didn't think that the pregnant and still emotional woman might be overwhelmed by such a beautiful gesture?"

"It's ok, Mom," Ava said, wiping away her tears. "I'm glad to know those two boys have grown up and become men. It may be hard to call them men for a while, but they have earned that right no matter their age."

Nodding, Kaen took the lifestone his wife had been holding and put it with the other one, wrapping them up again before heading toward the wooden chest they kept things in.

"I'm glad you are feeling better. I was beginning to worry you might have our children today."

Groaning, Ava shuffled toward the chair she spent time in and began to sit down until a grunt from her mother stopped her.

"We need to walk . . . again."

"Uggg . . . I'm tired, Mother. We have walked . . ." Ava paused, wincing as she held her side. "Fine, we can walk again."

Lady Hurem smiled. As Ava began to move to where her mother waited with an outstretched hand, Kaen saw his mother-in-law looking at him.

"Be a good dear and go retrieve my husband if you would. Tell him to bring the bag."

"The bag?" Kaen asked, tilting his head slightly at such an ambiguous name.

"He will know. Now go and hurry. If your wife is lucky, you two will be holding your children within the next day.

Kaen perked up, and Ava smiled, wincing for a moment.

"I'll be back, my love," Kaen said as he ran to Pammon.

"Oh, the bag!" exclaimed Lord Hurem. "That means it's time!"

"Seriously?!" Kaen shouted as his father-in-law ran to a door the servants usually used.

The older man said nothing until he opened the door and shouted, "BRING THE BAG!"

After he had done so, Lord Hurem took another breath and cupped his hands. "BRING MY CHEST!"

"Uh . . . sir . . . do we have time for a chest?" Kaen asked as the man hurried back to where he and Pammon were waiting.

"Time? Yes! I doubt I would need anything in the chest for your wife, especially with the amazing Amaranth there, but I will need something to pass the time as we wait for your children."

"Wait, you just said it was time," Kaen replied. "How long are we talking?"

Lord Hurem shrugged and made a face, suggesting he had no real idea. "It could be an hour, or it could be an entire day like my wife said. All we know is we need to hurry."

The door banged open, and two servants came carrying a massive chest with straps to keep it closed.

"You want to bring that with us?!"

"Please, Kaen, you and I both know that Pammon can easily fly with that, and you could lift that with one hand," Lord Hurem declared. "I'd ask you not to do that but to try and keep it level. There are lots of instruments and vials inside, some with your and Pammon's blood in them. Keeping them safe is always best, so I don't have to ask for more."

You better keep that chest level, or you may end up walking to this battle if you break something with my blood in it.

Kaen started to laugh, but his father-in-law backed up, sensing an aura coming from Pammon.

"Is he upset?"

"Oh, he just threatened me not to let any of your stuff break. It wouldn't be wise of me."

"Well, he is right! Pammon knows the value of things!"

Groaning, Kaen rolled his eyes and waited for the two servants, who started to set the chest down.

The door banged open again, and another servant came running, holding a rather large bag.

"Ahh, my good man, Kurt! Thank you for retrieving that!"

The servant was out of breath and sweating, having run farther than the other two. Lord Hurem took the bag from him and slung the leather strap over his shoulder.

"I'm ready if you two are, but I'm not certain what is the best way to get on Pammon with this chest."

"Wait here, I can help with that."

I swear this man is remarkable sometimes. Who brings a chest like that to their daughter's first birth? Kaen asked as he climbed Pammon's scales. *I mean, it's a twenty-foot or more climb without that chest, and he expects me to—*

Stop complaining . . . just get the rope and get this done. Amaranth is nagging me about being gone as long as we have been.

Stopping near the top of his dragon, Kaen looked at Pammon and frowned.

Is she having the baby?!

Soon. That is all Amaranth will say.

Groaning, Kaen reached the spot on Pammon's back where they kept things and dug through the packs that were always tied to the saddles. Finding the rope he was looking for, Kaen moved to the edge of his dragon's side and started to unroll it.

I'm unsure I can handle any more kids if Lord Hurem is always like this.

'You can choose your friends, but you can't pick your family,' Hess told me.

Groaning, Kaen finished unwrapping the rope and lowered both ends to the ground, keeping the middle section up top with him.

"Tie the sides, and I'll pull it up here!" Kaen shouted.

The servants ran forward and grabbed the rope, doing as Kaen had instructed.

With the chest halfway up, Kaen looked at Pammon and began shaking his head.

"Don't tell me that!" he exclaimed, starting to yank the rope up faster and not caring if it banged against his dragon's scales.

Yes, I was informed with a much more emphatic need to hurry, and so I suggest you get that up quickly.

"Dad, you better start climbing! We were told it's time!"

Lord Hurem yelped and ran to the scales, no longer afraid of being under the chest, and started scampering up Pammon's side.

"I'm sorry! The chest was a bad decision!"

Kaen ignored Lord Hurem's words and grabbed the chest, putting it next to the saddle and quickly wrapping the loose rope around it and the saddle.

"Sit!" Kaen exclaimed as his father-in-law reached the top.

The moment Lord Hurem's butt hit the saddle and the strap was clicked around him, Pammon leaped into the air.

Hold on, this is going to get rough.

As Pammon cleared the rooftop and angled toward the cave, Kaen grabbed the saddle with one hand and the rope tied to Lord Hurem's chest, which his father-in-law supposedly needed.

[Flight Burst Activated]

Hold on, my love, we are coming!

69

Two New Lives

Looking down at his daughter in his arms, Kaen couldn't help but smile when she yawned, her tiny hand stretching and the fingers opening when she did.

He kept his pinky wedged inside that tight little grip and stroked her cheek.

"She's beautiful," Kaen whispered as he glanced at Ava holding their son.

"They both are," Ava replied before kissing their son's forehead.

Some grumbling came from the couch, and Kaen saw his in-laws watching them. Lady Hurem did her best to stay on the sofa and give them a few moments with their children.

"I think she is dying," Kaen whispered as he leaned over and kissed Ava's head. "When do you think we should let her hold one again?"

"When you are tired of holding your daughter, you can give her to my mother. Until then, do not let her whimpering change your heart. When we leave for this battle, she will get plenty of time to hold them."

Kaen groaned and looked up at Amaranth and Pammon, who were both looking down at the two of them with their children.

Thankfully, neither of them looks like their sire.

Kaen laughed and shook his head.

It is good that both hands are taken, or I would use one to respond.

I could bite off that finger, and then what would you do?

Amaranth would heal it.

Pammon suppressed the thrumming that Kaen knew he almost let out.

"Two blond-haired-and-blue-eyed children . . . what are the odds?" Ava asked as she ran her finger across their son's cheek.

"We need to decide what names to give them."

Ava groaned softly. "It was easier when we thought it would be two boys or two girls . . . but choosing one of the two we came up with seems harder."

"Take your time for now, they will be fine," Kaen said.

I can feel the joy and pride emanating from you. It's like a wave of it.

How does one describe this moment? I fell in love with Ava, getting to know and spend time with her. Yet these two . . . the moment I saw them and held them in my arms, I would go to war with anyone for them.

I understand that feeling. When I first touched each of my children . . . a part of me connected, and that was why I said what I did about them a while ago. They are not pawns. They are a part of me.

Kaen smiled as he rocked his daughter in his arms.

He felt Pammon's heart and read his friend's mind.

Looking up, he smiled.

If you want to do that, I am certain Ava would not say no. Do you know how it will work?

I do not, but these will be the last two I can do. I am ok with that, though.

"Ava, my love, Pammon has a request."

Tilting her head upward, Ava saw Pammon looking down upon the four of them, his golden eyes shining as they reflected the soft light of the light orbs.

"What is it, Pammon?" Ava asked, smiling at the bronze dragon she had come to love.

Ask her yourself.

Pammon shook his head and adjusted his neck so he could get a little closer to them.

May I grant your two little ones the last of my teeth so that I can communicate with them? It will be like I did with you.

Tears began to form in Ava's eyes as she nodded, smiling and sniffing.

"I would be honored."

Moving his head back over the partition that rarely did its job, Pammon took a talon and collected the second-to-last one he had, bringing it toward the little girl that Kaen was holding.

Turn her around and hold her up.

His daughter fussed a little as Kaen adjusted and held her up so Pammon could reach her.

He leaned over, magic building up inside him till it flowed through his talons and into the tooth he had pinched between them.

In a way that seemed impossible, he gently lowered the glowing tooth till it barely touched her head, not disturbing the sleeping babe at all. It pulsed with the magic that came from his will.

I make this pact with your child to be a part of her life from the day she was born. If she calls, I will answer if I can. I will be there for her as I know her father is there for my children. We shall be of the same family.

The tooth vanished, and a mark appeared on her head for a moment, glowing brightly before it faded.

Their daughter let out a whimper, and then she cooed, opening her eyes to reveal those blue irises. It looked like she was staring up at the massive bronze dragon who gazed at her. As quickly as she had opened them, they were closed, and she was fast asleep.

"Did I just . . . Pammon?"

Kaen fumbled for words as Ava looked on, wondering what had happened.

I do not know, but I can sense her now. The heart that beats inside her is different from Ava's . . . I didn't know that was possible.

"What did I miss?" Ava asked as loudly as she dared.

"Pammon's tooth left a mark for a moment, but it's gone now. He says his bond with her is different from his bond with you—deeper."

Ava's jaw dropped as she stared at Kaen and then at Pammon.

"How?"

I do not know . . . Now, hold up your son so that I may do the same.

Turning her son around, Ava held him so that she could see his face as Pammon did what he was going to do.

Repeating the same process, Pammon channeled his magic again into the last tooth he would ever have for this gift.

It glowed brighter than the one he had just done.

Firstborn of Kaen and Ava, you shall receive my last blessing. I shall watch over you as I do your sister, and I will be there to protect you all your days. Like your father loves you and my children, I pledge my love to you.

The tooth turned so bright it almost made Kaen and Ava squint to watch. Their son fussed as Pammon pressed the tooth gently into his forehead. As the skin and tooth met, their son settled down and reached up with a hand. The light pulsed, and the tooth vanished, and once again, a mark was there for a moment.

"Dear spirits," Kaen muttered as he saw the mark for the second time and was certain of what he had seen.

The mark vanished, and the little boy yawned, holding up a hand, reaching for the talons so close to him. As if drawn by a thread, Pammon gently put his talon closer, and Ava began to tremble as their baby boy stretched out farther. When the tips of his fingers brushed the talon, a slight glow of light lit up Pammon's talon, and the dragon quickly yanked it back.

"What was that?!" Ava exclaimed, pulling her son back without thinking, jostling him more than she had intended. Yet the boy slept, a slight smile upon his tiny lips.

Kaen could feel what Pammon felt. There was a connection with his son that almost meshed with his own.

What is that? It's like I can almost feel his heartbeat.

I . . . I don't know . . .

Pammon's mind raced as he tried to figure out what had happened.

Your son . . . when he touched my talon . . .

Impossible!

Kaen glanced at his son, fast asleep in Ava's arms.

As certain as I know you are there and he is here, you know I am not lying. He said my name.

Kaen stumbled toward the couch and, with a weak smile, offered his daughter to Lady Hurem, who held out her hands and mouthed the words *Thank you* to Kaen.

"My love, what happened? You and Pammon are both acting weird."

Moving back to his wife, Kaen sat beside her and brushed the small few strands of blond hair on his son's head.

"When he touched Pammon's talon, Pammon heard our son say his name."

Scoffing came from Lord Hurem and Lady Hurem as they heard what Kaen said.

Ava's eyes widened more than any other time as her head spun toward her husband. "That's . . . that's impossible . . . isn't it?"

Shrugging, Kaen chuckled and shook his head. "I have no idea. All I know is we are loved and that for the first time in over a thousand years, people and dragons are a family again."

Closing her eyes momentarily, Ava took a deep breath and slowly let it out.

"Thank you, Pammon," she said as she glanced up at the bronze dragon, still looking down at her son.

Thank you, Ava Marshell, for loving me and my family.

Kaen's heart ached as he and Pammon left the cave. The children, along with their mother, had been fed and were asleep.

I'm not sure how to describe what I feel right now. I felt something like this come from you but never understood it. Forgive me for not.

How can one expect the rain to know that someone doesn't like getting wet? If you could not understand what I felt until now, I do not hold it against you.

Rubbing his friend's neck, Kaen let the cold wind rush over him as they left in the early-morning light.

Let us go. There is work to be done.

Soaring high above the land, Pammon and Kaen kept a lookout both above and below. They were in enemy territory right now.

I don't believe he is near, but we cannot simultaneously watch the land and sky. You need to look below, as I cannot see that far. I will let you know if they appear up here.

The armies are going to have a hard march. The roads have been blocked with stuff. Do you think they may be trapped?

Can you see anything out of the ordinary in the piles or in the trees along the road?

Pammon's eyes tried to focus on the section he had seen, but it was so high up that the details were not as clear as he preferred.

Unless we get lower, I cannot answer that question. There is nothing right now, but that can change in a few weeks. This is going to be hard on the army. The food will be a problem, especially if they have to spend days clearing blockades and more.

How many miles are we talking about? Four? Six?

Pammon ran his gaze along the road, counting the blockades.

There are more than six miles of stuff blocking the road, each a quarter of a mile apart. There are probably other traps hidden as well.

Rubbing his face with his hand, Kaen couldn't help but groan.

I read all those books back in Hoste's vault, and the elves had mentioned this. Stioks is already ahead in this fight. We need to make this harder on them.

That is a horrible idea, at least for now. We can do that the week we march, but there is still too much time.

If we use my bow and I charge the arrows, I can quickly destroy the rubble they have put on the path. We may even be better not clearing it until a day or two before the army reaches it.

And this will be their weakest moment. If Stioks was foolish enough to attack, we could defend, and it would be three against one.

Shuddering, Kaen nodded and scanned the sky again.

I still struggle to believe the rumors that Stioks killed all of the females. Letting his dragon eat one makes sense, but it has left him with no one. How insane is he?

Pammon thrummed before angling to turn around and head home.

We have established that that man is something else. A wild beast that needs to be put down.

70

An Unexpected Discovery

"Who's the cutest baby?" Sulenda asked as Hess made faces behind her.

"I thought I was the cutest baby," Callie said as her parents gushed over her nephew and niece.

Hess started to chuckle as Sulenda stood up and groaned.

"It's an expression, dear. Unfortunately, your father and I cannot say wow, those children thankfully look nothing like their father, or your brother might get upset," Sulenda replied, playing with Stein.

Callie laughed and glanced up at Kaen, who nodded.

"She's right, sis. Ava and I are always thankful you look like your mother, not the milkman."

Ava started coughing, trying not to laugh as she fed Anastasia.

"Why does everyone say that?" Callie asked.

"It's because they're full of shite, dear." Hess grunted as he gave Kaen the middle finger.

"Well, I think they're beautiful, and I am glad Mom and I get to help with them in a few days. I've always wanted a sister or brother."

Hess began to cough, and Sulenda started to groan slightly, causing Stein to look at her with his big blue eyes.

"If you hadn't told me what Pammon did, I'd wonder why these two seem so awake. Most children aren't like this after a few days."

Nodding, Kaen squeezed his dad's shoulder. "I wouldn't either, but even Pammon has said it's different. He knows when they are awake, and even when we flew out to the school the other day, he could sense when Stein woke up."

Hess stared at his grandchildren in amazement. "One shouldn't be surprised anymore, I guess. You have a habit of the impossible always happening to you."

* * *

"You're certain this is the best choice? Letting her come?"

Kaen started to laugh, being taken aback at that question. "*Let* her come? How many times have you *let* Sulenda do something?"

Sucking air in through his teeth, Hess winced. "Fair point. Perhaps I should reword that question, not that I think it would matter."

"It won't," Kaen replied as he finished stuffing some items in a pack for their children. "I'm just glad that Sulenda and Callie will be with our children and Ava's parents. We need to get them dropped off as the army heads out tomorrow."

"Eleven thousand troops . . . it is not the largest army, but I don't think anyone planned on ever doing what we are attempting."

Pausing as he inserted a few more pairs of clean clothes into the pack, Kaen turned to look at his wife, Sulenda, and Callie, who were sitting on the couch and playing with his children.

"I'm not sure I ever imagined my life with kids, but here it is. Every person who is choosing to fight is doing it because they love someone, as I love my children. This fight isn't about land or power, and you know it. It's about protecting those over there."

"Hairy dwarf balls, Kaen. When did you become so smart?" Hess asked, teasing the man he had raised for over ten years.

"I'd like to say you played a role in that, but we both know that can't be true," Kaen shot back, winking as he finished packing the sack. "Are you ready to lead an army?"

"No, but I'll do what needs to be done. Herb is staying back to provide leadership while Aldric is gone. Every general and advisor has been summoned, but after the battles on the walls, we are down more than I would like to admit. Only a few of the older ones remain. Even Bren is leaving his place and coming to fight. I never would have imagined a day that man would put on armor again."

As Kaen slung the pack over his shoulder, his jaw went slack for a moment. "I was just as surprised as you were, but I'm grateful for him being willing to. That man is still a beast at his age."

Kaen noticed Ava looking at him, and he nodded. She smiled slightly, her lips forced together. She knew what it meant to leave her children.

"Time to go, Dad."

As Kaen turned toward his wife, Hess grabbed Kaen's arm and stopped him.

"I'm proud of you, son. No matter what happens on that field, I want you to know that I have always been grateful for every day I have been a part of your life."

Grabbing Kaen in a one-armed hug, Hess squeezed the man who could now easily crush him in a fight.

"Is this where you ask for your ring back?" Kaen teased after they broke their embrace.

"No . . . I wouldn't get the bonus; besides, it's your wedding ring. You can't take that off."

Laughing, the two men walked to where their family awaited.

"Dear, this isn't my first time caring for babies. Sulenda and I will be fine."

Ava nodded, kissing both her kids for the hundredth time as Sulenda and her mother held one. "I know . . . it's just hard."

"You can always stay."

Ava saw the way her mother's lips were drawn back and her cheek muscles showing. She knew her mother was not happy about Kaen letting her go fight, but this was a battle they all needed to be a part of.

"No, I can't, and you know it. Now stop saying that and promise me you'll take good care of them."

"We've got them, Ava," Sulenda said, cutting in before Lady Hurem got herself in more trouble. "You go with our fighters and make sure they come home. Someone out there needs to keep a level head."

Laughing, the women gave hugs and kisses, masking the fear of who might not return.

"This is all I could make potionwise," Lord Hurem said as he handed Kaen a thick pouch and a small pack. It contained four healing potions and one dragon potion. "The dragon one should finally work."

Kaen nodded as he took the pouches and the pack from his father-in-law. "I'm going to only keep one for myself. Ava will have one, Hess will have another, and the last will go to Aldric."

Kaen slipped a potion out and handed it to Hess, who carefully held it in his hands and admired the glass bottle.

"These look almost like the ones you sold a decade or more ago. The color is a little deeper red, though. Why is that, Lord Hurem?"

"Ahh, yes! That is because I could break down and infuse a little bit of Pammon's blood with those. Not having a dragon's blood required us to find the rare herbs and get them magically altered. Those potions should not suffer the same effect as the others you had."

"You mean I won't scream inside my head?" Hess asked.

Shaking his head from side to side, Lord Hurem bit his lip as he squinted. "Hopefully. Again, I haven't had a chance to get these tested, but either way, everything else is in there."

Kaen had been listening to the two men talk and pulled out the massive potion Lord Hurem had made for Pammon. The thick glass container fit inside both of his hands, cupped together. Staring at it, Kaen noticed that the potion's color was different from the others he had been given.

"Why is this one different than the others you made?"

"Ah! You have a keen eye, my boy! That is because, like your potions, I mixed some of your blood with Pammon's! It took a while to get them to bond, as your life forces are different yet the same. One has to mix them for a long time to finally get them to mix together."

Kaen and Pammon began to think the same thought as Lord Hurem continued talking.

Do you think that is really the answer?!

Closing his eyes and igniting his lifestone, Kaen looked at the potion in his hand.

Inside the glass bottle, two colors of red swirled around each other. Even though they were mixed to the naked eye, to Kaen's ability to see life and magic, there was the same dance of magic on the glass inside the Dragon Rider vault.

Impossible! I mean . . . is it? Could it be . . .

You tried putting your blood on that glass and seeing if it would open years ago, but nothing happened. Do you really think it needs both of our blood?

Maybe, but are you willing to bleed so I can try?

Pammon groaned, and Kaen felt his dragon's frustration at that thought.

For you always, but I swear if this doesn't work, you'll have to let me stab you after this battle is over.

Laughing, Kaen nodded.

If that is what this takes, then so be it.

Opening his eyes, Kaen looked at the potion in his hands again and realized both men were staring at him.

Slipping the potion back into the sack, Kaen handed it back to Lord Hurem. "I need you to hold this, and I need a jar and that awful needle again for Pammon."

Lord Hurem's eyebrow rose, and the older man glanced up at Pammon, who was still groaning softly. "I can get those in a moment. Can I ask why?"

"Yes, but I'll answer later. I need to hurry and do this now." Turning to Hess, he smiled. "Stay here with Ava and our family. I'll be back in a moment."

"Now I want to know what you're up to like Lord Hurem asked, but I'll trust you, son."

Kaen nodded, handed the potion pouch to Hess, and then jogged over to Ava as Lord Hurem ran off to get his supplies.

"We leaving?" Ava asked as she watched her father leave the courtyard.

"I am, but I'll be back in a moment. Something I need to try once more. Are you ok spending a little more time with our children and mothers?"

Ava made a face, and Kaen started to laugh at it. "It looks like you have gas like Stein did the other day," he teased.

She rolled her eyes and frowned. "I'll be fine. Hurry back, my love." She kissed Kaen and watched as her husband ran off to where Pammon was anxiously moving about.

"What's going on?" Sulenda asked.

"He won't tell me, but it's some Dragon Rider thing. He said he would be back in a few."

I swear this gets worse every time.

Kaen pulled the massive needle from Pammon's gum. "Sorry. Just know I don't like doing it any more than you like receiving it," Kaen said as he handed the needle to Hess.

And yet I'm always on the receiving end.

Lord Hurem put a stopper in the two bottles he had filled and began wrapping them in cloth.

"These aren't as strong as the ones the potions are in, but unless you drop them, they should be fine with a little jostling."

Kaen nodded and waited for them to be secured in a pouch.

"I'll be back, and hopefully I'll have some good news."

Herb had been caught off guard when Kaen had shown up, papers and maps strewn all over his office. Yet when Kaen shared his thoughts, the man had dropped everything and raced through the maze of stairs.

As the lock clicked and the door began to swing open on its own, Herb bounced on his feet.

"You sure you don't want to come in?" Kaen asked, chuckling at how excited his friend was.

"No," Herb replied. "This is not something I can bear to watch. If it works, I would love to be in there, but if it doesn't, I'm not sure I could handle seeing it fail . . . right now, I've got enough on my plate that this is weighing me down. I'll stay out here praying to the spirits if you don't mind."

Kaen nodded and reached over, squeezing Herb's shoulder. "Thank you again for letting me do this."

Herb just nodded and watched as Kaen walked through the entrance to the vault.

He seemed very anxious. I think he is more anxious than you or I at the moment.

And yet I haven't been this excited in a while.

You mean since a few days ago when your children were born?

Kaen chuckled as he crossed the room. His dragon had a way of always knowing him better than he did sometimes.

Reaching the cabinet with the armor inside, Kaen touched the glass with his hand.

I guess there is no time like now to try.

71

A Need So Great

The color on the glass swirled as Kaen studied it.

It almost looks like that potion did. Here goes nothing.

Taking his knife from its sheath, Kaen sliced his palm open and pressed his blood against the glass. Sheathing the blade, he pulled out a bottle of dragon blood and pulled off the stopper, pouring it over his hand and the dragon glass.

Smearing them together, Kaen and Pammon watched, waiting and hoping to see if they had finally found the answer.

Seconds ticked past.

Nothing is happening . . . why?

Slamming his fist into the glass, Kaen growled.

I'm not sure! Those colors look almost like the colors on the glass. What are we missing?

Both tried to solve the problem. Kaen felt the blood start to dry on the surface, and his wound began to close.

Why would they put this behind a barrier like that? Dragon Riders aren't known for torturing their own kind like that. This is a test of some kind—a need so great we would overcome.

Kaen knew Pammon was correct. This was here for one reason only: to help a possible Dragon Rider if they ever came and their need was great enough. No one but a Dragon Rider could get in here.

I need you to share your magic and life with me momentarily. I think . . . no, I know that is what this needs. Somehow, we have to prove who we are, not with just blood but our connection. Perhaps someone could get past the door and find the blood of a dragon and a rider, but they couldn't fake the connection.

Laughter came through their bond, and Kaen couldn't help but smile.

You really are getting wiser. I will have to inform Ava that her assessment of you is not correct.

Kaen pulled out his knife again and reopened the cut on his palm.

Taking the last potion, he poured it over his hand and the surface, mixing the two, and dropped the bottle to the ground.

I'm ready.

Pammon's power surged through their bond, and Kaen's body began to fill with power. His own lifestone burned hot, and they watched as the colors on the glass vibrated.

It's working! More!

Their purpose and power mingled together in Kaen's body, and he willed it toward his hand. The lesson in the forest that he had thought was so silly now filled a purpose Kaen could never have anticipated.

Their lives, blood, and power surged through his arm and into his palm. His fingers vibrated from the power inside them.

It looked like the sun, with how bright his hand was glowing, and then Kaen saw the first real sign of success.

A crack!

I see it!

Seeing a change in the glass, both of them focused on what their lives together were about. Pammon envisioned in his mind his two children and the two mates that he had. The word he often used to describe Amaranth and Glynnis, *mates*, felt wrong now. They weren't just someone to enjoy physically or create more dragons with. They were a part of him. His family had grown beyond Kaen and Hess five years ago. Now it was filled with dragons he loved and humans who were just as important.

Kaen's body began to shake as Pammon found his reason for this battle and focused on it completely. The dragon knew this wasn't a battle just to win and defeat an evil man but to give his family a future no matter the cost.

The lifestone in Kaen burned hotter than he could ever remember. He grabbed the case with his other hand, panting as his lifestone matched his will. Years ago, he had found his purpose. He had solidified to it and then lost his way as his plans failed. Years spent in guilt, sorrow, and fear had stolen his power, yet now he was reborn. The faces of his children, Ava, Hess, and others flooded his mind. Pammon and his family filled his thoughts.

In a moment, their reasons for everything became one and poured out of Kaen through his hand.

The glass shattered, blowing inward, and in a moment, the entire surface he had been pressing against was gone.

Both of them dropped, their exhaustion from what they had done hitting them.

We . . . we did it.

Kaen could feel Pammon panting and trying to recover just as he was. On his knees, Kaen opened his eyes as his lifestone went cold, looking up at the armor he had dreamed of for so long.

We did.

Slowly, he reached out with his hand, his arm and fingers trembling from the exertion and excitement, toward the armor. They touched the purple scales where the knees would go.

"Kaen! Are you ok?!"

Laughing, Kaen nodded, not knowing if Herb could even see him.

He heard footsteps, and then they stopped a reasonable distance from him.

"You . . . you two did it," Herb said, his voice not hiding the shock. "How? I mean . . . no, don't tell me, but . . ."

The footsteps came again, and Kaen felt Herb's hand reaching under his armpit. "Here, let me help you up."

Standing with some assistance, Kaen turned and saw the massive grin on Herb's face.

"I can't believe we succeeded . . . we actually did it."

Herb nodded, staring at the armor no longer protected by the glass. He looked at Kaen and gave him a gentle poke in the side.

"I don't want to ruin the moment, but do me a favor and put that thing on. I want to . . . no, need to see it on you!"

Laughing, Kaen started to take off his outer clothing. "I can't say it's the most fashionable thing, but I'm also looking forward to seeing it on myself."

This fits like a glove. It actually adjusted to fit my legs, chest, and shoulders.

I guess it speaks of the magic inside it. I can feel something coming through our bond from it. There is no way to describe it other than that it belongs to you. Does that make sense?

Kaen nodded, trying not to ignore Herb, who was waiting for him to finish putting on the last few pieces.

Slipping on the boots, Kaen felt a shimmer run through him as the final one adjusted around his foot.

"Uh . . . I . . . you . . ." Herb fumbled for words, unable to make coherent sentences as he gazed upon Kaen, who gave a quick spin to display the whole thing.

"It fits, like, perfectly. How?"

Kaen shrugged as he ran his scaled gloves over the armor. Each glove felt like his own skin, with tiny green and silver scales on the top part. It made no sense to him how they could have been acquired.

"There is no bunching or anything. It's like someone, somewhere, long ago, made this exactly for me."

Kaen ran his hand over the massive red scale on the chest's breastplate. The dragon emblem that had somehow been etched into it almost seemed alive. The gold scales on his shoulders stood out even in the simple light of the room. The black helmet gave him perfect vision through the slits for his eyes, nose, and mouth. The armor was perfect, with each of the individual colored scales connected to the other black scales that made up the outfit.

Check your stats.

Kaen coughed and shook his head.

What?!

Check your stats.

Laughing, Kaen smiled at Herb, who was looking at him quizzically.

"One moment, Pammon wants me to check something."

Herb shrugged and continued to gaze at the sight before him.

[Status Check]
Kaen Marshell - Adult
Dragon Bond - One Soul 30%
Age - 24
HP - 5548/5548 (38%)
MP - 1297/1297 (38%)
STR - 61 (38%) +35 = 96
CON - 66 (38%) +35 = 101
DEX - 62 (38%) +35 = 97
INT - 59 (38%) +35 = 94
WIS - 51 (38%) +35 = 86
Emperor Helmet - +5 to all stats. Strong Willed
Emperor Chest - +10 to all stats. Fortitude, Second Life
Emperor Leggings - +10 to all stats. Quick Stride
Emperor Gloves - +5 to all stats. Quick Strike
Emperor Boots - +5 to all stats. Solid Footing
Wedding Band - +3% to all stats. Fortitude
Emperor Set Bonus: 5/5 Equipped. +5% to all stats. +50% reduction to all damage. +50% to all resistances.

Holy ogre shite!

Pammon said nothing, but Kaen could feel his friend struggling with the numbers just as he was.

I . . . no . . . how . . .

Our need was great enough. Now it is time to end this. Let us go and show the others what we have been given.

Kaen felt the shift in his heart as in Pammon's, each knowing there was nothing more they could do. The time had come.

Kaen enjoyed the discussion and comments, as everyone back at Lord Hurem's estate admired the armor. Ava reacted in complete disbelief when he shared his stats with her. There was still a dragon shield waiting for him back at their place, along with a few other items. Knowing that multiple stats would be pushed beyond a number no one believed was possible still boggled his mind.

I can feel you smiling. It is that large.

Should I not be smiling? Honestly, right now, you and I both know we have never been more prepared.

That does not mean we should forget we are still made of flesh and scales. One would be foolish to walk in and think themself invulnerable. Remember how that went the last few times.

Sighing, Kaen nodded as he watched the entrance to their home draw closer. With his arms wrapped around his wife, Kaen wished the helmet wouldn't block his lips, or he would have kissed her on the neck.

Regardless, she shifted back into him, letting him hold her close as they each knew tonight would be the last night they slept here for a while.

"You're stronger than me, my love," Kaen said after kissing his wife.

"And why is that?" Ava asked, her tone letting him know it might be a dangerous statement he was about to make.

"Childbirth, going to battle, leading an army. You don't have to do the last two, yet you have chosen to be by my side. For that, I am grateful."

Snorting, Ava shifted as she lay on top of him. "Just promise me you will come home to us and end this once and for all."

"No matter what happens, this battle will be over soon. This land will have a moment of rest and peace for as long as our family lives, hopefully longer."

Ava nodded and then kissed his bare chest. "I'll hold you to that. We have two beautiful children who need to learn what it is like to ride on a dragon."

Closing his eyes, Kaen imagined what that would be like. A child with him and a child with Ava, each getting to fly across the sky on the backs of Pammon and Amaranth. He could see their smiles, hear their laughter, and imagine how wonderful that would be. Inside his chest, his lifestone surged softly for a moment, and Ava lifted her head.

"Was that you?"

"It was, my love. I was just imagining what it would be like one day with us all flying together. My lifestone pulsed at that thought."

"Well, tell it to stop," she teased. "I'm worn out, and we need to sleep. War is coming."

72

Marching to War

It is time. Amaranth and Foros are ready to watch the skies, and the army will be there within a day. If we are going to remove those blockades, we must go now.

Using Pammon's vision, Kaen could see that a few more had been added closer to the border of Luthaelia.

Whenever you are ready, head down. I will see how much stronger this bow is against something like that.

Pammon snorted as he angled toward the ground.

We both know what it can do. Stop trying to act like you need a reason to test it out.

Kaen smiled at Pammon's humor. Both of them were doing what they could to keep their minds relaxed, as the first day of troubles had already been stressful enough.

Stop thinking about that mess. No one knew the carts would break down and block the pass that bad.

Logistics . . . all those books spoke about how much they matter during battles. I now see how right they were. We should be a few miles ahead.

Be thankful there has been no rain in the last seven days. The roads are in good shape, and people are making good time. Now, focus. Do what we can, and let us not worry about anything else.

Unhooking his bow from its spot, Kaen pulled out an arrow. Looking up, he could barely see the shape of Amaranth high above them. Knowing where to look would have made it harder to find her if it weren't for his connection.

They are fine. Ava is doing well, Amaranth says. Now, let's do what we can.

Looking at the first barricade, Kaen placed the arrow and began to draw back. His lifestone was burning, and its power flowed into the arrow.

Feeling how far he had to pull back the bow still felt slightly different after all those years of using the one his father had made for him.

When he let go, the arrow sped toward the barricade, its white tip ready, headed to where Kaen had aimed.

As they flew over it, an explosion erupted underneath them, but Kaen didn't pay it any heed, instead preparing for the next one ahead.

That worked well. Most of what was there is gone.

Tomorrow, we will be at the opening to the battlefield. Are you three ready?

We will be fine. Remember, this part of the battle does not concern you two. Focus on your goal and bring Pammon home safely.

Kaen could feel the fine thread of concern in Amaranth's tone, but he resisted the urge to tell her the same thing about Ava.

You have seen the fires burning at their armies. They need to be smart. I stopped counting at thirty siege weapons designed for us.

And the tips on them all look like the two arrows I have.

It would appear we did find where all that ore had vanished to. Stioks has not been wasteful with the time that he was given. Let us show him tomorrow that we have not been wasteful with ours.

Very well. Let's return to Aldric and update him on what we have seen.

"Those are a lot more siege weapons than we had hoped for," Aldric declared as he looked at the army Kaen had sketched out that they would fight. "How do you suppose we can get close?"

"That is a question for you and your commanders, my king."

Aldric frowned at Kaen's statement but gave him a simple nod. The tent was filled with his seven advisors as well as Hess.

"All I can tell you again is that they are prepared, and once you cross this line, their siege engines will reach you," Kaen said as he tapped the line he had drawn on the map he had created from above.

"And there are still at least thirty thousand in their army?"

Kaen began drawing small squares, returning his pencil to the enemy lines.

"How is Stioks making this happen? I have no idea. There is a massive buildup of orcs, goblins, and ogres on both outer edges of the army. In the middle are the people of Luthaelia. Behind them are more ogres and orcs. I assume that the orcs are keeping the people pinned, unable to leave, and forced to fight."

"This would mean a weak middle section, which would explain why the fortifications they built in the middle of the field are stronger and more dangerous."

Kaen nodded, tapping the three farthest barriers the enemy had built. "These are their range markers. Somewhere around here, they will attack with their long-range siege weapons. This next spot," Kaen said as he circled a few other barriers, "is probably where their archers will attack." Kaen made one more circle of a fortification and then tapped it a few times. "I'm going to assume that if you manage to get past those two things, they will rush you from the higher ground. The elevation isn't terrible, but it is enough to make things very difficult."

"What about our horses? Can the cavalry squad do anything?"

Kaen and Aldric turned to look at one of the older advisors, who had been studying the map more closely than the other six.

"Not in a head-on attack. They would be destroyed long before they got within range. Even our best casters can't reach as far as their long-range weapons."

The advisor nodded. "Permission to come closer and point out something."

"You're fine, Lester. Come and show us what you are thinking."

Aldric winked at Kaen and motioned slightly with his head as the bald-headed man approached. "Lester has been with me since I was a boy. I have learned a lot of tactics and battle plans from him."

"The king is too kind," Lester said as he moved to the side of the map. "He just likes to tell people I'm very old."

Aldric chuckled, and a few of the other advisors laughed as well.

"Here. You could send the cavalry this way, through this section, and have them come up out here. That would put them slightly behind the army and to the side. If they can get a full charge in with the element of surprise, it would open up the right side of the battlefield and remove a few of the siege weapons."

Kaen tapped his pencil against the table, looking at the spot where Lester had pointed. "Someone get me the larger map that shows more details," Kaen said suddenly. "I need to see if that spot is actually what I think it is."

People began to move around, looking through maps and occasionally bringing one to Kaen. Finally, the third map one of the advisors got was what he needed.

"What is your name?"

The woman holding the map gave a slight bow. "Penelope, sir. Advisor to the king."

"Thank you, Penelope. Can you hold it over here for a moment so we can all look at the map side by side? Feel free to point anything out that you might notice," Kaen said before turning and looking at the other five advisors watching him. "In fact, if any of you feel like something jumps out, don't hesitate to say something. Aldric and I might miss something you have seen."

Penelope and one of the other advisors held the map as Kaen asked, and a crowd formed around them.

"See here, this is a trail," Lester pointed out. "It's not anything more than perhaps a logging trail, but if it is old enough, the path should be safe for them to travel on."

"Unless it's been trapped or is being watched," Penelope added. "If they are prepared for someone to use that path, they would be trapped on all sides."

"Both of you are right," Aldric replied. "If that path is clear and safe, it wouldn't take but a few hours for them to make it to the backside of the army. We only have fifty men and horses. Can we afford to lose them?"

Lester shrugged. "What is fifty men and horses versus eleven thousand? Can you risk the entire army's lives on a path that will cause many to fall and not be willing to risk a few to save more?"

Frowning, Aldric nodded. "This is why I keep him around."

"He's right," Kaen replied. "One of the dragons could scout the path tomorrow morning to see if anything is there and return, dropping a flag to tell you if it is safe."

"It's a shame their siege weapons are pointed in all directions, or we could send a dragon to try and attack from the side," Hess said as he looked at the markings on Kaen's map. "If the cavalry succeeds, their main objective should be these two siege weapons. Removing those would open that side for Foros to attack."

We cannot get close enough to shoot arrows, either. I'm afraid, as I already mentioned, those weapons could possibly reach us.

Kaen grumbled silently as Pammon reread his thoughts on that matter.

If Hess is right and those two weapons were taken out, could Foros do anything there?

Pammon studied the section of the map everyone was focused on.

It's possible. He is small enough and, without a rider, could fly in such a way. There would be just enough space, and he has enough fire inside him to create chaos if he is successful.

Are you willing to allow him to take that risk?

The real question had been asked, and Kaen felt the weight of that decision resting on Pammon's mind and heart.

If this is the only way he is willing, I will not say no. Let him choose on his own.

I will leave that discussion to you and him, then. As long as I can tell them his decision by tomorrow morning, they can adjust accordingly.

Kaen felt Pammon begin talking with his son and turned to focus on the people watching him.

"Sorry. Pammon is talking with Foros. Hopefully, we will know soon enough if he can attack there."

Lester and Hess both started to point at the same spot.

"Go ahead," Hess said, motioning to the older man.

"If the dragon cannot help there, we must focus here with the cavalry. Either way, the risk provides us the greatest chance for the least casualties. If they can take out this siege engine and turn on the group we believe are the archers, it would clear a wide path that our fighters could advance on."

Lester glanced at Hess, who nodded. "I was thinking the same thing."

Aldric tapped the last piece to discuss. "Phillip, is he ok with being in the middle?"

"Sometimes, one doesn't get the luxury of being ok with something. We all know that our choices will affect the lives of many people and their families. Phillip is committed to that as well. He knows the danger and the risk. I trust him to do what must be done."

"Very well, unless someone has something else to say, we are finished for now."

No one said another word, so Aldric dismissed everyone except Hess and Kaen.

"I wish you luck tomorrow. Do what only you can," Aldric said as he held out his hand.

Shaking it, Kaen gave the king a smile. "We have come a long way. This ends soon."

Hess slapped Kaen on the back, then leaned against his son. "No matter what happens on that field tomorrow, you take care of what you must. Trust us with this."

Kaen nodded.

He will do it.

Are you certain?

It was his choice. He and Phillip discussed it, and they both agreed that there was no other way to defeat this army without risking so many lives.

Tell your son I am grateful for his courage and strength. I will tell Aldric the news.

"I'm not sure if that is good news or bad," Aldric said when Kaen's eyes moved from nowhere to his.

Kaen's face was hard, a slight frown pulled tight at how he knew his friend and partner felt. "Foros has agreed to attack that area if the cavalry can break through and destroy those siege weapons. The expression I currently wear is that of a father who can't imagine what it is like to risk one's son for a battle he could easily fly away from."

Both men stared at Kaen for a moment, each grimacing slightly at the truth of that statement.

"Somehow, some way, I promise I will try to repay Pammon and the rest of the dragons for what they have done for us," Aldric replied. "It may take the rest of my life, but make sure they all know that."

Kaen smiled and nodded. "Good luck tomorrow, you two. If you'll excuse me, Pammon and I have someone to find."

73

Searching for Stioks

It has started . . . where is that man?

Neither Glynnis nor Amaranth has seen him. The dwarves and wood elves started fighting a little while ago.

You're not telling me something . . . it's just as bad there, isn't it?

Telling you and distracting you isn't my goal. We have different objectives, and we must trust the others with theirs. Now, focus; we need to find him.

Kaen continued to search the sky as Pammon soared over the capital city of Luthaelia.

Kaen had used Pammon's eyes to look at the land below for the briefest amount of time, and his heart broke. Stioks had ravaged his own people, and there was filth and destruction wherever they looked.

Scorched ground that could only come from a dragon marked random places in the countryside. Entire homes and lines of structures were eradicated and melted to ash.

This man has enslaved his own people to the orcs. I have seen a few places where orcs are herding people like cattle into buildings.

The good news is the number of orcs is less. Imagine if we hadn't assaulted the castle—all those monsters we killed . . . and attacked. There could easily be thirty thousand more here.

Scanning the sky, Kaen didn't believe Stioks would be in the massive black castle positioned in the middle of the land.

Pammon's head turned upward, and he looked in every direction for a moment.

We need to fly down, and I want to grab a few trees. Perhaps if we knock gently, he will answer.

We are about thirty minutes from his castle if you feel it is safe. I am ready here.

Pammon grunted and angled himself toward the ground. As they flew lower, Kaen flexed his fingers around the grip of his bow.

I'll save my shot until I'm confident I cannot miss.

Pammon said nothing as he continued his dive toward the earth. It came at them quickly, as the bronze dragon did not want to waste time and put himself or Kaen at risk. In one quick motion, Pammon's massive back claws wrapped around the trunk of a giant tree and his bronze wings began to beat rapidly. The roots in the earth snapped in a moment, unable to resist Pammon's power. Dirt fell back toward the earth as the tree was lifted up into the sky, an awe-inspiring sight for anyone who witnessed it.

That tree is larger than I expected, yet you do not seem bothered by its weight.

Pammon grunted and looked back at Kaen as he continued to climb upward into the sky.

This tree weighs more than you believe, but I will be fine. That whelp will fall to me or you. If they appear, letting this tree fall will only take a moment.

Whenever Kaen thought he understood Pammon's strength, he was reminded that there was nothing like his dragon. None of the council would probably pick a fight against him, even without the ability he had to command. Every year, climbing up into his saddle took longer, as Pammon's neck rested easily at about thirty feet when he was sitting.

The number of people has not increased. There are some outside, but I wonder how many are still alive. Even if you look at the walls with my eyes, you will see that most of the defenses he built are gone.

Did he take his own defense for the army? Why would he do that?

Perhaps he bet we would assist there and wanted a chance to strike us down. The few weapons on the wall have no one operating them either.

Kaen looked around. They were only a few minutes away from being in position to drop the tree right onto the top of the castle.

Would he really want to force us to come inside? That might be the better play, as it reduces your size and maneuverability and limits our actions to the ground.

It would also limit your use of the bow; we both know how he feels about that.

Unable to help it, Kaen grunted at how this was happening. The battle he had imagined and played out in his mind multiple times was not going as he had hoped. Running through a castle he didn't know provided too many opportunities to fall into a trap or suffer some spell.

After you drop that tree, get me close enough that I can also do some damage. If Stioks won't come out at first, I will do what I can to force him to show his face.

Pammon snorted, and Kaen could hear the slight strain in his breath. No matter how large Pammon was, flying for twenty minutes with that massive tree in his claws was taxing his strength.

In just a few more moments, I will be ready.

A section of the stone castle fell, crashing into the ground below and sending up a cloud of dust.

Pammon began to circle, roaring as loudly as possible.

One minute passed, then two, yet no sign of Stioks or his dragon came from below.

Now it is my turn.

Arrow after arrow infused with his power fell upon the castle, taking out massive amounts of stone that fell to the ground.

I see people fleeing the castle. Where is this man and his dragon?! Why won't they come and face us?

Kaen was overwhelmed by Pammon's hatred for Stioks. Learning how the man had treated Pammon's mother had not helped at all and had only ignited the fire within.

Let me keep firing. I will bring the castle down upon him if he won't come out.

74

Frederick and Tazorath I

"Hold the line!"

The dwarves near him shouted back as Frederick clashed with the first barrier in their way.

Mother is very adept at doing what she did.

Tazorath's words confirmed what Frederick thought he had seen. The yellow dragon had done what he considered impossible, attacking the area where the siege weapons were. Though he couldn't see it all, the two weapons that fired at her had not missed by much, yet the dragon had turned, rolled, and flown in ways Frederick didn't know were possible.

Now the siege weapons were down, and they could press the middle as he had hoped.

Roars of anger and hate came from across the field where massive, topless fighters raised swords and axes, beating them against round shields.

How many more attempts till Glynnis is done taking out the weapons?

Frederick hacked at the barrier, his sword slicing through it in almost one hit. Once he had cut a section out, he moved through the opening.

"Protect my back, shields up!"

Dwarves followed behind him, holding massive shields and creating a wall of them as Frederick began cutting sections out of the wooden spike wall. He grabbed the pieces he cut with his free hand and flung them in one direction.

Roars and cheers came from his group of dwarves, and the barricade was slowly removed.

She says to give her another few minutes. She is trying to find the best angle to come from.

You two are doing great. How many more barricades are left on the right?

Tazorath went quiet for a moment, and Frederick knew she had just used her lightning again. She would run out of breath attacks soon. Thankfully, she could help clear the spiked walls that kept the dwarven army back.

Five. I can get maybe three more, and then they will be on their own.

You're doing great! Keep it up, and then get somewhere you can see so you can help me!

He could feel the joy from his dragon and wished he could turn and focus on her being amazing.

Two more swings cut the last section of the one he had been working on, and after tossing the last two pieces aside, Frederick turned to look at the army waiting to charge.

"Line up and spread out! Shields ready! Remember, they are going to try and run through us!"

Frederick ran back to the group of dwarves tasked with being his honor guard. Each dwarf was one Bosgreth had personally chosen for the task.

The redheaded female dwarf handed him back his shield and grinned. "Looks like we finally get to fight!"

The other six dwarves roared and formed up on both sides of Frederick.

"Let's go!"

The group ran up the incline, their feet pounding against the hard-packed ground. The snow was gone, but the field was still frozen and slightly slick from the cold temperatures that had frozen it every night.

As the dwarves began the first real push of the battle, the barbarians across from them started shouting and banging their weapons against their shields.

How much longer?

Almost done with the one and then one more.

Ok, the battle is going to start!

Glancing behind him, Frederick saw the dwarven army surging on his right, using the openings Tazorath had created. The sounds they made as they ran, shouting and the impact of their feet, filled him with a thirst for battle. He had fought many times with Phillip and a few others on the walls, and even when battling the kobolds, it was exciting, but this was a whole different feeling.

Looking back at the army before him, he scanned the crowd, searching for the person Kaen had told him to find.

A few hundred yards to his right, towering over the other barbarians, was a man wielding two large axes. The man had black paint all over his face, chest, and arms. He was waving his axes in the air and shouting something that was getting the people before him excited.

"We need to shift to there!" Frederick shouted over the noise, pointing in the direction he wanted to go.

The dwarves shifted, each keeping in step with Frederick, who made sure not to run faster than them.

The line of barbarians began to move slowly, and Frederick could see that they would be about fifty yards short of where he wanted them to be when they clashed.

"Protect yourselves and each other!"

"Don't hog all the glory!" one of the dwarves shouted, and Frederick grinned.

These dwarves are crazy.

Almost done, and then give me a minute. I'll be able to help!

And your mother?

Tazorath paused a moment, and Frederick could feel that she was frustrated.

She is having problems with the left side. They are adjusting for her, which is why they are not firing at the army anymore.

Rolling his eyes momentarily, Frederick tried to ignore how Glynnis and Tazorath occasionally argued. He knew how he had been with his mother and couldn't imagine what it was like having a dragon as one.

Just let me know. I'm going for their clan leader! I need eyes soon!

The barbarians were running now, their feet thundering against the cold ground as they descended the slight incline.

"One hundred yards! Be ready!"

The seconds passed faster than most could imagine, and within six seconds, the sound of shields and bodies slamming into each other rang out all around him.

Two barbarians came at him with their shields, bracing them with their shoulders, and slammed into Frederick.

He smiled, drove through them using the shield that King Aldric had given him, and collided with both men, sending them flying backward and into a few of their incoming allies.

The closest set of barbarians then started swinging their axes as their comrades slashed at the dwarves beside him.

Metal on metal, metal on wood, and then metal biting into flesh filled the air.

Yelling from both sides and cries of pain from those about to die limited the orders that one could give in these moments.

Keeping the clan leader in his vision, Frederick and his group began to cut their way through the solid wall of barbarians, all screaming and trying to land a hit on them.

75

Wood Elves and Dwarves

"Help that rider!" Sedel shouted as she pointed to the army of barbarians charging toward Frederick.

The dozen archers next to her drew back and unleashed arrows so quickly that the dwarves who stood near them, ready to replace the baskets, were in shock.

Like rain, death fell from above, arching over the battleground and into the mass of unprotected torsos. Screams of pain and agony ripped through the barbarian horde.

"What are those fools doing?" Dagan asked as he stood near Sedel. "Surely they would be wise to not rush ahead like that."

"Apparently they believe their shields will protect them," Sedel replied. She motioned to an elf beside her and the woman raised an orange banner. Two elves ran toward the fighting, each holding a wand in their hand.

"Make sure they don't hit my army!" Dagan shouted as he began making hand signals to his dwarves nearby.

The ones he had been signaling started blowing on horns, and banners popped up along the edge of their battlefield, halting the advance on the northern front.

When the two wood elves got close to the dwarven wall of soldiers, the line of troops split so quickly, someone might have wondered if it was done by magic. Upon reaching the front of the shield wall, each elf channeled the magic for their wand and brilliant motes of molten light erupted from the ends of them, racing toward the army of barbarians slowly advancing while hiding behind their shields.

The molten orange strands grew in size and shape, soon turning into fireballs the size of a wagon, and slammed into the front line of the barbarians. Flames splattered out and stuck like pitch to anything or anyone unlucky enough to be in its path of destruction. The people caught in the flames were set ablaze; the lucky ones in the front died immediately while others had to wait to succumb to the magical fire.

As if waiting for an attack like that, two shamans strode forward from the barbarian army, their own wands in hand. Darkness grew at the tip of their wands and like a stream, black liquid poured out from the tips, rushing as a wave that rolled across the frozen dirt like water over a fall.

"Sedel!"

She ignored Dagan's shout, already doing what she could. Her hand was plunged into the ground and magic was swirling around her, though no one could see it.

Short, thick trees sprouted up before the dwarven line, growing quickly and forming a hedge before them. Sedel was pale and sweating, pouring her life into this moment, ready to defend and give everything she had.

In seconds a nearly solid four-foot-high barrier stretched three hundred yards across the battlefield. The black sludge ran into it and like water against a dam, some crested over and continued its surge. Most had been stopped by the barrier she had created, a putrid smell coming from the two magics fighting against each other.

Where the black liquid spilled over, it rushed forward, almost as if hungry for flesh, until it found a row of dwarves and one of the wood elves holding a wand. Their bodies began to decay immediately upon contact, bones and flesh turning into a black goo on the frozen soil.

Horns roared and the dwarves still standing, having been saved from the spell by the barrier, began to spread out, rushing toward the sides where it was currently safe.

"Loose," Sedel said, her voice weak as she struggled to stand.

Dagan was next to her in a moment, offering his hand and lifting her up.

"Thank you for saving our people," he said, his voice carrying the weight of the hundreds of warriors who were gone in an instant. "I'm sorry for your loss."

A tear fell from the face of the new leader of the wood elves as she turned and saw that Dagan's statement matched his expression. His bottom lip was drawn in and his eyes were soft.

Reaching out with her hand, Sedel stroked his face with a thumb and smiled.

"I am sorry I could not save more of yours," she replied. "May the spirits watch over all those we lose today and not forget why we bleed together."

As Dagan nodded once, his steady gaze and strong expression returned.

The sounding of more horns made the two of them turn and study the field, which was in chaos.

"My king!"

Dagan glanced at a dwarf who had just arrived. Giving the man a bob of his head, the runner spoke quickly.

"The rider! He will be engaging their chief! The dragons have taken out their siege weapons!"

Looking across the field, Dagan saw that Frederick was close to the massive figure who stood above every other shirtless and paint-covered fool on the opposite side. The barbarian chief was their weakest link even though they considered him their greatest asset.

"That boy is a fool!" Dagan shouted. "Sound every horn! All lines rush forward!"

Two dwarves behind King Dagan began to wave banners, and horns all along the dwarf and elf battlefield started to belt out the call for nothing to be held back. Across the battlefield the sound of horns and soldiers shouting echoed, creating goose bumps all over Dagan's arms.

"He's not a fool, Frederick is trying to save lives," Sedel stated as she stared at the Dragon Rider and the band of dwarves with him. "This was his plan from the beginning, and you know it."

"Yes, but he was supposed to wait until more of them had fallen!" Dagan replied, his tone harsher than he had intended.

"And doing so would have cost how many more dwarven lives? You should be grateful he is willing to risk his own so that more of your people can survive."

Grimacing, Dagan felt the truth of Sedel's words pierce his heart. She was right. That boy, not even old enough to have fuzz on his chin, was braver than most dwarves with a foot-long beard.

"Forgive me . . . I was foolish in my speech."

Laughing, Sedel shook her head, color starting to return to her face. "Trust me, I have spent more time with his mentor, and I can say that whatever Kaen believes has been taught to that boy. He reminds me of a young man I lost badly to in an archery contest many years ago."

Chuckling, Dagan found himself smirking and studying Sedel. He could see she wasn't joking about losing.

"Now that is a story I look forward to hearing after this is over. Come, let's join our people and finish this!"

Nodding, Sedel motioned to her archers, and they picked up their basket in one hand and began to race ahead, moving to a position where they could safely attack the enemy without having to worry about hitting any dwarves.

"After you, King Dagan," Sedel said with a grin.

Groaning, Dagan hefted his hammer and took the shield his attendant had been holding.

"Play the drums! The king joins the battle!"

An earsplitting noise came and the roar of the dwarves shouting in excitement almost drowned out the pounding of the massive war drums that announced something not heard in a generation.

The king of the dwarves had come to fight.

Dagan glided across the battlefield, in armor that had been passed down for over a thousand years. Its metal had not been seen in a millennium, and those who did their best to care for it had no idea how it was once produced. Like gold it shimmered in the light, yet it weighed almost nothing but provided just as much protection as the dragon armor Frederick wore. Each link was so small that unless one was standing next to Dagan, they would believe it was one piece of metal.

The shield was crafted with a magical power long since forgotten, and inside the middle of it rested a golden dragon scale. Powerful magic would block almost any spell it defended against, and Bosgreth had taught Dagan how to activate the Reflect ability it carried, usable once a week, but able to send back the spell that struck it at the caster.

The hammer, Lightbringer, was a legend in the history of dwarves. Over two thousand years ago, a crafter had created it, gifting it to the king of the dwarves. It struck with the power of something ten times its weight and yet when swung, it felt like a thin branch in the hands of a dwarf. An enchantment bound the hammer to the king. No one but he could carry it or use it.

Seeing Dagan with it today as he rushed with his elite group of warriors confirmed in every dwarf's heart that he was their king.

76

Amaranth and Ava

I cannot hit them from here! You need to get closer! My magic just fizzles out from this height!

There is nothing we can do! Foros is not in position yet and we will be in danger of the siege weapons if I get closer.

Are you telling me that you cannot dodge them from this distance? I have seen you fly before and know that you are capable of that.

The sensation of frustration Ava felt coming from Amaranth made her wonder if she had pushed too much, but the troops were moving down below. There was no time to wait and if she could help at all with a few well-placed fire spells, it would be worth the risk.

No . . . I will not let you tempt me into doing something stupid. We will bring honor and pride to our families, but I will not allow you or myself to be put in a position where our children do not see us return.

Wincing, Ava knew Amaranth was right. She was caught up in the desire to help and was willing to take a risk.

Just wait. Foros said they are almost ready for us.

Amaranth released every ounce of anger and frustration she had. The roar felt better than any she had ever let out before.

Thank you for warning me! I could still hear and feel that even with my fingers in my ears.

They were zipping by and the troops below were moving up. Foros and the riders were working on the siege weapons and Ava had a moment to start helping.

Fireball after fireball leaped from her hand as quickly as she could form another, crashing down into the army at the outer edges. It wasn't much compared to the numbers before her, but it would help.

Hang on!

Ava grabbed the rope with one hand, thankful for the clips that kept her in the saddle as Amaranth rolled and dove downward, a massive bolt sailing not far above the dragon's body.

That was close!

Yes, but I need to help draw their fire.

Ava didn't reply, simply drawing upon her lifestone. It had acted differently, but Kaen had told her it might. The moment Amaranth had roared, it surged inside her. Power filled her and now with the way she felt, she began to unleash death upon the goblins, orcs, and ogres foolish enough to advance toward the troops that had moved up.

Body parts flew in different directions as her spells exploded in the midst of the group.

I'm coming around for another sweep. Look to the section between the three large ogres! There are some of the orcs with bombs like Kaen mentioned.

Twisting and turning in the saddle, Ava scanned the battle line and finally saw the ones Amaranth had mentioned.

I can see them! How close can you get?

There are two down, I can get close enough.

Amaranth banked and came closer to the enemy line. Arrows attempted to hit her but all of them were off by a good bit.

Ava pulled out the wand that Aldric had given her. The range was decent but what he had told her about the damage it would do was what excited her the most.

As she willed magic into it, the wand began to glow. She watched as it built up, lightning starting to arc on the tip and the crackling of electricity filling her ears. After five seconds of channeling into the wand, a bolt of lightning surged from the wooden tip, stretching across the air toward the field as a single bolt toward the group Ava had aimed at. In that brief moment of use, the battlefield was covered in a bright flash of light and Ava had no doubt that what came from the wand was far stronger than any spell she could ever hope to cast.

It streaked through the air, electrifying the section of orcs, ogres, and goblins she had aimed for. The spell arced through all the enemies, looking like one of those storms during which most people hid in their homes, afraid of the forked lightning coming from the clouds. An area of fifty yards or more was turned into a light brighter than any lightstone she had ever gazed upon, but even better was the explosion that ripped through their ranks as a pack of orcs intent on blowing themselves up did just that.

A smoking crater that had small tendrils of lightning still arcing over the ground was the evidence of their short-lived existence. Carnage and death surrounded it as a reminder that Ava and Amaranth had been there.

77

Phillip and Foros I

Phillip couldn't help but stare across the battlefield and wonder what Frederick was facing. Looking at an army of thirty thousand created a twinge of pain as the enemy roared and mocked them across the six-hundred-yard expanse between them.

"You certain we can take out those fortifications, sir?"

Turning to look at the officer assigned to him, Phillip nodded. "Sergeant Pulak, we don't have any other choice. For now, we wait for the orders to attack."

The man and the other warriors shifted nervously behind him, each comforted only slightly by the dragon circling above them.

"Understand, sir. I'm just making sure I understood the assignment."

Nodding, Phillip turned his eye to Foros. His dragon flew high above the clouds, scouting the area the cavalry were attempting to cross.

Two loud horn blasts sounded, and then a pause came, followed by a repeat of the two blasts.

How are they doing? Any trouble yet?

I find it strange, but no. The path is clear, and when I scouted early this morning, I saw no one and no traps. There appear to be a few remnants of orcs and goblins near where they will come out, but not enough to stop them. If all goes well, Mother should descend and roar in ten or fifteen minutes.

"Sergeant!"

"Yes, sir!" the man replied.

"Send word to King Aldric that we expect the battle to start in fifteen minutes. The green dragon will roar when the time has come."

From the corner of his eye, Phillip saw the man with sandy-colored hair glance up at the sky before nodding. "On my way, sir."

I wish I had learned to see through your eyes like Kaen can through Pammon's. Remember to be safe. I can't lose you.

Through their bond, Phillip felt the satisfaction of his words. It had changed after their bond had deepened, and the emotions and feelings that came now were sometimes jarring.

I will do what I must to help us win this battle. You need to focus on your goals. Once my job is finished, I will do what I can.

Phillip tried to center himself, breathing deeply as he gripped the axe in his hand.

I'll see you soon enough.

Time felt like it stretched on as the sound of shouts and roars from both sides of the battlefield echoed every so often. Phillip could sense the change in his dragon as Foros began to dive down toward the ground, signaling that the action was about to start.

They are charging now.

Phillip turned to the man on his left, who had different flags laid out on fifteen-foot poles before him.

"Wave the yellow ones four times and then the blue ones twice!"

He watched as the man grabbed the massive pole with the giant yellow banner and started waving it.

A horn blasted behind him, and then again after a four-second pause.

A long horn sounded when he dropped the yellow flag and began to wave the blue one.

Cheers and shouting began to erupt from the men, and Phillip pointed the axe he was holding toward the barriers and fortifications the opposing army had set up.

"SLOW! MARCH SLOW!" he shouted, his command echoing multiple times down the line both ways.

His group took a step and then another, not racing toward the area they knew would mark the attacks from the siege weapons.

Horns and roars came from the other side, and Phillip saw the enemy shifting in place as they began to move forward. There was movement from the far left of the enemy army, and a massive boulder launched into the air as someone fired a siege weapon.

The line of Ebonmount warriors froze as the boulder, which was larger than most horses, arced high into the sky and plummeted toward the ground. It landed a dozen yards before the fortification on the enemy side and bounced and rolled toward King Aldric's army.

For over forty yards, that rock bounced and moved, destroying a massive section of the enemy's defenses until it finally stopped, a long, deep furrow through the field where it had hit and rolled.

"Goblin shite!" someone cursed behind Phillip, and others mimicked the man's words with a few different variations.

His own heart had skipped a beat when he saw the rock and the destruction it brought. No matter who one was, getting hit by that would squash them like a bug.

"Don't be afraid!" Phillip roared. "Follow me!"

A few men roared, but more than half could not muster up the same courage as they had moments before.

Looking to the left, Phillip saw that the boulder had stopped about sixty to seventy yards from the army's line.

Tell me something good, Foros. Things are going to get nasty out here soon. We have seventy yards before their weapons will reach us.

They are minutes from the side of the line. Twenty or thirty orcs are dead, and an ogre as well. Three of the men are down so far. I know you can tell where I am. I will strike once they have taken out the weapons that can hit me. Mother is moving down as well and into position.

Up in the sky, the green dragon circled downward, her shape growing larger as she descended. Phillip snorted, as he had always considered Pammon large when he was young, and Amaranth was bigger than Pammon had been in those days, yet compared to Kaen's dragon now, they were so small.

"Be ready, everyone! Everything is about to change in a moment!"

Phillip did everything he could to keep the troops spirits high, practicing what Kaen had told him. When he turned around and pumped his fist and axe into the air, he could see the fear in the warriors. They knew the battle was necessary, but most were aware they would likely not make it home.

Yards slowly disappeared as they took a step every few seconds, a drumbeat signaling another step. Ten seconds passed, and another ten seconds. The sound of armor and weapons echoed across the clearing with each step.

Phillip's heart took off like a racehorse when Amaranth roared only a quarter of a mile above the field.

The army cheered as she announced her presence in full, and Phillip could sense what was going on near Foros.

They have broken through the sides and are cutting a path through the enemy. Some have noticed, but the majority have not, as Mother timed that roar perfectly.

The drum increased its tempo, now only five seconds between each step.

Amaranth dove across the battlefield from the north to the south between the two armies, roaring again as she faced the ogres and orcs that Phillip could only imagine might be less anxious in the coming moments.

One weapon is down, but a third of the cavalry is gone. Their army is noticing them!

Nervousness and concern flowed through their bond as Phillip knew that Foros was anxiously awaiting the outcome of the sneak attack.

Like a mindless creature, Phillip kept time with the drum, stepping as he was supposed to, but his mind and heart were focused on the rush of emotions surging through their bond. It was impossible to keep his own held back when Phillip realized Foros had gone in to attack.

Are they down?!

No reply came, and Phillip stared where he knew his silver dragon would appear over the tops of the trees in a moment.

One is, and the other is almost, but there is no time left to wait! The cavalry is almost gone, and five are left trying to push for the last one!

He wanted to plead with Foros to stop and wait, but there was no time. His dragon came over the treetops, dropping near the ground, and fire began to pour out of his mouth in controlled bursts. For a moment, Phillip stood there, unable to move or obey the instructions of the drums as he watched his dragon create chaos to his right. Two massive siege weapons were on fire already, and a different part of the army was burning.

A long gust of flame shot out, and Phillip saw a third weapon on fire.

Then the roar across the battlefield and the pain in his heart made him stumble.

FOROS!

No answer came, but Phillip saw his dragon desperately trying to fly toward his side of the battleground.

Amaranth roared again, and Phillip saw the flash of green as Foros's mother tore across the battlefield toward her flailing dragon.

Pain lanced through his body as his dragon fell toward the earth. The silver scales were covered in blood, and even from this distance, Phillip knew that his partner was gravely injured.

The army had stopped moving as the silver dragon lay on the battlefield, halfway between both sides, floundering like a fish on the bank of a river.

78

Frederick and Tazorath II

An axe head slammed into Frederick's shoulder, and the pain of it hurt from the impact but not a cut that would have killed many. The black scales that protected him there absorbed part of the blow.

The barbarian who had done it roared in anger, and as he tried to lift his axe and attack again, a hammer caught him in the chest.

Frederick didn't have to look to know the redheaded dwarf. Thoria had ended the life of another.

I can see you. You're going to have to move far to the right if you want to get to the clan leader. The barbarians are about five deep, and you are on the second row of them.

Slamming one to his left with his shield and hacking off the arm of one to his right, Frederick tried to keep his eyes on the constant barrage of weapons and objects all aimed at him.

Can we press through and then get to him?

Two axes came at him from a barbarian leaping over his friends, and Frederick dropped quickly, holding his shield over his head. He felt them both slam into the shield. The barbarian's weight then struck the shield, bringing it to a quick stop.

Frederick thrusted with his full might as he stood up, and the painted man was flung over his friends and back in the direction he had come.

On your left!

Without hesitating, Frederick pivoted and raised his shield as a huge two-handed axe slammed into it. Had he not gotten the shield there in time, the axe would have slammed into the side of his head and done some serious damage from the impact.

He jabbed forward with his sword, and it slid into the woman wielding the axe. Frederick was caught off guard for the slightest second as he realized it was a woman. The only thing letting him know was that she wore no shirt and let her girls fly free.

Focus!

Yanking his sword out, Frederick slashed to the right, taking off the head of a barbarian attacking one of his honor guard members.

Push through! You have two more lines to cut through! Do the spin.

Groaning, Frederick hated how Tazorath called that move but knew what she sought.

Planting his feet, he roared and drove forward into an attacker, slamming his shield into them. As they flew backward, slamming into the person behind them, Frederick spun quickly to his left, his arm snaking out and holding steady. The strength that Kaen had made him and Phillip earn through all that hard work paid off as his sword cleaved through flesh, bones, and shields like they were air. In one moment, he struck down five barbarians.

Now forward! Two left, and then you are behind them!

His eyes landed on the two that Tazorath was talking about, and they both hesitated for a second, having seen the carnage he had just created.

At that moment, he dashed forward, chopping down with his shield and shattering the shoulder of the man on the left while driving the sword through the open mouth of the woman on his right.

Help your allies! I'll tell you when someone comes.

Grateful for Tazorath and her eyes watching him, Frederick began to cut away the backs of those attacking his dwarven entourage. The death they received from behind was quick, with their heads coming off in a single blow or a sword piercing through the back of their heart.

Every time his arm swung, someone died.

Duck right!

Ducking, Frederick spun to the right, holding his shield out above his head while his sword sliced out at knee level.

A scream came at the same time a weapon skidded along his shield. The barbarian fell as their leg came off above the knee.

Block, parry right!

Spinning more to the right, Frederick brought his sword and shield up to protect himself, seeing the two axes approaching him. One banged into the shield while the other sliced its wooden weapon haft off on his sword.

The head of the axe continued forward and slammed into his chin.

Ignoring the pain, he sliced outward and down with his sword and cut the man's chest and stomach open.

It's clear. Move to the back. Your squad is with you.

Standing quickly, Frederick saw that five of his group had made it to him. A brief glance told him that they were all that was left.

"Your cut!" Thoria shouted before turning to slam her hammer into a barbarian coming at her.

Reaching up with the back of his hand, Frederick saw the blood and groaned. There was a good cut but no time to worry about it and nothing worthy of the only potion he had.

Where is he?

Coming toward you! Twenty-five yards on your right!

His head hurt a little from the axe and from Tazorath's yelling, but he knew she was worried and didn't complain.

"Incoming clan leader! Protect yourselves!"

A grunt came as they all turned and began making their way through the back line of barbarians. Some they killed, others they wounded enough to be no more of a problem.

Running at him was a man taller than Hess. He looked as wide as Kaen and had a rage in his eyes.

"Half circle!" he cried out as the barbarian clan leader, and they raced the last few yards at each other.

The man brought one axe down and the other across low, making Frederick parry with his sword and block with his shield.

As they collided, the massive man kicked Frederick in the midsection because both weapon and shield were being used to stop his axes.

Jumping backward, Frederick absorbed most of the impact from the kick and landed a few yards back.

All those times going against Kaen are finally paying off.

Focus! You're clear for now!

The barbarian rushed at him again, and Frederick didn't wait this time. He drove forward and held up his shield as the man brought both axes down at him. The collision and impact from the force left no doubt that the clan leader was strong, but even with his size, Frederick was stronger.

As he slashed at the barbarian's leg, an axe pivoted down and managed to deflect the blade inches before it sliced into his quad.

They began to trade blows back and forth, blocking and parrying as they felt each other out. While stronger, Frederick quickly realized the man was at least a thirty in his use of axes, as the technique and swings were almost always perfect. The few times they weren't, Frederick recognized them as feints, trying to draw him in.

The sound of battle rang out around them, and unlike the leader, who occasionally glanced to see if someone was coming for him, Frederick focused completely on the man. He knew no one would sneak up on him, which allowed him to start pressing the attack slightly.

The leader glanced to his left as Frederick noticed the dwarven warrior on his right.

An axe moved toward one of his guards, and Frederick didn't wait, rushing forward.

His sword lashed out, aiming for the unprotected midsection. A few inches away from connecting against the flesh, the clan leader's axe in his right hand came down, hooking the sword in the curved part and lifting it safely to the side. Frederick smiled as the large man pivoted to dodge the blow as he parried it.

[Shield Charge]

He burst forward, his shield slamming into the man's side and throwing him backward, tumbling along the ground for five yards. Frederick pressed the attack, not allowing his opponent to recover, slamming his shield down on the man's leg. Bones cracked, and the man yelled out in pain.

The barbarian had only one axe left, having lost the one in his right hand, and tried to slash at Frederick from a downed position. With his shield in the perfect spot, Frederick lifted it up, letting the axe slam into it while pushing it up and away.

Exposed, the clan leader couldn't stop the sword thrust that came, piercing below his rib cage and into his lungs.

A hand slammed into Frederick's arm and sent him backward, but all it had done was rip the sword out, blood gushing from the wound he had just landed.

Behind you, two!

Spinning quickly, Frederick saw the man and woman coming for him. Each had a black skull on their wooden shield and paint over their face and eyes like the barbarian he had just stabbed. They were frantic, and they shouted as they charged with their weapons high.

Sidestepping the man, Frederick brought his sword across, cutting through the wooden shield and slicing through the man's side and rib cage.

The woman surprised Frederick, stabbing through her companion with her sword, and caught him in the hand.

The scales stopped the sword from cutting his fingers off, but the impact was enough to make him let go of his sword.

Seeing him without a weapon, the woman ripped her sword out of her companion, who was falling toward the ground, taking his last breath, and swung her sword down at Frederick.

The dagger in his belt was gone, already in the air, and found a new home in the woman's throat as she stumbled toward him, awkwardly swinging downward at Frederick.

As she tumbled to the ground, he grabbed his dagger, pulled it out, and slid it back into his sheath.

That was close. You are safe. The barbarians around you have stopped fighting.

Looking for his sword, Frederick picked it up and walked over to where the clan leader was, his chest heaving as he bled from the wound that had just been inflicted.

A pitiful attempt of an attack came at Frederick, and he just let it go by, slicing the arm off at the elbow.

The barbarian tried to cry out, but blood came from his mouth as it filled his lungs.

Leaning over, Frederick slung his shield onto his back and then grabbed the long hair of the leader, pulling it upward as his sword cut the man's head off.

Standing, he lifted the head high and roared.

Barbarians all around him saw the head and began to shout something. A horn sounded three times, and the group of warriors ran away from battle, disengaging quickly.

His dwarven guard was down to four, and if one didn't get healing soon, Frederick knew the guard would not make it. However, they formed a wall around him as barbarians raced past them and back toward their homeland.

"Bloody hell!" cried one of his dwarves. "Did you know that would happen?"

"I had hoped that the information I got was correct. It appears it was."

Half the army was running away, and the other half, still alive, realized their time was done and began fleeing. Three sharp blasts on horns kept ringing out as the army ran away.

Frederick dropped his head and took a few deep breaths. "You all need to go get healed. I'm good."

"You sure?"

He nodded and pointed to the line of dwarven troops coming toward them. "I'm not alone. Great work, all."

As his dwarven squad approached the main forces, he heard people calling for healers.

Excellent work today, Tazorath. I couldn't have done it without you.

He smiled as he experienced the joy his dragon felt.

I was about to say the same. Now, if you don't mind, I would like to eat.

Laughing, Frederick smiled.

79

Phillip and Foros II

Like an arrow fired from a bow, Phillip was moving. The entire group was hesitating, not sure what to do, as one of their greatest hopes of winning this battle was down, and the other dragon moved toward it.

Tears were streaming down his face as anger and rage boiled inside him. Pain and agony like nothing he had felt before burned within. A barrier stood in his way, and with a single jump that he hadn't realized he could make, Phillip was over it, landing and rolling as he moved.

The trumpets and noise came from both sides of the battlefield, yet Phillip saw only one thing. He could imagine something far greater than anything else holding on to life by a thread.

No! Don't come!

Those three words pained his heart as Phillip ignored them. Amaranth was almost upon his dragon, and Phillip allowed himself a single moment to glance around. Both armies were rushing forward. The kingdom of Ebonmount was coming to assist and protect the dragon and its rider, who was racing toward his injured partner.

On the other side came a horde of orcs, goblins, and ogres, all intent on claiming victory over a pair of dragons.

Phillip's legs moved faster than he had ever known they could. The memory of this last half year and everything Kaen had made him do flashed in a moment, and he finally understood why Kaen had pushed them so hard. Now was the moment when all that mattered.

His shield and axe were out as he blazed across the last hundred yards, running to beat the throng of enemies coming toward his friend.

Run! Please . . .

The cry from Foros was weaker.

Never! We live or die together!

Those words fueled and drove him, and suddenly, his lifestone roared in a way he had never experienced before. Kaen had told him that one day it might act like this. His muscles felt infused with a strength and speed he never believed was possible.

Amaranth was behind her son, green light forming around her as she pressed her body against his, wrapping her wings around him for protection.

"TAKE HIM AND GO!" Phillip shouted as he leaped over the last barrier between him and Foros, charging headfirst into the wall of orcs and goblins.

A few slowed when they saw him approaching, but most charged ahead, unconcerned for a man wearing black dragon-scale armor when the true prize and glory were so close.

His axe moved quickly and precisely as Phillip reached the first orcs that crossed his path. Their heads were freed from their bodies, and his shield slammed into another, sending it flying backward and taking out a few of its allies.

Roars and shouts of the enemy surrounded him, but Phillip paid no heed as only one thing was on his mind.

Protecting Foros.

Every step he took carved an orc or goblin as he moved left and right, cutting down the approaching line of enemies that pressed closer to where his dragon lay on the ground.

He could feel the pain and a slight thread of hope coming from Foros as Amaranth tried to heal him.

Unsure of how long that might take, only the death of Phillip's enemies would buy the time he hoped Foros had.

Phillip zigzagged back and forth like a lightning bolt between the green and dark brown horde.

Piles of bodies formed in a small semicircle as he shouted at them, daring them to keep coming. They answered with their own roars and continued to surge ahead.

Go . . . left . . . I can buy time . . .

Don't fight!

His plea to Foros not to do anything didn't matter as a gust of fire roared to his right, setting a section of land at least ten yards long ablaze and turning the orcs advancing from that side into ash.

Pain lanced through their bond as Phillip knew Foros had injured himself with that attempt to help.

Stop!

He will not listen, Phillip! I need more time! The wound has pierced his entire chest, and I cannot move him! Defend my child, please!

Phillip didn't reply. He took the distraction his dragon had caused, slid his shield into the hook on his back, and drew his sword.

His arms became death for those foolish enough to get within his reach.

Another wall of fire sprang up farther ahead and Phillip was confused for a moment.

Ava is here. She is helping me and you!

Hope flooded Phillip's mind and he ran into the pack of orcs and goblins trying to make their way around the wall of fire. Every move he made resulted in body parts of the green and brown monsters in his midst littering the field.

The ground became slick from the blood that ran freely, and the few who managed to strike his body with their weapons received an attack from him. The armor stopped all the cuts, but the impact still hurt. His shoulder ached from a massive club that had hit, and his left leg had taken a solid strike from an axe.

Go!

I will never abandon you! We are one! Never forget that!

The distraction of talking with Foros resulted in an orc coming from behind and landing a hit with its club into his back.

A crack came, and Phillip gritted his teeth. Ignoring the pain in his body and the constant throbbing, Phillip spun. He saw the orc smile momentarily until its head was lifted from its shoulders.

A loud roar came, and as Phillip turned again, trying to keep track of everything around him, he spotted the ogre that was approaching.

It was one of the tier twos he had faced before, and it was killing its own army as it swung its sword through the crowd, running toward Foros.

Explosions rang out off to his right and behind. A quick glance showed that Ava was holding back the tide that tried to come at his dragon from the far side.

Cursing under his breath, Phillip tried to breathe, trying to regain the air in his lungs that was missing from the strike he had just suffered. All around him were fallen orcs, and the number of corpses he had created began to set in.

There were piles in some spots over four feet high from where he had struck down those trying to climb over their fallen allies. The wall of flames from Foros still burned, blocking off a place to come from, and as much as Phillip hated that Foros had hurt himself more by creating it, right now it was the only thing allowing him and Ava to hold back the army.

Phillip yelled, racing toward the ogre. The creature turned toward him, smiling as it hefted its massive sword into the air.

Phillip grinned as he sliced down two orcs between him and the ogre. Time had passed since the last moment he had faced one like this, and he knew this fight was his.

The ogre swung its sword in a wide arc, cutting through three orcs as it did, trying to cleave Phillip in one blow.

Its attack looked slow, and Phillip jumped into the air, leaping like he had over the boundary earlier. He flew over the blade and into the ogre's face. He brought both sword and axe down at the same time upon the beast's head and neck. The top half of its head was sliced off by the sword, while the axe buried itself into the creature's neck until it hit the opposite collarbone.

Blood and gore went everywhere as the ogre stumbled, its sword flying from its hand. Two black eyes looked at Phillip in shock for a moment before the light of its life vanished, and Phillip jumped off the falling body.

He had hoped the ogre's death might buy more time, but the sounds of more roars and the pressing of other orcs cut that thread quickly.

When he landed, he cut down four more creatures before retracing his steps to get closer to Amaranth and Foros.

"We have help coming!" Ava shouted.

A quick glance lifted his spirits. Only about seventy-five yards away came a rushing throng of the warriors of Ebonmount. One stood out, as Phillip had seen Hess pointing a sword in their direction, knowing the man was leading the charge.

To your right!

Amaranth's voice startled Phillip, but he didn't hesitate. He lifted his sword and axe as he glanced to his right.

A massive hammer struck where he had blocked with his weapons, and the ogre that had swung it sent him tumbling along the ground.

He rolled for five yards until he got his footing and stood in time to see another attack coming from the ogre. It was larger and wore chain armor. Its hammer was spiked on one side and had a flat section he had managed to block.

"Die, rider!" it shouted as it swung its hammer down at where he was trying to stand.

As he rolled to the left, the hammer slammed into the ground with enough force that dirt shot out, creating a two-foot hole with a single attack.

Phillip charged, his arms aching from the strike he had blocked. He had a potion but wasn't sure if he could still use it. The bottle might have broken in the pouch on his hip, and there was no time to check.

The ogre reacted faster than Phillip had thought it could and dragged its hammer along the ground and into his path. His sword's swing connected with the hammer's haft, and the metallic clang of the collision rang out.

In one move, the ogre spun the head of the hammer off the ground and brought it down again in a sideways arch from above.

It is stronger than you think! Use your skills!

Jumping backward and barely avoiding the ogre's weapon swing, Phillip felt the gust of air its attack had created.

There was no time to plan as another attack came at him, the ogre moving with speed and power. It shifted its grip on the long handle, allowing it to shorten its swings and speed up its attacks. Four attacks came in rapid succession as its fingers twirled the heavy weapon like it was nothing but a twig.

Every time, Phillip barely managed to escape the blow.

His eyes saw the pattern emerging and the weakness of its attack.

Feinting to the right, Phillip watched as the ogre spun his weapon again, twirling it for a moment before the head of the hammer moved in the direction he had feinted.

Lunging forward instead, Phillip swung his sword at its right leg, knowing what it was about to do.

As it had before, it twirled the hammer in its left hand as it deftly slid its right hand along the shaft and changed the direction of the weapon to block the incoming attack.

Phillip grinned as he took his axe and sliced upward, timing the movement of the hammer and sliding it along the shaft of the weapon.

The ogre wasn't fast enough to react as Phillip's axe blade sliced through its left hand's fingers, which had been manipulating the weapon with skill and precision.

Four fingers, the length of his entire hand, flew through the air, and the hammer flew to his left. The ogre could not control the momentum of the swing with only one hand.

A roar of pain and anger started to come from the ogre, but Phillip didn't care.

[Flurry]

Five strikes from his sword pierced through the ogre's abdomen and up into its chest.

The fight had shifted in a moment, and he watched as the ogre clutched the wounds with one hand.

Phillip roared at the defenseless ogre and, in moments, cut off its right leg while driving his axe head through its left hip.

The creature crashed into the ground, guttural roars of agony and rage coming from its mouth as it fell.

It bounced twice, and before it could move again, Phillip's sword drove through the back of its neck, slicing the chain armor it wore to protect against such an attack.

Straight ahead!

Barely able to withdraw his sword, Phillip saw another ogre coming, this one just as massive as the one he had slain but wielding a shield and a seven-foot-long sword.

Glancing around him, he noticed that the orcs and goblins had pulled back, giving a small fighting area between him and Amaranth and Foros.

"My turn," the ogre said in a tone that Phillip was surprised he could understand.

It charged, and Phillip shouted, moving to meet its charge.

80

Phillip, Ava, and Hess

Phillip's side hurt, and he felt the wet, sticky liquid running down his left leg.

Two more ogres lay on the ground nearby. The one with the shield had broken his nose with a well-timed kick but still died. The taste of blood and the pain of breathing had made the third fight harder.

The ogre with two clubs had waited its turn, happy to have a chance at being the one to defeat him.

Blood bubbled from its throat, where he had managed to kill it.

The axe throw was good, but there are three more coming. Hess is fighting through the crowd behind me. My tail keeps them at bay, but you must take the potion.

How is he?

Weak . . . that is why he has not spoken . . .

Phillip's hand trembled as he ripped the axe from the ogre's neck and watched another ogre approach him. The orcs had parted from where he stood, many snarling and shouting, but it was like he was a stone in the middle of a stream. None came at him or Amaranth directly. They all moved out of the way, leaving him for the ones who had apparently claimed this right.

Ava stood before Foros, panting. She was low on mana and Phillip could tell from the look in her eyes how low she was getting.

"You can pull back," Ava shouted.

"Would Kaen?"

No response came from Ava as she knew the answer.

His hip hurt, and Phillip knew Amaranth was right. There might not be time to take the potion later.

Sliding his axe into the loop on his belt, he fumbled with the pouch, his fingers aching and hurting from the moments of this day.

Horns continued to blow, and drums thundered all around. The sounds of people dying and weapons colliding filled the air.

Finally, he managed to open the pouch and pull it wide, revealing the bottle wrapped in multiple layers of cloth and padding. The red liquid was still inside, and thankfully, it had not broken.

"Well, at least the pouch would have kept it inside unless punctured," he said out loud as he pulled it out and used his teeth, wincing as he did, to pull the top off.

As he drank the liquid, his body began to shake, and he felt bones popping into place. His nose shifted, and he winced as his back and whatever had happened there adjusted.

His pain vanished, and his body felt amazing after a few deep breaths.

"I owe Aldric for trading my potion for his," he yelled at Kaen's wife.

"Don't be stupid! Fight smart!" Ava replied.

A pair of roars came, and Phillip watched as two ogres arrived thirty yards away from him. Both began shouting at the other, pointing at him as they declared who would have the first chance against him.

Each looked horrible to fight, but what really scared him was the one coming up slowly behind them. The ground shook even though it was fifty yards away. The orcs and goblins that were too slow to get out of its way were either squashed or swatted away when it swung the chain with a ball on it.

You may need to run . . . I am not certain—

No. I will not abandon Foros or you.

Phillip turned and looked at Amaranth. Her eyes were swirling between different colors rapidly.

You trusted me with your egg. Trust me now.

She nodded and then glanced back down at her child beneath her wings.

Five minutes. I should be able to move Foros in five minutes. Can you buy me that time?

Phillip smiled as he turned and started running toward the two arguing ogres.

I will buy that time no matter the cost.

An unexpected fireball blasted a group of orcs that were moving off near his right toward Foros. Ava continued to give everything she had, and for that Phillip was beyond grateful.

His lifestone had been lagging, and the exhaustion of each fight had taken its toll on him. He was tired and worn out, but knowing there was now a chance his dragon could make it energized him.

It roared to life, burning within his chest, and he moved with a speed that caught both of the arguing ogres off guard. He figured the one with the shield had to be easier than the one with the massive metal weapon resembling an axe. Hoping that the honor system he had seen would stand, Phillip flexed his fingers around each of his weapon handles and made his move.

The ogre with the shield saw him first and yelled something, but it was too late. The one with the axe had turned to the side, and the axe had been pointed at the other ogre, leaving itself open.

Coming from the side, Phillip slid along the ground as the ogre turned, swinging its left arm backward in hopes of hitting him with it.

The blade of his sword sliced through the ogre's Achilles tendon and ground against the bone of its lower left leg.

It roared as its leg gave out and started falling to the side.

Phillip jumped up and spun, swinging his axe, cleaving through the ogre's right hip. The sound of bones shattering brought a smile to his lips.

Without wasting a moment, he moved and hacked off the ogre's arm above the elbow with the axe.

The ogre roared in pain, trying to move and do something as it lay on its back, unable to get up or defend itself.

Pointing his sword at the ogre with the shield, Phillip grinned. "Perhaps you are stronger than this one!" he shouted before bringing his axe down on the fallen ogre's face.

Blood flew, and the ogre shook twice before lying still.

The one with the shield laughed and swung its sword to show that it was ready.

"Come, human, see if I am," it replied, excited and happy at what had just happened.

Phillip nodded and began to move back toward Amaranth slowly.

"Follow me. I do not want you to win because your friends helped you."

The ogre paused and then snarled. It roared loudly, and Phillip watched as all the orcs nearby moved away.

The one with the ball and chain stopped about twenty yards away and roared something at the one with the shield.

The ogre he had just challenged turned and shouted something Phillip couldn't understand. The exchange between the two was heated, judging by how they pointed at each other and roared.

Phillip's eye caught movement as the spiked ball the ogre had been dragging behind it suddenly snapped forward. The ogre he had just challenged raised its shield and braced itself for the impact.

The collision made a thunderous sound, and the smaller ogre was knocked backward through the field about seven yards. A huge furrow of dirt ran in a straight line as he withstood the blow. His shield was warped like a blacksmith had hammered metal over a ball around it.

Phillip could see that the ogre's left arm and shoulder were shattered, bones sticking out of the skin.

Time seemed to stop as the two ogres stared at each other, and the larger one slowly dragged its weapon back toward him, the metal ball of death bouncing along the ground.

You must run. There is no chance.

Will you leave your son and flee?

Amaranth said nothing for a moment, and Phillip knew her answer before she replied.

I cannot and will not.

Then that makes two of us.

Groans came as the beaten ogre rose from the shallow dirt it had somehow survived. It let the shield go, its arm hanging limply against its body. Without a word or even a glance at Phillip, it moved toward the back line.

Laughter drifted over the battlefield. It was guttural and dark.

"It is time to die, Dragon Rider," the ogre bellowed as it began to walk toward him. "I will smash you and suck the life from you. Then I will wear your head around my neck."

It laughed again as it came closer.

"Phillip! We need to run!"

Glancing to his left, Phillip saw Hess coming up toward him. He was covered in gore and blood. Behind him were a few students that he recognized, each looking worn and tired but appearing to be in decent shape.

"That's a tier four or five!" Hess shouted. "It is way beyond us all!"

The ogre stopped and looked at Hess and then at the half-dozen teenagers he had with him, each fighting against the orcs near them. "More fun and food! Fight me, you all!"

Phillip saw the ogre flick his chain, having brought the ball to his side. It flew backward a few yards, killing a few orcs that had gotten behind it.

"I won't leave!" Phillip shouted, hooking his axe and switching hands for his sword. He grabbed the shield from his back and took a few deep breaths. "My potion is gone, but my dragon is there. We need more time!"

Laughter came as the ogre watched them shouting and arguing about fleeing. "Stay and play. Stay and die."

Phillip glanced at the students who had moved up near him.

"We will follow you, Phillip. We owe you that much."

"Thank you, Gerald, but you're not strong—"

"Neither are you, sir, and you can't make us. If you won't go, neither will we. None of us signed up to run away."

Phillip trembled some at the words. He had spoken those words before on the wall during the first attacks.

"Very well. Pattern C, I'll lead. Get me an opening."

The eight students that had arrived spread out, each banging their weapon against their shield one time.

"Watch its range and speed! It's going to come fast! I need an opening like we trained!"

The ogre began to laugh louder, apparently amused by the teenagers preparing to fight against it.

"Hess, are you helping or not?"

A grunt came, and Phillip saw out of the corner of his eye the man who had kicked his ass more times than he could remember pulling something out of his pouch. Whatever had been in the vial had caused Hess to glow blue for a second.

"Tell Sulenda I love her," Hess said loudly.

Phillip opened his mouth to reply, but Hess was already moving. His shield was fixed to his arm and ready for impact, and his massive hammer was low and coming behind him.

"GO!" Phillip roared as he raced toward the ogre, angered at Hess's words.

Movement from the ogre signaled that its weapon was now in play as it snapped toward Hess.

When Hess charged, they were only fifteen yards from the ogre, and he had reduced the distance to seven when the ball collided with his shield.

A second before impact, the shield glowed, and the two slammed into each other.

The sound was overwhelming, and yet the ball dropped straight down as Hess came to a complete stop.

Phillip was now past Hess, his sword out and eyes scanning the ogre for what it might do. It seemed surprised, and that second of delay allowed Phillip to get within five yards.

Its wrist flicked backward as its body shifted, and Phillip saw the chain yanking the ball in his direction. It swung its right arm across its body, whipping its weapon as it tried to make up for the slack in the chain.

There was no time to smile, but if there had been, Phillip would have sported one. Seconds before the spiked ball would hit him, he slid onto his back, shield up.

A spike slid across his lifted shield as it passed by, causing it to roll in the air. He and Frederick had practiced that maneuver the last few months, and it paid off now.

The minor collision with the ogre's weapon slowed Phillip's momentum, but he was on his feet a second after it passed, rushing for the creature's legs.

Roar now!

There was almost no delay as Amaranth lifted her head and shook the area around her with the force of her roar.

His ears popped, but Phillip pushed through the pain, seeing that it had also affected the ogre.

[Power Slash]

His sword moved, and the entire three-foot section of his blade sliced through the ogre's right calf, cutting through the bone and almost slicing the bottom leg off.

The ogre's right hand jerked back as Phillip swung, and right after his sword connected, its oversized fist slammed into him.

Bones shattered inside him, and the sword remained in the ogre's leg as Phillip was sent flying. Like a small rock hit by a stick, he flew backward toward Amaranth and Foros, flopping and rolling along the ground. He slammed into a pile of orc corpses and came to a halt.

He struggled to stand and his body seemed to fight against his desire. Not allowing the physical pain to win, Phillip stood up, hopping on one leg as the other hung limply. Each hop sent a lance of absolute agony, yet there was no way he would give in.

The ogre was struggling to stand. Only one of his eyes seemed to be working. Cocking his head, Phillip watched as his students that he had trained rushed at a creature almost three times their size and beyond their limits without fear.

Spears and other weapons sank into the ogre as it fell backward. Someone had taken its injured leg out. He wanted to smile but couldn't.

"PHILLIP!"

It was Ava's voice yet it sounded so distant and so different. The blood that filled his ear on one side and the ruptured one on the other made hearing difficult, but he recognized his name.

Pain washed over him and he started to blink, choking on a cloud of yellow smoke.

He fell to the ground, unable to move, and the pain of the awkward landing almost knocked him unconscious.

Don't move! I am coming!

Amaranth's voice filled his head, and it hurt from the force of it.

Flames roared past him. An explosion took place closer than he could believe.

Breathing was getting harder, and Phillip noticed everything was darker.

He could feel the ground vibrating and knew it had to be Amaranth, but it didn't matter. He felt peace, and it was too hard to breathe. Phillip closed his eyelids, succumbing to the darkness that beckoned him.

81

Finding Stioks II

Kaen released a basket, untying the rope that held it, and watched as it fell into the ruins beneath them.

Three hundred arrows . . . that castle is no more and yet nothing . . . can he still be hiding somewhere?

I have watched the sky in every direction, and there is no way they can sneak up on us. Let me land, and we shall make one of those who fled the castle tell us what they know.

Do you want me to torture someone?

If you cannot ask in a way that will get them to answer, I am certain I can help loosen their tongues.

Sighing, Kaen nodded.

Very well, let's see what we can learn.

"Don't kill us!"

"We're not like him!"

Kaen frowned as the pack of about twelve people cowered beneath Pammon. They had tried to split up and run in different directions, but Pammon had herded them together better than most sheepdogs keep their flocks.

"Silence!" Kaen shouted, holding up both hands to show they were empty.

A few whimpers came from the group, but no one said a word as Pammon lowered his head. Each moved their eyes between the massive bronze dragon before them and the Dragon Rider on his neck.

"Where is Stioks?! Where has he gone?!"

"We don't know!" one of the men shouted back. "He left yesterday with his dragon Taerar!"

"What do you mean he left? Which direction?!"

The man shook as Kaen yelled, the fear of his master and the things he must have endured noticeable by the smell of urine that Pammon had commented on as he landed.

"South! Yesterday afternoon! That's all we know! Spare us, please!"

"Spare us!"

"Mercy!"

Their cries angered and hurt at the same moment. What Pammon and he had seen since they flew into the heart of this land was a sign of the monster Stioks really was. At one point, this kingdom had been flourishing, it had been said. Food, gold, art, and more came from here, and the people had thrived. Now it looked as bad as the place Tioanoe had fled. A mere fragment of a shell of its former self.

Where could he have gone? He wasn't at the battle with Amaranth and them unless he was hiding and waiting to strike.

Are you expecting me to have an answer? Could he have gone to the orc castle to take it over or bring more troops? Can he be waiting in ambush to attack my wife and son? Or would he have possibly flown south before changing directions and heading north to help against the dwarves?

Kaen cursed and saw how the people reacted, realizing he had said it louder than he had planned.

"You are free to go. We mean you no harm. Our goal is to kill Stioks and free the land from his grip."

The people all lifted their heads and stared at Kaen momentarily.

"Are . . . do you really mean that, sir? We were told all Dragon Riders were worse than him."

"Believe what you will, but unlike him, I will not sell your children to orcs and goblins. Once the battle is over, we will come back to try to free you from them."

A few began to cry, holding their clenched hands in the air as they thanked them.

"We need to go. Is there anything else you can think of that might help us find Stioks?"

They looked at each other, and Kaen could tell they could not help.

"Very well. Be safe!"

Pammon turned and leaped into the air.

This has cost us almost half a day.

Ask Amaranth and Glynnis if they have any news.

It will take time because of the distance, but I will ask. I'm sure they would have cried out if one of them saw him at all.

Rubbing his eyes with his gloved hands, Kaen felt lost.

I guess I'll fly in the middle of both armies. We shall see who can give us the most information and then perhaps go and help. That is the only thing I can do, unless you have a better solution.

Pammon flapped his wings as he gained altitude and adjusted his angle slightly between both armies.

He knew we were coming, and he prepared. His armies are fighting, and his home is left defenseless without him here. If we are to—

That's it!

Kaen's shout cut off Pammon's words, and as his dragon read Kaen's thoughts, both of their hearts sank.

It is the only thing I can think of, and you know it is true.

Then we must hurry. I will tell both Glynnis and Amaranth.

Kaen's heart broke when he realized what he could only imagine was happening right now. If Pammon told Amaranth, Ava would not stay.

Don't . . . don't tell Amaranth or Glynnis . . . please.

But—

You know I'm right, even though you don't want to admit it. If Stioks has gone to Ebonmount and Ava believes that, she will convince Amaranth to take her. She may even persuade Foros and Phillip to come. Together, those two would be no match for Stioks.

We both would lose more than we can imagine.

Pammon's heart and mind were reeling from the pain that Kaen was experiencing.

Your children . . .

Fly . . . as fast as you can. I will give you every ounce of power that I have.

Pammon felt Kaen's lifestone erupt with power. There were only a few moments in their life together, it had burned like this, and yet none of those previous times felt like now.

[Flight Burst]

Pammon lurched forward with a speed and intensity that neither had experienced before. Not even the day they saved Hess could compare to the angst both felt at the belief that Stioks would do to their home what they had done to his.

How . . . long . . . can you . . . burn like that . . .

Pammon struggled to speak as his body and core were flooded with Kaen's power.

Leaning against his dragon, Kaen pressed his gloved hands against Pammon's scales, willing himself to be drained completely.

Until I pass out . . . fly, my friend.

82

Ebonmount

Pammon was struggling to hold on when the mountains of Ebonmount finally came into view. The sun had been up for two hours, and an entire day and night had passed, yet they had made it home.

A sense of dread and hope came as they had achieved what both believed was impossible.

[Flight Burst Expired]

Kaen couldn't lift himself from his position, lying across Pammon's neck. Straining his head, he could see the mountains still hours away.

There is smoke . . . in the clouds . . . it has to be him.

Anger flooded their bond as Pammon beat his wings. He was tired, but he had grown strong enough to handle the stress of what they had done.

Kaen was spent. His lifestone was cold, as every ounce of his mana and energy had been shared with Pammon. Had he wanted to try using his dragon's eyes to see, Kaen doubted that he could even manage that.

They will be fine . . . they have to be. I . . . I need a moment . . . you are amazing . . .

Exhaustion took over, and Kaen closed his eyes for a moment.

As soon as he did so, he was tormented by nightmares of Stioks and the things he could be doing to their home. Even worse were the fears of what Stioks would do to his children.

Pammon said nothing. Using years of practice, he made certain that every time he flapped his wings, they maximized his speed. His body was tired, and Pammon had pushed past his limits. Grateful for the wind's help staying airborne, Pammon tried to recover for what was going to come next.

He could feel the fear and pain coming from Kaen as he lay there, passed out on his neck. He tried to convince Kaen to stop multiple times during the night, but his rider was committed. There was no way Pammon could fault him for that.

The clouds over Ebonmount continued to get darker as smoke from the bowl rose into the sky. Unlike most smoke, its magical nature didn't disperse as quickly.

They were five minutes from crossing the mountains, and Pammon felt what he had been seeking for so long.

One beat came to him. Fast as always, but it was there.

He lives . . .

Even though Pammon hadn't sensed Anastasia's heartbeat yet, if her brother was ok, she would also be.

What is that you feel? My children?

I can feel your son. Wherever he is, it does not appear he is in distress. If he is ok, then your daughter is safe as well.

Kaen sighed, letting go of some of the weight he had shouldered for so long.

Thank you, Pammon.

Pushing with his hands, Kaen sat up on Pammon's back and groaned, stretching to remove some of the stiffness from his position.

I am not certain what we will see, but we must be prepared. Control your thoughts and guard your emotions. You are still weak. I can feel it.

How can I separate what I feel from what drives me? You know that is who I am.

Pammon said nothing, but Kaen immediately knew what his dragon was thinking.

Cursing under his breath, he shook his head and slapped his face a few times to try to clear his head, as Pammon believed he needed to.

The amount of smoke below shows the destruction. The whelp may have exhausted his flame, which will be in our favor. Be ready; we will end this in a moment.

Kaen nodded and undid his bow. His finger traced along the two metal arrows in the quiver by his leg.

Just find them for me so I can shoot.

The mountains below slid past their view, and no matter how much they had prepared themselves for what they would find, both of them were genuinely unprepared for the destruction they saw.

The trees to the south that had just started growing again were burning with the green glow they knew to be magically started. Sections of the town where the people lived and worked were in flames. Some areas appeared safe, as they had the bricks they created years ago covering their roofs.

Farms that the kingdom had planted were nothing but ash, and Pammon couldn't see a single animal left alive.

To the west were the caves they had called home, and smoke drifted out of the openings.

Panic set in for a moment as Kaen considered what could have happened had their children been inside.

The keep was relatively undamaged, and Pammon saw that troops were still on the walls, each operating its weapons. Some had been destroyed by magical means, but there were still enough that had kept Stioks and his dragon away.

The adventurers' guild . . . use my eyes.

It took a moment, but Kaen was able to finally ignite his lifestone again. It had never been like this before.

That was harder than I expected . . . What are we—

Kaen's throat went dry, and circling above the adventurers' guild was Stioks's dragon. It had grown massive in the last seven or eight months, yet worse than that was the armor he saw on it.

Is that the same metal as my arrows? How can it fly with all of that armor? Why even wear armor?

Pammon growled as he began to descend.

To stop you. Stioks is no fool, and he has been preparing for your arrows. Our attack against Juthom gave him the knowledge about us that he needed. Your strength lies in the bow.

As Pammon's eyes scouted the area, Kaen saw that Stioks was not on his dragon's back.

Where is he? Surely you don't think . . .

Pammon's thoughts answered the question before he finished it.

Your children are inside, somewhere in the vaults. I can sense it. Stioks, it appears, is inside the guild hall. You need to deal with him. I will deal with his whelp.

Cursing, Kaen let the wind carry away his words as he clenched his hand around his bow.

I can't take this inside. Against Stioks and indoors, I will need my shield and sword. I can, however, shoot an arrow at his dragon.

A roar came, and Pammon growled. The dragon had noticed them and began to fly off south toward the city, leaving his Dragon Rider inside.

Kaen didn't hesitate. He had paid dearly for this skill and he was going to use it even if Stioks couldn't be the target.

The bow moved with a practice that he had spent a lifetime perfecting.

A longer metal arrow was nocked and ready, drawn to his cheek. His eyes followed the shape of the dragon that was flying quickly to the south.

You can't run . . . not this time!

[Homing Shot]

The arrow flew faster than Kaen had remembered when he shot one at Hess.

Both he and Pammon glided in the air for a moment as the arrow traveled across a distance not possible apart from magic. He had wanted to put mana into the arrow, but he had nothing left to give.

A screech came from Taerar as the arrow struck. The dragon floundered for a moment, falling down before his wings began to beat again, slowly gaining altitude.

I will deal with him. You must go deal with Stioks. Save your children. Kill that man. I will feast on his dragon tonight.

Pammon swooped down quickly, ignoring the fact that Stioks's dragon was getting farther away. Even tired there was no way the dragon could outrun him, especially if he was hurt.

This feels like a trap. Be careful.

Nodding, Kaen knew Pammon didn't need to see his acknowledgment of that warning.

By the right side, swing low, and I can get off on that roof and make it from there.

Pammon dove near the building Kaen had mentioned, and as he passed, Kaen ran and leaped off Pammon's back, landing on the roof and rolling a few times.

Getting up, he checked to make sure everything was still in place.

Adjusting his dragon shield and sword, Kaen jumped from the roof to a wall and down to the street below.

He frowned at the corpses of townspeople that were scattered along the street. Dried out, almost like someone had baked them in the sun for hours, they stood as testaments of Stioks's magic.

He has drained the lives of those who were obviously fleeing here. Be careful with his dragon. There is no telling what he may have done to it. Remember what Juthom said.

He will die regardless.

Kaen shook his head in frustration. He was angry, and Pammon was angry, but there was no reason for Pammon to act like this.

Do not be an eggling! Kill him but be smart. You also have children and a family waiting for you!

A trickle of a grumble came through the bond, and Kaen glanced to see his dragon flying higher into the sky and south of the capital.

Kaen stopped the sneaking he was doing along the wall and let his mind think.

Is he fleeing?

I'm not sure, but he is climbing higher into the sky. I am slowly catching up with him, but it would appear he does not want to fight in town . . . ahh, now I understand.

Groaning, Kaen knew what was happening.

We both have to win on our own. Stioks is separating us.

Kaen peered through a window and saw no one in the central area. There were corpses littered across the room. A few tiny corpses caused his lifestone to burn. It was painful and not as strong as it would typically be, but seeing the death Stioks was leaving angered Kaen enough that through sheer willpower, he made it burn.

Behind the counters, he saw the doors ripped off. The stairs to the vaults below were located back there. Herb had mentioned multiple times how protected they were, but part of Kaen felt that might not be true against a man as powerful as Stioks.

Considering going to the open doorway, Kaen felt uncomfortable about this setup. He was walking into a box he didn't control, and Stioks could be anywhere.

Even with his new armor, he was tired and drained. Everything he had to give would be his own.

Glancing at the area near him, Kaen saw a shrub with tiny green leaves.

Moving slowly toward it, Kaen touched the tiny branches and closed his eyes.

His vision changed, and the magic of the world surrounded him. It was harder than he had anticipated as he was tired, but still, he had hope.

"Forgive me, little one, but I need some help. Can I borrow your power? I'll return it one day."

The words felt right, even though he wasn't sure they would do anything. Soon the lights of magic and life that filled the tiny plant flowed to his fingers and into him. It wasn't much, but as he held on to the branch, Kaen felt more coming from the other shrubs and trees in the area. Power slowly trickled toward him as if the land knew of his need and what he had done.

A minute had passed, and Kaen opened his eyes to see that the shrub had become dry and dead. No life was in it, but he felt slightly stronger than he had before. It no longer took as much effort to keep his lifestone alive with power.

"Thank you, little one, I promise to return soon," he whispered.

Moving back to the windows, Kaen took a deep breath and let it out. The door was risky, but if he was going to announce his presence, it would be on his terms. He leaped forward with his shield out, crashing through the windows and rolling along the floor once.

Coming to his feet, he held the shield out before him, his sword in his hand.

No noise came from around the room. It was like a tomb. Only the dead were in here.

A smell and hint of evil lingered, filling his nostrils and scrunching his nose.

A thin layer of death and horror covered the surfaces of everything in the room. Whatever spell had been cast had killed them where they stood.

He is fleeing . . . we are already above the trees, and at this rate, I cannot return if you need help.

Kaen knew he was right. Stioks was committed to ending this fight just as much as he was.

Slowly, he crept around the room, staying near the wall, his shield out before him.

Every step he took seemed loud, yet Kaen knew he made no sound. It was his heart pounding that he heard.

The ground and the building suddenly shook and rumbled from underneath, and Kaen cursed.

Something is happening underground! I'm going in!

Tossing caution to the wind, Kaen ran toward the door that led to the vaults.

It was time to save those that he could.

83

Into the Vaults

Corpses occasionally lay in the hallway or leaned against the floor.

None were recognizable as their skin was pulled taut against the skull, and every ounce of hair was no more. The corpses were a reminder of what Kaen was about to face.

Running, his steps pounding against the floor, he came to the spot in the hallway where the hidden wall was no longer hidden.

Half of it lay tossed to the side in the hallway, and the other half had been pushed into the wall.

How strong is he? Can I do that?

Fighting the fear and the memory of a sword through his chest, Kaen pressed ahead, moving through the stone tunnel and toward the stairs that led down.

The hallway twisted and turned, and occasionally Kaen got lost as he searched for a clue, trying to find which way they had gone. He had chosen wrong twice, running into a dead end, and finally found the hallway where two bodies lay near the open doorway that was missing some of its stones. The hole wasn't as big as the first door, and it was apparent from the broken pieces on the floor that it had put up a fight.

The problem was he wouldn't be able to fit through that hole.

Sliding his sword into its scabbard, Kaen grabbed one of the pieces of stone that jutted out. He pulled with all his might, but it felt like an impossible task as the stone slowly shifted in his gloves.

He put his feet against the partially broken door and began to jerk back over and over. After about ten attempts, the brick shifted, and another five later, it came loose, sending Kaen and the door into the wall behind him.

Jumping up and shrugging off the impact, Kaen began again on another brick, each one taking fifteen or twenty-five tugs before it finally broke free.

With one stone left before he knew he could fit through, another massive explosion came from under him, and the building shook again.

You need to hurry . . . Stein's heart has quickened considerably.

Fueled by the fear of his son being in trouble, Kaen grabbed the last stone and yanked with everything he had. It began to budge, and with a groan, Kaen pulled harder, and it came loose, sending him once again into the wall behind.

Driven by fear of what Pammon had said, Kaen began twisting and turning to push himself through the opening. Even though it only took ten seconds for Kaen to squirm through, falling onto the stone floor on the other side, each second felt like minutes. Panic was fighting to overwhelm him, as Kaen could sense Pammon's concern through their bond.

Yanking his sword from his scabbard, Kaen took off running toward the first three-way passage. His mind raced, and he realized then where he was. He knew exactly where Herb had to have gone.

Turning to the right, Kaen sprinted down the hallway and saw the open stairs leading down.

They're at my father's vault!

He threw caution to the wind and used his shoulder to absorb the speed at which he descended the stairs, slamming into the wall and sprinting to the left.

Another body lay dead by a broken door, and Kaen winced at what it had to be.

Stioks has used the adventurers' guild members to lead him this way!

Pammon said nothing in reply, and Kaen stopped trying to communicate with his dragon.

The door was gone, blasted off the wall.

He knows I'm inside and is trying to hurry this up . . .

It could only mean one thing if Stioks was that desperate to get down to his father's vault.

Stioks knows about my children.

Racing down this hall, Kaen turned left, heading to the stairs he knew were open and waiting for him.

If he was correct, there would only be two more doors before his father's vault.

BOOM!

The explosion this time was louder and closer. It was almost directly underneath him.

Stone walls blurred past as he ran down the stairs, went right and then straight, finding a door still slightly smoking that was blown open. A body lay there, but this time he could see that it was decaying. Unlike the others, it hadn't reached the same level yet, and as he passed by the corpse, he winced, recognizing the face as it began to vanish from the rot.

"Mandy," he whispered as he tore through the tunnel. A clerk he knew from long ago, dead because of a man he despised more than anything.

Turning left at the fork, Kaen ran to the stairs and flew down them, holding his shield out to his left as he slammed into the wall.

Another dead body was there as he glanced over the top, and the door that had just been destroyed had a black mist rising from it.

No time was left as Kaen heard pounding through the tunnels. The man had reached the floor of his father's vault.

His lifestone roared with power, and Kaen moved at a speed that defied all odds. He ran through the door and turned to the right, using the shield to absorb the impact. He saw Stioks standing outside his father's door thirty yards away.

The man looked haggard, and when Stioks turned toward him, Kaen saw a green glow in his eyes. Whatever power he had built up to launch toward the door was cut early and pointed at him.

Pushing off the wall, Kaen dove back into the hallway he had come from and felt the magic power going past him and down the hallway until it detonated against the wall.

The sound made his ears ring.

"Stioks! It's time to settle this!" Kaen shouted as he held his shield up and quickly looked back into the hallway.

The man he hated hadn't moved. He was still standing before the door that led to where Kaen assumed his family was. He wasn't sure how they had gotten in, as the door was only attuned to Hoste, Hess, Ava, and himself.

There was no time to worry about that right now, though. Stioks had pulled out his sword and had a shield off his back.

It was made from green dragon scales, and Kaen now knew what had happened to one of the females Juthom had supposedly had.

"I had hoped to kill your children before I faced you," Stioks hissed, twirling his sword slightly as he spun his wrist. "It appears you figured out my plan much sooner than anticipated."

The man's snarling face looked like his skin was about to break. A black section of skin was cracked and bleeding near his eyes, nose, and lips, and the skin on the other half of his face looked like it was beginning to rot.

Kaen began to slowly edge toward Stioks. If he sent any spells, there was nowhere to dodge, but with the armor he wore, and his shield, Kaen anticipated being able to deal with anything that didn't require a massive buildup of power.

"Are you ready to die this time?" Stioks asked as he began to mirror Kaen's movement. "Even with that armor, no dragon will save you this time, grandson."

His lifestone pulsed at that word.

"We're not family, no matter what you want to believe."

Kaen was trying to formulate a plan. The hallway was large enough for two and a half men to stand shoulder to shoulder. It was only about nine feet high, so jumping and other maneuvers were going to be limited. Everything that happened here would be close and a brawl.

Kaen's eyes twitched slightly as he took in the room. Just as fast as before, Stioks came at him.

They collided against each other, each man's sword hitting the other's shield.

As they pressed together, Kaen knew what Stioks was doing. He was measuring his strength to determine what might have changed in the last seven months.

He allowed Stioks to slowly push him backward, giving the man some notion that he still held an advantage. Kaen had been tempted to go all out from the start, but Stioks was too dangerous. He would be behind if he failed to win that initial rush, and Kaen knew Stioks would whittle him down.

The older man drove into Kaen and kicked his leg forward, aiming for Kaen's knee.

Sensing and seeing the attack, Kaen moved back and watched as Stioks began the fight for real.

Their swords collided and they began parrying and blocking with weapons and shields. Sparks flew as their blades connected, and the magic within each of them clashed.

Stioks launched combo attack after combo attack, pushing Kaen backward with every strike. He knew the hallway would eventually end, but he wanted to see what he might learn from the man's attacks. Last time, it had ended so fast, and he hadn't gotten a chance to learn a thing.

A feint caught Kaen off guard, and Stioks's blade slipped past his shield and glanced off his leg, the dragon armor chipping slightly but not breaking under the attack.

Taking a step back, Stioks glared as he stared at the armor Kaen had on. "What is that, and where did you get it?"

Kaen ignored the question and the man's gaze. Instead, it was his turn to take advantage of Stioks's frustration with a fight that wasn't so one-sided.

Kaen lunged forward, his shield out, and shouted, "Shield Bash."

Stioks held up his shield, and it flashed green as Kaen smiled, instead slashing at the leg that wasn't protected by his shield.

His blade only cut about a quarter inch, right at a small gap in the man's knee protection. Stioks had recovered fast when he realized Kaen hadn't used a skill but instead made him use one.

The cut wouldn't kill him, but it would eventually slow him down. Kaen watched as the shield flashed green again; the skill Stioks had used was gone.

The moment it faded, Kaen lunged forward again and shouted, "Flurry!"

[Flurry]

Stioks didn't react until it was too late. The first two thrusts slid past his defenses, one of them piercing the armor on his side by an inch. It hadn't been where Kaen wanted it, but it had required Stioks to use another defensive skill as his sword flashed green and easily parried each of the other three attacks.

The man's eyes looked like they were on fire, a green glow surrounding them and blood running from the red wound on the burnt side of his face.

Stioks stumbled back, shaking his head and trying to deal with the pain in his side.

Kaen kept advancing, and Stioks continued to retreat. He countered or dodged each thrust, shield bash, or kick, but Kaen realized that he was even with or stronger than Stioks in every category.

Stioks's sword flashed green as Kaen attacked, and he felt the tip land against his leg, side, and arm before he could bound back and take any more attacks from the skill he knew Stioks had used.

"Two can play this game!" Stioks shouted as he lunged forward, his shield flashing green.

Kaen smiled and planted his feet as Stioks slammed into his shield. His eyes widened, cracking his blackened skin and causing more blood to flow, while he scowled in frustration at his grandson not being moved or injured from the attack.

A hiss escaped Stioks's lips as Kaen's sword caught the counterpart of his left leg, slicing through the man's armor again.

Stioks bounded back a few steps, looking like a rabbit as he made room, and Kaen waited for whatever curse or snide remark Stioks was about to say.

No words were uttered, but Kaen cursed himself as Stioks's hand with his sword glowed green. Kaen rushed toward the man, and Stioks continued to bound backward, aware of how much room was left, and the energy surrounding his fist began to get larger.

A devilish grin appeared on Stioks's face as he finished the spell, and a cloud of green and yellow gas filled the hallway.

Immediately, Kaen knew what it was. His skin began to itch and burn, and his eyes and nose were worse.

Even with all the resistance provided by his armor and items, he found himself blinking. The spell impeded his vision.

The glint of metal slid along the inside of Kaen's shield, thrusting into the massive red dragon scale on his chest. It almost knocked the wind out of him from the blow, but the scale held up against the attack, knocking him backward a step.

"You're going to die!" Stioks shouted at the sound of a sword hitting a wall in the hallway near him.

Kaen started backpedaling, knowing Stioks was going to come for him, and fought to suppress the anxiety growing inside.

He couldn't see through the mist, which burned as he tried to blink it out.

Closing his eyes, Kaen ignored the burning in his lungs and settled himself, ignoring the laughter coming closer toward him.

"Stupid boy, I'm going to bleed you to death," Stioks declared before he began cackling at his own words.

Stioks's blade continued to come at him. Holding his shield to protect his face, Kaen felt the blade thrusting against his armor. It hurt to get hit but so far none of the strikes had pierced through.

"Hiding behind dragon scales? No worry, I'll just take them off one at time!"

Stioks's laughter filled the hallway and Kaen moved back quickly, trying to find some space to recover.

84

Pain Leads to Adapting

Kaen ignored Stioks and his taunts.

He willed his eyesight to change and watched as the hallway was no longer obscured with a mist he couldn't see through. Magical light lined the floor, walls, and ceiling. Ten feet away from him came Stioks, spinning his sword as he smiled. The light of his body was different than most. The burnt side was almost black, with just a faint outline of life within the skin that surrounded him. The other side had an orange glow that wasn't like the light most creatures or living things emitted.

Kaen saw the smile as the man moved forward, not bothering to defend himself as he approached. Knowing that Stioks had no idea that he could see, Kaen assumed a defensive stance, holding his shield out slightly and putting the blade against the edge.

A tiny chuckle came as Kaen moved backward, and Stioks started to jog. The older man moved to the far left side of the hallway, sword out, prepared to slice downward.

When Stioks committed to his attack, leg planted and sword in motion, Kaen slammed his shield into the blade and drove his own at the startled man.

Stioks's shield moved but not in time to block the blow. Instead, it pushed Kaen's sword down and into his stomach.

Moving faster than Kaen had expected, Stioks leaped backward, yanking himself free of the blade.

Kaen continued to attack, his weapon swinging wildly, doing what he could to prolong the ruse that everything was nothing more than luck.

Stioks gasped and backed away. The man he hated with passion reached for a pouch, and in an instant the older man uncorked a potion and drank it all. It didn't look like the potion he and Pammon had; instead this one was pure black, and whatever it was made of seemed to move through Stioks's body and take away part of his glow.

"Are you ready to die?" Stioks asked as he tossed the bottle to the stone floor.

Like a charging beast, Stioks advanced, his shield and sword coming at Kaen. Keeping an eye on his swinging arm, Kaen used the sight he had gained when blind to deflect and block each attack.

A minute of constant blows and strikes passed, yet neither of them found his target.

"How?" Stioks asked as he panted, moving back a few steps from Kaen. "How can you see?"

Pretending to look around the hallway and swinging his sword around, Kaen smirked. "See? You just smell and make a lot of noise."

"Lies!" Stioks shouted as he raced toward Kaen again. His weapon glowed with magic and Kaen knew the only skill the man could have left.

Stioks's sword moved with the speed and precision only Blade Dance could have. Had he tried to block and parry those strikes with his normal eyes it wouldn't have happened, but by following the flow of magic, he was able to stay ahead by a mere fraction.

One thrust slipped by, striking his left hip, but the armor held, even if his bone felt like it had almost broken from the power behind the blow.

Another glow told Kaen that Stioks's skill had expired, and Kaen grinned. Activating the skill he had gained while fighting at the orc king's castle, Kaen showed just how strong he was.

[Blade Dance]

He moved with a counterattack, catching Stioks off guard and landing the first hit to the man's right arm, which was still extended. Blood flowed from the wound on his forearm. Two more attacks got past Stioks's defenses, piercing each quad almost enough to hit the bone.

When Stioks stumbled, Kaen's last attack found its mark.

The blade pierced Stioks's armor, sliding through until it hit the armor protecting his back.

Stioks's mouth was open, yet no sound came as Kaen drove him against the wall.

Using his shield to keep Stioks's sword arm pinned, Kaen pressed the sword harder, trying to pierce the armor on the other side of his foe's body.

Kaen saw magic pulse inside Stioks from his lifestone and race through the injured man's arm toward his shield.

As Kaen jumped backward, the edge of Stioks's shield slammed into his chest and arm. The power of that strike hurt more than Kaen had anticipated. Hess had warned him years ago that a shield slam when pressed against someone was one of the strongest attacks, and yet until that moment, Kaen had never understood why.

His arm ached, and his hand throbbed.

Stioks slid against the wall, gasping.

Kaen could see life and liquid seeping from the wound he had caused.

"Impossible . . . I can't lose . . . I spent hours searching for your children," Stioks said between gasps. "I wasn't sure if I would kill them or raise them . . ."

Anger flooded through him at the knowledge of how evil Stioks really was. Making himself move forward, Kaen fought against the pain from Stioks's attack.

His sword went on the offensive, ready to take his anger out on the man who had cost him so much. Stioks's lifestone pulsed and he was covered in a blue aura. Every blow that Kaen landed did nothing, bouncing off as if he were hitting a rock.

Grunting, Stioks ignored the onslaught of attacks and sheathed his sword, enduring the blows as he backed up a few steps. Holding his hand out, he continued to retreat toward the vault where Kaen's children were hiding. A wave of magic rushed through Stioks, and Kaen felt a force of air denser than stone slam into him and force him back. No matter how hard he pushed against it, the spell drove him backward, down the hallway still filled with yellow gas. He was forced past the stairs and Kaen shouted and screamed in rage as Stioks pulled another potion from a pouch, drinking it.

The once proud and confident older man gasped for air as the potion sent power flooding through his body. His hand fell and the pressure immediately vanished.

Stumbling backward, Stioks began to draw power from his lifestone. It flowed from every part of the man and into his right hand as he drew the sword from its scabbard.

Kaen saw power like nothing he had witnessed outside the life force of Pammon flowing into Stioks's hand and the blade.

His arm hurt, and it still hadn't lost the numbness, but standing where he was and waiting for whatever spell was about to come at him left Kaen with no good options.

Holding the shield up, Kaen rushed toward Stioks, watching the man shift into the middle of the hallway. More mana and magic flowed into the sword, draining the light inside the lifestone, and Stioks's blade began to glow brighter. Time was running out, and Kaen didn't have any options left to play. Whatever spell Stioks was preparing to cast was a power beyond any he had ever witnessed. Not even the spell Selmah was casting on the top of the cave the day Pammon revealed himself came close to the power in the sword Stioks was pointing at him.

Willing his body to run faster than he ever had, Kaen covered the distance in a moment. His arm was struggling to respond; something inside it had been injured from the Shield Bash, yet Kaen envisioned his wife and children and what would happen if he didn't act. Gritting through the pain, Kaen swung his weapon with every ounce of power he had left.

[Power Slash]

His sword slammed into Stioks's blade, and a crack and chip appeared along the edge and middle.

Stioks's eyes widened only after he realized that Kaen wasn't aiming for his body, expecting whatever spell he had cast to protect him from the attack. Instead, Stioks's sword was still pointed out, away from his body, exposed, and filled with mana.

Kaen's blade struck with so much force that both swords cracked, and Stioks began to scream as the power finished traveling from his hand into the now-fractured blade.

Hiding his head and chest as best as possible behind the dragon shield, Kaen saw the buildup and transfer of power, knowing what was about to come.

An explosion filled the tunnel, and shrapnel from the sword went flying in every direction.

Kaen felt himself knocked back, rolling along the hallway floor toward the stairs.

Time seemed impossible to measure. Smoke choked Kaen's lungs and he struggled to make sense of everything around him.

Everywhere hurt. Kaen's ears felt like Pammon had roared right into them. A hollow noise echoed within, and pain seemed to radiate from every limb in his body.

Trying to sit up, Kaen saw Stioks on the ground on his back, about twenty feet away. The man was barely moving, groaning in agony. His sight let Kaen see that there were pieces of metal inside Stioks's body. Some were shallow, and a few were buried deep within.

Kaen focused enough to check out his own situation. His armor was mostly intact, but a shard of metal five inches long and almost needle-like, similar to one that Lord Hurem had used on him once, was impaled in his left thigh.

Another long piece had pierced the forearm of his sword hand.

It was then that Kaen realized his sword was gone.

Letting go of his shield, he leaned over, grabbed the small piece of metal in his leg, and yanked it out, wincing as it came free. For some reason at that moment, Kaen knew he needed to apologize to Pammon for all the times he had mocked the dragon when giving blood.

The piece in his arm was barely sticking out, and he couldn't grab it with his gloves.

Looking at Stioks once more, Kaen saw that the man he had hunted for so long was barely moving. Each breath sounded raspy and raw as it came from down the hallway.

Kaen could see all the pieces of metal inside Stioks, and he looked like a pin cushion.

Letting go of the trickle of power in his lifestone, Kaen used his normal vision to see the area around them. A thin mist of fog and poison still hung in the air, but it was mostly gone. It was dark where he was; the explosion had destroyed the lightstones set in the wall. Pieces of the sword were lodged in the floor, walls, and ceiling.

Reaching down, Kaen grabbed the pouch on his hip and opened it. Liquid seeped out, and he quickly pulled it tight. His knife was gone, so Kaen picked up the sliver of the sword he had removed from his leg and used it to cut the strap that held the pouch on. He put the opening into his mouth, and it took some effort for his tongue and finger to open it and undo the cinched section of leather.

Warm liquid poured into his mouth, and Kaen drank deeply, trying to keep the small pieces of glass that flowed toward his lips out, straining through his teeth.

He squeezed the pouch to get as much as possible before dropping it on the floor and spitting the glass out.

He waited, wondering if he would scream silently or at all.

The metal piece in his arm began to stir, and Kaen winced as it was pushed from his skin and out the small hole it had created in his armor. A few other small pieces in areas he hadn't realized had been pierced came out, stuck between his clothes and the dragon scales that had protected him. The hole in his leg sealed without any issues, and for the first time in a while, Kaen realized he felt amazing. He was tired but even the exhaustion he'd felt when he first arrived outside was gone.

Standing, he grabbed his shield and looked at the floor. A longer piece of metal was sticking out of the stone. Bending down, he grabbed it with his gloves and yanked. It snapped off, leaving him about eight inches of metal. It wasn't wider than half an inch but would do what he needed.

"Time to die, Stioks. The world has had enough of you."

A rasping laugh came, followed by some choking as Kaen stood over him. Blood oozed out of tiny holes all over the man's body.

The hand that had held the sword was gone, burnt off at the end about three inches above where the wrist should be.

Stepping on Stioks's other arm, which still held the shield, Kaen leaned over and looked into the man's eyes.

"Tell me . . . what . . . do you see . . ." Stioks said between gasps.

Kaen sighed, angry and upset that both eyes were bleeding, peppered with metal shards.

Stioks chuckled and spat blood as Kaen said nothing.

"Not the . . . victory . . . you wanted . . . is it . . . finish me . . . you win . . ."

Kaen's hand trembled as he squeezed the metal shard. Stioks was right. This wasn't the way he wanted to end this fight. He wanted the man who had killed so many, killed his father, killed his mother, to look him in the eyes as he took his last breath. Pammon deserved to know that the man who had enslaved his mother got to see the Dragon Rider of the egg she had snatched away be the one to get revenge.

"You're right," Kaen growled. "It's not what I wanted or dreamed of, but I'll take it. Answer me this first. Why did you choose this path?"

Stioks coughed, splattering blood everywhere; it ran down the outside of his lips and cheeks. His chest heaved as his lungs filled with blood.

"Why . . . because I could . . . it's funny . . . your father . . . asked . . . the same—"

Kaen shook his head as Stioks made a gurgling sound. He wasn't going to let him finish that sentence. He couldn't bear to hear Stioks mention his father anymore.

As he leaned down to end it, a flash of light came from Stioks's hand.

His body reacted as Kaen's mind tried to figure out what had happened. The shield moved between Stioks and the blast that came. Lightning arced between the two of them and Kaen was knocked back once more.

The entire hallway glowed from the heat of whatever wand Stioks had just used. The metal shards embedded in stones had lightning jumping between them. On the ground Stioks's body shook from the spell that impacted both of them point-blank.

"Kaen! Wake up, Kaen!"

Something warm ran down his lips. His body ached and all feeling was gone. He wasn't certain if being struck by an actual bolt of lightning would feel worse.

His mouth was open and Kaen's mind struggled with the pain of a body that had been burned outside and within. Every nerve was screaming in agony having just endured a magic that could have decimated an army.

Suddenly the pain vanished. The liquid that he had been given had healed everything in a moment.

"Kaen! We're here!"

He blinked a few times, tears fell, and Kaen saw his father-in-law standing over him.

"Lord Hurem?"

"Yes! Come! Stand up!"

A pair of hands grabbed him and Kaen found himself standing. The hallway was torn apart, stones missing from both sides of the walls. The section that had been near his father's vault were gone. Next to Lord Hurem was Herb.

"Herb?"

"We're ok, and so are your children," Herb replied, motioning to the women with both babies that were slowly moving over the debris and into the dark hallway.

Callie was holding a lightstone, providing what Lady Hurem and Sulenda needed to ensure they didn't trip on the stones.

Behind them and to the side were the charred remains of a corpse. A small section of black dragon armor was still wrapped around the burnt flesh.

Glancing down, Kaen saw that his chest piece and leggings were basically destroyed. It was still connected in a few places, but most of the armor had borne the blast, protecting him while sacrificing itself.

Allowing himself to smile, Kaen felt concern coming through his and Pammon's bond.

It's finished . . . Stioks is dead . . . Your mother has been avenged.

Kaen felt across the space and searched for Pammon and some feeling or sensation.

An overwhelming sense of satisfaction came, followed by primal rage.

It is my turn to end this.

Pammon knew Stioks was dead not just because he felt it from his rider or because Kaen had told him.

When the man was gone, Taerar turned sharply in the sky and flew straight toward him.

You shall die! I shall rip your throat apart!

Pammon thrummed as the dragon half his size raced toward him. It had struggled as it flew south, putting as much distance as it could between itself and where Stioks and Kaen had fought.

The armor the whelp wore hid his natural scales, and Pammon felt sorry for the dragon. Taerar had been forced to be bound to a crazed man who desired nothing but his own gains.

Kaen's statement about avenging his mother felt like a mountain had been lifted off his back. Pammon now flew unhindered by a hurt that had never fully healed until this moment. With Stioks dead, an anger that had often fought to consume him vanished.

The dragon that was still half a minute away from him had lived an unfortunate life. If Pammon's mother hadn't managed to escape with his egg and leave him for Kaen to find, his life would be like Taerar's.

Never knowing love.

Not knowing joy.

Not having a family.

The massive bronze dragon knew what he had to do, out of pity. All the anger he had felt for Taerar disappeared when Stioks's life was snuffed out.

Killing Tharnok had been painful. Having to end the life of a mentor and father figure was harder than he had ever told Kaen. It was a bond that he longed for and would fight to ensure his children never missed out on.

Today would be different. He would rid the world of a dragon that would be a plague on the name of dragons if allowed to live.

Come, Taerar, let me end your suffering.

The young dragon roared, and flame formed in its mouth. Red fire washed over Pammon, splashing harmlessly off his bronze scales.

Grinning, Pammon waited until Taerar was a few seconds away.

The fire he unleashed wasn't red.

The color that came from his mouth wasn't orange or even white.

What came from inside him was a flame that was only possible when he had a rider like Kaen.

Blue flames came out of his mouth, and Taerar flew into them, unaware of what he was about to experience.

The young dragon tried to roar in agony, but the fire burned his scales and melted away the armor Stioks had promised would protect him. His flesh was stripped from his bones in midair, and as he fell under Pammon, the flames didn't stop.

Rolling like Glynnis had taught him, Pammon turned and chased the corpse. The dragon before him was gone; Taerar's head had been vaporized in a moment.

A blue ball of fire plummeted to the ground, and behind it, the one that had created it gave chase.

Pammon roared, his voice echoing across the bowl of mountains, announcing who he was and that he was the victor. It carried for miles as it echoed off the stone, and if anyone had been outside, they would have stared in wonder at the falling blue star of fire.

Pammon finished chewing, leaving the still-burning and smoldering corpse to put itself out in a few days. He swallowed the heart and leaped into the air, heading back to Kaen.

It is done. We have won this war.

Through their bond, each of them felt relief from the other.

It felt like their whole life had led up to this moment.

They had fulfilled their promise.

Epilogue

"You need to rest. Amaranth is right and so is Foros. You are lucky to be alive."

Phillip grunted, struggling with the loss of sensation in his left arm. An ogre with a wand had used it on him as he stood there in a weakened state, watching Hess and his students kill the large ogre.

Disease had riddled his body and Amaranth had healed him all that she could, but the damage to his left arm was never going to be fully healed. Even the potion Ava had given him had simply mended the bones and skin.

"I'll try," Phillip replied, sniffing as he fought back the anger and hurt he felt. "Foros will be back soon. You can go, I'll be alright."

Frederick shook his head and scooted the chair he was sitting in closer to the bed where Phillip was recovering.

"It doesn't work that way and you know it," his best friend informed him. "We've done the impossible and I know in time you'll be back to your old self. I mean, look at Kaen. He overcame blindness, getting diseased, and more. Just give it time."

Phillip nodded and saw Frederick's gentle smile. He could feel his friend squeezing his arm.

"Besides, from what everyone is telling me, you're the real hero of the battle," Frederick said. "The stories are greater than anything I have ever heard about Kaen. Practically all the mothers in town are offering their daughters up in marriage, even the nobles!"

Phillip chuckled and a small coughing fit came over him. Wincing, he tried to match the stupid grin on his friend's face.

"I'm tired of my stories . . . tell me about your fight again. And tell it better than the first two times. Pretend you're Kaen telling it to us."

Both of them laughed, each knowing they couldn't match the skill of their mentor.

"Well, there I was surrounded by ten thousand barbarians, all by myself . . ." Frederick said.

"How long has it been since the rulers of all the kingdoms have met?" Aldric asked Sedel and Dagan as they all sat facing each other.

The room was plain and even more so were the three wooden chairs around the small wooden table.

"I cannot recall," Dagan replied. "Perhaps we can work harder to not allow as much time to pass between them."

Aldric smiled as Sedel played with the cup in her hands.

"Sedel? Is everything alright?"

She nodded and gave a forced smile.

"The cost was high and even though my people suffered far less than both of you, I cannot wonder about what comes next. The kingdom of Luthaelia is going to be a problem we need to solve quickly. The people there are torn, as we know, between a hatred and fanaticism of Stioks. Yet the food each of us knows the other needs is growing abundantly and if nothing is done, it will rot and be wasted."

"Dagan was right," Aldric replied with a chuckle. "You don't beat around the bush. I agree, we need to solve that problem quickly and between the three of us, I would like to believe that the decision made will be the best for all people."

Each of them sat in silence for a moment.

Clearing his throat, Dagan drummed his fingers on the table.

"Now for the dragon in the room . . . Is it true that Kaen and the other riders may be moving somewhere else?"

Aldric frowned while Sedel smiled.

"He has mentioned that a few times," Aldric replied. "I can understand why. It will be difficult for us to continue to support them all, even while the dragons often feast on the animals on the other side of the mountains. In the end, it is their choice. I am not foolish enough to think I could bind one to my bidding."

All three groaned and frowned at the memory of Havannath and what his foolishness had cost the elven kingdom.

"They will not stay away," Sedel stated. "I know Kaen and Ava enough to know they will find a way to be a part of all of our kingdoms. Besides, the trees growing in each of your capitals will allow us to communicate a little better. My people will show you how they work before I leave."

Dagan's shoulders sagged and the dwarf leaned his head back, stretching and letting out a sigh.

The other two watched as the dwarf snorted and shrugged.

"Maybe you two are stuck up enough to worry about expressing what I know we all feel. We won . . ." Dagan said quietly. "We won!" He slammed his fist onto the table, his face lit up, and a massive grin came over his face.

"The fear that has kept each of us awake for a decade or more is gone! Other problems may arise, but we know that there isn't anything we cannot overcome if we work together and trust Kaen and Pammon."

Aldric took a deep breath and let it out, grinning as Dagan had earlier.

"You're right. Perhaps you three might be willing to celebrate with a fine vintage?"

Dagan roared with laughter as he nodded excitedly.

Sedel nodded slowly and smirked. "I guess leadership does require that I celebrate on occasion."

Sliding his chair back and standing, Aldric rose and motioned for the other two to follow.

"Come, I've got a room filled with drinks I never thought would get to be enjoyed. Today, they shall find their purpose fulfilled, toasting to our people and the dragons and riders who fought for us."

It feels different . . . like we both know it needs to be done.

Kaen nodded as he held Stein in his arms. Ava was next to him, holding their daughter Anastasia, tickling her gently.

"Sia is such a happy baby," Ava said. "Nothing like her brother, who is stoic."

Tell me again why she calls the baby by a different name?

Coughing to hold back the laughter, Kaen grinned at his dragon.

Sometimes people give other people nicknames. Ava wanted the name Anastasia because it is a family name yet also wanted to shorten it.

So will Stein be called Ein?

Unable to hold back, Kaen roared with laughter, and his son fussed a moment before returning to the steady gaze that always seemed locked on Pammon when he was around.

"Should I ask?"

"Pammon just wondered what Stein's nickname would be."

Nodding, Ava said nothing else and stared across the desolate ground.

Everywhere was burnt and the grass and life that wanted to grow was being held back by the taint of magic Stioks had used on Roccnari.

Burnt and ruined stone littered the area where the castle had been. Much of it had fallen completely as the spell destroyed everything. Yet there in the middle of the land, where two streams flowed around space the elves called home, Kaen held in his other hand the second seed Sedel had given him.

"I'm ready when you are," Kaen said, moving to the hole he had dug out with his boot. "It's time for one last thing before we build a new home."

"You're certain the other kingdoms and the remaining elves won't mind?"

"I'm not certain about anything besides my love for my family," Kaen replied. "This part has to happen. If people come and join where we are, so be it, but this will be our home. Our dragons and our family will make this land what it is by the sweat of our backs. Someday this might be a place that rivals the other kingdoms, but that is not my goal. For now, we will build a home."

Moving up next to Kaen, Ava nodded and put her hand on his arm.

"I'm ready."

As am I.

So am I.

Kaen and Ava smiled at Amaranth, who had been silent. She was nestled up against Pammon, and different since Foros and Phillip had gotten hurt.

Do not leave me out!

Glynnis was on Pammon's other side, not allowing Amaranth to hog him for herself.

"Then let us do it."

Kaen plunged his hand that held the seed into the ground.

Everyone waited for him to start the process.

His mind raged at memories that harked back to the events that had happened seemingly only a few weeks ago.

The massive dragon near him had once been so small that he could almost hold him. A chicken had injured that dragon's pride and yet served as a moment of laughter for so many years.

Hess had taught him how to be an adventurer. Shown him that life wasn't easy and that adventuring was pretty. It smelled, stank, required nasty things to be touched, and meant that death could come at any moment. The memory of Luca brought tears to his eyes.

Wherever you are, Luca, I pray that what I have done was worthy of your sacrifice.

Every adventurer he had known and the field where so many were buried brought pain.

A slight thrum came and Kaen turned to see Amaranth sliding her body against Pammon.

His family had grown when Amaranth and Glynnis had joined them. Unknowingly he saw them as just that. They weren't dragons to command or dictate, but individuals with souls and a choice.

They loved him, and he could feel it, and even more they loved his wife and children.

You are going to make me cry if you do not stop thinking about these things.

Kaen sniffed and saw that a few tears were falling from Pammon's golden eyes and along the bronze scales below.

Sorry . . . just . . . not a day goes by that I can begin to imagine my life without you. Everything changed that day we found each other. Thank you for never giving up on me and loving me.

Pammon's snout came close and Kaen felt the softest touch from the hardest scale he had ever felt against his cheek.

Thank you for loving me and not giving up on this eggling. No man comes close to you. So many would have given in to power and enslaved my kind. They would have given excuses about how the cost was worth it. Yet you . . . you proved why you're worthy of the lifestone in your chest. Thank you for loving me and my family.

Sniffles came from next to him and Kaen glanced up to see Ava blinking away tears.

"Gah, I can feel the emotion coming off the two of you in waves."

Laughing, Kaen nodded and focused on his lifestone.

"We did this to protect our families."

His stone burned with a power that was greater than any he could recall.

Pammon almost flinched from the power he felt through their bond.

"It's time."

Power from Amaranth, Glynnis, Pammon, and Ava joined together and flowed in Kaen.

Somehow the two female dragons gave theirs to Pammon and he was able to channel it through their bond.

The seed in his hand shot out roots faster than Kaen had expected. They burrowed deep into the ground, finding nutrients and life deep down where the magic had not managed to taint the soil.

Water ran deep in the ground and the roots sought it out like a hunting dog on a trail. The roots wove between the soft soil and soon found the rivulets of water waiting for this moment.

Deep down, near those tiny pockets of water, the roots also found a system of roots.

Gasping, Kaen could see with his eyes not focused on the magic of the world what they had found.

The tree! They found the roots to the great tree!

Power- and magic-infused roots from the seed Kaen had brought burrowed into the roots that already covered most of the dirt where the elven capital had once been. They started to join and intertwine with the network below, finding magic still hiding deep inside them.

Kaen's hand thrust upward and out as the root turned into a stem and then into a sapling. Within a minute it was a full-fledged tree, white bark and everything, growing so fast that Kaen had to back up as the trunk began to expand.

"Kaen! What is it?!"

"It's the tree! The elven great tree was still alive underneath! The seed has joined it!"

No longer did just his magic and the magic of the others feed into the growing tree, but a life force that had been waiting joined in.

Power from his body was pulled out, draining everything he and the others could give.

Ava backed away first, panting as she felt wore out, staring in amazement at the tree that was already over fifty feet tall and growing.

Kaen continued to focus on letting the tree take all that he could.

Amaranth bowed out next, and soon Glynnis was empty.

It is just you and I. Take what you must, I can feel what you feel from inside the tree.

You can hear it too?

It sounds like . . . singing and music . . . what we heard when we stayed here with Elies and Tharnok.

Kaen had thought at first he was imagining it but once Pammon pointed it out, he wondered what they were experiencing. It was different than the forest Sedel lived in.

Another minute stretched on, and Kaen's lifestone was coming to the end of its limit. There was more that the tree wanted, yet as the tree grew wider and he pressed his hand against the bark, letting it slowly move him backward, Kaen could barely keep standing.

Just a little more. There is more I can give.

Kaen felt Pammon's power change as it poured into him.

That's your life force!

It is . . . this is our home, and the place where we are about to live needs it. You cannot see why, but you will in a moment. It will be worth it.

Pammon's renewed power overwhelmed Kaen. It reminded him of when he had been shot in Minoosh and could barely move. Pammon had given him the strength to survive.

"I . . . do this . . . for my family!"

Shouting those words took more effort than Kaen imagined, but his lifestone changed colors. Like a golden beacon of light, the power it now drew wasn't based on a simple desire but on a changed purpose. The family that was standing around him.

Like rays of sunshine the power that came from Kaen and Pammon washed out over them and into the tree. His vision with the ability to see magic was overwhelmed and blinded him as the power radiated from his hand.

"Dear spirits," Ava whispered.

As if pure sunlight burst forth after a cloudy and dark month, warmth ran along everything.

The tree took it all and Kaen had no idea what it did with it.

Enough!

A claw pulled him back from the tree, breaking the bond.

There in his dragon's embrace, Kaen panted, feeling like he had come close to giving his own life in that moment.

Open your eyes.

Kaen's lifestone went cold, his body ached, and his mind throbbed. He had to blink multiple times to get his eyes to slowly focus but when he did, his jaw dropped.

"Is that . . . all this?" Kaen asked no one in particular.

"How . . . how did you and Pammon do this?"

Kaen stared at the ground around them. Green grass had replaced the burnt and black area. Now it was covered with life. The tree before them was over a hundred feet tall and the trunk was over twenty feet wide.

Why is it I feel that we will never hear the end of what these two have done?

Ava laughed first at Amaranth's question, but soon all five of them were laughing as Kaen and Ava turned, staring at the place, once desolate, that now looked ready for a new beginning.

Kaen turned to Pammon and smiled.

"I guess we'll need to fetch Hess."

Why?

"Do you really want to live in a place that I build?"

Pammon's thrum vibrated the ground.

As his dragon laughed, Kaen drew Ava close and kissed her on the forehead.

"We're home."

About the Author

Shawn Wilson is the author of the Last Dragon Rider and Ultimate Level 1 series. Movies, shows, books, and more provide inspiration for his stories. Wilson is a father of six and enjoys spending time with his wife and kids.